the spite date

USA TODAY BESTSELLING AUTHOR
PIPPA GRANT

Copyright © 2025

All rights reserved. This book or any portion thereof may not be reproduced or used in any manner whatsoever, including the training of artificial intelligence, without the express written permission of the publisher except for the use of brief quotations in a book review.

This is a work of fiction. Names, characters, businesses, places, events and incidents are either the products of the author's imagination or used in a fictitious manner. Any resemblance to actual persons, living or dead, or actual events is purely coincidental. All text in this book was generated by Pippa Grant without use of artificial intelligence.

Pippa Grant®, Copper Valley Fireballs®, and Copper Valley Thrusters® are registered trademarks of Bang Laugh Love LLC.

Editing by Jessica Snyder, HEA Author Services
Localization by Tracie Delaney
Proofreading by Emily Laughridge & Jodi Duggan
Cover, Edge, and Formatting Design by Qamber Designs
Edge Design embedded by Painted Wings Publishing
Cover Art Copyright © Wander Aguiar.

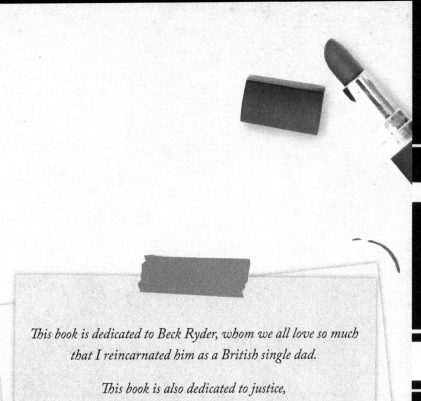

This book is dedicated to Beck Ryder, whom we all love so much that I reincarnated him as a British single dad.

This book is also dedicated to justice, vengeance, and plot twists.

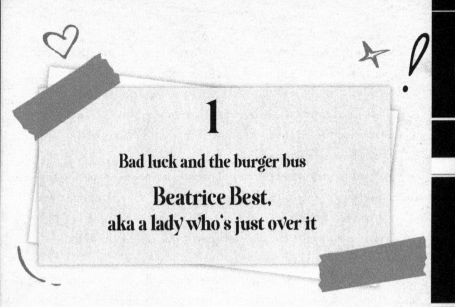

1

Bad luck and the burger bus

Beatrice Best, aka a lady who's just over it

The first time I sat inside a jail cell was a few months after my parents died. A lot of that initial time after the fire was a blur, but I distinctly remember Mrs. Camille being there, which meant that Hudson, my youngest brother, had to still be in fourth grade.

The spring of his Mrs. Camille year.

Every kid in Athena's Rest remembers their Mrs. Camille year. A kid who has her as his teacher when he's suddenly a homeless orphan remembers it even more.

Some of us even do stupid things like decide to date one of her sons years later and subject ourselves to her all over again.

But I digress.

Jail cell.

Mrs. Camille.

Hudson.

I was locked up behind bars because Mrs. Camille had looked down her nose at me during the fourth grade field trip to the police station—she loved giving the children a glimpse of their future if they didn't behave—and she said something like *that one looks like she belongs in jail*.

Hudson had laughed like it was the funniest thing he'd ever heard—his big sister was nothing if not the last person on earth who would ever break any laws—and since laughter was sparse in our family in those months after the funeral, I sucked up my fear of confined spaces and let Mrs. Camille and the officer lock me inside a jail cell.

I handed my phone over to my baby brother, and pictures of me as a jailbird were the prominent feature of the Christmas cards I designed but forgot to send that year.

It was a private memento of what I assumed would be my last foray into the bowels of the Athena's Rest temporary holding facility.

I was mistaken.

And now, at the end of a very bad week, here I am again.

In a small jail cell.

With one fluorescent light flickering overhead, the smell of sweat and urine and hangover lingering in the air, and smears of I-don't-want-to-know-what on the concrete floor.

Also?

I'm trying not to hyperventilate over being stuck in the old, tiny cell with cinder block walls on three-and-a-half sides, no window, and only a door-width of metal bars facing a cinder block wall across the tight hallway.

Oh, and I need to pee.

"C'mon, Logan," I call to the officer at the end of the short hallway, trying to keep the panic out of my voice. "You know you don't have reason to hold me, which means I have reason to tell the entire town you arrested me so you could try to jump your little brother's leftovers in prison."

Logan Camille.

Yeah.

That Mrs. Camille's oldest son is now a police officer, and he's just like her.

Which is to say that while half the community thinks he's the best police officer to ever walk to beat here in Athena's Rest, New York, in my experience, he's a power-hungry nightmare who loves scaring children, the elderly, and the weak of heart.

As is Jake, his brother, who's also directly to blame for my shitty week and now indirectly to blame for me being behind bars.

the spite date

It's an indirect blame that takes two or three squirrely twists and one minor logic leap to get to, but you still arrive here.

Though it's fairer to say that Jake's favorite actor on the entire planet is directly responsible, and yes, that's the complete, honest truth, which prompts the question—how, exactly, is this my life?

And why am I on the bad side of it?

Logan ignores me.

I shift to the right angle to see him sitting at a metal desk at the other end of the hallway, his feet propped up as he bites into a jelly donut.

Need to pee *so bad*. And also find fresh air, and lots of it. "The only reason Daphne never told the captain about your little indiscretion at the lake was because I was dating your brother. No reason for her to not spill the beans now."

He snorts as a glop of red jelly squeezes out of his donut on his second bite and drops onto his navy-blue uniform shirt, along with a spray of powdered sugar knocked off the donut by his snort. "No one believes anything Daphne says."

"Your mother does."

Ironic, but true.

The take-no-bullshit, should-see-a-proctologist-about-how-far-that-stick-is-wedged-up-her-ass Mrs. Camille loves my best friend and roommate and fawns over her every time they cross paths.

Maybe it's because she doesn't know Daphne's been disinherited from her hotel-chain family and Mrs. Camille is hoping to get a slice of the family pie, which honestly seems unlikely because Daph hardly keeps that information private.

Maybe it's because Mrs. Camille secretly wants to get tattoos and mermaid-inspired dye jobs.

I think it's most likely that Mrs. Camille wants Daphne to costar in one of the local theater productions so that her name brings in a bigger audience, but my brothers and Daph all laugh whenever I say it.

But also, see again, half the community thinks the Camilles are wonderful, and I think a good part of the rest don't have an opinion.

"One phone call, and Daph will spill the beans," I say.

Logan eyes me.

I stare back without blinking while trying to not let him see how fast I'm breathing.

He realizes I'm not blinking, and he straightens and stares back at me harder.

Dammmmmmit.

Now?

Seriously, a staring contest *now*? With a guy who's almost a decade older than I am?

When I have a hundred pounds of fish in danger of rotting outside in my food truck and I have to pee and I'm barely holding off a panic attack?

He rises and saunters down the hallway, eyes glued to mine.

Yep.

Apparently we're doing this now.

"I could file a complaint against you for unnecessary force and harassment," I threaten.

He keeps chewing on his donut and doesn't answer.

"C'mon, Logan. I gave you all of the documentation. I was supposed to be there."

"No, you weren't."

"I had every reason to believe I was." *Don't let him see you squeeze your legs together, Bea. Do* not *let him see you squeeze your legs together.*

He stops on the other side of the bars. "You know what I think? I think you set up the fake email account and booked the *party* yourself."

If I weren't staving off a panic attack, I'd roll my eyes at the idiotic suggestion that I booked a fake party so I could try to invade Athena's Rest's famous new resident's estate.

And if I didn't have to pee so badly that I was afraid my bladder was about to burst, I'd roll my eyes harder at the way Logan misuses the air quotes and puts them around *yourself* instead of around *party*.

"Why would I do that?" I ask him.

"Because you wanted to break into Simon Luckwood's house and meet him like the stalker that you are."

While my eyes are floating because of how badly I have to pee, his eyes are starting to water, and if I can see that from here, I'm about to win the staring contest.

Little victories.

I live for them.

They're all I get ever since his brother stole my dreams and dumped me.

"I don't have any interest in Simon Luckwood."

He snorts. "*Liar.*"

I'm never getting out of here. "Even if I did, do you honestly think I set up a fake credit card that paid me and a fake email account to book a party and a fake voice on the other end of the phone line that confirmed Simon Luckwood wanted my burger bus at his house?"

"Yes."

After I get out of here and can breathe again, I sincerely hope he and I are put against each other in pickleball this summer because I will fucking destroy him.

Specifically his gonads.

With my pickleball.

How can one family in town be allowed to torment so many of us and never pay for it?

Oh, right.

Because they also volunteer for everything and smile just right for the cameras and have this perfect public image that you don't realize is a façade until you make your way into their inner circle.

And really, most parents in Athena's Rest don't mind that Mrs. Camille is, as they put it, *a commanding presence in the classroom.*

Love requires good boundaries and all that.

"Do you know how much it's cost me to replace everything your brother stole from me when we broke up?"

He smirks.

No, a pickleball to his gonads will be too good for him.

I need something else.

Daphne will have ideas.

I keep my eyes trained on him, still not blinking, barely managing to not cross my legs and make it obvious how much overall discomfort I'm in. "And you'll never make detective if you can't piece together that, with my credit cards already stretched to the limit and nothing but a new business to show for it, there's not a bank in the world that will authorize me for a random extra throwaway credit card with a limit high enough to book myself for a party at a place I don't even want to go to."

He points at me with the donut. "And there's your fatal mistake. Again. *Everyone* loves Simon, and everyone wants to see what he's done with the old place. You're lying, and you are *busted*."

"Did you know that getting donut dust in your eyeballs can make you go blind? And that when you go blind, you can't masturbate anymore? Everyone knows masturbating too much makes you go blind, but no one ever talks about how the reverse is also true. The ability to pop a woody is controlled by the same nerves that control your eyeballs."

He shifts a glance at his half-eaten donut, then squeezes his bloodshot eyes closed. "That's not true."

I blink too while he's not watching. "I raised three boys, Logan. I had to know these things to keep them safe."

"You're threatening an officer of the law."

"When your boss sees the shitty work you did to put me in a jail cell because of a stupid grudge, he's going to put you on administrative leave. You might even lose your badge."

He smirks again. "You know absolutely nothing about how the law works."

"Considering I'm sitting in a jail cell for doing nothing wrong, it's pretty clear you don't either."

"Big words from someone who couldn't even make it through a full year of college."

That one lands, and I suck in a breath that I feel the exact wrong way in my bladder.

the spite date

The tiny bit of control I've had over my breathing and my panic attack recedes, and my fingers and toes tingle in warning.

I'm going to wet myself and hyperventilate.

The fish I bought for the private party that Simon Luckwood booked my food truck for will go bad.

The last thing I saw before Logan slapped cuffs on me was a notification on my phone from my bank that the payment Simon Luckwood made for that party had been reported as fraud.

And every single day, someone else tells me that my ex is finally about to open the restaurant he more or less stole from me when we broke up.

"*Camille*. Shut the fuck up." The door slams, and a very large, very intimidating man strolls through the door as Logan jerks backward, hopefully hitting his head on the wall behind him.

"Ms. Best," Chief says.

I breathe through my fury and panic and overfull bladder and somehow manage to pretend I'm fine as I finger-wave at him. "Chief."

"What are you doing here?"

"Being harassed by my ex-boyfriend's brother."

Chief Sosa's cheek twitches.

He and I could be on a first-name basis, but he hires officers like Logan, and my brothers weren't exactly saints while I was finishing raising them, even if they never ended up in jail.

I'm still not convinced Hudson won't do something to legitimately land himself exactly where I am before he's out of college and fully off my responsibility list, so I keep the chief at arm's length.

Even if I've wanted to hug him a million times since the fire.

His kindness and support, especially in the early days, helped me get through.

"She's—" Logan starts, but I interrupt him.

"My burger bus and I were booked to do a secret menu party at Simon Luckwood's place, but when I showed up, his security freaked out, said I wasn't supposed to be there, and they had me arrested. Look in my phone. I have email exchanges and records of a phone call to verify it was real, plus a receipt with Simon Luckwood's name on the credit card that paid me. It's since been reported as fraud, and I have a really good guess as to what happened, but I didn't break in. I had the code. I had every reason to believe I was supposed to be there."

Believe me. Believe me and let me out to pee and breathe.

The chief looks between me and Logan. "Did you look at her phone?" he asks Logan.

Logan's chair creaks as he straightens even more. "Chief, you know she's a liar. Look at all the stuff she spewed about my brother when they broke up. Calling *Jake* a thief? Come on. We all know Jake's not a thief."

"But *did you check her phone?*" the chief repeats.

"Chief, she can fake that stuff."

"Do you know who else can fake that stuff?"

"Boys," I answer for him.

As if I didn't have enough reasons to dislike Simon Luckwood, the fact that I'm nearly positive his sons are why this all happened makes me dislike him even more.

You don't leave thirteen-year-old boys to their own devices during their summer break.

I should know.

I went through two of my brothers' thirteen-year-old stage as their primary parental figure.

Doesn't matter how sweet and kind and good they might be most of the time, they still have thirteen-year-old-boy brains.

"Boys," the chief agrees. "Mr. Luckwood has twin teenage boys. And what do teenage boys with too much free time and access to an unlimited credit card like to do?"

"I can answer the first part of that, but my brothers never had access to an unlimited credit card, so they never got a woman thrown in jail for planning a party they didn't tell me about." My voice is getting higher and tighter, and I can hear the panic in it.

But Logan is turning an uncomfortable shade of burgundy.

The chief growls at him. "Release her and *be nice*. We can't afford a lawsuit."

"Neither can she," Logan points out.

"Do you know who she's living with again?"

Logan snorts. "Daphne doesn't have money either."

"Daphne has connections and a problematically strong sense of justice. *Let Ms. Best go and be nice*," the chief repeats.

Relief.

The bathroom is in sight.

And so is fresh air.

"Can I have his last donut on my way out the door?" I ask the chief. It's habit to be cheeky, I swear. I'm still too close to a panic attack.

He stares back at me, and it's not just his cheek twitching now.

But I tell myself the facial contortions are more because Logan is gasping in outrage that I want his second donut and have nothing to do with the cheekiness in my request.

"By all means." The chief himself unlocks the jail cell door and slides it open. "Anything else?"

Freedom.

Freedom.

I'm nearly out of here. Almost to the bathroom. Almost to fresh air.

But I still manage to look him in the eye and ask for one last thing.

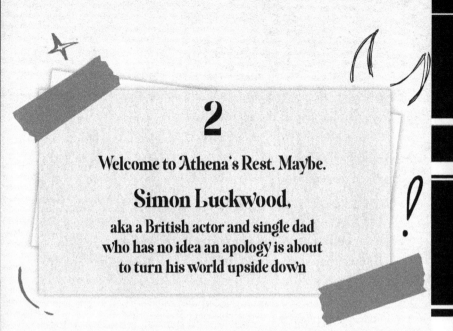

2

Welcome to Athena's Rest. Maybe.

Simon Luckwood,
aka a British actor and single dad who has no idea an apology is about to turn his world upside down

Well, this is awkward.

One minute, I've stopped short in utter delight at the sight of a food truck parked at the end of this street of shops in Athena's Rest, New York, thinking I'd like to finish my errands with a burger from this unique establishment, and the next, my security man is telling me that I had the owner arrested for trespassing at my estate while I was in the shower this morning.

"Was he on foot, or did he arrive by burger bus?" I inquire of Pinky.

Pinky growls low in his throat as he boxes me in between a building and a potted plant at the end of the street. His head is down over his phone, undoubtedly texting someone for an explanation.

He's a broad Scottish fellow who has the least patience of the three security men that the studio has insisted trail me and my boys since the unexpected breakout success of one of my television shows.

"*She* claimed you booked a party," Pinky tells me.

I peer through the bush at the food van.

Bus. The food *bus*.

Much larger than the food vans back in London or the food carts in New York City.

It's an actual school bus, painted with hamburgers stacked on their sides, a little pickle over the back wheel well, and above the window cut out for service, *Best Burger Bus* is spelled out and adorned with flowers that have hamburgers in the center.

"I didn't book a party, though were I to, I would certainly entertain the idea of having it catered by a burger bus. How adorably charming."

He stares at me.

And as I stare back, I have a bloody good idea what the man's thinking.

"You book a party and not tell us, boss?" he asks.

Rather than answering, I pull my own phone from my trousers pocket.

Heat is gathering on my neck. "You say you—*we* had her arrested?"

"She hacked the gate code. Got all the way to the front door."

I flip open my bank app and begin scrolling, though it's unnecessary to scroll far.

The day is quite warm, but not warm enough to justify the increasing heat at the base of my neck.

Fraud report—credit issued is the first entry on the list of charges.

With the vendor reported to be Best Burger Bus.

I clear my throat and continue scrolling.

"Do you recall when I misplaced my phone for a full day last weekend?" I say to Pinky.

He grunts.

I check the date as I come across the original charge to the Best Burger Bus, and I discover I'm lacking the correct word.

What, exactly, is more awkward than regular awkward?

A voice distracts me from my own embarrassment at the trouble I suspect my children have caused, and I turn to watch the burger bus again.

A brown-haired woman is leaning out of the service window and having a lively discussion with a police officer.

"You're over the line, Bea," the policeman is saying.

I squint closer behind my sunglasses at her.

"Is that her?" I murmur to Pinky.

"Yes."

She smirks at the officer, showing off her dimples. "Measure again and use your glasses this time. I can park this thing on a dime."

"You just got it a month ago."

"Yeah, and I got my bus driver's license when Griff started high school. Been doing this for years. Want to see me spin it in a donut?"

"Chief didn't approve that."

"But he *did* approve me selling my fish here this afternoon." She hands him a piece of paper. "See? Authorization directly from him, right here. You can keep it. I made copies. Had a feeling I'd need a lot of them."

"*It's over the line.*"

"It doesn't look over the line to me," a tattooed brunette standing next to the officer says.

She shakes her head, and—

No, not brunette.

Her short, straight hair has layers of blue and green in it that are only noticeable when the sun catches it right.

"Daphne has excellent vision," Bea says. "Do you want me to call the chief for a tiebreaking vote? I'm sure he'd *love* to hear another of his officers is harassing me today."

The uniformed gentleman winces.

Truly, I wince too.

This woman—Bea—she's had a dreadful day.

Because of me.

"I believe I owe this woman an apology," I say to Pinky.

"Bad idea, boss."

That's been the answer since *In the Weeds* became an accidental runaway success two years ago, propelling me into the international spotlight for the first time in my otherwise lackluster career.

Don't apologize. Don't admit to wrongdoing. Don't give anyone an opportunity to sue you when people know you have money.

Excellent advice, truly.

And I intend to ignore it.

I open my mouth to say as much but become distracted by a blond-haired chap who dashes out of the establishment on the corner. "She can't park that here," he says to the policeman. "She needs a permit. No permits given today."

"Chief okayed it," the policeman says.

The blond man folds his arms and stares at the police officer.

The police officer shrugs and repeats himself. "Chief okayed it. You got a problem with her, take it up with her. I can't make her move."

It's wrong to huddle behind this potted plant and watch this unfold, but I still find myself opening my note-taking app on my phone.

After months of not having any inspiration for a comedy series I'm contractually obligated to provide to the studio that made me famous, I'm feeling a whiff of creativity coming on.

Could be the warm, late afternoon summer air.

Could be the charming little road beyond the burger bus called Secret Alley, which is lined with quaint one- and two-story shops that seem to have come from a different time and where I just located my favorite brand of tea, much to my surprise.

Or it could be that this burger bus woman is utterly fascinating.

She has good energy.

Pluck, as they say.

Despite my own deep feelings of guilt for what I've put her through, I'm rather enjoying watching this.

Pinky audibly sighs. "We should go, boss."

"Shh."

The blond man is squaring up to talk to Bea.

"I know why you're doing this, and you need to stop stalking me."

Daphne—the woman with the multi-colored hair—chortles out a laugh.

Bea leans further out the window. "I'm not *stalking* you, Jake. I'm *annoying* you."

Good line. Well done.

the spite date

"Annoy me somewhere else," Jake snaps.

"Oh, you think I can just wave a magic wand and make somewhere else a better spot for customer traffic? I would *love* for the best spot in town to not be outside your father's office. Here's an idea. How about *he* moves? The Secret Alley could do so much better than an ambulance chaser's propaganda at the entrance. Don't you have extra office space in the building you stole from me?"

"*I did not steal it.*"

Daphne coughs *liar*.

Despite my own embarrassment at my boys' behavior and the situation they put this woman into, I can't stop smiling.

Bea, it appears, can't either, though her smile is harder than her friend's.

She tucks a lock of curly brown hair behind her ear and props her elbows on the windowsill. "Yes, and your brother didn't arrest me for the pure fun of it this morning. I could sue the police department. That would look *great* on his record."

"I have a friend in the city who needs pro bono cases," Daphne pipes up. "And helping a down-on-her-luck woman who hasn't caught a break since she had to quit college to raise her brothers after their parents tragically died is great optics. For my friend. Clearly, not for your brother. Or for Bea, but that's exactly why everyone would take her side over yours. She's sympathetic. You're an ass."

Good lord.

This was a terrible woman to have accidentally arrested.

I hope she's a fan of *In the Weeds*.

"Can you tell her to shut up and give us some privacy?" Jake says to Bea.

Bea snorts. "For you? No. Daphne. Get closer and keep talking."

"Like this close?" Daphne steps closer to Jake.

"Closer would be better. He hates when you're in his bubble."

"Ew. He smells like sulfur and pickles. But fine. *Fine.* Is this close enough?"

Jake stumbles back and almost trips on the curb. "I'm calling the chief."

"Have at it, you big stud." Bea makes a low, growling cat purr that takes both me and my cock by surprise. "You know how much I love it when you tattle to Daddy."

Daphne snorts again.

Jake growls and charges back into the shop he emerged from moments ago.

I adjust my trousers, then go back to typing notes to myself.

I'd prefer to use dictation, but I *am* on a street, making notes about the woman arrested on the order of my proxies this morning, likely to be spotted by any number of the people also strolling by or pausing to watch, and I don't need to speak out loud to draw attention to myself.

Not many Brits around.

I stand out by virtue of my accent, never mind my fame.

Still getting used to it, to be honest.

While it's thrilling to be asked for pictures, and going out in disguise is an amusing kind of fun, there are a few downsides.

Such as needing security.

And the way that they're terrifying.

Don't misunderstand—Tank, Butch, and Pinky are good at their jobs—but also terrifying.

Three security specialists are perhaps overkill, but then, the studio executives are familiar with my boys, so possibly not overkill after all.

The other biggest downside to fame is regularly being asked what's next.

I was happily rolling along in the obscurity of barely-not-broke-actor land roughly two years ago when an influencer live streamed herself watching the show that launched to crickets three years before that.

Overnight, I became a household name, and the studio is demanding that I cough up the contracted material for a new show without delay to capitalize on my moment in the spotlight now that we've rushed through a second season of *In the Weeds*.

Far easier said than done to deliver new material though, unfortunately.

Pinky nudges me. "Best get on with it."

Get on with it.

Right.

Of course.

I pocket my phone, and he and I step out from behind the foliage to approach the burger bus.

Scents of cooking oil and chips—pardon, french fries—permeate the air. People mill about the cobblestone pavements on either side of this charming side street off the main road, but the policeman has left and so has Jake. Daphne is nowhere to be seen on the street either. Bea is no longer at the window.

I approach it and rap on the windowsill near the front of the bus. "Hello?"

The woman I recognize as Daphne appears inside the vehicle, wiping her hands with a towel as she turns to approach me. "It'll be a few minutes. We're still warming up the—oh, fuck, are you serious?"

I smile pleasantly at her. "Could I please speak with Ms. Best?"

"Why?"

"To offer my sincerest apologies for the mix-up this morning."

"As opposed to your insincerest apologies?"

"Ah, yes, my insincerest apologies. I have been known to make those on occasion." I pull my sunglasses over the brim of my baseball hat so that she can see me wink. "I save those for when I accidentally mow down a man after he's been unnecessarily rude to a lady. Ms. Best, please?"

Bea herself appears behind Daphne. "Daph? What's wronnnnn—are you for real right now?"

"Ms. Best." My smile falters in the face of the unamused energy radiating off her. "I'm Sim—"

"I know who you are."

Complimentary, that was not. Not that I deserve for this to be easy. She should not have ended up in jail over me. "I see. I wish to—"

"I wish to see you gone. *Tally ho, good potheads, I do believe this is the end.* As it should be. Cheese shop is that way. You should check it out."

"Ah, I'm—"

"Lactose intolerant? I know that about you too."

My head might be spinning. This woman can quote *In the Weeds* and knows my stomach cannot digest cheese, but nothing about her suggests she's a fan.

There's likely another explanation, and this one has me smiling again. "You must know Lana."

My ex—the boys' mother, who's still one of my best friends, and who's rather tied up with family issues, hence my summer in her hometown to be the primary caregiver for the boys—she doesn't mince words.

Good or bad.

It's perfectly fine. I'm aware my shortcomings exist, and I'm very comfortable with forgiving myself for them.

Though this situation is a little more difficult than most.

This may be the first time someone has been arrested because of me, and I dislike that immensely.

Especially as she was very likely innocent in the whole ordeal.

She continues to frown at me. "Do I know who Lana is? Yes. Do I know her personally? No."

I open my mouth.

Close it.

And try once more. "Ms. Best, I'd like to apologize—"

"Sure. Whatever. All's forgiven."

All does not sound forgiven. "Is it?"

She squeezes her eyes shut, then sighs long and loud when she opens them again, as though my face is the last in a string of very bad things about her day.

"It is if forgiving you means you'll let me try to salvage the rest of this day and get back to opening my bus to sell my fish," she says.

I wince to myself. "So it doesn't go bad. Of course."

Daphne coughs again, and this time it's accompanied by a *dick*.

Bea shoots her the same kind of look Lana regularly gives the boys—half-frustration, half-exhaustion.

"Well, he is," Daphne whispers. "Apologies won't pay for the fish he stuck you with."

Heat once again gathers at the base of my neck.

Rather doubt it's because of the summer breeze.

More because I'm realizing Bea might be in the same kind of spot in which I've found myself more than once over the past fifteen or twenty years.

That is to say, in a financial pickle.

But this time, it's because of me. "And naturally, I'll reverse the fraud report. My accountant must have made it."

Did I mention the suspicious part of Bea's gaze? Because that's aimed fully at me now.

"Will you?" she says.

"Of course. I—fish?"

"Doubt that. Your biggest fanboy would've told me if you fished."

I'm rather wary of the tone she's using.

It's ominous.

I shake my head. "No, no—this is a burger bus. Why are you selling fish?"

"Called a secret menu, dude, and you ordered all of it," Daphne says.

A secret menu.

This is the best and worst experience I've ever had.

Highly inspirational.

Highly mortifying.

"Your kids did it, didn't they?" Bea says to me.

"I find there's no good answer to that question that doesn't ultimately leave the blame for your experience this morning solely on my shoulders. And I do apologize. For myself, and for the role my children may have played as well."

The two women share a look.

"Didn't expect that," Daphne murmurs.

"Still don't want to keep seeing his face," Bea murmurs back.

And I smile.

It *is* my default facial expression, but in this case—"You both rather dislike me."

It's odd these days.

Also oddly refreshing in a way I'd like to not examine.

Daphne pins me with a flat stare that makes uneasy tingles dance down my spine. "We don't know you, you pulled a double cross on my best friend and got her sent to jail, and I've met a few celebrities in my life. Too many of you think you can get away with anything just because you have a pretty smile. I'd say we're suspicious, but sure, we can use your words and say instead that we *rather dislike* you. Are you going to fix the payment problem or not?"

I've also met a few celebrities in my life—clearly—and while many of them are marvelous human beings, I can, unfortunately, understand her suspicions.

I dig into my trousers for my phone again. "I do apologize again. Little fuckers can be quite sneaky. I'll call the credit card company myself straight away."

"You know it'll take days to get this straightened out?"

"Of course. Happy to pay again. Immediately. The rest shall sort itself out in the wash."

They share another look, and then Daphne grabs a tablet, navigates the screen, and holds it out to me with the card reader attached.

I glance at the readout on the card reader she's extended my way, verify it's roughly what I'd expect, and I add a fifty percent tip.

Once again, the women eyeball each other.

Then they share a shoulder shrug.

And then they both look at me with matching *are we done now?* expressions.

Utterly fascinating how they're in sync. Now that I've made this situation right, I need to wrap this up so I can get home and take notes. Make some character sketches.

"Are you sisters?" I ask them.

They don't pause to share any glances before both staring at me as though they've never seen my level of idiocy in their lives.

To be fair, it's a rather ignorant question.

They look nothing alike. Bea's light brown curls that keep escaping her sloppy bun, and her bright green eyes, the twin dimples in her cheeks, and her long nose and wide pink lips are near polar opposites to Daphne's straight, multi-hued dark hair, brown eyes, button nose, and cupid's bow lips, which are stained a deep burgundy. Bea's at least two inches taller, though I have no idea what shoes either are wearing, which could clearly change their heights, but Daphne has a smaller frame to Bea's perfect curves.

She's far from a waif, but she's also noticeably smaller than Bea.

"No," they answer together.

My security man clears his throat.

I know that throat clear.

It means it's time to move on.

"I truly am sorry for your inconvenience, Ms. Best," I say. "I'll monitor the boys better to ensure this doesn't happen again."

"Where *are* your children, Mr. Luckwood?"

"I requested my other two security agents sit on them until I return. I'm sure they've not caused any more mayhem."

I smile at her again.

She doesn't return the expression, so I clear my throat. "Ah, they're with their mother. She picked them up over their loud protests that I didn't understand at the time—soon before you arrived."

"Hope you took their credit card away," Daphne murmurs.

"Of course. Yes. And Lana's a far better parent than I am. I'm certain they'll cause no more mischief while with her."

Ah, there it is. More silent communication between the two women.

I clear my throat again. "I'll also inform the staff that you're welcome to call round."

Bea's brows knit together. "Generous as that offer might be, it's unnecessary."

Daphne leans on the windowsill. "Or are you asking her on a date?"

"I—" I start, then realize I have perhaps made a miscalculation, but also—a date wouldn't be a bad idea. My head is absolutely spinning with ideas for a new pilot to show the studio after this encounter. "No. Merely that if it happens again—"

"It won't," Bea says.

"She's a little over men right now," Daphne says in a stage whisper. "Even famous British single dads with the world's most popular TV show. Or possibly especially famous British single dads who play total dicks on that popular TV show."

A murmur breaks out behind me. Daphne straightens and makes a *you're next, come on up* gesture. "Secret menu only today, and it's all on the house. Fish on a stick? It'll be ready in just a few minutes. We're still heating the fryers."

Fish *on a stick*?

That's odd.

I start to ask if I could have one, but then I hear it.

"Is that Simon Luckwood?" someone whispers behind me.

"Oh my god. It's Peter Jones."

"That can't be Peter Jones. What's he doing here?"

"Didn't you know? His baby mama's from here. Lana? Lana Kent? Remember? And *her* mom is fighting going into the memory unit at Shady Acres. *Oh my god, that's Simon Luckwood.*"

Pinky grabs me by the elbow and tugs.

I nod to the ladies. "Right, then. Thank you for your time. Apologies once again."

I smile at the crowd behind us while my man pulls harder. "Good afternoon. Lovely to see you all. Enjoy your fish—fish on a *stick*?"

This entire burger bus keeps getting more and more fascinating.

I turn back to the window. "How do you keep it on a stick?"

"Duct tape," Bea replies from deeper within the bus at the same time Daphne says "Superglue."

"Is it not so flaky that it falls off the stick?"

They share yet one more look while my man tugs even harder on my arm and I continue to ignore him, which I'll likely pay for later, but dammit, I want to see how this works.

Bea breaks eye contact with Daphne on a sigh.

"He did pay for it," Bea grumbles.

"Fuck him—he sent you to jail," Daphne replies. "He paid for your inconvenience. Not for fish."

"Peter—Peter—*Simon*. Sorry. Peter was just such an amazing character, I—can I get a selfie? Wait. Wait, in Britain, you call them an *ussie*, don't you? I saw that on another TV show. Can I get one of those?"

"Back up and let the man get his fish on a stick," Daphne says to the man crowding Pinky and trying to get to me for a photograph.

"*PETER JONES!*"

The scream comes from entirely too close, and if everyone in the entire town of Athena's Rest didn't hear it, I'll buy this burger bus myself.

But what I see when I turn—

Bloody hell.

That's the man Bea was arguing with.

Jake, was it?

And he's charging me, and he's close.

Too close.

I yelp and leap backward as Pinky growls and leaps forward, but Bea has beaten all of us.

One minute, a normal-looking-though-overzealous blond-haired, averagely built, American man is dashing at me, and the next, the woman I apparently sent to jail this morning is using a red ketchup bottle as a weapon.

Not by flinging the bottle at him.

Oh, no.

She's squirting ketchup directly at him.

And it lands.

The thick red liquid hits him squarely in the middle of his face, splattering everywhere and making me think for a moment that his nose has exploded.

Someone behind us shouts in terror.

Pinky grunts, I assume in surprise.

Highly doubt the man's ever considered using condiments to protect his clients.

Jake grabs his face and squeezes his eyes shut and yelps.

"Don't attack my customers, you dickweed." Bea holds the ketchup bottle straight out as the man I recognize as Jake begins screaming again.

But this time, rather than my character's name, he's doubled over, wiping his eyes and yelling, "My eyes! Assault! My eyes!"

The policeman comes running back from down Secret Alley.

I share a look with Pinky, who looks back at me as though he intends to throw *me* in jail for not going with him when he tugged my elbow.

"It was self-defense," a woman behind me yells. "She was protecting Peter!"

I try to not wince and miss.

Peter was…not a good person on the show.

That's one other minor discomfort in this whole fame thing.

People tend to assume I'm personally as big of a tosser as the character I wrote and played.

Much like Bea and Daphne have.

I've become accustomed to it.

Not that it took much accustoming.

Not with my childhood being what it was.

"Yeah, the security guy didn't see him coming, and so Bea had to do something," a man behind me agrees as the policeman skids to a stop.

"I thought he got attacked by an invisible bird that pecked his nose off!" a woman cries.

"She blinded me!" Jake yells. "*My eyes!*"

the spite date

"You're not blind, you prick," Daphne says. "Don't rush at people. It's not nice. And rushing at people with security guards is fucking dangerous. You did this to yourself. You, Luckwood. Get inside the bus. You're causing problems."

Bea growls at her.

Daphne rolls her eyes. "Seen this play out a time or two," she mutters. "Give him the chef's table. Can't hurt to increase foot traffic."

"Fucker," Bea mutters back.

I don't think she's calling Daphne a fucker.

"Mr. Luckwood—" the policeman starts.

"I didn't see the man coming at my client, and the burger bus woman saved him before I could intervene," Pinky says.

He slides me another look.

While Butch, not Pinky, regularly cooks dinner for all of us on top of his other duties, they're often in harmony, which means it's likely that in retaliation for me turning this into a far larger spectacle than it should've been, they'll conspire against me to slip cheese into one or two of my dishes this week. And I'll take it as graciously as possible, because I do, in fact, appreciate Pinky taking Bea's side.

I've caused her quite enough trouble for one day, and she *did* save me.

In a manner of speaking.

"*Inside*," Daphne repeats, pointing to the back of the bus while Jake keeps yelling about being blind as an older woman attacks his face with a paper tissue.

"Stop squirming and let me pour this water bottle in your eyes," she barks at him.

"All right then," I say. "I'll be inside the bus. Chef's table, you say? Fascinating. This is turning out to be my lucky day."

This is even better than all right.

I do believe I've finally found a muse.

3

All bad ideas start somewhere

Bea

My feet ache. My hair has melted to the back of my neck. My armpits smell like rotten oysters. We're nearly cleaned out—probably because we gave away our entire inventory today, but still, it's nice that people are finally trying my food truck—and freaking Simon Luckwood is *still* signing autographs from my chef's table at the back of my bus.

This time for freaking Mrs. Camille.

Jake and Logan's mother.

Fourth-grade teacher and president of the local theater association, which is a role my mom had until she died, which is extra irritating today.

The good news? Mrs. Camille isn't trying to talk Daphne into playing a role in this year's late summer production.

The bad news?

"Oh, you simply *must* join us in the Athena's Rest Players," she's saying to Simon. "You would be the best Willy Loman for us. I'm playing Linda, of course. You and I would have amazing chemistry on stage."

"That's a most kind offer," Simon says.

"Oh, and you'll love the murder mystery dinner we plan too. Here. I have a postcard about it. Save the date."

the spite date

I look at Daphne, and we simultaneously make gagging faces.

Naturally, Mrs. Camille and Simon are getting along fabulously. While sitting at the chef's table in my burger bus.

When one of her kids arrested me and the other has been a complete dick since breaking up with me.

It's aggravating as hell on top of the fact that all afternoon, I've heard Simon's British accent, and all afternoon, I haven't been able to stop myself from looking at him.

His dark hair is hidden beneath his blue baseball cap, and the logo for the nearby minor league baseball team on the cap is obscured by the sunglasses that he put on top of the cap brim. His blue eyes are sparkly and seemingly happy, with laugh lines creasing the edges almost more than you'd expect for a guy in his mid- to late-thirties. His cheeks are covered with a light dusting of dark whiskers, and his nose is the kind that annoys me.

It's just so *perfect*.

I don't trust people with perfect noses.

But it's the perpetual smile that has me truly irked.

The man hasn't stopped being happy for a single minute.

Smiling that much is unnatural in any circumstance. If that's not reason enough to not trust him, I don't know what is.

I wipe a towel over my forehead and glance at Daphne. She and Hudson, who showed up to help too, are pulling the last of the fish and chips out of the fryers and bickering good-naturedly, like they always do.

The first time Daphne and I lived together, Hudson was fifteen and still at home, so they're practically siblings too.

She play-attacks him with a fried fish fillet on a stick.

He leaps back. "Stop waving it around like that. It's gonna fall off."

"That's what your girlfriend said."

He grabs a handful of fries and throws them at her.

She shrieks and dodges, bangs her hip into the customer window, and makes an *erp* noise as the bus sways.

"Good gracious, they're all hooligans, aren't they?" Mrs. Camille says.

She's using a British accent that I've never heard her use in real life.

"If you two make this thing roll over, you're building me a new one," I tell Hudson and Daphne as I flip a burger at the grill. While we've mostly been handing out free fish all afternoon—it *was* technically already paid for—a few people have asked for burgers.

Expected it might happen since this *is* technically a burger bus, so I swung by the market to get extra supplies after the chief let me out of jail and I reclaimed my bus.

And honestly?

It's a relief.

The burger bus hasn't exactly had a strong start to its existence.

Likely due to the woman sitting at my chef's table with the guy who had me sent to jail this morning.

"I'm simply amazed that it doesn't fall off," the Brit in the back of my bus says as he lifts his own fish on a stick in the air.

Mrs. Camille sniffs. "Undoubtedly unnatural ingredients that someone who clearly cares about his body as much as you do shouldn't consume."

"Time's up," Simon's security guy says to her. "Next person."

Simon? I'd toss him off the top of my bus, and yes, fine, I admit it's partially because Jake made me watch *In the Weeds* so much that I'd dislike Simon under even the best of circumstances. I have *In the Weeds* trauma.

But his security guy? The guy he calls *Pinky*?

He might be old enough to be my dad and looks kinda scary with that scar through his eyebrow, but I'll kiss him in gratitude if he can get Mrs. Camille off my bus.

"Surely you can make an exception for a fellow thespian," she says to Pinky.

"No," Pinky says.

"Afraid he's the boss," Simon tells her. "But it's been lovely chatting, Lucinda."

She smiles at him. "We *must* do it again sometime. Maybe over a spot of tea?"

"Lovely," Simon says again.

Pinky hustles Mrs. Camille off the bus over her objections that there isn't actually anyone else in line, which makes me love him a little bit more.

"Make sure he gets whatever he wants," I murmur to Daph.

"Already slipped him a twenty to get him to make her leave," she whispers back.

I fucking love this woman.

When I told her I wanted to buy an old bus and convert it to a food truck so that I could launch a more successful restaurant than the restaurant Jake essentially stole from me, she took my idea and went wild. No smaller buses for us. She insisted on a full-size, seventy-capacity school bus that we could put a chef's table into for a premier food truck experience.

Fine by me.

I would've been way too claustrophobic in a regular-size food truck, and she knew it.

We pulled out the bus seats to make room for the kitchen and painted the whole interior a sunny yellow, leaving the back windows clear but obscuring the front windows with custom-printed static clings featuring family photos from over the years, before and after the fire, so our parents are in some too. We're grilling burgers and having food fights and doing dishes together.

My oldest little brother brought in someone he knew with a plasma torch to cut the service window.

My middle little brother hooked us up with a friend of his who'd worked in his family's food truck his entire life and had opinions about the best setup for a kitchen.

My youngest little brother sent memes about food trucks to the group chat.

We covered the rear windows with pictures of family meals.

The table itself is big enough to fit six. It's an avocado-green Formica table that Daphne found at a thrift store and convinced a friend to paint and cover with resin to protect it, so now the tabletop is a field of flowers where burgers with wings flit about, pollinating everything.

We added it in so we could charge a premium for people who wanted an exclusive, if quirky, experience.

And that table of honor is still occupied by a man I'd like to forget.

He once again holds up the fish on a stick that Hudson gave him right before Mrs. Camille showed up. "And in addition to not falling off, it's still flaky and delicious. Absolutely marvelous."

"My dude, you need to get out more," Daphne tells him.

"Quite right," he agrees. "What other marvels does this town hold?"

"Cheese curds," the three of us answer together.

He grimaces, then the bastard does the worst thing he could possibly do.

He cracks up. "You're rather funny, the lot of you."

What a weirdo.

Not that I don't have a sense of humor—I do. Kinda have to, considering all that life's thrown my way in the past decade.

But the last thing you'd ever expect is for the guy who played—no, wait, *wrote and starred in*—the most awful show about the most awful people to be so freaking *happy*.

And I'd bet even people who liked the show would say the same.

I finish the burger and pass it out the window, and as I straighten back into the bus, another shadow falls over the rear door.

I catch myself mid-eye roll when I realize it's not another Simon Luckwood-slash-Peter Jones fan.

Ryker, my oldest little brother, fills the doorway as he scowls at Simon. His straight dark hair is in need of a trim, there's dirt on his cheek, and his boots don't match, which pretty much tracks for Ryker. He cares more about the plants and animals on his farm than he does about his fashion choices.

the spite date

He was the only one of my brothers at home when the house caught on fire. The other two were on a campout with friends. While he won't often say it out loud, I know Ryker still carries guilt and PTSD from everything he saw and went through that night.

"Didn't do enough damage today?" he says to Simon.

"Erm—" Simon starts as I give Ryker the *knock it off* signal.

"I left the farm for this," Mr. Grumpypants says to me. "I'm gonna give him shit if I want to give him shit."

"Bro, think fast." Hudson tosses a fish on a stick, throwing it like it's a paper airplane, toward Ryker, who stands there with his hands tucked into his overalls and watches the fish hit the ground, then looks back up at Hudson.

"No," Ryker says.

"But it's *free fish*. And it's Bea's fish. And you *ruined* it." Hudson staggers with his hand to his heart as though this will be what finally does him in, and I have to actively suppress a smile.

My brothers are the best. We did a good job with them. Mom and Dad and me. I think they'd be proud of me. Of *us*.

Though I have no idea what they'd think of how little I know about what I want my life to be now that I've done my job of raising my brothers and can focus on finding my own future.

And that thought makes my eyes burn a little because time doesn't heal all wounds, so I distract myself with shutting off the grill to get ready for cleaning up for the day.

But I'm still watching out of the corner of my eye.

"Bro—are you brothers?" Simon straightens, no longer trying to be subtle about looking for his security person. "You are, aren't you? Bea's brother's?"

Ryker grunts and walks past him, ignoring the question. "You have enough help today?" he asks me.

"Can't have any more, or we won't fit," Daphne answers for me. "If you don't want fish, how about a burger? You look hangry. Not growing enough food out on the farm?"

"Out of burgers," I report, because I've delivered the last one to the customer waiting outside.

"You're a farmer?" Simon asks Ryker.

We all ignore him.

Ryker keeps aiming his broody grump face at me. "You went to jail?"

"Hours ago. Chief let me out, and now—"

"Hello? Are you still open?" a woman calls at the window.

"And now we've made more in sympathy tips today than I made the last three days combined," I finish on a whisper as I turn to the window. "One last basket of fish on a stick, and that's all we've got," I tell her. "You want it?"

"Oh, yes, please."

"Out in a minute. Just stand there."

"Are there three of you? Three brothers?" Simon points to the pictures on the wall. "There are, aren't there?"

Daphne moves between them, which is basically useless since all three men now in my burger bus are at least eight inches taller than she is and outweigh her by approximately a burger bus too.

But what she lacks in stature, she makes up for in attitude. "What's it to you?" she asks Simon.

"Simply learning the community."

Nope.

I don't trust him.

And not just because he was getting all buddy-buddy with Mrs. Camille.

"Ryker," I say, "get out of the way so we can get the last fish done. Hudson, throw more food and you're grounded. Daphne, please see our special guest out. We're closed."

No one does what I've asked.

Hudson sticks a french fry in Ryker's ear. Ryker shoves him out of the way and approaches the fryers like he's going to finish the fish himself.

the spite date

And Daphne—Daphne peers around my brothers and gives me a look that I'm very familiar with.

It always means something different, but the results are generally the same.

We head out to do *something*, our efforts go sideways, and we get stories that we'll tell our great-nieces and great-nephews someday.

Assuming any of my brothers or Daphne's sister want to have children.

"Can I talk to you for a minute?" Daph says to me.

Ryker looks at her, then at me. He grunts in clear disapproval.

Hudson looks at her, then me. He grins with pure mischief.

If Griff were here, he'd look at her, then me. And then he'd lean in to listen and suggest ten times bigger than whatever Daphne's about to suggest.

He's such a middle brother. And currently in Milwaukee for a weekend baseball series.

I don't acknowledge Daphne's request because I don't have to.

She's going to talk to me no matter what.

Here now, or at home later.

She slips past my brothers. "Finish up that last order and close the window," she tells them.

And then she pulls me into the entry well of the bus, which isn't private, but it's more private than anywhere else. She switches on our extra fan and aims it into the bus, which will make it harder for the boys to overhear.

Harder, but not impossible.

"You know what's coming up next weekend?" she whispers to me, clearly up to something in a way that reminds me of my brothers back in their high school days.

"Full moon? Paddleboard races at the lake? Summer knit-off on the square? A cheese festival?"

"JC Fig's grand opening."

I stare open-mouthed at the woman I would've called my best friend for the past five years. "Ex*cuse* you?"

"Bea." She puts a hand on my arm, grinning. "Do you know what the opposite of love is?"

"Hate."

"*Apathy*. The opposite of love is apathy."

"And paying attention to a twatnozzle's grand opening of the restaurant he stole from me is apathetic?"

She peers around me and into the bus, then cackles as she huddles closer to me. "Going to his grand opening would be being the bigger person."

"Fuck being the bigger person."

She drops her voice even lower. "Even if you went on the arm of his favorite actor?"

My chest heaves inward as a noise I've never made in my life flies out of my mouth.

It's not quite a gasp, not quite a hiccup, but definitely something horrified.

Her entire face is squeezed up in unmitigated joy. "Right? Jake would shit himself. He'd have to serve you nicely without looking like the fuckwaffle he finally showed you that he really is, and you know what Jake loves more than anything?"

"I'm gonna go with a tossup between Peter Jones and himself."

"Eating food full of butter and cheese."

"*Daphne*."

"He won't be able to cook a single thing that Simon Luckwood would eat or like. I'll handle the reservation. I know all the right things to say so that they'll know a celebrity in disguise is coming. You know Jake'll eat that up because his socials game is shit without you, and I only know next week is his grand opening because I'm a petty bitch who wants to know my best opportunities to make him feel the way he made you feel."

the spite date

"How is it possible to perpetually have a girl crush on you while also sweating in horror?"

"Because this means you have to take another turdnugget on a date." Her face freezes, and she leans around me to peek into the rest of the bus again. "Okay. Phew. I don't think he heard me."

I eyeball the mirror over the driver's seat that's left over from the bus's schoolkid-carrying days.

Ryker and Hudson are both watching us.

I squint past them, and yep.

Simon Luckwood is *also* staring up at the front of the bus.

He's holding his phone close to his mouth, lips moving like he's dictating a text.

"One problem—okay, *many* problems, but the biggest problem—there's zero chance said turdnugget would want to be seen on a date with me in public."

Daphne snorts. "The man who's fascinated by how we keep fish on a stick and you having three brothers and who keeps looking at all of your family photos and smiling? The celebrity who made a point to come apologize for getting you thrown in jail when I can promise you that every single person from his agent to his security guy to his massage therapist would've told him not to ever accept blame for anything that could get him sued? You think we can't make that man feel guilty enough to talk him into taking you out for one very deserved dinner at a fancy restaurant now that he's seen how hard you work?"

"He already paid for the fish. And then some, if I was looking over your shoulder at that tip right."

"And he's been creating distractions for us all afternoon."

"Bringing in more business than we've seen since we opened, you mean?"

I know it. Daphne knows it. Simon could probably figure it out if he wanted to give it half a thought.

She ignores me. "The worst he can say is no."

"You're devious."

"Only about ten percent. The rest of me is a very nice person. We just happen to need my devious side today."

"*Need?*"

"Rocking chair test."

Rocking chair test. It's what we do when I'm telling her something's a bad idea and she's positive it's a good idea.

Seventy years from now, when we're sitting in the rocking chairs of the farmhouse where Ryker, Griff, and Hudson's grandkids all come see us for cookies and stories about the good ol' days, is this one more memory we want to share with them of the trouble that we got into and the fun that we had?

"Dammit, Daphne," I mutter.

Hey, kids, wanna hear about the time your great-aunt Bea blackmailed a famous Hollywood actor into taking her on a date to troll her ex-boyfriend?

Yeah.

This passes the rocking chair test.

And she knows it.

She cackles and claps her hands. "So, do you want me to do the talking, or have you got this?"

"I've got this."

Because honestly?

The idea's rapidly growing on me.

Jake Camille is the most charming man on the face of the earth when he wants you. He makes you feel like the center of the very universe when he's lavishing attention on you. He volunteers his time all over town. He donates to charity, and he knows how to do and say all of the right things at nearly every moment.

Meeting his celebrity hero is apparently not one of them, but trust me.

Any other time, if there's an audience, he's performing, and they're buying it.

But the man puts the dick in dickwad when he decides he's gotten his maximum use out of you.

And he got maximum use out of me.

The press coverage of my family last year was insane. Griff got called up to Atlanta from the minors, and everyone wanted to hear the story of the baseball player whose sister made sure he could still play ball after their parents died in a tragic fire.

Jake was by my side for all of the interviews.

By the end of the season, we were talking to reporters about how we were going to open a restaurant in honor of my parents together. I put together marketing materials. Started socials for updates on our progress. Planned the menu.

And then, mere weeks after signing the papers to finally buy the building and make our dreams come true, Jake dumped me.

Said *it just didn't feel right* anymore.

That I was *too high maintenance* for a guy who was about to open a new business.

He already has a new girlfriend who's telling anyone who will listen that I'm cold and uncaring and that Jake was the victim in our breakup.

Such utter bullshit.

He used me.

He used me, he used Griff's fame, he stole my dad's dream, and he knows I can't do a fucking thing about it because I used most of my parents' insurance money to make sure my brothers could do whatever they wanted after high school to live the lives they want.

I'm scrappy. I'm frugal. I can go back to college more or less for free anytime I want at the school here in town that my mom used to work for. I still have the world in front of me as my oyster, and I would've worried more about my brothers if I hadn't done what I knew my parents wanted to do for them.

There's just enough left for a small emergency fund for me, and after not having any kind of emergency fund immediately accessible when my parents died, I'm terrified to touch it.

So while I'm not broke, I'm also not feeling solid.

And everything I planned for my future with Jake?

I'll benefit from none of us.

My name wasn't on the purchase paperwork for the restaurant.

He had all of the passwords for the social accounts, so he changed them and locked me out.

He's still using the marketing materials I made for him and doing interviews where he still uses my name and Griff's name to get more attention for the restaurant that was meant to honor our family, not his.

So making Jake look bad?

Yeah.

Yeah, count me in.

And Simon Luckwood can always tell me no.

That's what I always told my brothers.

Ask. The worst they can say is no, but the best they can say is yes. Don't say no for them. Give them the chance to tell you yes.

I swing myself up the stairwell and back into the bus. "Luckwood," I call from across the whole vehicle.

His face lights up, which again, *so weird*. Especially after all of the hours Jake made me watch that show, where he was always scowling and plotting ways to help three brothers murder each other in a fight over inheriting a weed farm in rural Maryland, and after the way all of us have continually ragged on him all afternoon.

"Yes, Ms. Best?"

"We're not quite even. I want you to take me to dinner next Saturday night at a new restaurant that's opening up on the lake. And then we'll be done and I'll forget all of this ever happened."

Ryker growls.

Hudson chokes on the french fry he should've put in the last basket of fish, so that serves him right.

Daphne leaps over to pound Hudson on the back.

Simon's brows do a slight lift. "You'd like me to take you on a date?"

"I want a free dinner," I lie. "I miss men buying me dinner while I wear fancy clothes."

"No," Ryker says.

"Oh, yes," Hudson says between coughs.

Ryker frowns at Daphne.

She grins back at him.

"Will it just be the two of us?" Simon asks.

"Unfortunately."

His smile grows almost as broadly as Daphne's. "Brilliant. When shall I pick you up?"

"Told you," Daph whispers.

"Still very suspicious," I whisper back.

"Duh. He's a man."

"Hey, I can hear you," Hudson says.

Daphne smiles at him. "Good. Don't be that man."

"I'll make the reservation and let you know," I tell Simon. "Assuming I have your phone number?"

I don't know how it's possible, but the man smiles even bigger. "You do indeed. I believe you called it and talked to one of my boys when you confirmed their party."

He's ridiculous.

Next Saturday will be…something.

Unless I get cold feet and call the whole thing off.

But a chance to torment Jake after the way he left me?

No chance I'm calling it off.

He fucked around.

And I'm entering my *help him find out* era.

4

If you give a teenage boy a burger

Simon

I never wished to be a father. I expected I'd be dreadful at it, given that my parents taught me that children are a nuisance who are never good enough and will always require *something* inconvenient, whether it be larger clothes or a bedtime story or a day off school because of illness. I assumed I'd resent the time and patience required of me to raise any little fuckers with minds of their own.

But then I met Lana.

She was newly out of law school and working for a prestigious firm in New York City.

I was serving tables at a restaurant near her office between acting gigs.

We started flirting, then fucking, and lo and behold, despite our best preventative efforts, I knocked her up.

It was her choice to keep the boys, which I begrudgingly accepted.

I was a complete twat about it, warning her that I'd be a dreadful co-parent and that she'd have to carry the majority of the load.

But now, approaching fourteen years later, I'm grateful that she was infinitely wiser than me when that pregnancy test returned with a positive result.

That she forgave me for being a twat.

the spite date

That she carried the vast financial burden of providing for them—and sometimes me as well—while I was still attempting to make it in the acting world.

That I now have two young men in my life who are both so much like me that it sometimes hurts, while also being so very different from me that they confound me on a regular basis.

I'm not prone to declarations of people being my very world, but if I were capable of assigning such magnitude to another human being, it would be for my sons.

Since they were born, my life has been split into the months that I've acted as their primary caregiver while Lana was exceptionally busy with work and the times when I've felt as though I've misplaced a body part when I would land a role that would take me away from the boys for anywhere from days to weeks at a time.

Having an entire uninterrupted summer as their default parent, as Lana calls it, to watch them grow into young men is a treat.

Except for moments like now, when I must act as the disciplinarian.

"You're to apologize to Ms. Best for booking her services without properly alerting me so that I could ensure security would allow her on the premises without issue," I tell them both as we navigate the car park where a line of food vans are all set up at the edge of the lake in Athena's Rest's Harmony Park.

Mondays are food-trucks-at-the-lake days in the summer.

How bloody brilliant to take the sting out of the start of the week by encouraging outdoor lunches.

I've been told the town population is at a low point, with students from the nearby university mostly away for the summer months, but the shady areas around the small lake are nonetheless full of picnickers. Business people and business casual people and parents and children and people who seem to be on dates are seated at various picnic tables and on scattered red checkered picnic blankets.

Quaint and perfect.

"Is she truly the best, like her name says she is?" Eddie, the older of my twins, asks me. He's more like me in the face, with my blue eyes and square jawline and my nose, and for the most part, he sounds fully American in his speech patterns. He was an early bloomer, so his voice is fully deep as a man's and he's nearly as tall as me to boot. I had to replace his casual shorts just last week, and his shoulders are testing the limits of his favorite cartoon T-shirt today too. He also confessed to being the answerer of the phone call to confirm the party they had booked with Bea's burger bus.

"Probably not," Charlie replies. He has Lana's lighter hair and more delicate features, and his voice has only begun to crack. He's more prone to Britishisms, as Lana and Eddie call them. Charlie's wearing a hoodie, jeans, and trainers despite the summer temperatures, which disturbs me only because he's fought against wearing a coat every winter for the past three years. The child's internal temperatures must be inside out and upside down. "She could've at least left us some fish."

"Definitely not the best then."

"We're the victims here."

"Neglected."

"Overlooked."

"Undernourished."

"Overdramatic," I interject.

The boys share a smile and bump fists.

This apology will clearly go swimmingly well.

Much like me being the disciplinarian in this parenting gig.

The boys find it difficult to take me seriously. Likely because I'm rarely serious.

Had enough of that in my own childhood.

But I shall do my best to reinforce the importance of apologies today. "I wouldn't have saved you any fish if you'd got me tossed in jail either. You're lucky she hasn't insisted you wash dishes for a month to compensate for your misbehavior."

the spite date

They look at me, then at each other, and then they make a scene by laughing so loudly that Tank, Butch, and Pinky all three heave matching sighs and huddle closer around us.

Clearly, I've done an excellent job parenting and they take my threats seriously.

"We're nearly there," I mutter to Tank, who's both the smallest and the kindest of the three of them. "They're simply being children, and children are loud."

"Butch could've cooked you burgers." He's clearly put out.

I can hardly blame him.

Butch does make excellent burgers.

But if Bea Best makes fried fish as magical as the fish I sampled on Saturday when it's not even on her regular menu, I can only imagine the culinary delight her burgers must be, considering her bus is named after them.

They certainly smelt otherworldly on Saturday afternoon, but a smart man knows when he's already pushed his luck, and I had pushed my luck too far to ask to add a burger to my order.

One could've argued I'd paid for it, but I would argue back that making a woman serve jail time unjustly does require bigger reparations.

And I'm anticipating our dinner on Saturday more than I acknowledge that I should.

I can't quite convince myself it's merely inspiration for the show that I've become obsessed with plotting and scripting during my working hours.

Not when I keep remembering the smiles she gave to her customers, the way she ruffled her brother's hair, the whispers and giggles she shared with her friend.

It's entirely possible I would like to win over Beatrice Best and have a summer fling with her.

Which is absurd.

But also appealing.

For multiple reasons.

"I like Butch's burgers." Charlie's voice pulls me back to the car park, and I glance about discreetly to make sure no one seems to have noticed my head wandering.

"No one's burgers will ever be as good as Butch's burgers," Eddie agrees.

"That's why we requested the secret menu fish."

"Why pay for what you can get at home for free?"

"Excuse me, boys, but food and Butch are not *free*." I *tsk* to punctuate the sentiment, then inwardly wince. My mother used that sound on me time and time again in my own childhood. Have I become my mother? Is this our turning point when they realize I'm an arsehole?

There's a reason Lana plays, as she calls it, *bad cop*.

I'm utterly incapable of intentionally being the disciplinarian that my parents were.

Or possibly that's *willfully* incapable. Intentionally incapable.

Too terrified that my boys will one day feel the same about me as I do about my own parents.

Eddie grins at me. "They might not be free, but you're rich now, so what does it matter?"

"Plus, whenever your parents kick the bucket, we'll get all of their money, so it's not like me and Eddie will ever have to worry about not being able to afford burgers," Charlie agrees.

As I said.

Children are terrifying and confounding, and I am clearly a terrible parent.

I rub my brow and suppress a sigh. The boys are generally funnier than this. Truly funny. Not obnoxiously funny. "Please don't say any of that in front of your mother."

They share a matching grin.

Little bastards are fucking with me.

Though they're not wrong—I'm quite the disappointment in every way beyond giving my parents a new generation to pass their assets to when they kick the bucket so that their wealth can stay in the family without going to their embarrassingly useless failure of an only child.

"With your grandmother in the state she's currently in—" I start, and instantly regret it.

Because both boys' smiles have now fallen away and they're sharing another look.

I should be pleased.

This look holds guilt, and they *did* inconvenience Bea quite thoroughly a few days ago.

But I've held enough guilt in my lifetime for all of us, and I dislike making my boys feel it.

Even when they need to.

And especially knowing that watching Lana's mother slip away is their first true experience with grief. Her father died before they were old enough to remember him.

"Well, well, well, what do we have here?" a feminine voice that I've been hearing in my sleep says from above us.

Bea Best leans out the window of her burger bus. Her light brown hair is hidden beneath a tie-dyed bandanna that matches her tie-dyed *Best Burger Bus* T-shirt. Sweat glistens on her forehead, which she wipes away with her forearm as her green eyes dart amongst the six of us.

I shake away the melancholy and give her my brightest smile. "Bea. You're here. Lovely day for a burger in the park. I'd like to introduce you to my children. This is Eddie, and this is Charlie, and they have something they'd like to tell you."

"Hello, Eddie and Charlie," Bea says.

She doesn't add *nice to meet you*.

That's very distinctly missing.

"Hello, miss." Charlie squints at her. "You know the United States has laws against false advertising."

Eddie pokes him.

Charlie elbows him back.

I put a hand on each of their heads and separate them as I step between them. "That's not what we discussed that you would say."

"We don't want to say what we discussed," Charlie mutters.

"We would've told you about the party, but you were too busy with meetings and dinners and phone calls, and then you wouldn't listen to us when we tried to tell you on Saturday," Eddie adds. "You just said *stop arguing and go on with your mother now.*"

So I'm to be thrown under the bus.

Specifically, this burger bus. "I was *not*—ahem. Please apologize to Ms. Best. You had ample opportunity to ensure her visit could've gone off without a hitch, and she was rather inconvenienced by your actions. Or your inactions, as it were."

"Her socials thanked the community for their overwhelming support." Eddie flashes his phone at me, showing me a picture of the burger bus on an app I'm unfamiliar with, where the post has garnered two likes and apparently a single comment, which seems to have come from one of her brothers.

Charlie nods on my other side, which I can feel because my hand is still on his head. "That's code for *we got a lot of tips and made more money than we would've if I hadn't been thrown in jail.*"

"When did you get social media? Your mother doesn't want you on social media. It'll rot your brains."

"We have to do something to stay informed," Charlie says.

"Where do you think we found out about your favorite new fish and chips joint anyway?" Eddie adds.

"Was I like this when I was their age?" someone asks from inside the bus.

Ah, one of Bea's brothers is working with her today.

The younger one.

Hudson, I believe she called him. The one with the same eyes as Bea and darker curls that he's let grow wild on his head. His apron is covering a matching tie-dyed T-shirt.

"You would've been if there'd been two of you," Bea replies.

the spite date

She's smirking, but it's not an arrogant smirk.

More of an amused-with-an-edge smirk.

Her bright emerald eyes meet mine. "First time raising teenage boys?"

"First and only."

She chuckles. "Relatable. How's Lana's mother?"

"Dad. Dad. There's an ice cream truck over there. Can we get ice cream instead of burgers? We can have Butch's burgers for dessert when we get home. His burgers really are the best."

"A little worse than expected," I tell Bea. "Apologies for my demon spawn. They're generally far better behaved."

She leans her forearms on the ledge and looks at each of my boys in turn. "Are you close with your grandma?"

They freeze as one, and my heart squeezes in sympathetic misery.

Lana's mother is my third-biggest critic—right behind my own two parents—though I fully understand and appreciate her being hesitant with praise for the man who knocked her daughter up and then couldn't provide as well as I should have over the years.

However, she's always been there for the boys.

And I am more grateful for that than I suspect she would ever believe.

Charlie lifts a shoulder. "I guess."

"Sometimes," Eddie agrees.

Bea gives them a soft smile. "It's hard watching someone you love slip away."

Both of them eye her warily.

I clear my throat. "Yes, well, the boys wanted to—"

"It's not fair," Eddie says. "She's not even seventy yet. She promised us she'd live to a hundred and four so that she could see our kids get married too."

Charlie's hands are balled into fists. "I don't want to have kids, but if she lived to a hundred and four, she could see me win a Nobel Prize for solving dementia. And now she won't."

"You like science and math?" Bea asks him.

"I will for her."

"He's trying his best," Eddie chimes in. "That's all Gramma ever said we had to do. Just do our best, and nothing would hold us back."

"She used to visit us in the city all the time, but she hasn't been in two years. She missed seeing my art project win first prize at school."

"Your art project took first prize?" I ask. Where was I? Was this when I was back in England for filming? "Your mother didn't mention—"

"And she missed my orchestra performance too," Eddie says. "She's never missed it before. It was like, why am I even playing?"

I peer at him. "You're in the orchestra? And your grandmother has been to see you and I haven't?"

"What do you play?" Bea asks him.

He pauses.

Both of the boys lean around me to share a look.

"What *do* you play?" I echo.

My god.

My children are musical and artistic geniuses and I had no idea.

I'm as terrible as my own parents.

I am.

Worse, in all actuality.

Who doesn't know their children are musical and artistic?

Especially when I've lived near enough that I should've been attending their performances and displays.

Mostly.

I did travel a bit for projects the first half of the year.

"Violin? Clarinet?" Bea prompts.

"The soundboard," Eddie says. "I played the soundboard."

A relieved sigh slips from my lips while Charlie covers a snort of laughter.

I was well aware Eddie's taken an interest in technical, behind-the-scenes production, and that he wished for me to not be there to cause a scene.

the spite date

I thought I'd missed that he'd taken up the tuba, for which I would've snuck into the theater to watch.

"It's not funny, Charlie," Eddie says. "If it weren't for the crew, there wouldn't be performances at all."

"That's quite right," I agree. "The tech crew is invaluable in any production. Could we please get on with apologizing to Ms. Best? And then ordering burgers for all of us, which we will enjoy because they're delicious?"

"We're sorry we missed you on Saturday," Charlie says.

"It sounds like it would've been a great party," Eddie agrees.

Bea purses her wide pink lips together, clearly suppressing a smile.

"They're very sorry," I tell her. "Genuinely sorry. We're still working on expressing our regrets."

"So you're in charge while Lana's getting her mom settled?"

"Yes. And I'm only in meetings or working three or four hours a day."

"It feels like thirty or forty," Charlie says.

"Every day," Eddie agrees. "He works so long that he adds hours to the day, which is astrologically impossible."

"Astronomically," Charlie corrects.

"*Astrologically*. It means big, you dumb butt."

"Astrology is that baloney about Capricorns and horoscopes. Astronomy is about the stars. *Astronomically* means *humongomously*."

"Humongomously isn't a word."

"You're not a word."

"You're here for burgers?" Bea interrupts as they attempt to shove each other around me.

"I want Butch's burgers," Charlie says. "His are better than yours. You do false advertising."

I stifle a rare sigh. "We don't know that until we try them." I hear the phrase *hang you out the window by your toenails* flit through my head, and I wince once again.

So now I'm becoming my worst nanny too.

"When's the last time you ate?" Bea asks.

"Three days ago," Eddie says at the same time Charlie replies, "We've been punished with lack of food."

My god, they're about to get *me* arrested. "They had nine eggs and four pieces of ham and seven tomatoes and at least a full can of beans between the two of them for breakfast."

"How many hours ago?" she asks me.

"Three. Four. And they ate four large pizzas and a gallon of ice cream last night when my meeting ran—it was the first meeting that ran long in weeks. I worked *five* hours yesterday. We played Frisbee golf. And they bested me in cricket too."

Hudson appears behind Bea, and she turns and takes two cardboard trays from him, then hands one to each of my boys.

Hamburgers.

Chips—pardon, *fries*.

A pickle spear and lettuce and tomato and onion slices.

My boys both grab a handful of fries from their burger baskets and shove them into their mouths in sync.

They're fraternal, not identical, but their mannerisms are often indistinguishable.

"That'll be seventy-five dollars," Bea says to me.

Hudson leans out of the bus and taps a QR code displayed prominently beside the window. "And don't forget to tip your servers."

Butch growls softly.

Tank folds his arms over his chest.

Bea rolls her eyes. "Oh, don't act like it's highway robbery. I'll get you all burgers too. No extra charge beyond the seventy-five. Ask Pinky. They're worth it."

Remarkable.

My emotions feel as though someone's playing ping-pong with them, but Bea Best tries to rob me, and I'm suddenly smiling again.

Her fried fish bewitched me.

And I don't mind.

the spite date

"There's no way this will be as good as Butch's burgers," Charlie says around me to Eddie.

Eddie nods and talks with his mouth full of fries. "But it's food."

"I'm starving. There's nothing to eat at home."

"I wasn't like that, was I?" Hudson says to Bea.

"You once made yourself an omelet with a dozen eggs, a half-pound of cheese, and six slices of bacon, then went to a friend's house for a birthday party and cleaned out the pizza *and* the cake. I sent the parents apology money since they had to order three extra pizzas so everyone else could eat something."

"No, that had to be Griff."

"*He* got a job stocking the cheese shop before school because I told him if he was going to eat that much steak, he had to pay for it himself."

"Seriously?"

"Seriously."

"He told me he got steak because you liked him better and his nutrition was more important."

"You believed that?"

"No, I thought you were compensating because you liked *me* better and didn't want him to feel insecure."

She smiles at him, and my brain once again betrays me by wondering how it would feel to have Bea Best smile at *me* like that.

She undoubtedly has no idea she has this effect on me, but there was something about watching her interact with her customers the other day and the way she ran the small staff that has stuck with me.

"Go make more burgers so we can solve the hangry security people problem too," Bea says to Hudson.

"Can I do it after I call Griff and tell him I'm your favorite and that I was Mom and Dad's favorite too?"

"*No.*"

He grins. "Too soon?"

"You'll be in your fifties before it's not too soon."

While I stand there smiling at this fascinating relationship of siblings who are also parent and child, both of my boys moan.

I sweep a gaze over both of them, ready to rush them to the nearest hospital if something's been done to their burgers, but—

It appears the only thing wrong with their burgers is that they're delicious.

Burger juice drips down Charlie's chin as he moans again and eats a full third of the burger in one more bite.

Eddie's conquered half of his burger, and his eyes are rolling into the back of his head. "Dis ish *ooo* guh."

"I nee anuvva," Charlie says.

"Mo fies."

"Awwa fies."

"Do you speak teenage boy with their mouths full, or do I need to interpret that for you?" Bea asks me.

"Four more burgers to our order, please, with extra fries. And naturally, I'm happy to pay for it."

The success of *In the Weeds* couldn't have come at a better time.

Without it, I'd be going into debt helping pay for these two to eat.

"They're getting ice cream after all of this too, aren't they?" Hudson calls.

"Betting that depends on if they're also lactose intolerant," she calls back to him.

"I like her," Charlie says before wolfing down the last of his burger.

"Is she the one you're taking on a date this weekend? Is she just kissing up to us?" Eddie asks.

"It's not a date," Bea says. "It's an apology dinner."

"So you're going to bang him?" Charlie asks.

"One, inappropriate, and two, I'd have to want to for that to happen, and I don't."

"Are you sure?" Eddie asks.

"Eat your fries," I tell them, ignoring the sinking in my stomach.

She doesn't want to sleep with me?

the spite date

That'll put a damper on my dreams.

My boys hold up matching empty trays.

Butch appears with two large ice creams in oversize waffle cones. One chocolate, one vanilla.

The boys pounce.

"Thank you," I say to Butch.

He nods and grunts once.

Probably means *we all benefit when their mouths are full.*

"Go sit," Pinky says to the three of us.

"We'll get the rest," Tank agrees.

"Take the boys. I'll be along in a moment. I need a word with Bea."

My children are thankfully distracted by the ice cream and allow themselves to be led toward an open picnic bench in a shadier area close to the trucks.

Bea leans her forearms on the windowsill again and looks at me expectantly. "You want to plan another party?"

Her dry sarcasm makes me smile broader. "Your friend Daphne isn't here today?"

"She has a day job saving wildlife through a non-profit, so she only helps me on the weekends. Did you want to ask her out too?"

"No. Not at all. I simply wish to go into our evening together prepared. You're using me for publicity for your burger bus. Is that correct?"

Her eyes go flat. "Are you always this blunt?"

"Naturally. I don't object, by the way. Simply saying I wish to know the role I'm playing."

"You don't care if people use you for your fame?"

"I'm quite happy to let the right people use me as they'd like."

Hudson's head jerks toward us. "Did you just ask my sister to have sex with you?"

I clear my throat. "No. Not that I wouldn't have sex with her—I've rather enjoyed the time I've spent with her so far—but I'd keep that proposition more private. I know how prudish you Americans can be."

The two siblings share a look.

Bea's is exasperated. Hudson's holds a scowl.

She turns back to me. "That's very kind of you to let me use you."

My smile broadens. "Fantastic. So glad we aired that out. I'll prepare to be as charming as ever, and I'll leave the gossips and busybodies so convinced that you're the catch of the century that your burger bus won't be without customers for the rest of the summer."

She gapes at me.

"That *would* achieve your goals, would it not?" I ask.

"Yes, but—you're happy about being used. Who's happy about being used?"

"The gods have blessed me with success, Ms. Best. It gives me pleasure to use it for good."

"Are you for real?"

"I assume so. I've never contemplated the philosophy of realness, so I suppose it's possible I'm not."

"Why do you smile so much?"

"I quite enjoy it. Don't you?"

"Not *that* much. And Peter Jones—"

"Such a cunt, isn't he? And not the good kind of cunt. Not like a mate-cunt. Like a twat-cunt." Americans always need that explanation too.

She opens her mouth, then closes it again.

"Do you have the budget for a new dress? If you're going to make a splash, let's make a splash."

"Am I being punked?"

"I only punk my children, but more often myself."

It's the entire truth.

But thankfully, in this case, I'm going in with my eyes wide open. No punking here.

All will be well, and Bea and I will be cosmically even.

Her publicity, my inspiration, and my conscience will be at peace.

5

Do go on with the gossip

Simon

When Lana arrives to visit with the boys early Wednesday evening, I'm battling a case of an overactive conscience.

Not because I've allowed the boys to climb the trees in the sprawling back garden of this estate, but because of the notes I've been scribbling all afternoon.

Though Lana's displeased side-eye after her double take at Charlie's leg hanging off a branch makes me reconsider if I should be allowing my conscience to feel guilty about multiple things.

"If they fall, you get to explain it at the hospital," she tells me.

"We won't fall, Mum," Charlie calls. He's intentionally chosen to call her *Mum* since some little twat mocked him for it in preschool, and he insists it adds to the charm of half of his heritage. He uses Britishisms at every opportunity for the same reason.

One might say he comes by the spite attitude naturally.

If one wanted to consider such things.

"We're expert tree-climbers," Eddie adds.

"Wait until you see us jumping branches like the squirrels."

"We can't be squirrels, numb-nuts. We weigh too much."

"You weigh too much."

"You're an arsehole."

Lana narrows her hazel eyes narrower at me. "And they're cussing now?"

I clear my throat. "Boys, it's fine to explore the proper use of all of your words while at home, but I expect you'll use polite language whenever you step off this property. And at your mother's house. And in her presence."

They both giggle my rules.

I hear they'll eventually outgrow giggling, so I soak in the sound, hoping it's not the last time I hear it.

Though it would serve me right if it is.

I likely don't deserve to enjoy the sound of children's laughter.

Not with what I'm doing.

Lana shakes her head at the boys' giggles and drops into the chair beside mine. She's barely five feet tall and always brings to mind the blond pixies in that old animated *Peter Pan* movie. She's also the one and only woman I've formed any sort of real relationship with in my entire life outside of professional circles.

I'd say that was necessary since we share two children, but she *is* a good friend.

A good friend who lost all romantic interest in me when she realized I'm a hopeless disaster in personal matters, which is just as well.

I'm a far better friend than romantic companion.

"That wasn't the *watch your language* warning I would've used," she says to me.

"Your American prudishness aside, if you stigmatize the words, you give them more power. Far better to maintain power over your words by understanding how to use them all." I gesture to the teapot and cups on the tray between us. "Tea?"

"Is it caffeinated?"

"Of course."

"Then no, thank you. I want to sleep tonight."

"Ah. You've reached *that* age."

the spite date

She shoves my arm. "You will too when you get called back to London to put your parents in a home."

"Oh, no. That will be the boys' duty. They who inherit the kingdom must do the work."

Her eyes go large as saucers, and when I crack another smile, she shoves my arm again. "*You* are the asshole."

"Indeed."

The boys have gone suspiciously quiet, and we both look out at the large maple trees in the sizable garden beyond the brick patio.

"Eddie? Charlie?" Lana says.

One of them replies with a noise that sounds similar to what I expect a sick jungle bird might make, and the other hoots like an owl.

I sip my tea and smile.

Lana relaxes back into her chair. "I really will kill you if one of them falls out of the tree. I don't have the bandwidth to handle broken bones on top of getting Mom prepped for moving into the home."

"'Tis a risk one takes when one decides their children cannot live on electronics alone, and lucky for both of us, I have all the time in the world to play nursemaid if necessary."

She points to the notebook balanced on my knee. "Did your computer finally die?"

Ah, the computer.

My lucky laptop computer.

I've written all of my best scripts on it, and it's so ancient that it now runs at a speed that could be outpaced by a drunken snail who has forgotten how to move. It also randomly orders my equally ancient printer to spit out random web pages, old scripts, and the occasional email chain.

"She's operating as well as ever," I tell Lana.

"That's not the flex you think it is."

I smile.

"Is the fresh air helping with inspiration?" she asks.

The lovely thing about Lana is that I don't have to keep up pretenses.

So I have no problem letting her see me grimace as I, too, look down at my notes. "I find myself in a conundrum."

"That must be uncomfortable."

"I've found a plot for the show the studio ordered."

One of her delicate eyebrows arches. "And the problem is…?"

I could lie to her. Invent some ridiculous reason that this is a problem. Blame a cowriter.

But this could affect her too, and if there's anything that I owe the mother of my children, it's honesty.

Especially as I know the studio well enough to know it's likely they'll love this pitch and greenlight it immediately.

She'll see the entire thing on television soon enough.

"It's rather inspired by living…here."

She purses her lips together and stares at me.

I shift in my seat.

"This house here?" she asks.

"Did you know that the former owner of this house held a weeklong wake in the sunken living room for her husband when he passed? I was unaware that was a tradition here."

"Zada Young used it as an opportunity to show off her house since no one had been inside for twenty years. I came to the wake."

That was meant to be a distraction from confessing my sins, but instead, I scribble a note about the wake amidst my other notes. "Fascinating."

"The wallpaper's the same that I remember from that day. So are the fake flowers. You're living with wake flowers."

I note that as well.

"Simon."

"Yes, Lana?"

"The house isn't your inspiration."

She says it as if she's the boss of me, and heat that's likely a manifestation of my conscience trickles over my neck. "Is it not?"

"You can't lie to me, Luckwood. I'm raising your children, and you all have the same tell."

the spite date

"I haven't *lied*."

"You haven't told me the full truth either. Also, I can see your notes from here."

I flip my notebook over.

Lana clucks her tongue. "So you're taking Bea Best to dinner on Saturday night so that you can get more information about her life to make a TV show about it."

"You make it sound so filthy."

"Have you told her why you want to take her out to dinner, or does she think it's an *I'm sorry for having you thrown in jail* dinner?"

"She's using me for publicity for her burger bus. It's fair. And seems necessary. This woman with the community theater and some murder mystery dinner—Lucinda Camille—has accosted me twice in public to tell me how terrible the burger bus is, and the lack of traffic when the boys and I went to apologize on Monday suggested that the community believes it as well, or is at least wary of even trying it. Good burgers though. There's a secret ingredient. Fish that's unexpectedly delicious too. All very tasty. I see no reason that the burger bus shouldn't have a queue down the street, and I'm willing to stake my reputation on it for her."

Lana stares at me as though I've no idea how big of a stupid oaf I am. "So you're doing a burger bus date? Are you cooking? Or making *her* cook?"

"No, we're attending a restaurant opening."

Her face performs the same style of gymnastics that Charlie's does when Eddie's being a little prat and insisting that one of them doing their homework is the same as both of them doing their homework as a method of trying to copy Charlie's work.

"What restaurant?"

"Something something Fig. By the lake."

She makes a strangled noise that might be a laugh or that might be a gasp.

I'm not entirely certain.

But she finishes the noise with a broad smile. "I see."

"I'm afraid I don't see whatever it is that you seem to think you see."

"Mom! Mom, want to see me swing like Tarzan?" Eddie calls.

She peers back out into the yard. "No, I want to see you with both feet firmly on the ground, with all of your bones intact, no blood, so that you can give me a hug and thank me for bringing you fried chicken for dinner."

"Fried chicken?" Charlie echoes. "Which kind?"

"The kind from the little place on Secret Alley."

"Did you get the mashed potatoes too?" Eddie asks.

"Am I the best mother in the entire world who would never deny my sons mashed potatoes when I know they're their favorites?"

"She got the mashed potatoes!" Charlie crows.

"I'm gonna beat you down," Eddie announces.

"Nuh-uh."

"Yuh-huh."

"I'm faster."

"You're uncoordinated."

"But only young men who use their manners and don't fight get the mashed potatoes," Lana adds.

Charlie drops to the ground, lands in a squat, and rushes us. "Love you, Mum." He bends over and hugs Lana as Eddie *oofs* to the ground behind him.

"No fair! You got a head start because you didn't go as high, you idiot."

Charlie grins and dashes for the house, his hoodie hood flapping along behind him. "Potatoes!"

"I've authorized Tank and Butch to separate you if necessary," I call after them.

"Excuse you, hugs first," Lana adds.

Eddie huffs, rapidly changes direction to give Lana the barest hug and a peck on the head, and then he's off for the house too. Leaves cling to his hair, and a large smear of dirt mars the back of his shorts.

Lana rises.

I bolt to my feet. "You were saying, about my dinner on Saturday?"

"I wasn't saying a thing."

"Your face was."

the spite date

"That was me letting out all of the expressions I didn't want to make in front of Mom all day."

"What do you know about this restaurant? Or about Bea?"

She purses her lips together and looks up at the blue sky.

"Truly, Lana. If there's something terrible, I should know."

"For inspiration?"

"So that I may cancel the date if necessary."

"Did Bea actually tell you she wants to use you for publicity for her burger bus?"

"Naturall—" I play the conversation back in my head. "Ah. Hmm. I suppose I suggested it. Though she didn't contradict that she intends to use me."

Lana smirks. "You are such a man sometimes, Simon."

"What else could she want me to take her to dinner for?"

She starts toward the house. "What do you know about Bea?"

"That she was in her first year at university when her parents died in a house fire, and she moved home to raise her three brothers, and now she owns a burger bus. Oh, and she was wrongfully arrested last weekend—my fault—and her ex-boyfriend's brother was the arresting officer."

"Mm."

"*Mm?* What does that mean? Have I got my facts wrong?"

"What do you know about her ex-boyfriend?"

"What do *you* know about her ex-boyfriend?"

"He was two years behind me in school, but he did band, and he used to poke me in the back with his clarinet, but someone else always got blamed for it because no one believed that Lucinda Camille's son could *possibly* ever misbehave. Whatever Bea has planned for you on Saturday night, I approve."

I slap my hand over the rear door to the house as Lana reaches for it. "Whatever she has planned for me?"

"You're going to JC Fig's grand opening?"

"Yes, that's right."

"Do you know who owns JC Fig?"

"Should I?"

"Her ex-boyfriend, Simon. Her ex-boyfriend is opening JC Fig."

Bea's ex-boyfriend.

Bea's ex-boyfriend is opening the restaurant she wants to dine at for their grand opening on Saturday.

"Was it a cordial breakup?" I ask Lana.

"From what I hear, Jake and his family have all been quietly spreading borderline defamatory rumors about her and the reasons for the break-up. If Mr. Camille—Damon—wasn't an attorney, they'd probably be all the way into slanderous territory."

"Then why would she—oh. *Oh*."

Her ex-boyfriend.

Jake.

The man who rushed me on Saturday.

The man she squirted with ketchup.

A tingle touches my fingertips as my shoulders tighten and my chest constricts.

"She intends to use me to make him look bad," I breathe.

"It's been a long time since I lived here. I'd like to think people can change. But from everything I've heard, Jake's an even bigger public charmer now than he was in high school, which probably means he's still metaphorically stabbing other people in the back with his clarinet, but with more resources. I just have this gut feeling about him. So if that's her plan— to steal his thunder by making the entire night about you and whatever you do at the grand opening—then like I said, I approve."

My hand curls into a fist.

How lovely for Lana that it's so easy for her to approve of me being used as a pawn in a lovers' quarrel.

She sighs, then touches my elbow. "She's not your parents, Simon."

"Bloody well aware of that," I grouse.

"So ask her. Ask her if she's planning something bad for the restaurant's grand opening. I don't know her—she was several years behind me in school, probably close to ten or eleven, actually—so we never really met. The boys were three or four when her parents died. I remember one of them shitting in a houseplant when I was on the phone with Mom while she was telling me about the fire."

"You didn't know her, but you remember that?"

"Their house was three blocks from Mom's, and it's the biggest tragedy to ever happen in Athena's Rest. Also, it's the only time either of the boys ever shit in a houseplant. The memories are forever linked."

"That's…astonishing."

She studies me. "You're angry."

"I dislike being used for revenge against current or former romantic partners." And I dislike being angry.

I enjoy being happy.

I make a point of being happy.

"You *did* get her thrown in jail. And you *are* using her life as inspiration for your script."

I suddenly don't feel guilty about that anymore.

Not in the slightest.

How lovely.

"You're not going to talk to her, are you?" Lana says.

"Thank you for the information. You should go and enjoy some time with the boys. They're likely to be well-behaved now that you've offered them four chickens and a field's worth of mashed potatoes."

"Simon…"

"If you'll excuse me, I need to prepare for a role."

"If I needed you to show up in court just to intimidate opposing counsel who'd been a dickwad to me but thought you were the greatest actor on the planet, would you?"

"Did you date opposing counsel?"

"Pretend I did."

"This is nothing like that—"

"Isn't it? It's interesting that they broke up and now they're both in the food industry, even though I know he's still in real estate and I heard she was working as his admin assistant for most of their relationship. Makes you wonder if there's more to the story, doesn't it?"

"She's deceived me, likely for her own benefit and for my downfall. Why are you taking her side?"

She grins. "Because she's a woman, which is always enough for me. But if you need more, because I also know her ex, and I don't care how many hours he puts in planting flowers and how much money he donates to local causes, I just have this feeling that he's a still a twatwaffle underneath it all."

I continue frowning.

She ticks more reasons off on her fingers. "And because I know you. And because you'd be a lot happier if you went to therapy to deal with what your parents did to you. And because if you're using a real person as inspiration for your next show without telling her, you're going to be begging me for legal help sooner or later, and I want you to remember this moment—right now, when I tell you that you deserve to suffer before you ever do all of the things that I'm telling you that you both should and shouldn't do. It's like a pre-*I told you so*."

"I'm hardly an amateur. I'll change enough details."

"Keep telling yourself that."

I stifle a sigh.

It's frustrating being frustrated.

I prefer to be happy.

Even if only out of spite, which is why I originally set out to be happy many, many years ago. But being happy is habit now.

And speaking of spite—I suddenly have bigger plans for this date with Beatrice Best.

6

It's not too late to back out

Bea

Cold feet are supposed to be reserved for weddings, bungee jumping, and picking majors in college, yet here I am with cold feet about a simple Saturday night.

"I changed my mind," I tell Daphne as I stare at my reflection in the full-length mirror on the back of her white bathroom door. Hudson and I are living here in her apartment with her this summer. Possibly longer for me, depending on if the family renting the house I bought for us after the fire decides to renew their lease.

"About what?" she asks.

"Going tonight. You know what's going to happen when the first picture gets out of me looking like this while on a date with Simon Luckwood? And you *know* Izzy at the boutique will let it slip that he ordered me a dress. And shoes. And this ridiculous—what even is that bag? I don't care what kind of NDA he's using with her. She'll let it slip. And then everyone will say—I don't know what they'll say, actually. But a man doesn't buy an outfit for a woman without it meaning *something*. You know?"

Daph adjusts a strap on my slinky, glittery red dress. "You don't have to go. You can cancel."

I could.

She wouldn't judge me for it.

Wouldn't throw anything back in my face or call me a chicken later.

That's the thing about Daph—she's great with plans, good and bad, but she doesn't always have to have her way or insist you're making a mistake if you don't do what she wants you to do.

"And then Jake wins," I sigh.

"He doesn't *win*. He lives his life. You live yours."

I smooth my hands down the gown Simon sent. It hugs my hips and breasts and the evidence in my belly that I like chocolate chip cookies. "And if I don't go, I spend the next eternity obsessing over how I had this chance to show him what he lost out on and I chickened out."

"I'd pick binge-watching baking shows over going out to a fancy restaurant."

"Is JC Fig the fanciest restaurant you've ever seen?"

She snorts. "God, no."

"So it wouldn't be a great sacrifice for you to skip it."

She grins. "Let's try another angle. You like running your burger bus?"

I meet her gaze in the mirror. "More than I expected to."

It was honestly a revenge plan. Scrounge up enough money to buy and convert the bus so that I could run a more successful food truck than Jake could run a whole-ass building. I'd quit the job I had working in the mayor's office to be his admin assistant when we started dating, and then we were building a restaurant together. It was going to be our thing.

And then it was gone.

Everything was gone.

Job. Restaurant. Home. Future.

Now, despite my cold feet, I know I have to do this. For me.

I need to get even.

You could say my revenge era has started. But I'm having second thoughts because I don't want to spend my life ruled by a need for vengeance.

Even if I still want Jake to suffer.

the spite date

If it weren't for Simon's massive tip for the party that wasn't, and then the attention he attracted when we were already giving away the food for free, this month would be firmly in the red. Even with his payment, I'm barely able to afford my own meager salary.

Running a burger bus is a little bit more of a financial stretch than I thought it would be. Plus, my socials haven't taken off the way the socials for JC Fig took off.

It's likely a combination of changing algorithms on the platforms and a lack of the extra attention that we got for doing interviews about Griff, but part of me wonders if Jake has the right contacts to get my accounts suppressed somehow.

So yeah, add paranoia to my list of problems after the break-up.

"Think you'll still be running the bus in five years?" Daphne asks.

I make a face.

She knows the answer to that question.

And the answer is, I've spent my entire adult life taking care of my brothers and a few boyfriends, and I've never had to figure out what I actually want for myself.

Ironically, that's the biggest reason she and I are friends.

Because when we met, neither of us actually knew what we wanted to be when we grew up. In her case, it got her disinherited from a massive fortune. In my case—

Well, in my case, I just lived with the knowledge that I was a walking, breathing testament to failing my dead parents by not having my life together enough to know what I'd want to do with myself if I weren't raising my brothers.

That I just went wherever the wind took me, professionally speaking.

Before Jake and our shared restaurant dream, it was Will who worked too hard at the bank, and I switched up my hours at my part-time job at the furniture store so that I could make him dinner and be home when he got off work. Before Will, it was Andreas, who was massively into the outdoors and talked me into not working at all so that we could go hiking or fishing or snowshoeing while my brothers were at school, since *you have that insurance money, babe, so enjoy this life for the moments that it is. You'll figure out more money later if you have to.*

And before that, I didn't date much because I was driving the school bus route for my brothers' schools and trying to take classes and stressing over what I'd do whenever I finally had the time to figure out what I wanted to do.

So it's great that I can take free classes at Austen & Lovelace College since my mom worked there for so many years, and I still get occasional calls about filling in for the bus driver who took over after I quit to be a free spirit with Andreas, but I don't know what I want to do, and so long as I'm running the burger bus, I don't have to think about what comes next.

Who I am.

What I want when I'm not taking care of everyone around me and executing revenge plans.

Daph fixes a lock of my hair. "So enjoy tonight for what it is."

"Which is?"

"An opportunity for a professional boost because of a bad thing that happened. Simon Luckwood knows *exactly* what will happen when photos leak of the two of you. He straight-up told you so. And he hasn't been seen with a woman other than the mother of his children in like a year and a half, and he has to know that means this will be extra big. You have nothing to lose and everything to gain, and I can coach you through all the right things to say when you suddenly have customers around the block wanting to know if Simon's on the bus on any given day."

"And when people realize we're not actually dating? That this was a one-time thing?"

"They'll have tried your burgers and your secret menu items and you'll continue to flourish all on your own. Seriously, whatever you put in those burgers—chef's kiss, Bea. And I say that as someone who's eaten burgers all over the world. You're gonna rule this town with your burger bus. With your *fleet* of burger buses."

"I don't want a fleet of burger buses."

the spite date

"But what if this turns out to be the best thing you ever did? What if this *is* what you're supposed to do with your life? Just because you stumble into something sideways doesn't mean it can't fit in the end. Look at me and my job. I had serious reservations when I started because of where the funding comes from, but it's what I'm supposed to do. It's what makes me happy. Just keep your mind open to the possibilities, okay?"

"Can I please survive tonight first? Why did I think this was a good idea? Not that your ideas are ever bad. They're just sometimes more—actually, just *more* than what I'd ever do on my own."

"The fucker used your family's story to steal your dad's legacy. *And* he let you give him money to help pay for it, then didn't give it back when you broke up. Your *rent payments* for living with him, my ass. But again—if you don't want to go, *don't go*. You don't have to keep torturing yourself with him."

I don't.

But I'll have regrets if I don't take a public stand about *something*, and this opportunity to do it with Simon won't come up again.

I meet her gaze again while she adjusts my hair. "What if Jake gets extra attention because of this?"

"Jake can't cook, and there's zero chance he's keeping his chef happy. He's too much of a micromanager, and he can't keep up his *I'm such a great guy* façade forever. Why do you think he's gone through so many assistants at the real estate agency? Eventually, people see through him."

"Do they?"

She doesn't answer that. "All Jake's getting out of this is a temporary boost that'll fall flat within months, whereas *you* are getting the opportunity to prove to people that you're more than a burger flipper whose ex-boyfriend's family likes to spread rumors about you. Here. Let me see your eyes again."

I obediently turn and tilt my head down. "If he'd just opened his own restaurant somewhere else, with someone else's inspirations…"

"Exactly that. Tonight, you're gonna look like a fucking queen." She attacks my eyelashes with more mascara. "You're doing your ex-boyfriend the favor of showing up on the arm of a celebrity for his grand opening."

"You're calling in a bomb threat to the restaurant, aren't you?"

She cracks up. "That was five-years-ago Daphne, and that Daphne only would've done it to save the polar bears. *This* Daphne prefers psychological mind games, and Jake will lose sleep for weeks over this."

"Do you think he's smart enough to realize I'm playing psychological warfare? If your opponent doesn't understand the game, is he worth playing with?"

"That's why it's brilliant," Hudson calls from the bedroom. He's flipping through a gaming magazine, on his back on Daphne's bed, which is also piled with laundry and the ancient stuffed lobster she's had for as long as I've known her. Hudson's enjoying every minute of what's likely to be his last summer vacation since he's planning to try to get an internship somewhere next year. He's in school to be a teacher, but he's obsessed with music, and he almost landed a summer job at a record label in New York.

He knows tonight's full plan because he knows Daphne and he knows me and he has a very logical brain. He basically called us both on it the minute Simon left the burger bus last weekend.

And he's clearly still in favor of it. "You show up and you're all *oh, Jake, this is so beautiful, you did such a good job*, and he'll be so confused that he'll spend the night trying to make his little pea brain think bigger thoughts than it's capable of."

Daphne laughs. "Can you do that voice again? Bea's a little higher pitched."

"Fuck you," he replies with a grin in his voice. "Bea, if you bring Jake's favorite actor of all time, he won't be able to talk or walk straight because he'll be so flustered. He might even forget Simon's lactose intolerant and serve him something with cheese. When people talk about his opening, it won't be about the food, it'll be about *why was his ex-girlfriend there with Simon Luckwood*, and you've made his night about you. You've stolen all of his attention and all of his glory. You win. Any way

the spite date

you look at this, you win. And you can't take Simon somewhere else tonight and win the same. You *have* to crash the grand opening."

"And then the rocking chair test on top of all of it," Daphne murmurs. "But if you don't want to go, don't go."

"For the record, I object," Ryker calls from the short hallway outside the bedroom. He's been here for about an hour. Probably because he also has concerns about what I'm up to tonight.

"You'd object to breathing if it wasn't necessary," Daphne calls back.

I smile at the accuracy of her statement.

"Okay, Bea. You're ready. And now the first test of the night is if Simon can be on time."

She's barely finished speaking before the doorbell buzzes.

Hudson flings himself off the bed and dashes out of the room.

Ryker's not one to run, but I can still hear the two of them tussling in the hallway, making me wonder if Ry's breaking his preferred grumpy-slowpoke routine to battle Hudson to get to the door first.

"Too bad Griff couldn't be here too," Daphne says. "Can you imagine Simon facing all three of them together?"

"I might be dreaming about it before the night's over. Probably with Griff's bat too. Do you think Simon really smiles that much all the time, or is it an act because he's prepping for a role that's like, the opposite of playing Peter Jones?"

"Margot says he's smiley all the time."

"Seriously?"

"Yep."

"Huh."

"Right? I would've thought it was fake too."

If Daphne's sister says Simon smiles all the time, then he just might. While I don't know Margot nearly as well as I know Daphne, she's been to visit enough that I call her a friend. Plus, Daph adores her despite the unpleasantness of Daphne being disinherited while Margot's still on the fast track to taking over as CEO of their family's hotel mega-chain.

They grew up filthy rich in a family with multiple homes in neighborhoods full of other rich and famous people. They went to school with famous people's kids, and Daphne was regularly invited to famous people parties until she was disinherited, so it doesn't surprise me that Margot, who's still in that world, would've crossed paths with Simon, even if his fame is relatively new.

I check the mirror one last time. "How's Margot doing?"

Daph rolls her eyes. "Working too much and pretending she's not thinking about her ex-fiancé."

I don't know the full story of Margot's big breakup—it happened about the same time Daphne was disinherited four years ago or so—but I know enough to make a face. I also appreciate that Daphne's letting me ask questions to distract myself from what I'm about to do.

"Why's she thinking about him now? It's been forever since they broke up."

"Because his dad's getting out of prison soon and *our* father is apparently talking about trying to merge the companies again. Or so she says. I wouldn't know. I don't talk to him directly."

"Wait. *Prison?*"

"Yeah. Prison. Embezzlement and wine fraud. You didn't know that?"

"*No.*"

"Yep."

"How did I miss *that?*"

"Bea. You were in classes and I was moving in and Hudson got the flu and strep all at the same time and you kinda had other things going on than worrying about my sister's break-up."

"But her ex's dad went to *prison?* And your father still wants to merge companies? What does Margot's ex's family do?"

"Long story. No more time to spare. You have a hot date."

I am *so* getting this story out of her later. But for now, I check my reflection one last time. "An overly smiley date that I don't trust."

Something crashes in the living room, and then the apartment door makes its usual squeak, and then something else crashes.

the spite date

"Who are you?" Hudson says in a tough guy voice that cracks Daphne up and makes me cringe.

"If you're going to try to get into my sister's business tonight, I'll get into *your* business, you get me?" Ryker says.

"Hold on, I can get Griff on video call in two seconds," Daphne says. "I don't think his game today is for a few more hours."

"Do *not* call Griff too." I lower my voice as the two of us dash to the bedroom doorway and hover, listening to my brothers. "I think he fell down the *In the Weeds* rabbit hole and would probably *also* crap his pants."

"Good evening, gentlemen," Simon says. "Lovely to see you both again. I have the utmost respect for your sister and intend to try absolutely nothing beyond accompanying her on what I sincerely hope will be an enjoyable evening. Unless *she* wants something, of course. Which I also would not confide in either of you, because a lady deserves privacy."

"Where are your kids?" Ryker asks.

"Pizza and movie night with their mother, who's missed them quite a bit while she's been tied up helping her own mother this week."

"Bodyguards?" Hudson says.

"One with Lana and the boys, two downstairs with the limo."

"A *limo?*" both of my brothers say.

Ryker's question is skeptical. Hudson's is delighted.

Naturally.

And you can practically hear Simon's smile in his response. "Yes, one of those stretch SUV numbers. Did you truly expect me to make this evening anything less than grand to apologize for accidentally having your sister arrested?"

"What time will you have her back tonight?" Hudson asks.

"Whenever she wishes to be back."

"Turn your pockets inside out," Ryker orders. "I need to see for myself that you're not carrying condoms and hoping for a quickie in the bathroom."

"Oh, no, I sent those in the handbag that accompanied the dress and shoes."

Daphne and I trade glances, and both of us lunge for the clutch on the bed.

I'm not in the killer heels yet, so I beat her just as I hear Simon chuckle out in the living room.

"I jest, I jest. There won't be any hanky-panky initiated by me this evening. I'm well aware of my standing with your sister, even if I hope to eventually convince her that I'm not the devil I play on television."

"She knows karate," Hudson says.

"No, she doesn't, but she doesn't need to if she decides you've crossed a line and need a lesson," Ryker says.

"Sorry, Bea's loins," Daph murmurs over my shoulder as I open the handbag and verify for myself that there are no condoms inside.

My loins are still too skeptical of smiley Simon to agree that they need sympathy. Who's that happy all the time? And what celebrity doesn't care if they're used for publicity for a random small-town burger bus?

This is all fishy.

And not like my secret menu is fishy. That's good-fishy. This is bad-fishy.

But my heart melts the teensiest bit as I take in what *is* inside the bag.

Tissues.

Eye drops.

Makeup wipes.

Butterscotch candies.

"Did he do this himself, or did he steal an old lady's bag?" I whisper to Daphne.

"One way to find out. Get your shoes on, and let's make your grand entrance."

"You're making my grand entrance with me?"

"Of course."

"Because you think I'll fall over in these shoes?"

She flashes me a grin and very distinctly doesn't answer me. "If you really don't want to do this…"

the spite date

"How much of your actor money have you blown on alcohol and drugs and gym memberships that you don't actually use?" Hudson asks.

"Okay, okay, I'm going." I shove my feet into the sparkly red heels and only wobble a little as Simon's answer wafts down the hallway.

"Do you count inhalers as drugs? One of my boys has asthma, and the other has been known to break a bone here or there and require painkillers. And I send money to my favorite charities every month as well."

"Is he still smiling?" I whisper to Daphne.

"Sounds like it. I wonder what it would take to fluster him?"

"His children. They definitely fluster him."

Okay. Shoes on. Bag in hand. Hair done. Makeup done. Dress smoothed.

It's time.

"Bea?" Daph says softly.

"Yes?"

"Jake's gonna lose his mind when you walk into his restaurant in this dress. Everyone's gonna see what he gave up, and everyone will realize what a complete moron he is. You're fucking gorgeous."

"More to a person than how they look, Daph."

"In this world? I wish you were right, but you're not." She shoves me gently. "Go on. Go make a scene. I'll make contact with my spies so I can be there in five minutes flat if anything goes wrong."

I eye my friend once more.

She grins. "I will not be what goes wrong. Swear on the lives of every polar bear to ever walk the earth."

I hug her quickly. "I adore you."

She squeezes back. "Adore you more."

My brothers are still discussing Simon's qualifications and worthiness, and it's rapidly devolving—Ryker just said something about high school test scores—so I square my shoulders, straighten my spine, and walk out of the bedroom.

It's time for a spite date.

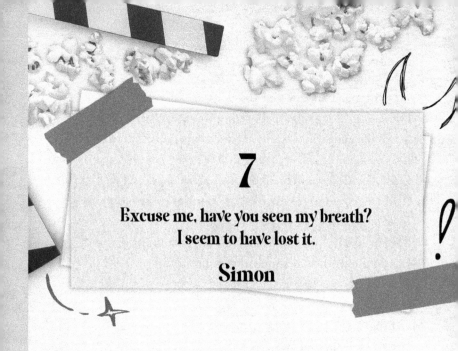

7

**Excuse me, have you seen my breath?
I seem to have lost it.**

Simon

Despite my reservations over being used as a puppet for some plan against Bea's ex that I'm not privy to, I do believe this date was an excellent idea for inspiration.

Bea's brothers haven't stopped peppering me with questions in the three minutes since they let me inside the apartment, and I'm making mental notes of every inquiry to analyze later.

Overprotective brothers are something I've not experienced regularly in my own life.

I'm an only child. Lana's an only child. Our boys watch out for each other, but it isn't the same as this overprotective-guard routine that Bea's brothers seem to have perfected.

"Aren't there three of you?" I ask after answering how much I can bench press—unknown, as I prefer running and push-ups to the gym routine, if you're wondering.

"Yes," Hudson says as Ryker replies, "What's it to you?"

"Your other brother doesn't live here too?"

Hudson coughs.

Ryker narrows his eyes. "Until we see how you treat Bea, you don't get to know anything about where our other brother is."

"Or isn't," Hudson chimes in.

Sincerely, it's fascinating.

So much energy put into protecting family.

I hope my boys stay this close as they age.

"What does it matter where he is?" Ryker asks as movement behind him catches my eye.

The short hallway is lit only by the natural light streaming in through the open doors on either side of it, which isn't enough to see clearly, especially without my glasses.

My low-light vision took a turn for the worse when I had my vision laser corrected, which is something that I didn't know could be a side effect of the surgery and which I'm lamenting at the moment.

My pulse is acutely aware of who's coming down the hall.

The click of stilettos on the wood floor, the shapely curves, hips swinging with every step, hair pulled up save for a few curls framing her face, and—

Dear god, she's stunning.

Beatrice Best in a form-fitting, sparkly red dress and sparklier red heels, with plump, bright red lips to match, her green eyes larger and softer—I have made a terrible miscalculation in thinking that I would be the main attraction for this date.

My lungs have ceased to exist, much less work.

My mouth has gone so dry that my teeth may have turned to dust.

And my heart—that useless little organ that beats for two people and two people only in this world, ever—shudders out a protest that the rock guarding it from the world seems to have cracked.

I don't remember how to blink.

Or how to close my mouth.

Not when the cheeky burger bus lady with the twin dimples has unveiled her goddess side.

She makes eye contact with me, and her eyes flare wider, her pupils darkening before she blinks.

The slight smile curving her luscious lips dips away, taking her dimples with it, and she looks behind her.

"*Now* he quits smiling?" she mutters.

"It's because you're pretty and he doesn't know how to cope with that," Daphne replies, much louder.

And that does it.

That almost snaps me out of my trance, as I'm certain Daphne had something to do with this master plan to use me.

But only almost.

Perhaps this was a terrible idea.

Perhaps this was the worst of terrible ideas.

I'd planned to stay on my guard and be ready for whatever twists and turns she throws at me tonight, but instead—

Instead, I'm rather enamored, and not nearly as unhappy about it as I should be.

Both of Bea's brothers cross their arms and shift so that they're a wall between me and their sister.

"Best. Behavior," Ryker growls.

"If you don't think she's pretty when she's sweating in her burger bus, you don't get to think she's pretty when she slaps on a dress and some lipstick and mascara," Hudson says.

"Better. Than. Best. Behavior," Ryker says.

"Oh, stop, both of you." Bea pushes between them. "This is just an apology date. Can we please get on with it?"

Daphne claps her hands, clearly thrilled with how this evening is going thus far. "Tonight is going to go down in the history books."

It certainly is.

Have I ever had a date that made my pulse uneven and sweat gather at my neckline? One which rendered my lungs still unable to function properly?

I don't believe I have.

Isn't that the cherry on top of the injustice pie?

the spite date

"You better not be thinking that you bought that dress so you get to take it off her because we *will* get our other brother and no one will ever find your body," Hudson says.

I shake my head. "Providing a dress is the least that I could do for a woman who deserves the night of her life." The words leave my mouth, and my cheeks get nearly as hot as my neck.

Were I unaware of her secondary reasons for wanting me to take her on this date, I do believe I'd mean every word I just said.

Even knowing her intentions, I might mean every word I just said.

Even knowing that the last thing I need is to develop a schoolboy crush on anyone merely because, as her brother said, she donned a dress and swiped on makeup.

Possibly it's been a mistake to forego companionship while I've been adjusting to my newfound fame. I'm rather out of practice at accompanying a beautiful woman for an evening, it seems.

And that puts me at one more disadvantage.

I clear my throat, blink twice, and then find my smile again. "You look lovely. Shall we?"

I offer Bea my hand.

She glances at Daphne, who's slipping her phone back into the pocket of her cotton shorts.

Daphne's smile doesn't contain dimples, but it does hold as much mischief as the smiles of the fairies tattooed on her arms.

Pictures.

She likely took pictures.

I should not have insisted my security detail wait for me downstairs.

Tank will likely gloat.

As he should.

"I'm coming with you," Ryker announces.

"*No*, you're not." Bea stands straighter. In her stilettos, the top of her head almost reaches his nose. "I'm going to go have a…nice…meal… while drawing attention for the benefit of…my burger bus."

This is when my instincts should kick in and remind me that she's a terrible human being who deserves to have a horrible time tonight, but my god, she's lovely.

Have I ever had a woman this lovely on my arm?

Are my lungs working again yet?

Ryker scowls at her. "I'll be across the street."

Hudson grins. "I'll babysit him."

"Tank and Pinky will also be there," I remind them.

The two brothers share a look. Hudson grabs a pair of trainers from near the door. Ryker shoves him and grabs a pair of work boots.

Daphne smirks at me. "I'm staying home and managing the online bets about if you two have another date after this. Might watch TV too. Catch up on my favorites."

"*Stay here*," Bea orders her brothers.

They ignore her.

She makes a face I've seen Lana make at our boys when they ignore her as well.

Her frustration shouldn't make me smile, but I relate to how she's feeling, which should annoy me since I don't want to relate to her feelings.

But I can't deny that it's also attractive that she understands raising teenagers. She *did*, in fact, raise teenagers, so of course she would understand.

"If we can't stop them, we may still be able to arrive before them," I tell her.

She eyes my hand, still out, then lifts her gaze back to mine.

Wariness.

She's nervous.

As she should be.

I daresay this evening won't be quite the evening she's hoping it will be, which I won't be letting on until it's time for *my* plans to fully fall into place.

"Or we could stay here and critique Daphne's telly choices," I offer.

the spite date

Say yes, a soft voice whispers in my brain.

Give yourself an out so that I can enjoy how lovely you look without the pain of knowing what you're about tonight.

The boys tromp out of the apartment.

Bea looks to the ceiling with an exasperated half smile tilting her lips once more. "Going out in public with a serial killer is preferable to watching Daphne's favorite shows."

Daphne winks at me and mouths *you're welcome.*

"I only played a serial killer hired to suss out a man's son's true intentions," I say. "Despite the number of deaths at Peter Jones's fictional feet, I have not, in fact, ever murdered anyone, though I do pride myself on reading between the lines."

"That'll serve you well tonight, mate," Daphne says.

Bea shoots her a look.

But I can't quite contain another smile.

Because of inspiration.

Yes.

Inspiration and inspiration alone.

"One question before you go," Daphne says. "Who stocked Bea's handbag?"

"I did."

Both women goggle at me.

"How did you pick what went in it?" Daphne presses.

"That's more than your one question. But if you answer one for me, I'll tell you my secret."

More suspicion rolls off Bea. "What do you want to know?"

"Were you truly on the line with your bus last weekend? At the Secret Alley entrance?"

They share a look, then a smile.

"I was three inches over," Bea whispers.

"Bloody brilliant. I thought so."

"How'd you decide what to put in Bea's bag?" Daphne repeats.

"The internet. Ta-da! My greatest magic trick. Now. For the last time before I'm convinced that you're playing games with me, shall we be on our way? Wouldn't want to miss our reservations."

Bea gives her shoulders a slight shake, straightens, and looks me dead in the eye. "Absolutely. Let's do it."

She finally takes my hand, and an electric current jolts my skin from my fingers to my palm, across my wrist and up my forearm.

Rather glad I'm in a long-sleeve shirt so that she can't see the gooseflesh rising on my arm.

But I get the pleasure of seeing it erupt on her arm.

Or rather the torture.

Why must the woman I'm most attracted to in years have secret intentions that will likely be disastrous for both of us?

And why must I insist on subjecting myself to the torture?

Ah, yes.

Art.

Art will always be torture, and also worth the torture, even if the attraction will not.

So we'd best get on with it.

8

Surely nothing will go wrong if we add bubbly to the mix

Simon

I say goodnight to Daphne, and Bea and I step into the apartment hallway. It smells of curry and ginger, and for a moment, I feel as though I'm back in London despite having spent as little time as possible there since my early twenties, before the boys were born. Bea drops my hand and leads me to the lift. When she presses the button, the doors open nearly immediately.

And then we're inside.

Just the two of us.

In a very small space with ivory walls and the curry and ginger scents from the hallway lingering with a hint of cigar smoke.

Bea presses 1 on the button panel beside the silver doors as they slide shut.

I stand in the middle of the car, unsure of how much space I should give her now that it's just the two of us and the elephants that she doesn't seem to realize have also boarded the lift with us.

"Have you lived here long?" I inquire as we begin our descent.

"I moved in with Daph when—when I broke up with someone a few months ago."

"Ah."

"How long are you in Athena's Rest?"

"Through the summer, likely. I'm due in Los Angeles in September."

"Filming your next show?"

"A movie. They've delayed production to accommodate my schedule with the boys this summer, in fact, which still feels rather odd."

She makes a soft hum of acknowledgment while I tell myself to stop talking.

The lift shudders to a stop, the doors open, and Tank greets us to accompany us out to the waiting SUV limousine.

This is quite a different experience from the last time I dated anyone.

Not that this is a *date* date. The real kind.

Even if a very small, inconsequential part of me wishes that Bea's intentions were merely interest in me as a person.

Possibly more than a small, inconsequential part of me.

Definitely a part that needs to shut up.

One can hardly be inspiration for a script without also being fascinating. Were I not in need of a script, I daresay I'd still be interested in learning more about this woman who raised her brothers and serves burgers and fish out of a converted school bus.

Her brow wrinkles as Tank opens the rear limousine door for her, but she also smiles and thanks him before stepping inside.

I follow.

Tank closes us in.

The divider is up between us and the driver's seat, so it's just the two of us back here.

And my hands are suddenly sweating.

Because I'm being an utter bastard in using her back?

Or because I suddenly don't know what to do with an attractive woman sitting so close that our knees are touching?

Am I back in primary school?

I don't get nervous around women.

the spite date

"Was the limo too much?" I ask Bea. "I didn't consider that what would do in a city might not work in a smaller town."

She's in the side seat, her red dress riding up her bare thighs as she inspects the buttons and levers that control the seats and open the cupboards hiding snacks and beverages.

"Maybe. Do you always pick up your dates in limos?"

"I don't know."

She studies me with those bright green eyes. "You don't know how you pick up your dates?"

"I haven't dated since I could afford to pick up dates in style."

Is my tie getting tighter?

She studies me closer and crosses her legs, which I actively try to ignore.

Her legs, that is.

Though the scrutiny is also rather uncomfortable.

The car pulls away from the curb, and I lunge for the cupboard to my right. "Champagne? To celebrate the pending success of your burger bus?"

I slide out the tray holding two flutes and an already opened and chilled bottle of bubbly.

"Is that Dom Pérignon?" she asks.

"It *is*. I've never had it before. Seemed a marvelous time to try it, while taking you out for a publicity date. Do you think they'd let us sneak it into the restaurant?"

She blinks slowly at me, making me wonder if she's aware that I'm aware of her other intentions. "I think we'll have to find out."

"Brilliant."

"You really don't care that I asked you to take me out for my own benefit?"

"I'm hardly getting nothing out of this evening. I do believe I'll be receiving a fair amount of attention myself, and you know how the celebrity world is. Always best to be at the forefront of your audience's minds."

She visibly swallows. "You really haven't dated at all since *In the Weeds* got popular?"

"No."

"Because it bothers you to not know who would've liked you before your success and who only likes you now because you played a popular character on TV?"

"Oh, I don't mind if the women I date like me or not. But I do mind if they intend to sell photos of me in positions I'd rather my boys not see me in. That's been the biggest deterrent."

"You don't care if they *like you or not*?"

I pass her a champagne flute. "Not at all. That would only matter if I intended for anything to become a permanent situation. I find I'm physically attracted to people whose personalities I don't like. They're good in the sack, and I never have to see them again if I don't want to."

Hence my current situation.

I *am* attracted to Beatrice Best, and I dislike her personality immensely.

At least, the part of her personality that thought this evening would be a good idea.

The part of her that understands teenage boys and shares smiles with her best friend, who gave up her own educational ambitions for the good of her brothers, who provided my boys with extra fries and burgers at no additional charge the other day—and yes, I noticed that—those parts of her personality fascinate me.

It's good that she wishes to use me.

Otherwise, I would be in over my head with this woman.

She goggles at me once more, then tips her head back and laughs. "Wow. That's a philosophy I never would've considered."

"Lana regularly tells me I should speak with a therapist, but until I'm unhappy with my life overall, I fail to see how discussing my unique philosophies with a professional would improve anything."

"Um, maybe for the example you're setting for your children?"

the spite date

"They don't meet the women I merely tolerate for their personalities but enjoy in the bedroom. Certainly not in the capacity as their father's companion, at any rate."

She's still shaking her head, lips still tilted up. "So this is what Daph meant."

"About what?"

"About British people being far more forward about sex than we Americans are."

"Yes, and we're rather comfortable with the word *cunt* as well."

She cringes, then laughs at herself. "Just a word…"

Americans. Truly.

I shift in my seat and change the subject. "Do you wish to get married someday?"

"*No.*" She laughs lightly. "Maybe. Probably not. But maybe—no. No, probably not."

"Your certainty is refreshing."

She hits me with a smile that makes her eyes sparkle and her dimples pop out on both cheeks.

My cock goes lightheaded.

Is that even possible?

I shift in the seat again, and yes, yes, my cock is most definitely lightheaded.

My hand is also shaky as I pour myself a flute of champagne.

"I wouldn't be an easy person to marry," she tells me.

"Whyever not?"

"Because I'm a sixty-year-old empty-nester in a twenty-nine-year-old's body. I love my brothers, but finishing the job our parents started wasn't easy, and I don't want to do it again. Ah-ah-ah. Don't say *maybe you'll feel differently once time has passed and you meet the right man.* The only right answer is *you did a great job with your brothers, Bea, and you've earned time to focus on enjoying your life for yourself now.*"

I smile broadly at her terrible English accent, tipping my flute to hers in a silent toast. "You raised at least two men who clearly adore you with all of their hearts and souls, and you deserve every happiness you gift to yourself. Is your other brother as kind and charming and brilliant as those two?"

"No. And he has even worse taste in television shows than Daphne does."

"So he's an *In the Weeds* fan?"

"You said it. I didn't." She shifts her gaze away as she takes a sip.

I sip my bubbly as well, amused at her reaction to the show. "You're not a fan?"

"Of a show about middle-aged men trying to kill each other over marijuana and money with the blessing of their shithead of a father? I realize I'm in the minority, but it's not my personal cup of tea, and let's be real. It's been done over and over and over again. Where are the shows about women murdering their cheating spouses and abusers and getting away with it? What about the shows where women are the mobsters and the mafia bosses? *Oh my god.* Why are you smiling like that? I'm basically insulting you, and you keep smiling bigger and bigger. *Who does that?*"

Someone who's rapidly realizing how to write the next cult hit. "No, you're right, the show was dreadful. I wrote it as a comedy and it was directed as a drama and it's a hot mess."

"*You wrote it as a comedy?*"

"That was my intention. If not straight-up comedy, satire at the very least."

She stares at me as though I'm a man who's lost his puppy and needs reassurance that it will be found one day even though she knows it's actually dead in the street.

As if I'm deserving of all of the world's pity for my situation.

Rather than offering comfort at my clear lack of worthwhile talent though, she purses those plump red lips together and looks away as though she's embarrassed for me.

It's a refreshing reaction, honestly.

The show was complete rubbish. Bungled all to hell by trying to make it into a true drama. And successful despite its best efforts to not be. Both seasons now. "Is that why you were immune to my charm last Saturday?" I ask.

"No, I was *immune to your charm* because you had me sent to jail and I almost had a panic attack because I hate enclosed spaces and my stupid ex's brother was the cop and he wouldn't let me pee and you had the nerve to be smiley-smiley-happy-happy like an *I'm sorry* was supposed to brush it all away when—sorry, this is rude—I was very, very tired of seeing your face to begin with."

I shift in my seat again because, while I'm comfortable talking about sex and inviting women to have sex with me, I'm also well-trained on not walking around with my flagpole up—there *are* lines—and I find it highly attractive in a woman when she insults me and holds me to a high standard.

Clearly, my body recognizes Bea as someone I could fuck and leave.

Also, perhaps Lana's right about seeing that therapist.

"And also because it's easy to confuse you with the character," she adds on a sigh. "I know I shouldn't, I just—you see Peter Jones smiling, and you wonder what he's planning next."

"A man intent on proving to the mother of his children that he can, in fact, afford to help pay for their school supplies will do anything for a meager salary," I tell Bea. "Including participating in the butchering of a show he wrote and loved, requiring him to play a man who's far worse than he was written to be."

"Are you just telling me this because you think it's what I want to hear?"

"Heavens, no. I don't tend to have that affliction. Though the studio does prefer that I not state my real feelings on the production while on press tours and late-night talk shows."

She's smiling as she sips her champagne. "I honestly can't make you out at all. Is this real?"

"As real as I get."

"So not *all* real. Just as real as you're willing to show people."

The lady is correct, and I should be as on guard as she appears to be. "Ah, we're almost here. Would you like a top up? I'm sure it's against proper etiquette to arrive at a grand opening with our own beverages, but I've discovered people let me get away with terrible behavior since they expect far worse from me, and it *would* draw extra attention to both of us."

She's quite pretty when she's smiling that *you are entirely too much* smile, and I do love the way her dimples deepen as her smile broadens.

Though her brother was right.

She's also quite pretty when she's working in her burger bus.

There's something undeniably attractive about a woman in her element, and Bea clearly enjoys interacting with the public and takes a great deal of pride in her mobile business.

She holds out her glass. "I would love a refill. Thank you."

The limousine glides to a halt, and I pour bubbly into her glass until the bubbles pour over the edge.

"A thousand apologies. Let me get you a serviette."

"I've got this." She switches hands and licks the champagne off her fingers before I can reach for a cloth, and my cock once again goes lightheaded.

So this is to be my punishment for the evening.

Watching an attractive woman lick her fingers and knowing there's only the slimmest of chances that she'd be up for a roll in the hay afterward.

Though the night is young.

And I still have many, many opportunities to be the world's most perfect publicity date.

Especially since I know more secrets than she thinks I do.

I pass her a serviette anyway, and she uses it to dry her licked fingers and swipe around the glass.

She's just finished when Tank opens the door for us.

I look at Bea. "Are you ready to make your public debut?"

She tugs the hem of her dress and smiles a smile that doesn't dimple or shine as brightly as usual. "As ready as I'll ever be."

"Then let us go make an entrance."

9

Don't fuck with karma

Bea

The fucker didn't get the fountain fixed before the grand opening. It shouldn't bother me that Jake took shortcuts, but it's the first thing I notice when I step out of the limo.

At least the grass has been cleaned up. Last I saw, it had overrun the brick patio in front of the converted Victorian mansion that once belonged to the first president of Austen & Lovelace College.

She named the house Ada Jane when she lived here.

I always thought it fit so well.

Now, there's a banner drooping in front of the bushes beneath the front windows announcing the grand opening of *JC Fig*, which also pisses me off.

Dad never wavered in saying he'd call his own restaurant *Jane's Fig* if he ever saved up enough money to buy the old place. Partly to honor the original history of the place, partly because my mom's name was also Jane, and partly because her favorite treats were the fig cookies he used to make.

Grief smacks me like a punch coming from inside my chest.

Dad should've lived. He should've lived and taken a leap with his dreams.

Mom should've lived. She should've been right by his side, the way they were always there for each other.

They should've been here tonight, with Mom working the floor while Dad managed the kitchen, and I should've been here with my brothers to help out, and we should've caught them stealing a kiss in the walk-in fridge and pretended we were horrified when really, we were all so happy that they were happy and that they taught us to be the same.

And instead, I'm here on a date with a man who's growing on me by the second, but who's actually a tool in a revenge scheme against the man who stole my parents' dreams.

Heat floods my eyeballs and my chest gets tight, and I realize I'm clutching my champagne flute tight enough to break it.

"Are you all right?" Simon asks me.

I shake my head and shove the emotions back down.

They can come out and play later. When I'm in a safe space to let them all out. "Let's do this."

He can't offer me his hand, as one is holding the bottle of champagne and the other his own champagne flute, so after a quick furrow of his brow as he studies me, he offers me his elbow.

The other couple arriving for dinner gawks at us.

They're not dressed as nicely as we are.

Actually, they're not dressed as nicely as *I* am.

Simon's in suit pants and a button-down with a tie, while I look like I should be on a date with a guy in a tuxedo.

Did he set me up to look too fancy?

Or did he set me up to outshine everyone else here tonight?

I should've told him.

I should've told him what this is actually about.

But I didn't, and now we're here, and if I tell him now, will he back out?

Not worth the risk.

I take his elbow. Tank shuts the limo door behind us, then hustles us to the new restaurant's door.

the spite date

"A grand opening," Simon says. "Quite the date."

I clear my throat and try to not squirm. "They get the biggest crowds."

"Is this a thing regularly done in America? Converting old houses into restaurants?" Simon murmurs to me.

"It's not uncommon."

"Will it feel like a home inside?"

"That depends on—on what the new owner did with it."

He smiles broadly. "Do I get the impression you're hoping it's dreadful?"

"I'm undecided."

"Why?"

I gulp. "The thing about small towns is, there's always history between all of us, and nothing's ever cut-and-dried."

"Then I'll follow your lead. If you grimace, I'll grimace. If you smile, I'll smile. If you lose your dinner—well, I'll try, but I have a remarkable gag reflex and it's astonishingly difficult for me to force myself to be ill."

I squint up at Mr. Smiley-Smiley as Tank opens the door for us. I'm not sure I deserve him tonight, which is a crazy change of opinion to happen over a week. "Can you do that?"

"I *am* a trained actor, darling. Who would've thought I could've pulled off Peter Jones? I deserve an Emmy."

"Fair enough."

The house's foyer has been converted to the host stand, naturally. I'm relieved to see the old wood trim hasn't been painted over, but some of the stained glass has been removed.

There's a page on the college's website with a walk-through of the old house.

Everyone in my family knows this building inside and out.

I loved the stained glass.

I also loved the chandeliers and the grand staircase that I can't quite see ahead of me and the banisters and the wallpaper and the worn wooden floors with the rectangular stains where rugs once protected those portions of the floor from being faded from the sun like the rest of the wood.

The hostess slides into the foyer and looks up at us as she reaches the mahogany stand, then blanches. "Oh, shit."

"Reservations for two and a half for Barney," Simon says pleasantly. "Do you need the email confirmation?"

"Oh, shit shit *shit*," she whispers again as her eyes flit between us.

I squeeze Simon's elbow, mostly because I suddenly don't know what to do.

The theory of arriving at Jake's grand opening on the arm of his favorite actor to make a scene is a lot different from the reality of being *in the scene*.

I'm better at pulling my brothers out of trouble and being a smart-ass in places where I'm comfortable than I am at causing trouble behind enemy lines.

Parking my bus three inches over the line of where it's supposed to be?

Child's play.

Getting arrested when I have proof I did nothing wrong?

I can handle that, even if it was awful.

Making a large public nuisance of myself on purpose?

I need to tell Simon.

I need to tell him *right now* what's going on.

"My man called an hour ago to alert the staff that *Barney* was a pretend name," he says smoothly, and I realize he has no idea she's *shit-*ting because of me.

He thinks she's having a reaction to *him*.

Breathe, Bea. Breathe breathe breathe.

I need to tell him.

And I will.

Once we're seated.

the spite date

"Yeah, but I thought *Barney* would be like, Margot Merriweather-Brown or like, one of the Rutherford brothers," the young woman says with another terrified glance at me.

"The Rutherford brothers? With the Razzle Dazzle family?" Simon asks.

The hostess sends another panicked look my direction. "They live over in Albany. I mean, they used to. They still come around sometimes when they visit the area."

Wait.

I know this woman. "Olivia? You're Olivia, right? From Griff's class?"

Her smile is so pained, I want to take a Tylenol for her. "Hi, Bea. Welcome to JC Fig. We're so glad to have you for our grand opening."

Simon's smile, on the other hand, seems completely genuine. "You know each other. Brilliant. Not to be *that celebrity*, but could we possibly be seated quickly? Before we cause a scene in your lobby? I'm eager to try the meatloaf to see how it compares to my favorite from the city. Your menu looks positively delicious."

Olivia grimaces.

I nearly grimace for her.

"Chef made a fixed tasting menu for tonight. No meatloaf."

"A tasting menu! Brilliant. Clearly, I must return another night for the meatloaf." He winks at her. "Provided the tasting menu is as delicious as I hope it will be."

She blinks at him.

Then looks at me and grimaces again.

Then looks back at him. "You can't bring in your own alcohol."

There goes his smile, doing its smile thing. "Can't I? Just this once?"

If she winces any harder, she's gonna get a charley horse in her cheek or eyebrow. "It's against the rules."

"I noticed you don't have Dom Pérignon listed on your online menu, and I prefer it to any other bubbly."

She looks behind her while I manage to not let my face show that he's lying.

Either to her, or to me in the car.

Then she peers behind us, where Tank is looming so close that I can almost feel him breathing.

And then she closes her eyes and takes the largest breath I've ever seen anyone take.

When she opens her eyes again, I lean into the stand. "I feel like your boss would really want celebrities to be happy," I murmur for her ears only.

"What's that now?" Simon asks.

"Fine. *Fine*." Olivia winces once more, then grabs two leather folios and a drink list and leads us into the converted house.

We walk past the old sitting room on the right, which has had its wallpaper replaced with plain blue paint, and the former library on the left, which has had its bookcases removed, probably to make room to squeeze in two or three extra tables.

The old crystal chandeliers have been replaced with iron fixtures, and the walls in both rooms are adorned with mirrors, which fits Jake.

He knows he's handsome, and he loves to bask in it.

All of the tables are draped with white cloth and have candles dancing in the centerpieces, which makes me shiver.

We don't do candles at home.

Especially exposed candles.

Simon glances at me and lifts his brows, like he noticed me shivering.

He's stupidly handsome tonight. Hair perfectly in place, five-o'clock shadow hinting at scruff to come soon, and he's already rolled his sleeves up his forearms. His suit pants fit his ass better than baseball pants fit my favorite players, and there's mischief brewing in his blue eyes, drawing me in like a bug to a zapper.

"Long story," I murmur.

Olivia leads us up the central stairwell between the two front rooms before I can see any more of the first floor, and my heart cramps again.

Jake replaced the banisters.

the spite date

Instead of the intricately carved deep-brown wood, they're iron with glossy black wood railings.

He ruined my house.

I know, I know, it's not my house.

But for a few months, I thought it would be. I was here when he closed on it. I transferred money to him to help pay for the down payment, which he claimed later was rent money since I'd moved in with him. We had sex in the kitchen.

And now it's all his, and he ruined it.

My eyes start to burn again, this time for me instead of my parents, but I shake it off.

I'll feel sad later.

When I'm alone.

Right now, all I want to feel is rage.

At the top of the stairwell, Olivia leads us down a short hallway and turns into what was once a bedroom.

Six four-person tables are squeezed in here, and all but two are occupied, and my shoulders relax as I realize none of the people in this room are Jake's parents.

I was sure we'd run into them.

So far, though, we have not.

Olivia seats us at a table in front of a window overlooking the lake.

Simon sets the bottle and his flute on the white-clothed table so that he can pull out my chair for me.

Tank takes the other table in front of a closed door that's hiding a bathroom.

I wonder if it's still a bathroom or if it's been converted to storage. My vote had been to leave it as a bathroom with the clawfoot tub on display behind glass.

So it's probably storage.

Dammit.

Murmurs go up around us, and Tank glares collectively at the whole room.

"Aileen will be your server tonight," Olivia tells us. "She'll be around with the bread presentation soon."

Simon moves forward as if he's going to lift his hand and ask for something, but then slouches back in his seat.

And then Olivia's gone, and once again, it's the two of us.

Except we're on display.

I recognize half of the other couples in the room.

None of the women are in sparkly red dresses.

Worse, Quincy and Wendell Thomas are here.

Or possibly better.

Quincy is *the* gossip in Athena's Rest. If you want the entire town to know something, you tell him. If you want to keep a secret, you avoid him. If you want to start a rumor about someone though, he's not your guy. He only deals in truth.

And he's likely Daphne's spy.

This should be a good thing.

But my stomach hurts.

"Can you eat butter?" I ask Simon as I pinch the flame on the candle between us. "I know how to avoid peanut allergies, but lactose intolerance wasn't something any of my brothers' teachers ever asked the parents to worry about."

"In small quantities." Mr. Smiley's nose wrinkles. "Are you familiar with ghee?"

"My dad was a chef. I'm familiar with a lot of food."

And the smile returns. "Was he?"

"He was."

"Did he teach you to make your burgers?"

"He did."

"With whatever magical secret ingredient you use?"

I smile. I could give credit to using produce from Ryker's farm, but I know half the success of my burgers will be because of Dad's secret ingredient, which will go to the grave with me.

"Yep."

the spite date

"And he introduced you to ghee?"

"It's delicious."

"It's marvelous. All of the taste, none of the risk of discomfort. Tell me more about your father. Did you cook with him often?"

"I used to go to work with him on the weekends. Ryker did too, right until our parents died." I glance around the dining room.

Yep.

They're all staring.

Waiting for the show.

Reason enough to grab more bubbly.

But none of my story is a secret. Everyone in town knows it.

"What did your mother do?" Simon asks.

Tell him, Bea. Tell him why we're here.

I ignore myself. "She was a professor in the math department at Austen & Lovelace."

And twice a year, she acted with the local community theater for a hobby, which she adored, and which I am absolutely not telling Simon.

Both because since Mom died, Lucinda Camille took over running the theater, and also because I don't want to draw the correlation between Mom's hobby and his job.

Not when I'm afraid it would make me feel like her local success was less than his international fame since they'll move an entire movie production's schedule to accommodate him. Even when fame and fortune from acting was never what she ever wanted.

Weird, right?

"Were they awful?" Simon asks the question with that bright smile on his face, and I actually burst out laughing, then remember I'm on display, and I start coughing to cover the laughter.

Simon passes me his water glass, which is both incredibly endearing and also completely unnecessary since I have one in front of me as well. "Are you all right?"

I wonder how many times he'll ask me that tonight. "That has to be the worst question anyone has ever asked me."

He grins.

I crack up again.

I'm still half giggling when I finally answer him. "No, they were not *awful*. They were the best. And that's not a rose-colored rearview mirror. Our house was the one all of our friends came over to hang out at. Dad would cook for everyone. Mom never yelled. They both laughed all the time, and they'd kiss and hug in front of us and gross us all out. I got in trouble once for punching a boy who snapped my bra strap, and Mom showed up in the principal's office and read them the riot act for trying to punish me for defending myself, then took me out for tea and told me how proud she was that I stood up for myself. Truly, truly the best."

"Fascinating," he murmurs.

"Were *your* parents awful?"

"Oh, goodness me, no. They were far worse than awful."

He says it with that happy-go-lucky, no-worries-in-the-world expression on his face, but his voice—his voice doesn't quite match it.

"Are they still alive?"

"Alas, if karma were real, I daresay your parents would still be here and mine would not."

"Wow. They're that bad?"

He lifts the bottle of Dom and tops himself off. "I'm afraid even four of these wouldn't be enough to prompt that full story. Tell me about your brothers."

"Their feet smell, they team up against me, and none of them ever make me dinner."

"Just like my boys."

"Well, you could've raised them better. Mine were already broken when I inherited them."

He chuckles as a short young woman with a purple streak in her blond hair, wearing the black pants-and-white shirt uniform for JC Fig, appears at our table with a basket of bread. "Oh my gosh, I love you," she whispers to Simon as she sets the bread down. "Okay. Okay. I'm going to be normal. Hi. Aileen I'm. I mean, I'm Aileen. I'll be your server tonight."

"Hello, Aileen," Simon says. "Lovely to meet you."

Her whole face flushes red as she shifts side to side on the balls of her feet. "Take your time looking at the menu. Not that you have a lot of options. The chef did a fixed menu for opening, and I just need to know which soup, which salad dressing, and which flavor of ice cream for dessert. It's homemade right here in our kitchens. Oh, shi—shoot. Crap. Shoot. I'm supposed to tell you about the lobster mac. Our main dish tonight is Chef's famous award-winning version of everyone's favorite comfort dish. It features fresh-caught lane mobster—*Maine lobster*—and a creamy three-cheese fennel sauce over cavatappi noodles."

I pinch my lips together and cast a glance at Simon, who hasn't stopped smiling. "Sounds brilliant." He reaches into his breast pocket, pulls out a pair of reading glasses, and slides them on as he glances down at the menu. "Tell us about the soups."

"You have the option of cheddar broccoli or lobster bisque."

I pinch my lips harder, and not because Simon in glasses is weirdly even hotter.

It's because I didn't know about the menu.

I mean, I knew the regular menu was cheese-heavy, but I didn't know there would be a tasting menu *without* the meatloaf Simon mentioned wanting to try.

Or, you know, any single option at all that isn't swimming in butter and cheese.

He keeps smiling. "Marvelous. Could you give us a few moments?"

"Oh, absolutely. Of course. Take your time. Would you like another bottle of wine? Or tea or something else? We can get you anything you'd like. Oh, and here's the fondue."

"Fondue?" My voice comes out strangled.

"Only the best here at JC Fig. Why stop at butter when you can dip your bread in cheese fondue? Be very careful—it's hot."

She steps aside while another server sets a pot of melted cheese on the table.

I reach out a hand before he can light the fuel beneath the pot. "Please don't."

He glances at me, and his face does the kind of gymnastics you'd expect from someone connecting *Bea Best is here—parents died in a fire—don't light the candle—boss's ex-girlfriend—messy breakup—oh shit, that's the boss's favorite actor with her.*

He visibly gulps as he holds eye contact with me.

"Please," I repeat.

Is sweat breaking out on his forehead, or was it already there? "It'll get cold and lumpy pretty fast, Bea. Jake would want you to have, erm, creamy fondue cheese."

I twitch, wondering how good Simon's memory is for names. If my face isn't the color of a tomato, I'll eat these stilettos. "I'll handle the lumpy cheese problem," I force out.

"Lumpy cheese is a risk we're willing to live with," Simon agrees.

The young man looks between us, then back at the cheese, then back at me. "Fuck, you're epic," he whispers.

"I dislike dining with anyone who is less than epic," Simon says. "That will be all. Thank you."

His voice holds an unexpected authority that has both of the servers scurrying away from the table as if they know they've been dismissed.

"Bea?" Simon says quietly to me as he peers at me over the top rim of his glasses.

I gulp champagne. "I didn't know it would be a cheese- and cream-based fixed menu. I mean, I expected half the dishes on the menu would be cheesy, but not *all* of them."

"Ms. Best."

"Yes?"

He removes his glasses, then leans into the table with his nose right over the warm pot of cheese. "Are you afraid of fire?"

I need to tell him.

the spite date

I need to tell him why we're here.

Because any minute now, Jake's going to walk into this room to see his favorite actor, and Simon has no idea, and—

"Would you like me to request that everyone else put their candles out too?" Simon asks.

I am an asshole.

The biggest, assiest, holiest of assholes.

I've set this man up on a spite date and he's offering to ask everyone in the room to put their candles out in deference to my discomfort around open flame. "Can we open this window? It's hot in here. Are you hot? I'm hot."

I'm hot. My dress is too tight. My shoes are too tight. My handbag is too tight, and I don't know how that even works, but it is.

"You're stunning, in fact," Simon says. "I believe I made sure of that."

Mr. Smiley has left the room, and in its place is a man watching me with compassion and concern.

We could leave.

Bolt right now.

It's not like he can eat anything on the menu. And then Quincy will tell everyone we fled the restaurant because there was nothing Simon could eat, and I don't have to see Jake, and why can't I be more like Daphne for just one evening?

Buying a burger bus to make it more successful than a restaurant out of sheer determination to one-up my absolute douchenoodle of an ex is one thing.

This date—this is something else.

"Can I ask you something?" I say to him as I fan myself and Quincy Thomas giggles across the room.

"You're welcome to ask me anything." He winks. "But I might not answer."

"Do you ever get mad?"

His smile spreads broader across his lips, but it doesn't hit his eyes.

My stomach grumbles.

And it's not the champagne.

And it's not that it's been six hours since I ate anything.

It's a gut feeling that Simon Luckwood is *not*, in fact, the happy-go-lucky man he presents to the world.

And he might not be happy right now.

Because he feels obligated to be here and put on a show?

Or is it something else?

"Certainly," he says smoothly. "Everyone experiences anger at times."

"Have you ever been so mad that you do something you regret?"

His blue eyes flicker over my face. "Is there something you regret, Bea?"

"No. Yes. Maybe. I—"

There's a muffled squeak at the side of our table, and we both look up to see my ex standing there.

Clearly having overheard.

I gulp and use my champagne flute as a shield against the death lasers flying at me from Jake's eye sockets.

He looks at Simon, stutters something incoherent, looks at me again, glares harder, and then he finds his spine in the face of having to talk to the only man in the universe who could make him stutter.

"Mr. Luckwood. I didn't know you were joining us, or I would've greeted you myself. Welcome to JC Fig. We're delighted to have you."

Jake's voice is shaking and too high pitched. Sweat beads on his forehead. He's in black slacks and a white button-down, and you can already see—and smell—that his antiperspirant has failed.

My heart starts beating faster.

This was a mistake.

I shouldn't have done this.

It's cruel, and I don't like to be cruel.

"Thank you," Simon says. "I'm sorry, old chap, I missed your name. Are you the maître d'?"

He shoots, he scores.

And he doesn't even know it.

"I—I'm the owner," Jake stutters.

"You look familiar. Have we met?"

"N-no." Jake shoots me another death glare.

I reach for the Dom and top off my glass.

Simon snaps his fingers. "Last weekend. At the burger bus. You were the chap who—sorry. I didn't recognize you without—" He pauses and gestures to his face.

I barely stifle a whimper as Jake's face goes even redder than the ketchup I made him wear last weekend.

This isn't good.

This is *not good*.

If Simon can recognize a man without ketchup on his face, Simon knows who he is.

He's probably known all night.

I should not have done this.

Yes, you should've, I hear Daphne's voice whisper. *Jake fucking stole this from you. Did the man ever love you at all? Or did he just use you?*

I know the answer to that.

The answer is that he used me.

He saw where Griff's career was headed, saw the publicity coming toward our family, wanted to use it for his real estate business, and then saw a bigger opportunity when I told him about my dad's dreams.

Jake deserves every bad thing he has coming to him.

Simon holds out a hand. "Good to meet you, old chap. Call me Simon."

"S—Simon. Right." Jake shakes too hard, which you can tell from the way Simon's body jerks. "Simon, I am absolutely your biggest fan."

Tank starts to move.

"He is," I agree, as if Daph's speaking for me. Or Hudson. Or Ryker. Or Griff, who hasn't been as outwardly pissed as my other two brothers at the situation with Jake, but he'd probably go along with this too. "Jake would have Peter Jones's babies."

Simon's eyelid twitches as he extricates his hand from Jake's before Tank can take down my ex-boyfriend. "That's a new level of dedication. I appreciate the support."

Jake obviously can't figure out what to do with his hands now that he's not shaking Simon's. He's probably contemplating never washing them again.

"We have better tables," Jake says. "More private tables. We thought—someone else was coming. Someone less important."

Oh, barf.

Okay.

This is helping my regrets.

Simon looks between me and Jake. "I have no objection to this table. Bea? Any problems?"

I smile back as nerves make my belly gurgle.

He knows.

He has to know, but he doesn't seem fazed by it at all.

"Great view," I say. "Several witnesses. I'm good here."

"Excellent. We're good here."

Jake's gaze drifts to the champagne bottle, and his face goes even redder as he snaps his mouth shut.

I know that face.

That's the face he wears whenever anyone offers him a bottle of wine that costs more than thirty dollars.

He was about to offer the best wine in the house, on the house, but he can't top Dom Pérignon.

He can't come close.

He always relies on everyone around him not knowing that he's passing off fifteen-dollar bottles as hundred-dollar bottles. Every time we were invited to someone's house for dinner, he'd grab something with a label that looked high-end enough to convince them that he'd paid the world for it.

In retrospect, that should've been a clue that he was all show.

But right now, I could kiss Simon.

Right here. In absolute gratitude for his pettiness.

At the same time, it's putting me on guard.

Will the petty end here? Or is there some petty coming for me too?

As if I'm one to talk.

Karma is going to bite me on the ass for this.

But at the same time, I'm starting to have fun.

And I *was* having fun with Simon before Jake showed up.

One more surprising thing about tonight.

"If you need anything, anything at all, you just ask for Jake." Jake slides another look at me. "Including finding yourself a better date."

Okay, yes.

Regrets are over.

Jake can choke on a bag of dicks.

Simon barks out a laugh. "Ah, you're a funny one, aren't you? A better date. When mine is this stunning, inside and out?" He takes my hand and presses it to his lips, and an involuntary shiver glides up my arm, making me break out in goose bumps for at least the second time tonight. "We're perfectly fine, thank you. And I'm hopeful this is the first of many, many more opportunities to enjoy your—ah, this lovely woman's company."

Butterflies flit through my stomach.

He's acting, I tell myself.

This is a game, and he's winning, because he's known all night—he has to have—and I've been sitting here sweating over if I'm the asshole for not telling him.

But that's a problem for later.

Right now, my rage is coming back.

Find you a better date.

Jake deserves this.

"Could I ask for a favor, though?" Simon says pleasantly.

"Of course. Certainly. Anything you'd like, Mr.—Simon."

"Is there possibly something without cheese or cream or butter on the menu this evening?" He drops his voice. "Dairy and I don't get along."

Jake's eyes bulge. "Oh, fuck, I forgot," he whispers.

"I didn't," I tell Simon.

He beams at me. "Yes, I noticed. So observant and thoughtful."

"If they have ground beef in the kitchen, I could make you a burger."

"Like the one you made us the other day?"

"As long as the beef's good."

"That would be—"

"I can make a burger," Jake interrupts.

I squint at him. "But can you?"

"*I can make a goddamn burger, Bea.*" He huffs, squeezes his eyes shut briefly, and then forces a smile at Simon as the murmured conversations around us stop completely. "Apologies. It would be my honor to make you a hamburger."

Simon's eyes are positively twinkling. "Thank you kindly, old chap."

"My pleasure. I'll—I'll get right on that. Ask for Jake. Anything you want."

"May I please have whipped honey butter and sourdough bread?" I ask.

Jake's eyelid twitches.

Someone at the table closest to the door snickers, then coughs.

"We only have—"

"Oh, I adore whipped honey butter," Simon says. "In small quantities. Heavy on the honey. Light on the butter."

Jake's jaw clenches. "Right. Yes. Yes, of course."

I give my ex-boyfriend the fakest of my smiles. "Thank you so much."

He growls and turns to the door, trips over his own shoelace, straightens, and marches out of the room.

Every other couple stares at us.

"Are you sabotaging his grand opening, Bea?" Quincy whispers into the silence from across the room.

Simon laughs again. "Sabotage? Rather think we're helping the old boy out with publicity."

I make an *mm* of agreement over my champagne even as I become fully convinced that Simon has known about me and Jake and my real plans all night.

Maybe it's not that bad.

Maybe he's really this happy and nice and he has a petty streak or a protective streak or a *something*.

Quincy cackles.

A woman at the next table frowns at him, and Wendell shushes him.

"What?" Quincy says to his husband. "If you dumped me the way Jake dumped Bea—the version *I* heard, which I know isn't the version that Jake's sharing—I'd absolutely show up to your next installation opening with your favorite actor on my arm."

"No, you wouldn't, because Liv Daniels isn't your type."

Quincy gasps. "How dare you. You know I would be straight for revenge."

"I bloody love this town," Simon murmurs.

"Best place on earth," I agree. "Usually."

"All you need to do is replace the cheese shop with a kebab restaurant, and it would be perfect."

I mock gasp. "The cheese shop is *sacred*. No one disses the cheese shop."

"I will."

"No wonder Lana never married you."

He tips his head back and laughs, and once again, the conversations that had picked up around us go quiet.

And I get it.

I don't *like* him, but I don't dislike him either.

He's charming in his own way. Magnetic, if you're prone to falling for that.

Which I'm not.

I refuse to be.

I put my napkin on the table. "Will you excuse me for a minute? I need to run to the ladies' room."

"Of course."

"Don't wait for me if the bread gets here. I can hear your stomach growling."

"I believe I can survive another five minutes." He rises as I rise, and heat floods my face as Quincy murmurs, "Manners are so *swoon*."

They really are.

And that's why I need a little escape.

Just a tad bit of breathing room.

And then I'll face the rest of the night.

10

There's an issue in the loo

Simon

Bea Best is a remarkably charming companion, made more remarkable as she flashes those dimples at me before she turns and strides out of the room and toward the hallway.

I quickly retake my seat so as to hide my once again overactive, backstabbing cock from view.

Watching her hips swing in that dress as she leaves the room does things to my body.

She has a lovely arse.

Round and grabbable.

Perfectly sized for my hands.

Why do the worst of them always have the best bodies?

And why do I always have to notice?

Especially when I have an audience and cannot scowl about it without being noticed?

Top on my list of things to scowl about—I am, unfortunately, stupidly happy to be here.

I still have questions for Bea—research questions that I have no qualms about asking without telling her why—but until Jake appeared at our tableside, I'd almost forgotten that I was ever irritated with her.

Aileen strides into the room with a silver pitcher and starts refilling water glasses at the other table.

The two gentlemen who took an interest in Bea's intentions are first.

"Not to be that person," the taller of the two says to Aileen, "but service seems…slow. We finished our fondue twenty minutes ago."

"First night kinks." She casts a glance at me, catches me watching her, and turns back to them, lowering her voice. Lucky for me, I have excellent hearing. "And you didn't hear this from me, but Jake and Chef are fighting about menu modifications."

Both men peer at me.

I pretend to not notice as I drain the last of the champagne.

Such a pity.

The bottle's run out.

It was quite delicious. I can see why it's popular.

And I gave half of it to Beatrice Best.

The trickster.

I wonder if she's ever been called Trixie as a nickname. I shall have to try it.

It fits her devious little mind.

All the better if she doesn't like it.

"An all-cheese menu was never a good idea anyway," the shorter of the two men whispers. "Do they not know what that does to a normal person's digestive system?"

"That's what Chef said too. And you didn't hear that from me either. I'm like, the *only* person on staff who seems to think so."

I stifle a smile that pops out automatically.

And then a hiccup.

Possibly I shouldn't have drunk a half bottle of champagne on an empty stomach.

The Asiago bread is likely worth the risk of later discomfort.

Goodness only knows I say things I shouldn't when I'm tipsy. Wrong crowd for that tonight.

the spite date

"How bad is the fighting?" the shorter man asks.

"I really shouldn't say if I want to keep my job," Aileen whispers back.

"They should sell tickets to a table in the kitchen. I'd pay a mint to see Jake Camille actually losing his shit in public."

"You're such a weirdo, Quincy," the taller man says.

The shorter man—Quincy, it would seem—winks at him. "Love you too, babe." Then he looks at me. "Excuse me, can I ask you a question?"

"No," Tank says.

"By all means, ask away," I reply.

Tank growls.

I ignore him.

"Are you here just for Bea to embarrass Jake, or are you here because of what Jake was rumored to have done to Lana in high school?"

I sit straighter. Not because I'm unaware of either woman's issue with the owner of this establishment, but because I'm curious what the town says about them. I discreetly burp, remind myself I'm tipsy and need to tread lightly, and smile as though I'm confused.

At least, I hope that's what I'm doing. "Excuse me?"

"Shut up, Quincy," his partner says to him.

Quincy waves a *shush* hand at him. "You know. Because of that time that Jake put live goldfish into Lana's locker in high school? But no one ever called him on it because they couldn't completely prove it was him, and his dad's sued like, everyone in town, and his mother runs the fourth grade like a dictator, but also the whole school secretly since every principal at the grade school has always been afraid of her too. They're the terror couple."

One of the women at a different table makes a noise of protest.

"Shush, Gertie," Quincy says. "Just because he's always charming to you doesn't mean he's charming to everyone. Honestly, I thought Bea could do better when I heard she hooked up with Jake, but I imagine when you're used to taking care of everyone around you, even breadcrumbs of affection feel like riches."

Aileen is refilling water glasses at the next table.

Tank is glowering at me.

And I'm uncertain what to say in response.

Lana didn't mention goldfish.

Which I most definitely need to not say out loud.

"Oh, you didn't know," Quincy whispers to me.

"Didn't I? Or am I merely curious if you're getting the story right?" I smile, quite proud of myself for making sense.

Bubbly.

Bubbly makes me tipsy faster.

His mouth forms an O. "Oh my god, is there more to the story? Tell me. Tell me *now*."

I attempt to lift my brows in a *sorry, mate, not for me to share* look that I've found most gossips understand.

It's apparently a universal enough expression that Quincy gets it too.

He softly slaps a hand on the table. "What if I told you everything I know about the house you're living in? It's a good story. And you should know to watch out for what happens in the shed during a full moon."

"Nothing happens in the shed during a full moon," his partner says.

"That ghost was real, Wendell. I saw it myself."

"That ghost was Logan Camille taking advantage of you being drunk because he liked picking on people who were smaller than he was."

"That, I absolutely believe," a woman at the next table murmurs over her wine. "He's not the same kind of sophisticated that Jake is."

"Still can't believe they let him become a cop," the woman's companion says.

"*I know*, right?" Quincy says. "And of all the bad luck, for him to be the one to answer the call when Simon thought Bea was breaking into his house. You know he loved cuffing her, and I mean that in all the bad ways that it can be taken."

Another night, another situation, I'd be enjoying this more.

the spite date

Except I'm now wondering if this is a setup.

I'll go to the bathroom so the local gossips can sing my praises and tell you how awful my ex and his brother are so that if you're mad that I didn't tell you, you'll feel sorry for me instead.

And it's fucking inspiring.

Who doesn't love a town of people who stand up for the lowly against the corrupt power family? This will be an excellent addition to my script.

Bloody hell.

I've bent my spoon, and I didn't even realize I'd picked it up.

At the same time, I'm smiling so hard that my cheeks hurt, because this town is charming and hilarious and very nearly perfect.

Why must I be both drunk and angry and happy?

Not both when there are three things, my inner editor says.

So I haven't drunk enough to turn that off yet.

Rather unfortunate.

"Are you going to file a complaint against Logan on Bea's behalf?" the first woman asks me.

Be charming, Luckwood. Be fucking charming. "Oh, I'm sure Bea can handle any complaints herself. She's quite adept at anything she sets her mind to, is she not?"

"*Swoon*," Quincy whispers.

"Swoon *again*?" Wendell replies. "My god, you're a pushover."

"And aren't you lucky for that?"

"How long have you two been together?" I inquire.

"Twelve years this Thanksgiving," Quincy says.

And even grumpy Wendell smiles. "It was hate at first sight."

"Who's the overdramatic one now?"

"It was. You hated me because I was a stuck-up asshole."

"And now you're my asshole."

They share a look, then they both giggle.

"More water, sir?" Aileen says to me. "Or I can get you a new bottle of champagne. Or wine. Or tea. Anything you'd like. Except bread quickly. Sorry about that."

"Your best wine, please. Red."

Am I tipsy, or is she wincing? "We're a little low on reds tonight."

"Whites go with cheese," Quincy says.

"Ah. Then your best bubbly."

Tank makes a noise again.

I ignore him again.

A server rushes into the room with a tray of salads—dear god, even the salads are swimming in shredded cheese—and as each table is served, their attention drifts from me.

I tap my fingers and look out the window at the lake, where a few paddleboarders are still enjoying the last of the summer evening.

Has Bea been gone a long time?

Has she run out on me?

No, that would make little sense. Not that I'm currently capable of making sense, but there's no sense in giving me the opportunity to commiserate with her ex-boyfriend about how terrible she is.

That would make him look good.

I peer across the table.

Her handbag is on her chair, and I can see her phone sticking out of it, so she's not texting someone more diabolical plans from the loo.

Unless, of course, she has a secret second phone.

I look across the room at the two men again. "Excuse me, but could you tell me why you're here supporting a man whom you claim is awful?"

Quincy smiles broadly. "For the gossip."

"And to enjoy the food before the place folds," his partner adds. "Chef's good. I've had his food in Rochester before."

"Wendell doesn't think he'll last two weeks," Quincy whispers.

"I always wanted to see the inside of this house myself," the woman at the table beside them says. "That's why I'm here."

the spite date

"Jake's a good guy," the man at the last table says. "All of that stuff is just rumors. No substance to it."

Jake rushes into the room again with a bottle of bubbly in hand. "Apologies for the delay." He takes on a slight accent himself that wasn't here his first go-round, much like his mother did when she cornered me at the chef's table in Bea's bus last weekend. "Chef had insisted no substitutions, so we weren't prepared, but we're getting cheese-less bread post-haste. It's coming right up. The best hamburger you've ever had in your life too. Cheerio!"

He blinks at me.

I blink back.

"Where's Bea?" he asks.

"Using the ladies' room."

His eye twitches. "If she vandalizes it—"

"Bea would *never*," the woman behind Quincy says. "You should be kissing her feet for the attention you'll get for her agreeing to go on a date here, and with Simon Luckwood? All for you to accuse her of a petty crime that she's not committing? For shame, Jake Camille. For. Shame. I'm starting to wonder if you're behind those rumors about people getting salmonella from her burger bus too."

The man's facial muscles will likely be sore tomorrow if the way they all keep twitching and bunching are any indication. "Sorry, Mrs. Cranford," he mutters.

He lowers his voice and leans in to me as he untwists the wires holding the bubbly's cork in. "Be careful. She's crazy. She lit my underwear on fire before she moved out. I had to break up with her because I found her snooping in my bank records. I think she was going to try to rob me blind. And I *did* hear people are getting food poisoning from her food truck."

"She lit your underwear on fire?"

He nods ominously.

I look at the put-out candle on the table, then at the fondue without fire beneath it, and then back at Jake. "Yes, I can see how that would absolutely be within her character."

He freezes like he recognizes by my sarcasm that he's been caught in a lie, then turns his attention to the bottle. He pops the cork, and it shoots into the ceiling, straight into a light fixture, which breaks into a million little pieces and rains down on Tank.

I gulp.

Jake gasps.

"Oh my god, someone shot the light out!" Quincy yells.

"Oh, stop it, you know that was just the cork," Wendell says as people start crowding into the entryway.

Tank rises, shaking his head, and glares at Jake, who shrinks.

"Get them a new table," Tank growls. "No glass."

Where on earth is Bea?

Did she set this up?

But no—I ordered the bubbly, which is spilling out of the bottle.

Likely stored wrong.

And she didn't pop the top herself.

She—

"Mr. Camille?" Aileen pushes through the small crowd that has gathered in the doorway. "Mr. Camille, there's a guest stuck in the bathroom. The door won't unlock."

I look at Tank.

He looks back at me.

"Oh, dear," I say. "I'm afraid that must be my date."

Is my date a witch?

Is that how she made the bottle of bubbly explode? But how would she have known I'd order another bottle? And how would she have known to be away when I did?

Did she plan this with Lana?

the spite date

Impossible. Lana would've ordered ahead to make certain there was red wine for me. Except did they know that the menu was all cheese and that red wouldn't be available?

How the bloody hell does a restaurant not have red wine? They'll need it tomorrow, will they not?

Tank turns toward the door. Jake does the same.

I grab the champagne that Jake has set on the table and follow them.

There's a door at the end of the hallway, and the hostess—Olivia, I believe Bea called her—is leaning against it. "Try turning the handle the other way," she's saying.

"I've tried turning it every way you can turn a handle," Bea's voice replies.

It's high.

High and panicked.

Do her fears extend beyond fire to enclosed spaces as well?

She said as much, did she not? Why is that little nugget stuck in my head?

I frown as the wall bumps into me.

Or possibly that's me bumping into the wall.

Would it be uncouth to sip straight from the bottle?

"Quit playing games and open the goddamn door, Bea," Jake says.

"If you speak to her like that again, you'll find yourself one with the door," I hear myself say.

"Simon?" Bea says.

"Yes, darling?"

"If I get out of this bathroom alive, I swear I'll cook you whatever you want for dinner to apologize for being a complete asshole to you."

"Not in my kitchen," Jake says.

"Touch grass, you fucking codpiece," she snaps back. "Also, Simon?"

"Yes?"

"Will you please go across the street to the miniature golf course and find Ryker and tell him that the fire truck that's on its way is because I'm stuck in a bathroom and not because there's a fire?"

"*You called the fucking fire department?*" Jake says.

"*I'm fucking stuck in your bathroom because your doorknob is fucking broken.*"

"*Because you broke it.*"

"I did *not* break your damn doorknob. And I don't have my phone, so I didn't call the fire department. Your staff did because it's what they're fucking supposed to do."

I share a look with Tank.

Bea sounds rather breathless and almost at the point of tears.

And that's likely what makes the bubbly do more talking for me. "Jake, old chap, get the fuck out of my way so that I can rescue my date."

"How much is she paying you to do this?" he growls at me. "*Tell me.* How—*urp.*"

Fascinating.

I wish I were sober enough to fully understand whatever move that is that Tank has just performed on the bloke to get him twisted up like a pretzel and out of the way of the door.

But I'm not sober enough, and I don't honestly give a rat's arse how it happened.

I simply know it's time for this portion of my date with Bea to be over.

"Beatrice, back up," I order. "I'm going to break the bloody door down."

"You—*what?*" she says.

"Step away from the door, darling. I'm about to be your hero once again."

11

I would like off of this ride, please

Bea

I hate small spaces.

Hate them.

Like the way Ryker hates flame. That's how much I hate them. And Ryker *haaates* flame.

This bathroom is a fraction of the size of the jail cell that had me almost in a panic attack a week ago.

And it's a full story and a half above the ground, and the window is too high and too small to climb out of, and I'm going to die.

So I'm not thinking clearly enough as I huddle against the door, rattling the knob and trying to make it let me out, to actually process that Simon's serious about being my hero.

The massive *thump* that rattles the door has me scrambling back though.

As far back as I can go in this little room with the tile floor and lone high window that's barely big enough for the pedestal sink and ancient toilet when my knees are shaking and my breath is coming in short bursts, anyway.

"Bloody hell," he says, his voice muffled by the thick wood. "That wasn't aimed right, was it?"

My legs bump into the toilet, and I quickly shut the old wood lid and climb onto it.

My heart is racing. I'm sweating like I've been in a sauna for an hour instead of trapped in a bathroom for ten minutes.

This adventure will pass the rocking chair test tomorrow.

Right now, I need to get the hell out of here.

I didn't break the doorknob on purpose.

I really, really didn't.

I just wanted to stare at myself in the mirror and give myself a little pep talk about how *I can do this*, and instead—well, instead, karma decided to remind me that I shouldn't use people.

There's another thud, but this one is accompanied by the crack of splintering wood. The door flies inward, making a breeze hard enough to lift the wispy flyaways of my hair that have escaped the fancy 'do Daphne put it in.

And then Simon steps into the open doorway, his sleeves rolled up his forearms, his hair slightly disheveled, tie loose, with a bottle of champagne in one hand while his other hand hangs casually at his side.

Like *no big deal*.

Like *just busted a door down to save my date*.

While holding a bottle of champagne.

He eyes me, takes a swig off the bottle, and then pulls a face like he got bubbles up his nose.

My heart hiccups.

He's handsome and funny and innately charming, and just looking at him is calming my racing pulse.

He shifts his gaze to the broken door, splintered where the knob was, slightly crooked on its hinges now, and he nods as if he's pleased with the work he's done.

"There now. That does it. Come along, Bea."

Tank is deeper in the hallway, holding Jake in some kind of twisted-up position.

More people are beyond, staring at us.

the spite date

At least two are holding phones aimed directly at me.

My heart thuds.

My eyes sting.

My knees wobble, which is extra bad because I'm still squatting on top of the toilet.

In a dress.

I think I have a crush on Simon Luckwood.

And I don't think it's because he's saved me after going on this awful date with me. I don't think it's an adrenaline crash, and it's definitely not that he's ever been my favorite actor.

It's—well, it's *him*.

He shoulders into the bathroom. "Hold this," he orders.

I take the bottle without thinking, and then he's lifting me off the toilet, cradling me in his arms like I'm a precious treasure in need of protecting.

My eyes burn hotter.

"I'm such an asshole," I whisper.

"Indeed," he agrees.

It shouldn't be funny.

It really shouldn't.

But a snort of laughter escapes me anyway, and just like that—I can breathe again.

My heart can't quite join my lungs in working right, but I can breathe.

And that, too, makes him heroic in my eyes.

He helped me breathe.

He carries me out of the bathroom, and I wrap my free arm around him and bury my face in his neck to avoid looking at anyone.

Yes, yes, fine.

Also because this is never happening again and if I'm having a fairy-tale-princess moment, I'm going to enjoy the hell out of it before reality destroys it all.

I could tell him that I can walk.

That I'm fine. Just a bit wobbly. It'll pass now that I'm out of there.

But he's carrying me down the hallway as if I'm light as a feather, and he smells like my dad used to—like bergamot and patchouli and safety—and I don't want to let go.

"Is this another situation like you parking three inches over the line even though you claimed you were right on it?" he murmurs to me.

It takes me a minute to realize what he's asking.

Did you fake being locked in the bathroom the way you faked having your bus on the line instead of three inches over?

"No," I whisper.

"So you're terrified of fire *and* confined spaces?"

"No. Yes. Sure."

He chuckles, and the sound reverberates against me. "Sounds like quite the story."

I don't deserve this, but I *want* this.

To be taken care of.

"I really didn't break the doorknob. I mean, apparently, I did, but it wasn't on purpose. That wasn't part of the plan."

"I believe you."

"You shouldn't."

"Because you *did* break the doorknob?"

"Because I didn't tell you why I wanted to come here."

"It's quite all right. I'm rather tipsy, so I'll probably accidentally dump you down the stairs as I try to finish this role of playing hero tonight."

I jerk my head up.

He gives me a lopsided grin.

"Oh my god, put me down."

We're almost to the stairs.

Tank is behind us.

Jake is nowhere in sight.

"I'm eighty-three percent certain that I can make it to the bottom of the stairs just fine."

"*Simon.* We can't leave. We haven't had dinner yet."

He grins. "I bloody well can't eat it without paying for sins I haven't committed yet, so I daresay that your intentions will be best suited with us leaving this way instead."

And then he sways.

Tank grabs him by the shoulders. "Put her down, boss."

"Such a spoilsport." He takes the first step down the staircase. "Tell me, Bea, what sort of meal were you planning to cook me to thank me for being the world's best—*hic!*—date?"

"Nothing if you don't put me down. I can't cook with a broken arm."

"I can make it," he insists as he takes another step.

"So we're definitely leaving?"

"Yes. In protest of the menu." He hiccups again as he takes a third step.

If I try to fight to get down, we're rolling all the way to the bottom of this staircase.

"But my bag—"

"Tank shall—*hic!*—retrieve it."

Two more steps. We're two more steps down.

"Oh my god, are you *acting*?" I whisper.

His smile grows exponentially larger. "Darling, I am utterly charmed by your belief in my acting skills."

That wasn't a yes.

It also wasn't a no.

We're halfway down now.

I lift the champagne bottle and take a gulp of it myself.

Maybe if I'm buzzed, falling the rest of the way down the stairs will hurt less.

"You haven't answered my question about what you're serving me for dinner," he says pleasantly.

We're on full display for half the people dining on the main floor, plus two couples peering around the hostess stand.

Oh god.

Oh shit.

Oh fuck.

There they are.

Mr. and Mrs. Camille.

Jake's parents.

And—*fuck me.*

Logan. Logan and a date.

Watching Simon carry me down the stairs of Jake's restaurant.

I think this is good.

Or possibly bad.

Maybe both.

Simon sways on the steps as he looks at me, waiting for an answer.

"Secret menu," I blurt.

"Oh, Ms. Best, I am *intrigued*. Your last secret menu item was—*hic!*—remarkable."

Two more steps.

We're almost there.

He pauses and lurches to one side.

Tank growls and grabs his shoulders again.

"Don't worry," Simon says to me. "He won't quit. The studio pays him too well. Mostly because of my boys, but, alas, also because of me. Tank. Please pay the hostess for our meal. I won't have anyone saying we didn't behave honorably in this sordid affair tonight. Charge it to the company card."

Oh my god.

I think I've found a real-life hero.

Simon steps dramatically to the floor on the ground level, and this time, he sways hard.

Then hiccups.

Then giggles as he straightens both of us.

"Simon! Simon, wait," Jake calls. "She's playing you. Everyone thinks she's this perfect, wonderful person, but they don't know her like I do."

Simon sighs deeply, lifting me with his inhale and somehow settling me even closer to his chest on his slow exhale.

the spite date

And then he turns and looks up at Jake, who's halfway down the steps. People crowd around at the top of the stairwell.

All conversation has stopped in the two rooms on either side of us.

"When everyone else is always the problem, old boy, it's time to look in a mirror. Lana sends her—*hic!*—regards. No, wait… That's not what she said." He squints at the ceiling as though he's thinking. "Ah, yes. Lana sends wishes that you spend your every day with the same affliction that I would have if I were to have dined on any of your dishes this evening. And I daresay a number of your diners tonight wish the same. Good day, sir."

I spot Quincy at the top of the stairs, his mouth spread in a wide-open smile.

Simon carries me around the hostess stand—without knocking me into a doorframe or the stand or swaying at all—and strides past the Camilles without another glance, and directly out the door.

"That was—" I start, but I cut myself off when I spot the firetruck rolling into the circle drive. "Oh, shit."

Three firefighters leap out as Ryker races across the street from the miniature golf course.

My brothers love that place.

"All solved, gentlemen," Simon announces to the firefighters. "I saved the lady from the restroom. Though I daresay you might wish to inspect the remainder of the loo doors for broken locks before you depart."

He sets me on my feet, holding me steady while I wobble.

The firefighters continue into the restaurant, probably for confirmation that a random drunk guest isn't making things up.

"There's no fire," I call to Ryker. "I got locked in a bathroom."

He slows.

Hudson, who's on his heels, slows too, but he also grins. "No shit?"

"It was an accident."

"Excuse me, gentlemen, but I haven't finished my date with your sister." Simon takes the champagne bottle and lifts it for a long drink that has my eyes watering from watching him.

That's a lot of bubbles down his throat at once.

"And you have to be drunk to finish the rest of this date with my sister?" Ryker says.

He's still studying me head to toe.

Cracking his knuckles too.

"Absolutely," Simon says. "Alcohol always makes tricksters more bearable."

"Tricksters?" Ryker repeats.

"People who lie about their intentions."

Hudson rolls his eyes. "Dude, I was there. You jumped to a conclusion about what Bea wanted and you just assumed you were right without asking her if it was possible that you and your ego got it wrong. Pop off. Bea, let's go home."

Simon eyes me.

My brothers eye me.

The limo glides to a stop behind the firetruck.

I could go home with my brothers.

Call it a night.

As far as my original intentions go, this has been a success.

But I hear Daphne whispering *rocking chair test*.

And it makes me smile. "No, you go home. I owe Simon dinner. The entire menu was cheese."

"Including the salads," Simon announces. "They were cheese salads. I saw them myself. Cheese salads with cheese dressings. Why on earth has this place been named after a fruit when all they serve is gastrointestinal distress?"

Oh my god.

I like him.

I do.

I don't care if the smile thing is all an act.

He's hilarious and he's kind and I'm almost positive he's drunk.

The man needs food.

Who am I to deny him that?

12

When a man loves a corn dog
Simon

The burger bus is delightful when I'm drunk at sunset.

The yellow paint is alive as if my eyes are kaleidoscopes, making the colors swirly and bright. Evening insects are chirping and humming and singing as the sun sets over the trees at the edge of the apartment building's parking lot. The pictures of Bea's family are moving.

Not the framed photographs themselves, but rather the people in them.

I can smell the grilling burgers and see her father flipping them and watch as her mother sets more places at their picnic table, and that's merely *one* moving photo.

"Eat," Bea's mother says.

Except that's actually Bea, setting a basket of a corn dog and chips before me.

Yes, *chips*. I refuse to call them *fries*, no matter how long I have lived primarily in the States.

You cannot make me.

So there.

She balances in a chair across the table from me, still in that sparkly red dress I bought for her. One would think alcohol would render my cock useless, but it's quite happy right now.

She made me corn dogs and chips while wearing that dress.

It's likely nothing could render my cock useless after watching her make me dinner in that dress and those heels. And it's not the bubbly making the show erotic.

It's simply *her*.

And a smidge of the bubbly.

Definitely a smidge of the bubbly.

To include the third bottle that I opened in the limo on the way here.

I hiccup.

Bea smiles, and it's so charming and ridiculous at the same time. How is one woman's smile more charming than another's?

"*Eat*, Simon," she says.

I lift the corn dog and study the one dog that appears to be three. "Do you make burgers—*hic!*—on sticks too?"

Her low, throaty laughter makes me temporarily forget where I am. "I'll look into that."

"What about your chips? Do you intend to place them on sticks too?"

"I'd have to charge extra for a basket of fries on sticks."

She bites into a chip and smiles at me again.

My lightheadedness goes lightheaded and my horniness grows hornier.

I want to lick her dimples.

I want to lick her dimples and her lips and her neck and her—dear god, what *has* this bubbly done to me?

The bottle stares at me.

I frown back at it.

It giggles conspiratorially.

"Do I have to feed you?" Bea leans across the table and pushes my hand toward my mouth, the warmth of her fingers and palm making my skin want to lick her skin too. "Eat the corn dog."

That's an excellent idea. But I wave my three corn dogs at her.

My one corn dog.

Just one. One that looks like three. "I only eat if someone tells me a secret."

"You need a dinnertime secret?"

"Yes."

"Do you need bedtime stories too?"

Ah, bedtime.

My favorite topic. "If the correct—*hic!*—storyteller is present and naked."

She shakes her head and shoves the corn dog straight to my lips.

"Secret first," I say against the fried dough.

This smells delightful.

Even better than the fried fish.

That *has* to be the champagne doing my thinking for me though. Nothing could possibly be as good as her fried fish, though her burgers come close.

I cross my eyes, and the three corn dogs become two.

"What kind of secret do you want?" Bea asks.

Tell me what you look like naked, my overactive cock and the bubbly team up on me to demand.

We dislike her, I remind them.

That makes her perfect for naked time, they remind me back.

"Simon?" Bea says.

I jerk my head back up to look at her, as I was apparently glaring at my crotch, and my head nearly floats off my neck.

Good grief, I'm plastered. "Yes?"

"Your lips are moving, but you're not actually saying anything out loud."

I giggle.

Giggle.

Whoops.

"Oh my god, *eat the corn dog*."

I lift it as though I am a medieval knight and it is my sword. "But first, a secret!"

She laughs. "Okay. A secret. Here you go. Our last name used to be *Beste*. With an *e* on the end after the *t*. But no one knew if they were supposed to say *Bestie*—which was technically right—or *Best*—which was wrong—so my grandfather dropped the e when he married my grandmother."

That *is* quite the secret. I shall have to write it down later. If I remember. "Truly?"

She nods, which my brain processes in slow motion. "I think he made the right choice. I'm very particular about who I'm besties with, but I enjoy being *the best*."

"Is there anything about your life that's not fascinating?"

"No. I'm even amusing when I scrub toilets. Have to make it fun or I won't do it, and that's not an option when you live with three boys. Well, *lived*. It's just habit now. And that's two secrets. Now *eat*."

I obediently bite into the corn dog, pause to moan in utter delight, and lose my train of thought.

Do my thoughts have trains?

I think not this evening.

I'm fairly lucky my thoughts exist at all, given how light my head feels.

Being drunk is glorious. Why don't I do this more often?

"Is that a good moan or a tortured moan?" Bea asks.

"I dislike you, so both."

The blasted woman has the audacity to laugh at me. "You don't like me?"

"Goodness, no. I *detest* you. You've put me in the same position my parents did all through my childhood, using me as a pawn in a lovers' quarrel. I think you're awful. And I rarely—*hic!*—think anyone is awful. Aside from my parents."

My vision has crossed from the absolute glory that is this corn dog, so I can't tell what that face is that Bea's making at me.

the spite date

And even if my vision were working, I daresay my brain isn't up to it, so I don't know that I would be able to decipher it regardless.

Oh, look.

The corn dog looks like a willy.

I giggle again.

"You're very happy for a man having dinner with a woman he doesn't like," Bea says.

"I have the extraordinary talent of being able to be happy in *any* circumstance."

"That *is* a remarkable talent."

"I trained myself—*hic!*—without any assistance from the people who should've wanted me to be happy. Heaven help me, I could eat three more of these."

"Finish this one first."

"Tell me another secret."

"It's your turn. You get to eat another corn dog when you tell me a secret."

Fascinating.

I believe she's right.

I try to do the maths in my head about our conversation, and I find I can't recall what I just said, which means she must be right.

She's not nearly as pissed as I am.

Drunk pissed. The good kind of pissed.

The enjoyable kind of pissed.

"Do I know any secrets?" I ask Bea.

"I'm sure you do. Tell me how you and Lana met."

"I made a terribly inappropriate pass at her while serving her spotted dick, and she was unfamiliar enough with us Brits to be enamored with awful pickup lines delivered in my charming accent. Though if you ask me, *she* is the one with the accent."

I bite into the corn dog again and moan.

Her lips twitch up in a smile.

All six of them.

And her eight dimples.

What a treat, to watch Bea's *eight dimples*.

"You don't drink much, do you?" she says.

"Never. I tell all of my secrets when I—*hic!*—drink too much."

"Are you really mad at me for taking you to Jake's grand opening?"

"Furious."

"That's more believable when you say it without smiling."

"And that's my greatest trick, Beatrice Trixie Best. I have managed—*hic!*—to fool you into thinking you know what I'm thinking because I am the world's best—*hic!*—smiler. I'm a smiley smiler who smiles the blues away and fools—*hic!*—everyone."

"Eat more corn dog."

She looks out the rear door, and she frowns before looking back at me. Her dimples have gone into hiding.

I reach toward her, intending to poke her cheeks until I locate her dimples, but she shoves my hand back.

Ah.

Right.

I'm holding the corn willy. Some women are so fussy about being touched on their faces with willies.

I giggle once more.

Bea shakes her head. "*Eat*."

"*Talk*," I parrot back in her American accent.

"I'm beginning to understand why Lana never wanted to marry you."

"Only beginning? Rather slow, aren't you?"

Her eyes widen, and she tips her head back for a bloody good laugh once again.

I mentally pat myself on the back for temporarily outsmarting the alcohol long enough to amuse her.

Her laughter is music.

A veritable symphony that I'd like to bathe in three times—no, four times a day.

Do I remember how to count to four?

I lift my hand, see the willy on the stick, and giggle again. "Tell me another secret."

"Are you going to remember this in the morning?"

"Every word."

I don't actually remember how I got here, so that's probably not true.

Cheers to me for continuing to fake it.

"Daphne saved my life once."

I sit straighter. "Truly? Did she save you from drowning? *Hic!* Or were you in a gunfight? Did she rescue you from a rabid animal?"

"That's really where your brain goes?"

"I am *very* creative, Ms. Best."

"Clearly."

I wave my willy dog. "Carry on with the secret-telling, if you—*hic!*—please."

"You don't recognize Daph?" Bea asks.

"Should I?"

"I guess not. Some people do, some people don't. Her family owns the Aurora Gardens hotel chain. They get covered in gossip pages sometimes. Daph most of all, until a few years ago."

"Ah, I see." I nod, and my brains slosh around inside my skull and request that I not nod again.

"She moved in with Hudson and me about four years ago when her parents disinherited her after she was kicked out of Austen & Lovelace."

Oh, that is juicy.

Almost as juicy as the hot dog inside my corn dog that's really a willy dog, which I've very nearly finished. "Go on."

"You don't know this story?"

"How the—*hic!*—hell would I know this story?"

"It was all over the news, and you were living in New York too, weren't you?"

"New York high society doesn't care what I know about London high society. I—*hic!*—don't care what I know about London high society. And out of spite, I refused to acknowledge—*hic!*—that New York society exists. They are all, every one of them, welcome to lick my boots."

Oh, my.

I do like watching Bea eat her corn dog.

Her lips sealing around the thick tip is giving every part of my body ideas about what else she might put in her mouth.

Specifically, yes, my cock.

Her gaze freezes on me with that corn dog in her mouth, those lovely red lips wrapped around it, and I wonder if my evening might not have a happy ending after all.

I do like happy endings.

Though I like happy endings more when my head isn't sloshy and when I have more certainty that I'll have memories of the happy endings.

Bea finishes biting the end off and chews slowly.

She's growing rather fond of you, the champagne tells me.

I giggle.

I do believe it's correct, and isn't that just hilarious?

Even if I cannot remember why?

I start to bite into my corn dog again, then wonder how this must look to her.

And I decide I don't give a rat's arse.

Prudish, I am not.

Bea clears her throat. "So Daphne was disinherited, and she—"

"What did she do? *Hic!* Was it scandalous?"

"That's her story to tell. All I'll say is that she had to leave school and needed a place to stay."

"So it *was* scandalous."

"There aren't any sex tapes, and she's never been arrested for murder, if that's what you're asking."

"Bah. *Hic!* I prefer the scandals where she's sleeping with her brother's fiancée."

the spite date

"She only has one sister, and she is *not* sleeping with her sister's fiancé. *Ex.* Ex-fiancé."

"Unfortunate. That's a brilliant scandal."

"Simon Luckwood, are you a gossip?"

"Of course," the bubbly replies for me. "Where do you think I get my best ideas from? Do keep up, darling."

She laughs again. "It is absolutely impossible to read you."

"Excellent. *Hic!* What role do you play in New York high society that you were able to gain an introduction to the heiress of the largest hotel chain in the known universe?"

Would you look at that?

I'm able to speak long sentences.

And I do believe I'm tracking this conversation.

That deserves a pat on the back.

Bea's eyes go comical as she watches me pat myself on the back with what's left of my willy dog.

"Daph and I met at the local college here. I was taking a couple classes since Hudson was my only brother left at home and I had a little more bandwidth for trying to work toward my degree again, and she'd transferred here and was in both of them."

"Do children of the rich and famous often come to university here?" I inquire.

I believe that's what I ask, at any rate. It seems a logical question. And when Bea answers, I applaud myself once again for managing to keep up the appearance of a man who knows what she's saying.

"It's a pretty exclusive school, so rich and famous students aren't uncommon. I didn't know she fit that category—she was just someone who seemed a little older than most of our classmates, like I was too. I don't remember why we started sitting next to each other in both classes, but we did, and then one day, she caught me in my car before class having a complete meltdown over my refrigerator breaking two days after the washing machine bit the dust."

"Arsehole washing machine."

Bea laughs. "Exactly."

I bite into my corn dog again and sigh in satisfaction. "Carry on. Your voice is lovely, and I am quite—*hic!*—tipsy, and it's an excellent combination."

She squints at me, but then her lips are moving again, and I could watch her lips for hours.

Days, even.

Months.

Years.

With the dimple.

The dimples.

All of them.

"I told Daphne I was dealing with homeowner crap, she offered to buy me new appliances, and I thought she was kidding. I asked her if she could buy me three extra days every week instead to get all of my shit done. I'd bitten off more than I could chew with two classes, my job, *and* Hudson. Daph insisted on taking me out for tea, and then she really did buy me new appliances."

I lift my willy dog's stick in salute. "Jolly well done. My parents once nearly divorced over a household appliance."

"That doesn't sound like a healthy relationship."

"Who needs healthy when you thrive on dysfunction?"

"Are you talking about them or yourself?"

"Excuse me, darling, but *I* am the one running this inquisition. Please remember your place. Carry on. Tell me about the appliances."

She murmurs something that sounds like *worse than my brothers*.

"Of course I am," I reply. "I have many more—*hic!*—years of experience."

She laughs again, and I drown in her dimples again.

It would be so warm and cozy to live inside her dimples. To escape the rest of the world, right there in her face. To be in her cheeks. So close to her mouth.

Good god, have I ever been this drunk? "Ms. Best."

"Yes?"

"Can one truly fall in love over household appliances?"

She shrugs, which somehow makes the entire bus tilt sideways. "Who wouldn't have fallen in love with someone who managed everything from picking them out to overseeing same-day delivery? It wasn't the money—I offered to pay her back. It was the time and mental energy. I was so grateful that it was something I didn't have to handle solo that I cried all over her and then made her my dad's butternut squash risotto and barbecue chicken with his secret sauce to thank her."

"I was unaware that was an option for dinner this evening."

"It wasn't an option for dinner tonight."

"Tomorrow night, then."

"Simon. We are not having a *tomorrow night*."

Is it getting woozier in here, or is it my bubbly? "Why not?"

"Are you the same person who just said you don't like me?"

"That's no reason to never see each other again."

"Maybe not for you. But I like hanging out with people who like me and who I like back."

"Do you not like me?"

Of course she likes me.

I'm incredibly likable. And charming.

And stinking drunk.

"It's irrelevant if I like you," she tells me.

I blink slowly at her, and it takes her entirely too long to come into focus when I open my eyes again. "Why?"

"I'm getting over a breakup. I don't want to date a single dad because I already raised three kids and I'm done. I need to put my energy into growing my business. I like my life the way it is. You're famous, and I don't want that level of scrutiny on me or my brothers. Should I go on?"

I roll my eyes heavenward, which makes my entire body feel spinny and swoony. "Ms. Best."

"Yes, Simon?"

"Could you please write down the rest of your answers to the rest of the questions I ask you while I fall asleep? I—*hic!*—don't want to miss a thing, but I…"

But I.

Yes.

But I.

And that's the last thing I remember before the world goes a cozy shade of dark.

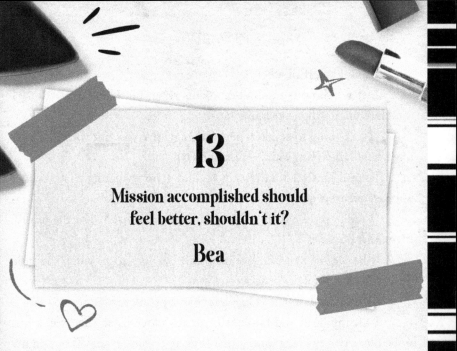

13

Mission accomplished should feel better, shouldn't it?

Bea

The next morning, I'm sitting sideways at the little nook in Daphne's kitchen where we regularly have coffee and tea together, frowning at my computer that's resting on my pajama-clad knees, as I scroll my social feeds.

Everyone in town has an opinion about the opening of JC Fig.

It's three posts about Simon and me for every one post about the actual restaurant opening. And of the posts about us, over half of them mention him breaking down the restroom door—while holding a bottle of champagne—to rescue me when the doorknob broke.

Which the firefighters confirmed.

The doorknob was broken. There's no way I could've gotten out on my own, and there's no way I could've broken the doorknob, or if I did, it was because it was so old that it was bound to break no matter what.

And now I'm vindicated.

Mission accomplished.

With dozens and dozens of pictures of Simon carrying me out of JC Fig floating around local social media to boot.

Several of them with the Camilles gawking awkwardly in the background.

I should be thrilled.

Instead, Simon's rambly comments about not liking me because I used him are rolling over in my head.

"I was going to come in here and high-five you, but you don't look like it's a high-five morning," Daphne says.

I scroll and read another post, and I frown harder. "It was…an unexpected evening."

"I didn't rig the door to break and lock you inside. For the record. I wouldn't do that."

"She did try to order seventy cheese fondues to go when she stole my credit card though," a new voice says.

"A thousand dollars is like less than a penny to you."

I lift my head and blink at Daphne's older sister, then feel a real smile bloom on my face for the first time since Simon passed out on my burger bus chef's table last night. "Hey, Margot. I didn't know you were here. Sorry for taking your usual room."

She's taller than Daphne by a couple inches, a little more slender, with blue eyes and hair that indistinct shade right between light brown and blond. Her pajama shorts are adorned with cartoon mice, which is the last thing I ever expected the first time I saw Daph's uber-elegant, strait-laced, CEO-track sister.

She reaches into a cabinet for a coffee mug and smiles back at me. "No problem. Good excuse to make Daphne clear off her bed so we could have a slumber party."

"A snoring party is more like it." Daphne grabs the electric teakettle and fills it with water. "You need to see a doctor to get that addressed. Or maybe—I know this is gonna sound crazy, but hear me out—maybe you should sleep well enough during the week that you don't crash so hard every weekend."

Margot casually flips her off, and I smile bigger.

"Could you all shut up?" Hudson mutters from the couch in the next room. "Some of us need fourteen hours of sleep every night."

the spite date

"Like you're not partying your heart out and sleeping no more than five hours a night at college," Daphne calls.

"Yeah. Duh. That's why I need sleep in the summer."

"Ryker has a spare bedroom," I remind my brother.

"So you go live with him."

Not a chance.

He wakes all of his guests up by five-thirty to go check on his goats and chickens.

"No Bea, no Hudson," Daphne says. "You're only here because I love your sister."

He grunts, and the couch squeaks, and then all is silent again in the living room.

Margot digs into the tea drawer that Daphne keeps stocked for her, and that I've been taking advantage of while I'm here.

"Paris tea? What's this?" she murmurs.

"It's a new level of delicious," I tell her. "You should try it."

Daph hits the start button on the coffeepot, then on the electric teakettle, and sounds of multiple appliances boiling water fill the air. She reaches into the fridge for a pizza box and drops it on the table, then slides into the booth across from me.

"Are you seeing Simon again today?"

I snort. "No. I'm working the sports association carnival this afternoon." It's an annual fundraiser for youth sports clubs in Athena's Rest. I'm taking the burger bus and donating proceeds, even if things are tight and I can't quite afford it yet.

"Simon stocked her bag with tissues and eye drops and butterscotch candies," Daphne whispers loudly to Margot, as if that has any relevance to the sports association carnival. "How cute is that?"

"Why did he have any business putting things in her bag?"

"He bought her a new one to match her dress." Daph looks at me again. "I know you made him dinner in the bus last night. I saw you. But I didn't see him leave."

"He was so completely toasted that he fell asleep at the table and his security guy had to carry him out to the limo to take him home."

"So you're taking him a hangover cure?"

I make a face. "No. He was fun, but—no."

"He's fucking hilarious," Hudson calls. "I watched a bunch of interview videos."

"Go back to sleep. Nobody asked you," I call back.

"I've met him once or twice, but not enough to get a feel for him, so I asked around my circles," Margot says. "The most dirt anyone has is that his parents are insufferable. Otherwise, everyone thinks he's great. Even ex-girlfriends."

"That's a red flag," Daph says.

Margot pulls a face at her. "It is not."

"He probably paid them to only say good things about him."

"He barely had enough money to help pay for his kids' clothes and food until *In the Weeds* hit big."

"Ooh, did you pay someone to go through his financials?"

"No, Daphne, it's straight-up logic. His parents have more or less disowned him, and he was working at restaurants between acting gigs."

They both look at me as if I'll be the tiebreaker in their debate, and I don't cover the wince that I'm wincing fast enough.

"What's with the face?" Daphne asks me.

"I didn't make a face."

Margot gives me her *don't bullshit me* CEO face. "You made a face."

"I know you're not judging him for being disowned and broke," Daphne says.

I set my laptop on the table and straighten. "Of course not, but since when are you on his side?"

"I'm not on his side, but I *am* disowned and relatively broke most of the time, so I want to make sure that's off the table for things we judge him for."

"I'm not judging him for being broke."

"Then what's with the face?"

the spite date

"Just tell them why you made a face so I can go back to sleep," Hudson calls.

"He just—he mentioned last night that he doesn't like his parents, and that's so foreign to me that I'm still processing it," I lie.

Daphne stares at me.

She knows I'm lying. We've regularly discussed how awful her parents are when she starts to feel guilty for going no-contact with them. I'm well aware bad parents are a thing.

Margot doesn't know I'm lying though. "Understandable. I've actually met his parents. Not because of him. Because of other things. They didn't pass the vibe check."

"Our parents don't pass the vibe check," Daphne says.

Margot ignores her, but she undoubtedly is still getting points from Daphne for what she asks next. "Are you seeing him again, Bea?"

"Oh, I don't think so."

Hudson ambles into the room with his curly brown hair sticking up all over. "You're all fucking loud."

I smile at him. "Buy you breakfast if you come to work with me today."

"Real breakfast? Bacon and eggs and sausage and biscuits and potatoes?"

"I was going to offer tea and scones."

"It's too early for you to be funny," he grumbles.

"Have I ever told you how much you remind me of Ryker in the mornings?"

He flips me off just like Margot flipped Daphne off a minute ago.

Daph and I share a high five.

We're killing it this morning.

"So, back to Simon," Daph says with a mouthful of pizza as the coffee maker starts to sputter and whine at the end of its cycle. "Why don't you want to see him again?"

"Because I don't want to date anyone right now."

Daphne pauses with her pizza halfway back to her mouth. "That is so not a reason."

Margot grabs the teakettle and pours hot water into her mug. "Agreed. You can't plan timing on love."

"*It's not love*," I say.

Hudson eyes the coffeepot. "I wouldn't mind him being my stepdad-slash-brother-in-law."

"Stop. We are *not* seeing each other again. While he's funny and charming and weirdly handsome when he's not playing a total douche-weed on TV—oh my god, you should see him in his reading glasses—he's leaving in a few months, and I'm just not interested in falling for him."

That last part.

After everything that happened at JC Fig and then in my burger bus last night, that last part is the biggest problem. Even bigger than the things I'm not saying—*he doesn't like me, I hurt him, he doesn't want to see me again, and I feel bad about it*.

And I think everyone in this kitchen knows it.

The part where I'm lying that I'm not interested in falling for him.

I'm still working through how I feel about him not liking me. I'm not ready to share the part where I actually *do* like him out loud yet.

Hudson heaves the most massive sigh that he's capable of heaving. "*Fiiiinnne*. We can get your stupid tea and scones for breakfast, and then I'll help you at work today."

Margot rubs his hair. "You're such a good little brother. I wish I had a younger sibling as awesome as you."

Daphne throws a slice of pizza crust at her.

Margot shrieks and ducks it, then dives into the booth to tickle Daphne like we're all seven instead of nineteen to thirty.

Hudson stares at them, not blinking, not entirely horrified, but close. "That would be a lot hotter if you all weren't my sisters."

"Quit being such a hornball." I rescue my tea as it sloshes over the sides with the ruckus happening on the other side of the table, then scoot out of the bench and set my computer aside. "I'm going to shower. And I'll take you to the diner instead of making you have tea and scones. Just because I love you."

He makes eye contact with me, half grinning like he knew I was going to take him to the diner all along, and for a split second, I see my dad in him.

The way his lips quirk. The light in his eyes. Definitely his nose.

I'm seeing Dad in him more and more these days.

And I'm not at all sad about that.

I like knowing our parents are living on in us.

"Do you love me enough to let me shower before you take all of the hot water?" he says.

Margot and Daphne are still giggling at the table, but they both look at me, then at each other, and then they simultaneously roll their eyes.

Hudson glances at them. "Don't start, water hogs. Bea, give me five minutes. I need a shower."

"Who's a hot water hog?" Daphne says. "You better be fast. Margot's taking me cheese shopping, and I don't want to smell like I'm the cheese when we walk in the building."

"I said I'll be five minutes," Hudson says.

"And we all know that means forty, because you're going to the diner, and we all know who works at the diner on Sunday mornings."

He flips her off and saunters back out of the kitchen.

She grins at me. "Your turn, Bea. What's it gonna take for you to flip me off too? My day isn't complete until I've annoyed *everyone* around me. And don't smile while you do it. I need to know I *seriously* annoyed you."

"How do you tolerate her every single day?" Margot asks me, also smiling.

"She's like the fourth brother I never had."

Margot laughs.

Daphne does too.

"Oh, hey, you know what we should all do after cheese and the carnival?" Daphne says.

"Eat and watch television and pretend I don't have to go back to the city for work?" Margot says.

"We should go see Madame Petty."

Margot slides a glance at her sister.

I pause with my tea halfway to my mouth.

"No," we say together.

"Come *on*," Daphne says. "It'll be fun."

I shake my head. "There's nothing fun about letting Madame Petty tell our fortunes."

"This is the same fortune teller we saw right before you were cut off?" Margot says. "The one who more or less told you that you were about to be broke?"

"She's super good for someone so young. I want to know what she thinks of Bea and Simon."

Someone knocks on the door before I can once again tell her no.

I set my tea aside and head to answer it. My heart picks up a little.

Is Simon back?

Did he sober up and want to talk?

Don't be stupid, Bea. He's not coming back.

But my pulse is acting like a sugared-up middle schooler and I'm straightening my posture and swinging the door open with a smile as if he is.

As if I'd be glad to see him.

Which I would be, even if I don't want to admit it to myself.

I'd like to know he's not really angry with me. Not like I could've guessed I'd hit a nerve by using him to make my ex ragey when he didn't care if I used him to get publicity for my business.

Or maybe I could've.

Actually, I probably should've.

And—oh, fuck me.

He's not here.

Jake is.

the spite date

Smile gone.

Jake's in jeans and a casual blue button-down, with his hair immaculately in place, his cheeks freshly shaved.

I square my shoulders for battle instead of for flattering my posture as my pulse kicks even higher. "What do you want?"

He blows out a breath, then looks at me with a muscle ticking in his jaw. "Fine."

"Fine?"

"Fine, I'll take you back."

Daphne makes a strangled noise.

Or maybe that's me.

Possibly both of us.

All I know is, I'm caught so off guard that I can momentarily only gape at him.

"Is that her ex?" Margot murmurs.

"Yeah. Watch how this is done," Daphne murmurs back. "The part where an ex wants you back and you don't take them back because they're an ex for a reason."

Margot *hmph*s. "We're not discussing this."

"But we should."

Jake rolls his eyes. "Can we talk out here?"

"No," all three of us say together.

I shoo the two of them back. Good thing Hudson's in the shower. He was supposed to have a full bedroom at Jake's house all summer.

You know. Before Jake dumped me and stole my parents' dream.

"There's nothing to talk about," I tell Jake. "We're not getting back together."

His expression turns suspiciously patient. "Go on. Get it all out."

"Get what out?"

"All of the reasons you want to yell at me."

I don't like this.

I don't like this at all. "I'm not going to yell at you."

"You're not?"

"No. I'm going to close this door, and you're going to leave and never come back."

He sticks his foot in the doorway. "Come on, Bea. We know this was just our temporary breakup to see how we could handle life without each other. And now it's time to get back together."

"What happened?" Daphne asks. "Did your chef quit?"

His cheeks flush. "No."

"What about—what's her name? Kim? Aren't you dating Kim Womack?"

"Yes, but you know that doesn't mean anything. She's just a whore who likes to—*fuck*, Bea." He leaps back, clutching his foot.

Yes, the foot that I just slammed in the door.

"Don't call women whores, asshat." I succeed in shutting the door this time. Then I lean in to it and raise my voice. "And in case you need it said again, I don't want to get back together with you."

"Simon Luckwood was using you, you moron," he yells back. "If you think he wants anything other than in your pants, you're wrong."

"He's really dumb, isn't he?" Margot murmurs.

"It's his ego. It squeezes all of the air out of the other parts of his brain."

Margot looks at me.

Then at the door, which Jake is banging on again.

Then back at me.

The apartment door locks automatically when it's shut, but I flip the deadbolt and add the chain lock too.

Just in case.

"It's a man problem," she says.

"Testosterone is the worst," I agree.

We both look at Daphne, who's wandered back into the kitchen.

She has her mischief face on, and it gets more mischievous as Jake pounds on the door again. "You know it's inevitable, Bea," he yells. "You know you want me. You know last night was you trying to get back with me. Don't play hard to get. This is your last chance."

the spite date

"No hot coffee," I say to Daphne the same time Margot says, "If you're planning to kick him in the family jewels, you get one shot."

"I was just thinking I'll take the building super some donuts tomorrow. And get the hallway security footage. And maybe anonymously send it to the Athena's Rest Business Association. And also, Bea, I think you should go see Simon."

"I am not going to see Simon. He helped me do what I wanted to do, and clearly"—I gesture to the door, which gives one more shake as Jake hits it—"it worked."

Margot's frowning. "If he bangs on that door one more time, I'm calling the police."

I glance at Daphne.

She grins. "Worked so well that you should do it again."

But that's the thing.

I don't want to see Simon just to get back at Jake.

Now I want to see Simon for the simple joy of seeing Simon, when I suspect Simon never wants to see me again.

"Just think about it, Bea," Daphne says. "Just think about it."

I'll think about it.

And I won't do anything about it.

Because I've done enough to Simon, and this one is mine to handle.

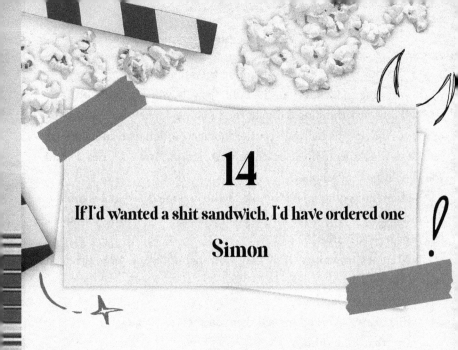

14

If I'd wanted a shit sandwich, I'd have ordered one

Simon

Someone is sticking an ice pick in my skull and shining a spotlight directly into my eyeballs and someone else has loaded my stomach with lit dynamite and I am never, ever, ever, *ever* touching bubbly again in my natural lifetime.

"Don't let them toast me when I die," I whimper.

I would prefer to never touch bubbly in my natural afterlife either.

"Epic date?" the mother of my children says above me. "Or epic after-date?"

"I—"

Bloody hell.

I can't remember.

Were I able to remember, I don't believe I'd want to talk about it either.

Am I eating cotton balls, or is there some other ailment of my mouth that requires a doctor's attention?

"Dad! Dad! Dad, there's a carnival today." The earth shakes around me, and the dynamite in my stomach threatens to explode.

"Will you take us? We were angels for Mum. We deserve to go to the carnival."

"Bet they have funnel cake."

"And lemon shake-ups."

"And fried Oreos."

"And burgers."

"And cotton candy."

"And fried fish."

I groan and clutch at my head.

If I clutched my stomach, I fear it would revolt.

"Boys. Off your father's bed," Lana says.

"But we missed him, Mum."

"Not that we didn't love being with you."

"Of course not."

"We just missed him too."

"You won't miss him much longer if he pukes on you." Lana's cheerful voice reminds me of another reason I never married her.

She's evil when I'm ill.

"Is it already eleven?" I whimper.

"It's eleven-thirty," one of the boys reports.

The ice pick picking at my skull hammers harder as my children climb off the bed. The sudden stillness makes me feel as wretched as the bouncing initially did, and I take several deep breaths to keep from losing the contents of my stomach.

This is bad indeed if I'm this close to vomiting.

I never vomit.

"We're hungry," Charlie says.

"And there's a carnival," Eddie says.

"With food."

"To feed us."

"We're starving, actually."

"Near to dying."

"Out," Lana says. "Go find something in the kitchen. Let me talk to—never mind. Kitchen was the magic word."

The bed sags, and I whimper again as the sound of the boys' footsteps fades beyond my bedroom.

"Saw the pictures," she says.

Pictures.

Date.

Champagne.

Bea.

Bus.

Fuck.

She made me dinner in her bus.

I remember a willy dog.

And very little else. "Why don't I remember half of last night?"

"Pinky said you drank three bottles of champagne almost all by yourself. That might've done it."

I'd groan again, but groaning drives the spikes deeper into my skull.

"Mom was great last night for the caretaker, but she's having a rough start to her day. I can't stay long. And the boys are right. There are all kinds of hangover foods at the carnival today. It's at the lake parking lot."

"Rides?"

The world spins at the idea of carnival rides, and my stomach threatens to rebel.

"No rides. Face-painting, games, fortune-telling, and I think maybe a house of mirrors. Maybe. There was an incident a few years ago, and I'm not sure all of the mirrors ever got replaced." She touches my shoulder. "Much as I wish I could go, I'm out. I'll tell the boys to be good and ask your team to keep a close eye on them. You'll feel better once you puke and shower. Might as well get it over with."

She's unfortunately not wrong.

It takes nearly two hours, but I manage to get myself out of bed, showered, and semi-hydrated. And I also force my mood to improve after I realize I've missed a call from my parents.

Though I wouldn't say I *missed* it.

the spite date

Simply did not see it ring through, and would not have picked it up even if I had.

When I finally appear in the sunken living room, where the boys are playing a video game on the large-screen television, they pause the game and immediately hop to their feet.

"Can we go to the carnival now?"

And that's how I end up dragging my hungover arse back out to the Athena's Rest lake area.

I'm in a baseball hat and the darkest sunglasses I could find in my collection. All three of my security agents are amused at my hangover. My boys are oblivious though.

There's much grabbing of my arms and tugging of my body this way and that as we approach the carnival. The noise is causing my headache to return before we've hardly reached the edges of the game booths, and the mixed smells of all of the food trucks are triggering more than a smidge of nausea.

But the nausea gets worse as I spy Bea's burger bus.

Did I make an utter fool of myself?

The restaurant memories are clear. I do recall breaking down the toilet door to rescue her when the doorknob broke.

I recall returning to the burger bus.

I recall Bea frying corn dogs and chips while wearing that red dress.

And everything is hazy and murky after that.

"Burgers!" Charlie shouts, drawing the attention of half the carnival goers, who have now spotted me.

Whispers and murmurs race through the crowd.

Tank sighs.

Pinky sighs.

Butch sighs.

"Do we have extra painkillers?" I murmur to Butch.

"Two more hours before you can have more," he replies.

I suppose this is my punishment for having a retired army medic in my security detail.

"Mr. Luckwood will sign autographs by the bounce house after he's had a chance to enjoy the carnival," Pinky tells a small crowd of people approaching us.

Translation: I'll interact with the public once my hangover has died down a bit more.

"Can we get burgers, Dad?" Charlie says.

"I want a double patty with triple fries, and I still want to try the fish," Eddie says.

"Do you think she has fish today?"

"Why wouldn't she have fish? It's a good day for a secret menu."

"But if no one knows, will they order it?"

"That's why you go on socials, you jackass." Eddie whips out his phone and shoves it at Charlie.

I peer over their shoulders and spot an advertisement for Bea's burger bus announcing secret menu items at the carnival today. Fewer than a dozen people have liked the post, and none have commented.

So odd.

Her food is delicious, and heaven knows she handed out enough free fish last weekend that she should have gained a larger following.

"See?" Eddie says. "She has fish. Let's go get some."

"It might not be fish. It might be a secret something else," I point out.

Both of my children roll their eyes at me, then take off at a much-too-fast clip for my liking.

Both because my body still prefers slow and sloggy, but also because I don't quite know what to say to Bea today.

Or why I'm feeling as eager to see her as my boys are to have more of her food.

"Did Ms. Best get as drunk as I was last night?" I murmur to Tank.

"She was sober as a doorknob before the two of you got in the burger bus," he replies.

One of my eyes twitches.

I daresay that broken doorknob was the beginning of the end of me last night.

He smirks.

"Have I said thank you for delivering me home safely?" I ask him.

"All part of the job."

We reach the comparatively short line for the burger bus, and I get the advantage of watching Bea and Hudson moving seamlessly inside as they wait on the two customers before us.

She's in her tie-dyed shirt again, but the bandanna holding her curly hair back is blindingly pink and her apron is blindingly yellow. Her face is makeup-free, her smile is smiling, and her dimples are dimpling.

She's a veritable flower.

One that I can't fully appreciate because the bubbly is still impairing my senses and making very little enjoyable.

Except she's enjoyable.

Watching her work—it's spreading the bad kind of warmth in my chest.

The kind that says I like her, that whatever happened last night that I can't remember, she was sympathetic about it and made me feel safe enough that my subconscious has decided I'd be a fool to continue being angry with her for setting me up to be her tool of revenge against her ex.

Especially after having met said ex.

Wanker only touches the surface of how I'd describe him.

You can tell when she spots me because her face freezes, then puckers, and then she gives me a pained smile before returning her attention to the order she's taking.

Tank snickers.

"You caught that too?" I ask him.

"Everyone here caught that."

"Do you…do you recall if I said anything I shouldn't have while we were having dinner?"

"Wasn't listening."

"The next time I ask for champagne, please tie me up so that I may never again do this to myself."

Once more, the man smirks at me.

And soon, it's our turn to step up to the window.

"What's on your secret menu?" Eddie asks before Bea can say a word.

"It's fish, isn't it?" Charlie says.

"No, Dad's right. It can't always be fish or else it wouldn't be a secret."

"*Ooooooh*, is that what he meant?"

"It's what I think he meant."

The boys both look at her.

"Well?" Charlie says. "What is it then?"

"Corn dogs," she tells him.

Is it just me, or is she intentionally avoiding looking at me?

Whatever did I say about my willy—my corn dog?

And why do I keep thinking of it as a willy dog?

"No fish?" Eddie whines.

"We take what we can get without causing a ruckus," I tell him.

"Yeah, Eddie," Charlie says. "I want two corn dogs and a burger. Do all of those come with fries, or do I need to order fries separate?"

"They all come with fries," Bea says.

"Good. Do you do onion rings?"

"Oh, sneaky sneaky, are we?" She smiles at him. "Did you know that's the secret menu side today, or are you just an onion ring kind of guy?"

"That's my secret, but I'll tell you if you tell me if you shagged my dad last—"

I clamp my hand over his mouth. "Enough, young man. Only *one* corn dog for him with his burger, and no onion rings."

Eddie grins. "Can I get four corn dogs and a burger and two onion rings if I don't ask if she shagged you?"

the spite date

Hudson leans out the window. "Are you two talking shit about my sister?" he growls.

Both of my boys leap back, clearly startled.

None of my security team attempts to protect them.

"And that's what happens when you don't mind your manners," I tell them. "Apologize to Ms. Best."

"You're being a stick-in-the-mud like Mom," Eddie mutters.

"We don't ask ladies who they're shagging." My head hurts entirely too much for this. Why did I think the toddler years were difficult? "It's rude at best and will land you in a police cell for harassment at worst."

"Speaking of jail, you didn't have to sleep it off at the pokey palace last night, did you?" Bea asks me.

The pokey palace.

Calling a jail cell *the pokey palace* would be bloody hilarious were I not suddenly sweating merely because she looked at me.

"We got him home safe and sound as promised," Tank tells her.

Finally, she smiles at me, those dimples popping out and warmth coming into her lovely green eyes. "Feeling okay?"

"Bloody awful," I confess, though her smile, when aimed at me— it's helping.

Tremendously.

I might be in a spot of trouble here.

"Awful in a you-need-another-corn-dog kind of way, or awful in a please-just-give-me-fries-and-a-Coke kind of way?"

I straighten. "Fries and a Coke, please."

"You got it. How many corn dogs, hamburgers, fries, and drinks for the rest of them?"

I look at my boys in turn, releasing my hold on Charlie's mouth.

"We're sorry, Ms. Best," Charlie says.

I almost believe him.

Hudson clearly doesn't if the scowl on his face is any indication. I do believe it's got even scowlier with that apology.

Eddie shrinks against me. "Really, really sorry."

"We won't ask anyone who they're shagging again."

"We'll forget the word even exists."

"You better," Hudson says. "That's not funny. It's rude and inappropriate in every situation."

"Yes, sir," they both chime.

He draws back, clearly horrified. "And don't fucking *sir* me. How old do you think I am?"

"Thirty?" Eddie guesses.

"At least twenty-eight," Charlie adds.

I rub my brow and sigh.

"I'm spitting in their burgers," Hudson says to Bea.

"Don't think I'd stop him today," Butch muses.

Her smile beams brighter than the sun. "I'm so glad I'm not parenting teenagers anymore."

I do very terrible maths and order a bunch of food for all of us, then we step aside and wait.

While I watch her with her other customers.

She doesn't look my way despite my every wish that she would.

When Hudson calls our number, Tank, Charlie, and I step up to the window to pick up the food.

"Bea?" I say.

She glances over in the middle of writing down an order. "Yes?"

"How long are you here today?"

She checks her watch, and I look at it too, though I'm more interested in her slender wrist and the red nail polish I didn't notice last night.

It sparkles, much like her dress did.

Had I not got plastered last night, I might have had the opportunity to peel it off her.

The dress, of course.

Not the nail polish.

Though I wouldn't have minded had she left some of that nail polish embedded in my back after—

I clear my throat and tell my cock to stand down.

"About two more hours," she says, answering a question that I'd quite forgotten I asked.

I shake my head, regret it instantly, and suck in a breath while my cock calms all on its own thanks to the headache.

Ah, yes.

I remember what I was about. "Would you like to walk around the carnival with us when you're done?"

The couple beside me giggles.

Bea's cheeks flush. "I—"

"Yes, she would," Hudson says. "She's free in an hour, actually. Daphne's coming to relieve her."

"She is not," Bea hisses at Hudson.

"She will when I tell her you need her to."

"Margot's in town."

"Margot's a workaholic who'll be relieved to have time to hit a coffee shop and catch up on email."

The couple waiting for their food titters harder. I'm aware they're studying me, and I refuse to look back.

After a round of silent communication between Bea and Hudson, she smiles back at me again.

It's an edgy smile. Not an altogether happy smile. Possibly a suspicious smile. "Can you check back in an hour?"

"Certainly. Thank you."

I retrieve the last of the food with Tank and Charlie waiting for me, and we join Eddie, Butch, and Pinky on a small patch of grass that they've claimed behind the car park.

The chips and soft drink help immensely, and by the time we're done, it's been nearly an hour.

I spot Daphne stepping into the back of the bus, and a few moments later, Bea departs the same way that I assume I did last night.

Except for the part where she's awake and not being carried or dragged along by a security team.

She's traversing the ground on her own two legs.

I jump to my feet, only to realize that my body is still operating on bubbly time. My body teeters, then totters, and I quickly resume my position sitting on the ground, sending a shockwave from my tailbone up to my neck.

Mostly because my legs have insisted upon it.

And my head is in solid agreement.

Too soon for quick movements.

A dark haze clouds my vision momentarily, and when I blink through it, Bea's kneeling before me, holding out a basket and a bottle. "More fries and another Coke?"

And I'm once again reminded that I don't care that I was angry with her before.

Not when she's an angel with a hangover cure.

15

The future's looking corn-doggy

Bea

It hurts how much I'm enjoying watching Simon leap on the food. Mostly because I don't want to enjoy this.

I don't want him to be absolutely adorable in his awkwardness today. Not being able to stand on his feet, rubbing his head, smiling like a lost puppy being given a treat—hungover Simon is too endearing for words.

Add in that he's wearing a T-shirt for a women's soccer team and that hat for the local minor league baseball team again, and he's honest-to-god attractive.

He has to know it matters what he wears.

That any pictures of him taken in public will be circulated widely.

That people will talk about the teams whose logos he's sporting.

Daphne's told me stories about how much implied endorsements matter when you're famous and regularly in the gossip pages.

Like the time the lead singer for her favorite band went on a public rant about women—it was ugly, and that's all I'm saying about it—and then, because she'd been photographed at one of their concerts and often wore their T-shirts, she had to make a statement condemning his words.

Protestors showed up at her parents' house because they didn't think it was enough.

They didn't think anything she did to condemn what he said was enough, and she'd still been a teenager.

So what celebrities and gossip-magnets wear?

It's important.

"Why are these magic?" Simon asks me as he shovels a handful of fries into his mouth.

I barely resist smiling broader at him. "Carbs and grease are the rock to alcohol's scissors."

"I don't know what that means, and I don't care."

I lower myself to the ground and eye his kids.

They eye me right back.

"Do we have to wait for you to finish to go and play?" the smaller boy in jeans and a hoodie asks Simon.

"Yes." He twists the top off his Coke, takes a swig that reminds me of him downing the champagne straight off the bottles last night, and then sighs as one of his normal smiles stretches to his cheeks. "You shouldn't be unattended."

I glance at the three security guards.

When I look back at Simon, he's watching me.

He's in dark sunglasses, but I can still tell he's watching me. "Bea."

"Yes?"

"How old were your brothers when you let them run loose?"

"Ryker and Griff already had a lot of freedom when I moved home to take care of them. With Hudson, probably eleven? The whole community here helped watch out for him. They knew our situation. It was both good and bad."

He turns his head in his boys' direction.

"We're thirteen," the taller one with the deeper voice who's in a T-shirt and shorts says.

He looks more like his dad and is almost as tall as Simon too. He's the one who took the call telling me the party was real, I'm certain.

the spite date

"I know," I tell him. "You smell thirteen."

"We *smell* thirteen?" the smaller one says.

I nod. "It's a very distinct smell. Like day-old pizza, dirty socks, and boundary-pushing."

Simon beams at me. "That *does* describe the smell quite well."

"Griff was thirteen when he became my responsibility. I've done thirteen-year-old boys twice. They all smell the same."

"Nevertheless, would you like to join us as the boys attempt to win every stuffed animal and a multitude of pastries here at this carnival today?"

Is he for real?

The man who last night told me he doesn't like me because I didn't tell him I was trolling my ex with our date now wants me to walk all around the carnival with him?

I like that he seems to like me today, but I'm also wary.

Happens when you're in one too many relationships where you realize you've been used.

What does Simon *actually* want?

"If you aren't needed back at work," he adds hastily.

Almost awkwardly, in fact.

I glance around.

As expected, several groups of people sitting on the grass around us are blatantly watching us.

No doubt listening in.

Daphne's also mentioned a few times how being in the spotlight got old. That if she'd been born into a normal family, no one would've cared if she'd attended protests and talked about her favorite causes while she was at parties. Or wore a T-shirt supporting a band she didn't know was problematic until after the fact.

She would've been one more face in the crowd known as the overall population on Earth.

But she wasn't one more face in the crowd, and she knew she could use the attention to her advantage, no matter how she felt about the lack of privacy.

Ironically enough, embracing the spotlight to take advantage of her family's name to bring attention to injustices toward the world's animals is what eventually got her disinherited.

She was a blemish on her family's reputation.

I don't know how much Simon cares about his reputation, but I'm sure he cares about his sons' privacy.

So I tread lightly with my answer. "Are you sure you want *me* to come with you?"

He smiles at me as he munches on the last of the fries. "Why not? You're a marvelous conversationalist, you know all there is to know about this town, and I daresay you could teach me a thing or two about keeping thirteen-year-old boys on their best behavior."

This isn't adding up with the things he said about not liking me while he was tipsy last night. But again, I don't want to call him on it while we have an audience. "At this stage in my life, I'd rather teach teenagers all the ways to annoy their parents since I don't have to live with them anymore."

He tips his head back and laughs, which draws even more attention.

But then he clutches it with both hands and draws it back to center.

And I crack up.

I can't help it.

"You are *really* hungover, aren't you?"

"So very, very much so."

"Mum said he got pissed last night," the smaller of the twins tells me.

"Charlie. You know to tell Americans it's *drunk* and not *pissed*. Bea will think I'm angry otherwise."

The smaller boy—Charlie, it seems—grins.

The bigger of the twins—clearly Eddie, if I've identified Charlie correctly—is also grinning.

I'd keep smiling too—it's way more fun being on this side of watching teenagers push boundaries—but I'm working through being confused and wary.

I arch a brow at Simon. "So you weren't angry?" I murmur.

the spite date

His attention snaps to me so quickly that I imagine he's feeling it in his head. "I—did I...say I was?"

People are watching.

So I don't answer.

He slides his sunglasses down his nose and makes real eye contact with me.

My skin tingles, and I resist the urge to rub my nipples, which have contracted so fast and hard that they ache.

All because Simon is staring into my soul with those blue eyes.

It should be illegal for a man to be this attractive.

And it's not just the perpetual smile that I'm still suspicious of, or those perfect blue eyes, or the way he carried me out of the ladies' room last night, or how he's wearing a women's soccer team's T-shirt.

It's all of it together.

I swallow hard. "You don't remember last night, do you?"

His Adam's apple bobs, and he shoots a glance toward his kids before sliding his sunglasses back up his nose. "Are you decent with any of these carnival games? I'm certain I'll be rubbish at all of them, but I can hardly teach my boys that they must try if I don't try myself."

If he weren't Simon Luckwood, and if I had any interest in dating someone, I'd be planning to set up a time to talk to him later about what happened last night.

But he *is* Simon Luckwood. Beloved world-famous actor with a big life that's likely to only get bigger. And I'm a small-town girl who's gotten everything I want from the spotlight, and whose ex has gotten far more by abusing my short time in the spotlight, so we're definitely not talking about this later.

There is no *later*.

This is—fuck.

What is this?

Tying up loose ends?

Sure. Let's go with that. "I'm banned from doing musical chairs, but otherwise, I'm as good as anyone else."

"Why are you banned from musical chairs?" Charlie asks.

"They think I cheat."

"Why would you cheat at that dumb game?" Eddie wants to know.

"Because every prize is a full-size cake."

Both boys' eyes go round, exactly as you'd expect of teenage boys being told they could win a whole cake for themselves.

"And you can't play? For real?" Charlie says.

I nod. "Six years ago, when Hudson was about your age, I won three out of every four times I got in line. Natural talent. I haven't been allowed to participate ever since."

"They still have it? We can still win cakes?" Eddie asks.

"Yep. And they save the best cakes for last. Mrs. Snyder makes this carrot cake that will turn your world upside down. And don't get me started on Mrs. Johnston's red velvet cake. I don't even like red velvet cake, but I'd do things I can't actually say out loud in front of minors to get her red velvet cake."

"You should play for us," Charlie says.

Eddie's head bobs up and down. "We'll tell them you don't cheat."

"They'll believe us. We get away with everything now that Dad's famous."

"It's true. Last year, we got caught trying to smoke grass under the bleachers at school, but as soon as Mom told them she was sending Dad to get us, they said it wasn't a problem after all. They didn't want to bother him. But our principal did want his autograph."

Deep breath, Bea. Deep breath.

They are not my kids.

I don't have to—nope, I can't hold it in. "*You were smoking grass?*"

Simon chuckles. "Plucking it right out of the ground thinking it was the real weed," he says cheerfully.

"Next time, we're not using notebook paper and dandelions," Eddie says.

"*Next time* being when you've reached the age of maturity," Simon says.

"And when your prefrontal cortexes have fully developed," I add.

"Exactly what Ms. Best said." Simon smiles at his boys. "Otherwise, I will have to tell your grandparents that you two are hooligans."

Both of them freeze.

I decide to actively not wonder about their relationship with Simon's parents, because I don't want to know.

He dusts his hands on his jeans. "Shall we go and enjoy?"

"Simon."

He looks at me. "Yes, Bea?"

"My ex-boyfriend came to my apartment this morning to ask me to take him back."

What is it about a thick five-o'clock shadow over a tic in a man's square jaw that has my lady bits fanning themselves?

Possibly it's that he's somehow smiling while his jaw ticks.

Or possibly it's that I'm letting my imagination run wild with the idea that the mention of Jake is spurring primitive instincts inside of him, and he's picturing himself punching Jake, and while I'm not really a *fight for me* type of woman, I can't deny there'd be some satisfaction involved in seeing someone punch Jake.

Especially someone rich and famous who'd actually get away with it.

"Is that so?" he says.

Tread lightly, Bea. Tread lightly. "He thought our date last night was my play to get him back."

"And did you disabuse him of that notion?"

Simon's British accent? Hot.

Simon's British accent with a hint of possessiveness? Lava.

I swallow. "I did. I don't want him back. He's a manipulative ass—jerk."

"We say *arse* and *ass* all the time at home," Eddie says.

"But only at Dad's house. And only so we learn to do it properly. We're to mind our manners at Mum's house, even if Dad thinks words shouldn't be stalagnatized," Charlie adds.

"Stigmatized," Eddie corrects.

"Whatever."

"Cussing is so much cooler than smoking weed," I say to them.

"Not really," Eddie says.

"Our dad got famous because of weed," Charlie adds.

Simon winces. "And we really must be going, or we'll miss all of the games."

He climbs to his feet and offers me a hand, and I'm back in the bathroom last night with him lifting me off the toilet seat and cradling me in his arms like I'm the most precious package in the world.

Our fingers touch, and my hand is suddenly hot and cold at the same time. Tingling as if it's coming back to life after I slept on it wrong.

I don't need to tighten my grip on him to get to my feet, but I do anyway.

And when I'm on my feet, I realize we're very, very close.

The heat radiating off his body permeates my space bubble. His breath fans over my face. I swear I can almost feel his heart beating, and mine starts racing.

This is *I want to kiss you* close.

I'm hyperaware of the flick of his eyes behind his sunglasses, the blunt tips of individual hairs in his scruff, the way his lips tip up more on the left side than the right when he smiles.

"Do let me know if he attempts to win you back again," Simon murmurs.

The right answer is *what the hell is this? You told me you didn't like me for using you against him.*

But the right answer doesn't come out of my mouth.

Instead, some guttural version of *okay* is my body's instinctive response.

"I only want to do the games where we can win food," Charlie says.

"Duh," Eddie answers.

Simon shifts away, and an electric current snaps hard between us, shocking me back to reality, where everyone around us is staring and my breath is coming too fast and my knees are just this side of wobbly.

"Are you two ever not hungry?" he asks his sons.

"Once, I wasn't hungry, I was just tired, and then Mom said I grew two inches overnight," Eddie replies.

"I'm just always hungry, but you knew that," Charlie says. "Maybe someday I'll sleep and then grow a few inches too."

"Bea?" Simon glances at me again, but with his eyes shielded from the sunglasses and the distance between us now, I can't tell if he's looking at me or avoiding looking at me.

I'd like to avoid looking at him.

If I don't, he might see how much I'm starting to like him.

"Yes?" *Shit.*

I'm still breathless.

"Do you know the best games for boys who are perpetually hungry to win food that is *not* cake?"

"I—"

"Mum!" Charlie suddenly shrieks in joy. "It's Mum! She's here!"

"Mom's here? *Mom's here!*" Eddie whoops too.

I turn and spot a short, slender woman approaching from the opposite direction of the burger bus.

Both boys charge her.

Simon watches them, that perpetual smile settling deeper on his face, like he's even happier for seeing his boys' mom and how happy they are to see her.

And I suddenly feel like the most awkward person in the world.

I'm not his date. I'm definitely not his girlfriend. I'm—I don't actually know what I am, but I know Lana Kent is more intimidating to me than Simon could ever be.

She's put together in a cute summer dress with perfect blond hair and a light coating of makeup, and she's easily hugging both boys back at once, despite both of them being taller than she is by at least six inches.

Eddie probably by nine or ten. He's nearly as tall as Simon is.

"You came to see us win all the games!" Charlie says.

Eddie's nodding along. "The burger bus has onion rings and you should get us some. Dad won't let us have any more because he says we were rude."

"He's starving us."

"It's so unfair."

"We're still learning our boundaries."

"How are we to know what's inappropriate if he doesn't teach us?"

"I learn better when I have more onion rings."

I glance at Simon again, who's now wearing an exasperated smile.

"They're always like this, aren't they?" I say.

"Even in their sleep."

"That's fabulous."

"You're far too gleeful about this."

"Did my time. This is funny now."

Lana disentangles herself and joins the little circle made mostly by the security agents standing behind us. "Starving them again, Simon?"

People are starting to pull out phones.

Probably expecting a fight.

"I don't believe there is enough food in the world to keep them from starving," Simon says to his ex.

Still pleasant.

More so, if anything.

Yep.

I definitely do not belong in this group.

I'm the not-even-new-girlfriend.

I'm the woman he was mad at last night for tricking him into a spite date. And I'm incredibly wary of how happy he's been to see me.

"Your mother?" Simon asks Lana.

"She settled down. Two neighbors came over to sit with her when they heard you were here solo with the boys."

"Very kind of them."

the spite date

"They're the best." She turns to me, still smiling, though not as big as Simon usually smiles. "Hi. I'm Lana. And you're Bea Best. My mom used to send me articles about your family. Nice to finally meet you."

I shake her hand, and the anxiety and weirdness immediately fade. "The good articles, or the bad articles?"

"The bad ones. Better for gossip, unfortunately. But I crashed my bike at your parents' house once, when I was eight or nine, and your dad gave me a cupcake to make me feel better. I always remembered him because of how nice it was to get a treat for crashing instead of being yelled at to get off his lawn."

That sounds like my dad. "If you'd been two houses over…"

"Don't I know it." She shudders. "The Stoffels were the worst."

"Still are."

"Only the good die young," Simon murmurs.

Charlie flings an arm around Lana's shoulder. "Mum. *Mum.* Mum, can we have cotton candy?"

Eddie crowds her other side. "You haven't bought us cotton candy in forever."

"Not since we were babies."

"So long ago we can't even remember."

"I bought them six meals apiece," Simon tells her.

Lana smiles again. "Clearly, you should've done seven."

"And we want to do musical chairs," Eddie says.

"But Bea can't come," Charlie adds. "She's banned."

"She'd be bad luck."

Lana looks at me.

"She's terrible luck," Simon agrees. "The worst kind of awful."

"The best kind of bad is what we call it in my house," I tell them all. "You know. Because we're the *Best*s."

He suddenly looks at me. "Bestie."

"Yes?"

"Did you tell me a story about your name being *Bestie*?"

I blink.

Then blink again.

He definitely doesn't remember last night. "I did."

Lana purses her lips together, clearly trying to hide a smile. "I'm taking the boys to play a few games. Simon, don't get into any more champagne. Bea, lovely to meet you. Don't let this guy give you any trouble. He's a marshmallow. A marshmallow with commitment issues, but a marshmallow."

"Excuse me, but—" he starts, but the boys both dive on him and hug him tight.

"Bye, Dad!" Charlie says.

Eddie thumps him on the back. "It's not that we're abandoning you. It's just that we want cake and we know you want to walk around with Bea, and she's bad luck."

"We'll still acknowledge you if we see you when we're all walking around. Unless it's at musical chairs. Then you don't exist."

"Don't sign too many autographs. Make the people work for it."

And then they're off, dragging Lana through the crowd and toward the games.

Simon looks at his security team, and even though he doesn't say a word out loud, two of them immediately take off to follow his family.

"I was wrong," I tell him.

"About what?"

"You definitely have it worse than me with raising teenage boys. Two at once, *and* they know you have deep pockets? You're in so much trouble."

"Your sympathy is touching."

He smiles at me.

I smile back.

It's involuntary.

I don't want to smile at him.

Mostly because I don't want to fall for him.

But I'm starting to think it might be too late.

16

This is all a load of old bollocks

Simon

I'm uncertain how I feel about Lana arriving and taking over parental duties at the carnival.

On the one hand, the boys will remember this day with her rather than with me.

But on the other, I did buy them a month's worth of food before Lana arrived. *And* I pulled myself out of a drunken stupor to do it.

Plus, being without the boys gives me more freedom to do exactly what they expected I'd do, which is to sign autographs for people as Bea and I make our way through the artist tents and toward the games.

The locals will eventually stop asking as I become more familiar, and it is far easier to oblige the requests than to give myself a reputation as a crank.

And who wants to be a crank?

Certainly not me.

"Are you two dating?" a younger woman with round cheeks asks Bea at one point as I'm signing autographs for two older gentlemen.

"We're trying to see how much trouble we can cause," she replies before I can say a word. "You know he got me tossed in jail for a hot minute?"

"I heard your apology dinner was completely ruined because Jake rigged the bathroom door to lock you in."

"I have no idea why the door broke, but clearly, things happen when Simon and I are involved."

I slide a glance her way as I finish with the two gents.

She's wearing that devious smile that somehow makes her dimples even more attractive.

And I desperately wish to know what else I said to her last night as she was cooking me willy—corn dogs.

The *Beste* memory came out of nowhere, and it was accompanied in my head by rainbow disco lights and a dancing cartoon crocodile.

Certainly not a solid memory.

Eventually, we reach the edge of the arts and crafts booths, and we have a rare moment where no one stops to talk to either of us.

And that's when I spot it.

An enclosed tent.

With a bright sign declaring *Madame Petty's Fortunes*.

I nod toward it. "Have you ever—" I begin, but Bea cuts me off abruptly.

"No."

"No, you have never, or no, you do not wish to?"

"Both."

"Truly?"

"Ryker and a bunch of his friends went to see her three weeks before the fire, and she told him his life was about to get hot. Daphne went right before she was disinherited, and Madame Petty told her that she needed to hoard cash. My mom went once, and two weeks later my grandma died."

"Did Madame Petty predict your grandmother dying?"

"I don't know for sure, but at the visitation, I was hiding with some friends because I didn't want to look at her body, and Madame Petty came in, and I swear I heard her tell her friend that she called it. And what's really eerie is that she was twelve. Not even kidding. She started doing fortunes like other kids do lemonade stands, and everyone humored it because it was funny. Until it wasn't."

"Does Madame Petty only predict bad things?"

"No, Daph went back to her after the great disinheriting, and apparently Madame Petty told her that she'd do great things in her life. And Griff was at a bachelor party where she was booked, and Madame Petty told him that he'd find the love of his life near death—wait. Yeah. That one was dark too. We're still not sure if she meant he'd save her or if he'd lose her, but I definitely have more anxiety every time he travels. Which is basically every week. Why are you smiling? Why are you smiling *bigger*?"

"If Madame Petty can truly tell the future, do you not want to know what your future is to prepare for it?"

"You believe in fortune tellers?"

"Not a bit. But I do believe in fun. And in the unorthodox. And in puzzles."

People continue to glance in our direction, but no one stops us as I steer Bea toward the fortune teller's tent.

"You're doing this one alone," Bea tells me.

I cluck like a chicken.

"I prefer to live my life without guessing what's coming next," she insists. "I wake up enough nights as it is, worried about my brothers being out in the world on their own. I don't need to fret about myself too."

"Do you truly?"

That earns me an exasperated glance. "Wait until your boys are driving, then come tell me it doesn't give you an entirely new level of anxiety."

"Perhaps Madame Petty will have good news."

"Doubt it."

"Is that her real name?"

"No."

"Did she pick it after the musician, or the racing driver, or because she's terribly petty?"

"You can ask her that one yourself."

The tent is exactly what one would expect of a fortune teller. Round, with ivory walls hung with twinkling lights intermingled with greenery that is distinctly simpler and more natural than the greenery my mother used to hang at the holidays. The tent isn't large, but not so small that— "Did you tell me last night that you dislike small spaces?"

She squints at me. "Seriously, Simon—how much do you remember from last night?"

Not answering this question is likely in my best interest. However, I would like to know what I told her.

The way she was watching me as we all ate suggests I said things I shall regret...once I know what they are.

"Not as much as I wish," I reply.

"That's a vague answer that could mean anything from *nothing* to *I don't want to tell you.*"

"I'll tell you the truth if you come with me to have our fortunes read."

This tent, and a fortune teller who calls herself *Madame Petty*? I'm intrigued.

Fascinated.

Excited to see what other inspiration could come from this town by way of a psychic medium.

I don't at all believe she can tell the future, but I am terribly curious what she will say.

Bea stares at me, then at the tent, lips pursed.

And a guilt knife stabs me in the kidney.

Metaphorically, clearly.

Pinky wouldn't let anything actually stab me.

"Will you wait for me while I have my fortune read?" I ask her.

Her brows furrow for the slightest moment, and then she heaves a mighty sigh.

the spite date

"Fine. *Fine.* I'll go get my fortune read with you. Only because if I don't go with you, Daphne will probably drag me later. But if it gets creepy, I'm out, and we're never discussing it again."

That makes me far happier than it should.

She's still the woman who set me up as a lackey in her lovers' quarrel.

But I don't believe she's a bad person.

Simply a complicated one.

I can appreciate complicated.

I'm rather complicated myself.

"Marvelous." I glance back at Pinky. "Do you need to check this out, or are we free to enter?"

"You're free to come in," a wispy voice says from inside. "I've been waiting for you, Mr. Luckwood."

"That's not creepy at all," Bea murmurs.

Pinky steps around us and lifts one of the tent flaps to peek inside, then gestures that it's safe for us to enter.

"Come in, Mr. Luckwood. Ms. Best. It is good that you came to me today."

I glance at Bea.

She's cringing, but she slips inside the tent as Pinky holds the flap up.

I follow.

And then I'm smiling again.

This is both exactly what one would expect and also completely at odds with what one would expect.

More tiny white lights twinkle on the inside of the tent, and a mixture of scents fills my nose. Sandalwood, sage, rosemary—it's a fascinating combination.

Madame Petty herself sits on the opposite side of a low, round table topped with a black cloth. There is no crystal ball, but I do spot several decks of tarot cards among the lit candles and other talismans on a small shelf beside her.

Her blond hair is tied up in a messy bun, and she's wearing a Grateful Dead T-shirt. Her cheeks are smooth. Her forehead too.

Bea was serious. This woman cannot be more than thirty years old. Likely younger.

Unless she's engaged in witchcraft to disguise her age.

Which I don't believe in, though I do admire people who do.

It would be lovely to believe in magic.

"Please sit," Madame Petty says, gesturing to two large deep-purple cushions on this side of the table.

Bea glances at the candles.

Candles.

Yes.

She dislikes fire. I remember that much from last night.

"Could you—" I start, but Bea puts a hand to my arm.

"It's okay," she says.

"You don't like fire," Madame Petty says to her.

"Not exactly a secret," Bea replies.

"And how is Ryker?"

"You tell me."

"I see him seeking satisfaction and peace in a green area..."

"He's a farmer," Bea mutters while we both settle onto the cushions. "You just described the job that everyone knows he does."

"And we are here to talk about you, not your brothers." Madame Petty smiles at Bea. "You wish to know how many children you two shall have."

I succumb to an unexpected coughing fit.

The light flickers inside the tent, extra sunbeams suddenly bouncing about the interior as though someone's opened a window.

Madame Petty looks behind us. "The future is often surprising," she says to someone over our shoulders. "Coughing, choking, and gasping are natural responses to what I'm likely to discover."

I glance behind me and spot Pinky, backlit in the doorway as he peers in on us.

Bea looks at Pinky too, but she rolls her eyes at him.

He briefly studies me, smiles, and shuts the flap again, plunging us back into dimness.

While I've had my back turned, Madame Petty has extinguished all of the candles, and the interior of the tent is quite blurry to me now.

I failed to bring my glasses, as I didn't expect to be in a dark room. Everything is hazy inside.

Everything except Madame Petty's voice.

"Beatrice, shall we discuss your future first?"

If it's possible to feel a person stifle a sigh, that's exactly what I believe I'm feeling Bea do right now.

"Let's get it over with," she says.

Madame Petty's figure nods. "Good, because I've been feeling something ominous brewing for you for a while now."

"That was last weekend. Jail. Bet you heard."

"No, it started before that."

"When that tree fell on my car and Ryker's dog disappeared and the glitch happened with Hudson's tuition and he had to reregister for fall classes but couldn't get into half of them that he needs and the toilet backed up in Daph's apartment and we were without water for almost two full days?" Bea says.

I make another noise. "Good grief, when did this start?"

"The week before you got me tossed in the slammer."

"*All of that* happened within a week?"

"Yep. Probably something with Griff too, and he's just not telling me, but honestly, he's twenty-three and a professional athlete. If he can't handle himself now, I made a lot of mistakes."

"Having met your two other brothers, I'm certain you did a wonderful job with the third as well."

"Someone will betray you," Madame Petty announces, interrupting us.

"Shocking," Bea replies. "That's so out of line with everything else that's happened lately."

"Someone close to you," Madame Petty continues.

"Like Daphne?"

"I see a man…"

They both look at me.

Even when I can't see well, I can see that they're looking at me.

"He distrusts the world… It has been cruel to him…"

Ah, she's not referencing me.

She must be referencing someone else.

I don't distrust the world. Merely several parts of it. And it's been no more cruel to me than it has to other people.

I daresay it's been worse to Bea.

Especially lately.

"What's his sign?" Bea asks.

I nearly choke again, but this time, for trying not to laugh at her dry delivery.

She's quite funny, this one.

But Madame Petty doesn't hesitate with her answer. "He is a Scorpio."

Again, they both look at me.

As though they are aware that my birthday is in early November and assume that it must be me.

Actually, it's likely that Bea would know my birthday if she knew I was lactose intolerant. "Fully eight percent of the population must be Scorpio, if my maths are correct."

"It's closer to ten percent," Bea says. "Scorpios are born nine months after Valentine's Day, so it's one of the most prevalent astrological signs."

I did not need to think about when my parents might have conceived me.

Given how much they dislike one another and their penchant for having affairs, I've decided I'm not even biologically related to my father.

The idea gives me peace.

Most of the time.

"You're a Capricorn, are you not, Bea?" Madame Petty says.

"No idea," Bea replies.

"You know the most common astrological sign but not your own?"

"I'm complicated like that."

She's amusing is what she is. Amusing, and quick-witted, and utterly lovely.

"I sense that you *are* a Capricorn," Madame Petty says.

"You could just ask me what my birthday is."

"It's more enjoyable to guess based on your aura. And your aura says Capricorn."

"I've always wanted to identify as a Leo though. I love the idea of being a lioness."

Before I can agree that she'd make the best lioness, Madame Petty is speaking again.

"Capricorns and Scorpios make excellent partners. Until they don't."

"That tends to be the life cycle of every relationship that ends, which are most of them when you think about it."

"Did you two attend school together when you were younger?" I ask. "I would never claim to be psychic, but I do detect something of a history between you."

Something bigger than what Bea told me outside.

"I'm fifty-eight," Madame Petty says.

"She's twenty-four," Bea tells me. "And she has a history of wrecking hearts."

I wish I could clearly see the expression Madame Petty is aiming at Bea right now.

I'd like to know if I need to call Pinky back into the tent.

"I no longer acknowledge my earthly age, but rather my soul age," the fortune teller says. "Now you, Mr. Luckwood. You will be very, very lonely in the near future."

Bah. I smile in her direction. "It happens from time to time."

"Not like this."

"And I shall get through it."

"Not like this."

"My boys—"

Madame Petty cuts me off with an ominous noise that has me pausing.

I've been lonesome before. Regularly when I've been on set filming away from the boys.

And away from Lana.

She *is* my best friend.

As best of a friend as I've ever allowed myself to have.

But this sounds as though the fortune teller is warning me that I'm in danger of losing all of them.

"My boys and I talk every day when I travel for work," I say.

She clucks her tongue. "Oh, they are definitely *not* gonna be on your side here."

Bea shifts beside me. "Do you *ever* give positive fortunes?"

"Have you not met this world, Bea?" Madame Petty replies. "It's dark and tragic and no one is immune forever. And having misfortunes in your past doesn't make you immune to more hardships in the future."

"Is it so wrong to let people live with hope?"

"When there is hope to be had, I share the hope."

"Or you can't see the hope. Or don't want to, because you know darkness sells."

"Darkness is reality."

"But we don't all need it lurking around every corner. If I'd known my parents were going to die—no. Actually, no, I can't even imagine that. I don't want to. I don't want to think about knowing my parents were going to die without being able to do anything to stop it. That would've been worse than suddenly losing them. I don't want to be afraid something will happen to my brothers all the time. I don't want to worry that Daph won't come home one day. I—"

"Oh, Daphne is definitely not going to come home one day."

I clear my throat as I reach for Bea's hand and squeeze it.

She's breathing quickly. Just as she was when I pulled her out of the toilet last night. "Ah, perhaps we've had enough fortunes for one day?"

She squeezes my hand back, and something odd happens in my chest.

Something that feels disturbingly like protective instincts roaring to life.

The bitter taste of guilt floods my mouth.

More changes need to be made to my script.

She cannot ever suspect she was the inspiration for it.

That I might be the person Madame Petty suggests will betray her.

I could stay angry with Bea for the situation she put me in, but I don't wish to.

She apologized.

She made me dinner.

She leaked zero photographs of the events that transpired in her burger bus.

She told me upfront today that her ex wants her back.

Madame Petty pulls a trinket from her shelf. "Your children will get a dog," she says to me. Then she looks at Bea. "And your brothers will live long, happy lives, and all four of you will have children."

"I'm not having kids," Bea says quietly.

"I'm merely telling you what the spirits are telling me. Take it up with them if you don't believe it."

"My boys would love a dog," I interject. "Marvelous idea. Thank you, Madame Petty."

"Tell Daphne not to do anything stupid," she says to Bea.

"Sure," Bea replies, though her tone says she will definitely *not* be passing along the message.

"I'm so for real right now. She's going to do something stupid, and it might cost her everything."

"You're a few years too late. Some people might not learn their lessons, but Daphne? She's not doing anything to fuck her life up again.

She's finally happy. She's finally at peace. Leave her alone and let her stay that way. She's earned it."

Madame Petty sighs.

Bea's squeezing my hand hard enough to cut off circulation.

And more guilt joins the first round of guilt.

I badgered her into this.

"I'm suddenly craving a steak pie. Bea, did I see a truck selling pies?"

She looks at me as though she knows exactly what I'm doing.

Deflecting.

"They're sweet. Not savory. And probably closed up for the day."

"I see them reopening for a celebrity request," Madame Petty says.

Even in the semidarkness, with my terrible night vision, I see Bea roll her eyes.

I smile at her. "I quite agree," I murmur.

And then I rise, still holding her hand. "Our gratitude for your services, Madame Petty. Do enjoy the rest of your day."

"That's fifty bucks each," she says.

Bea makes a noise that her brothers are likely familiar with from times that they frustrated her. "Your sign says ten."

"That's for people who don't argue about disliking their first fortune."

I see to it that she's paid—it never hurts to not anger a fortune teller—and then follow Bea back out into the sunshine.

"Apologies," I murmur. "You were rather spot-on with your expectations."

She rolls her shoulders back. "I'm an easy mark in there."

"Do people often take advantage of your life tragedies?"

She slides a long, slow glance at me that has sweat breaking out at the base of my neck.

As though she's aware that I too am essentially taking advantage of the tragedies of her life.

the spite date

But her answer—her answer is even worse than I could've anticipated.

"I've never thought of it exactly that way before, but yes. Yes, I think you've just described why every boyfriend I've had in the past decade noticed me."

Wonderful.

Fabulous job, old boy.

You're using her life tragedies, *and* you've suddenly busted her rose-colored glasses.

I turn us toward the games. "Perhaps you live in a place where people care more than they take advantage. This *is* a lovely town. And I've only begun exploring it."

She's quiet as she turns to head in the direction of a familiar laugh rising above the rest of the noise.

My boys are clearly having the time of their lives.

I hustle to follow Bea, worried that I've ruined the day for her.

"Another cake, Mum!"

"We'll be sugared up into the next millennia!"

Bea smiles softly, but she doesn't say anything.

"Are you quite all right?" I inquire. "I shouldn't have pushed—"

She glances around, then stops short of entering the rows of carnival games. "What are you doing, Simon?"

"What am I doing?" I echo dumbly. I'm well aware of what she's asking, but I don't have an answer.

Nothing beyond *enjoying your company*, which is the wrong answer for all of us.

For many, many reasons.

"You told me last night that you didn't like me. And now—now, everyone in Athena's Rest will be talking about how we're essentially having another date."

I swallow. "I...said what now?"

"You told me your parents always put you in the middle of their—their relationship problems, and you were mad that I did the same to you with Jake."

Bloody hell.

"You don't remember, do you?" she presses.

"I am unfortunately rather more affected by bubbly than I'd like to be."

"Which means what, exactly? That you lie when you're drunk, or that you told me the truth and just don't remember so you're trying to butter me up to ask me what else you said?"

The world is spinning.

The world is spinning with the fact that there is no good answer to that question.

I could lie and tell her I'm being kind merely because I appreciate her kindness from last night.

I could tell her a partial truth, that I don't remember, but I'm not attempting to butter her up so that she'll tell me more.

Or I could tell her the full truth—that I am absolutely enamored with her story, with her life, with *her*, and that I'd like to get to know her better, and to hell with being angry about last night.

I dislike being angry.

But I like Bea.

And I dislike that I like Bea, because the last time I let myself like a woman—well, I don't regret the boys, but I certainly hope I learned my lesson.

"Hey, mister, win a teddy bear for your lady?" A man under a tent holds out a ping-pong ball. Rows of goldfish bowls are lined on the table behind him. "Sink this in a bowl, and you can have your pick of teddy bears for your lady."

"I'm not—" Bea starts, but I cut her off by slipping an arm around her waist.

She glances up at me sharply.

Likely because I haven't answered her question.

the spite date

And I'm well aware that not answering and touching her is kind of its own answer.

"Is that all it takes?" I inquire of the man.

He flashes a smile at me. "Harder than it looks."

I glance down the row of games, where my boys have stepped back into the line for musical chairs.

"I rather doubt that," I declare. "Bea, would you like a teddy bear?"

She's still looking at me.

Possibly calling me a chicken for not answering her question.

But it's answered one of mine.

What did I say last night?

Entirely too much.

"She doesn't think you can do it," the guy calls to me.

"I certainly can't if I don't attempt it," I reply.

Bea sighs. "Simon. No one ever wins this game. There are actually petitions every year at city council meetings to ban him from setting up his games at any of the local festivals and carnivals. It would be more efficient for you to just make a donation to the youth sports fund."

"But far less fun," I reply.

"Screw that game," another voice calls. "Screw the teddy bears too. I've got one that'll really impress her."

A different man is standing with a mallet in front of a test-your-strength booth.

"Is that one also rigged?" I ask Bea.

"I don't like the way you're smiling right now."

"You should do it too. I'm certain you have far more strength than the rest of us." I hustle her toward the booth and nod to the man holding the mallet. "Sign us up. How much for a swing?"

I buy us each three chances to hit the target hard enough to lift the weight all the way up to the bell, and I gesture for Bea to take the mallet. "Ladies first."

"So you know how much harder you have to hit it for me to not show you up?"

"Because I have manners, Ms. Best."

Last night, I giggled and told her I liked her willy dogs.

Manners, indeed.

Her brows lift as she smiles, as though she's fully aware which memories are sifting back into place, and she takes the mallet.

The board is marked with measures of strength for the weight to lift above, and I'm unsurprised when Bea's first attempt sends the weight two-thirds of the way to the bell, all the way to the *You might be able to win an arm wrestling match against a three-year-old* line.

This standard of measurement is quite judgy.

Bea shakes her head, grins, then steps back and swings the mallet even harder.

It's fascinating watching the arc of her body. The strength in her arms and her legs. The flush of her cheeks as she smiles broader when the weight reaches nearly the ninetieth percent mark.

Though the marker is far less complimentary than it should be.

You got lucky once, but you'll never get higher than this, the board reads.

"You've handled a mallet before?" I ask her.

"I help Ryker split wood at his place every fall. Great stress relief."

"Still can't make it hit the bell," the gentleman running the booth says to her.

"Go bake a pie, Larry," she replies.

He scowls at her.

She grins even broader, and—her dimples.

I fantasized about licking her dimples last night.

Did I say those things aloud, or did I keep them in my head?

"Larry here spent seven years telling everyone he made the best pies in town, but no one deserved them," Bea tells me.

"Just swing the damn mallet, Bea," Larry says.

"Or the right berries weren't in season, or the flour for the crust wasn't fresh enough at the market, or he was too busy with his day job…"

"He gets it, Bea. Swing the mallet and move on."

the spite date

"A little belief in your contestants would go a long way toward making people like you more," Bea replies. "Maybe redo your board with some motivational messages instead of trash talk."

"Trash talk is motivational."

"And yet you're getting all pissy about me trash-talking your pies… Interesting double standard, don't you think, Simon?"

"I believe you'll hit the bell, Bea," I reply.

She grins at me, and once again, my lightheadedness goes lightheaded.

So.

Fucking.

Lovely.

Full of mischief too.

You can tell by the way she swings that mallet as though she's the star of one of those YouTube channels dedicated solely to wood splitting.

And it's zero surprise at all when the weight lifts all the way to the bell, ringing out loudly for all of the carnival goers to hear.

She drops the mallet and holds her arms wide in victory as she looks at me. "Go ahead. Beat that."

I swoop her up and spin her around. "Well done, Bea! That was incredible."

And then I remember myself.

Standing here, in the middle of a public carnival, with people watching.

I set her down, and she stares up at me, smile gone, a look of singular concentration crossing her face.

I clear my throat. "Lovely swing. Congratulations, darling. You've quite the talent with swinging a mallet."

A mechanical voice cuts off whatever Bea was about to say. "Standing on the target is cheating. Prize forfeited."

Pinky makes a low growl. "You got five people recording this on their phones."

Five people.

Phones.

And I've just swung her in a circle as though we're friends.

Better than friends.

Remember your surroundings, you arsehole.

The rumors will circulate that we're dating.

When I make a point to not date anyone.

My publicist will need a call.

Immediately.

"Here's your prize, Bea," Larry grumbles. He holds the mallet out to me. "You still wanna do this?"

I believe he's asking if I want to risk not performing as well as Bea has.

And the obvious answer is, of course I fucking do.

"Stand back, Bea, and let a novice show you how this is not to be done," I say.

She stares at me without blinking for another long moment, and then she laughs. "How far back?"

"Oh, very far. I fear I shall be quite unpredictable with my swing."

Larry takes six steps to his side.

Pinky sighs heavily and pushes Bea back another four feet as well.

I test the weight of the mallet and find it heavier than expected.

Rather unlikely my swing will crack the *did you even touch the target?* line.

But I wind up anyway, doing my best to imitate the way that Bea lifted the mallet, swinging it back over my head, only for the weight of the thing to suddenly and drastically change as I attempt to bring the mallet down.

A woman screams.

Larry does too.

When the mallet strikes the target, it's missing its head.

The sound of splintering glass crashes through the air.

"My goldfish!" someone yells. "Save my goldfish!"

I spin.

Pinky blocks me with one beefy arm while shoving Bea beside me. Several people have ducked, huddling close to the ground.

And it's suddenly clear what happened.

The mallet head detached from the handle at just the wrong moment to fling itself into the booth behind us.

The booth of the ping-pong balls and goldfish bowls took a direct hit from the mallet head.

"You would think the fortune teller could have warned us about *this*," I murmur to Bea.

She whimpers.

It's a soft whimper that has me immediately spinning to face her. "Are you injured? Did it hit you? Are you—oh."

She appears unharmed.

Unharmed and highly amused.

"I didn't hit it hard enough to break it," she says between fits of laughter. "This isn't funny. Someone could've been hurt. But *oh my god*, the way it went flying—and then you took out half of the goldfish bowls—you might've just solved the biggest problem in the carnival game circuit here."

People have begun helping the gentleman scoop up his goldfish to deposit them into the bowls that survived the mallet attack.

"It's a single mallet head." I look at Bea, who's bent double, wheezing. "How the hell did it take out that many fishbowls?"

"Like billiards," Pinky says. "They were touching. Hit one right, it's gonna break the ones next to it."

"Dad? *Dad!* Are you okay?"

Charlie reaches us first, followed closely by Eddie, Tank, and Butch.

Lana's taking a leisurely stroll toward us, loaded down with at least two cakes and a bag of candy floss.

"We're fine," I tell my boys. "There was, erm, a mishap with a mallet."

"Basically your dad isn't allowed to ever help anyone in town split firewood now," Bea says.

She's still giggling.

It's beautiful.

Music.

"Go and help your mother," I say to the boys as Bea steps around Pinky to head toward the fishbowl disaster.

I should help.

But the moment I take my own step in that direction, Butch and Tank block me.

"Glass," Tank says.

"Emotional people," Butch says.

"Time to go."

Of course.

And they're correct.

Naturally.

We've begun to attract a crowd.

"Bea—" I start, but my entire security team gives me a look that tells me I'm fighting a losing battle.

To them, she's a dalliance.

A distraction.

And she's managing herself without issue, navigating the broken glass and grabbing a fish and chatting amicably with the rest of the carnival goers who are converging on the tent to help.

I am not needed.

Worse, I am likely a distraction. And the cause of the mayhem.

That seems to be the story of my life since *In the Weeds*.

One would think I should be accustomed to it by now.

She doesn't glance our way as we leave.

And that makes me far sadder than it should.

17
We are never ever pretending to get back together
Bea

He left.

Simon just left.

No goodbye. No warning.

One minute, he was there, being charming and smiley and a little awkward, and the next, I was finishing helping pick goldfish off the ground and he'd disappeared.

The boys were gone.

His security team was gone.

Even Lana was gone.

It was like they were never there.

So after everything's picked up, with only a few weird looks aimed my way from the people around us—probably because people know I was walking around with Simon and want to know the gossip, including why he's no longer with me—I head back to the burger bus to help finish cleaning that up too. Daph and Hudson report that we've sold more than any other event this week, even if we didn't sell out like the rest of the food trucks.

And the way my brother and best friend are looking at each other, I know there's more.

"What?" I say.

"Don't—" Daphne starts, but Hudson interrupts her.

"Lucinda Camille was supposedly making the rounds, telling people that she heard from a friend that someone got sick after eating at your bus."

I squeeze my eyes shut and take a deep breath. "Implying I've made people sick when she'd say to my face that she never said I made them sick?"

Hudson nods grimly.

"You're going to have to fight back eventually, Bea," Daphne says. "People who are like her—they fight until they win."

"Jake already got the whole fucking restaurant," Hudson says.

"You two should go," I say. "I'll clean up. Thanks for your help."

They both look at me like they each want to say something more about the Camilles, but I shoo them away.

I baited Jake last night.

He got terrible press for Simon leaving without eating.

And I spent some of today hanging out with Simon in public again.

I *am* fighting back. Even if I don't like *how*.

So it's good that Simon disappeared.

I need some perspective. Some time to figure out what *I* want.

How I want to continue this battle.

"You want to go cheese shopping?" Daphne asks Hudson. "It's all on Margot."

He shakes his head. "I'm staying to help Bea."

"You don't—" I start, but he cuts me off.

"I won't say a word about the devil. But you're working too hard. I'm helping. Okay?"

I blink back the burn in my eyes, then smile at him. "Thank you."

He grunts. "Least I can do."

With two of us on the job, it doesn't take long, and soon, I'm driving the burger bus back toward the apartment.

the spite date

Hudson lounges in the lone front seat that we left in the bus for cases just like this, when someone's riding with me.

"You gonna talk about the other elephant in the room?" he asks me.

"What elephant?"

"The one where Simon Luckwood liiiiiikes you?"

My heart hiccups even as my brain tells me he's wrong. "He doesn't like me."

"Bea. I know when a guy's making googly-eye faces at my sister."

"He was wearing sunglasses."

"And you could tell even with the sunglasses. So why the long face?"

"One, he doesn't like me. He told me so. Two, I'm not interested in dating right now, so it doesn't matter if he does or doesn't. And three, even if he did, he basically abandoned me after he destroyed the fishbowl toss game. Who does that?"

"Guys whose security team recognized that the crowd was gonna get hella big once everyone realized he put the game out of commission. Everyone hates that game. He's a hero now. A hero who liiiiiikes you."

And this is why I don't want to talk to Hudson about it.

Because he'll say things like that and make me think he's right.

And what's more complicated than my ex-boyfriend's favorite actor giving me all the signals to suggest he likes me when I've already weaponized the appearance of our relationship and turned the town's worst family against me with it?

"What do you care?" I ask. "You were all overprotective caveman when he came to pick me up last night, and you're making excuses for him today?"

I catch sight of him lifting a shoulder in the rearview mirror. "I don't know. He just—he seems like he needs a friend. And you're a good friend. And *you* could use some new friends too. People who weren't here when Mom and Dad died. People who can honestly not give a fuck what the Camilles say about you and your burger bus. So you don't have to ask if they only became your friend out of pity or spite or if they actually like you. That's why Daphne's so great. No history. Not that far back. So you know she likes us for who we are now and she doesn't give two shits about what Jake and his family do either."

That's remarkably insightful.

And it doesn't help me battling the *I like him, I shouldn't like him, he doesn't like me, so why is he acting like he likes me?* conundrum still pinging around my brain.

"Explain this *he needs a friend* thing."

"Bea. *No one* smiles that much. He's trying too hard to make people like him."

"Maybe that's Hollywood."

"Not according to Daphne. Or logic. He wrote and starred in the world's current biggest show. Everyone wants a piece of that, whether he's smiling or not."

I don't have a good answer for that, so I drive us the rest of the way home, caught up in my own thoughts.

Once we're in the apartment, I head straight for the shower while Hudson collapses face-first on the couch.

And that's how I expect to find him when I get out of the shower, but it's not.

No, when I wander into the living room in my rubber ducky robe with my wet hair pulled up in a towel on top of my head, Hudson's in the kitchen pulling mozzarella sticks out of the air fryer.

And on the other side of the front of the apartment, Simon is sitting on the couch.

We lock eyes—his wary, mine likely wild with surprise—and his gaze drifts down to where my robe is gaping open and showing off my cleavage.

I muffle a shriek and retreat to the bedroom as Hudson calls, "Hey, Bea, Simon's here to see you."

"I daresay she's figured that out." Simon's voice holds all of the normal cheer that doesn't match the hint of caution I noticed in his eyes.

Maybe I was imagining it.

Maybe he was startled too and I misread his expression.

Maybe Hudson threatened to disembowel him and invite Ryker over to help.

Or maybe Hudson's right and Simon needs a friend and he doesn't know how to say so.

Or maybe Simon's here because he wants to know more of what I remember of last night that he doesn't.

The more I think about it, the more I'm convinced that Simon wouldn't have told me he didn't like me if he hadn't been drunk.

So this has to put him in an awkward position.

And if there's one thing I've learned about Simon Luckwood in the past week—he doesn't send his team to do his work. Dirty or otherwise.

He apologized himself—once alone, once with his boys—for putting me in jail. He went on an apology date with me. He broke down the bathroom door himself to rescue me last night.

And Hudson's probably right that his security team is the reason he didn't stick around to save the goldfish.

So of course he's not sending an assistant or a security guard to ask what he said.

He wants to know himself.

I dig through the clean laundry pile in the corner of my room between my queen-size bed and the lone window, telling myself I'm looking for a bra and underwear while I toss aside shirts and shorts and skirts and pants that I'm suddenly not feeling like wearing, because what *does* a woman wear to meet a guy in her living room when the guy gave her the most awkward date of her life—no, wait, *dates*, because I think today counted as a date too, and both of them were awkward.

And also kind of awesome.

Not because I was on a date with a guy I've watched for countless hours on TV—Jake *loved* that show—but because he's nothing like what I would've expected.

He's too real for that.

Too normal.

Male voices drift down the hall and through the hollow wood bedroom door.

Video games.

They're discussing video games.

I finally locate my favorite bra and my skimpiest panties—I'm feeling like a strong, sexy woman today, okay? It has nothing to do with Simon being here after he abandoned me at the carnival—and I decide on olive green linen shorts and a loose white sleeveless blouse.

After finger-combing my curls and shaking them out, I decide wet hair will do and stroll back out of my bedroom, where the scent of fried cheese hits me in the face.

"And what does that one do?" Simon's saying to Hudson as they huddle over his phone, one empty plate of leftover mozzarella stick breading on the table in front of them.

I eye Simon.

He didn't eat cheese, did he?

Wait.

No.

Not my business.

But what's he doing here?

Hudson shifts on the couch, making it squeak. "That's either the slingshot of death or the slingshot that'll help you hunt for birds to eat."

"Croaking Creatures?" I ask as I settle into the easy chair beside the couch.

Simon glances at me, does a double take, and then smiles. "Hello, Bea. You look lovely."

My entire body flushes. "Funny. You look like a guy who ran away from a good time."

Hudson's back to being the protective brother. He scowls at Simon. "Quit looking at my sister like—oh, shit! Look at this. They just added Doc Rover's evil twin and a flying squid of death."

"Death by flying squid," Simon muses. "How fascinating."

"It inks your eyes out."

"And that's…good?"

"You want your creatures to not die, but also you get more points when you do die in more horrific ways."

"I'm a tad confused."

"Sometimes I think parental confusion is the entire point of half of what they do," I say.

Simon beams at me. "I said that exact thing to Butch not thirty minutes ago when my boys were arguing with each other over a pinball machine until I intervened, at which point they teamed up on me."

"You teach them to ask about a woman's sex life?" Hudson asks.

Simon sits straighter. "Of course not. I'm teaching them to be respectful, and didn't realize that was an area that needed attention."

"Lighten up," I tell Hudson. "Or else I'll tell the story about you and your buddies and the school trip where you all—"

"Okay, okay," he grumbles. "Fine. Thirteen-year-old boys are boundary-pushers. Especially when there are more than one, and especially when their parent dates."

"I know you're not blaming me for what you did at Joey's house when I was *not* dating his dad."

"You *were* on a dating app. And so was he. And you matched."

"And I'm your sister, not your mom, and I most definitely did *not* accept his invitation to *anything*."

"Oh, dear, that looks like it hurts." Simon points to something on Hudson's phone. "Is the arrow supposed to stick out like that?"

"Yeah, and if it's a—"

Simon sways back and away from Hudson, clearly horrified.

"Bomb arrow!" Hudson crows. "If I'd been holding a kitten of death at the same time, it'd be quadruple points."

"I worry so much about the youth these days," Simon murmurs.

"You've got two chances to do better than Bea did."

"Don't you have somewhere to be?" I ask my brother.

"Yep. Right here on this couch. I worked hard today. Even harder than my boss. She took a couple hours off."

"She also gave you money for new shoes that you haven't gone out and bought yourself yet."

Hudson scowls at me. "Are you telling me to leave?"

I shrug with my eyebrows. "Am I?"

Simon watches us both, the smile coming back on his face. "You have the most fascinating relationships."

"It's ninety percent love and ten percent resentment," Hudson says. "Can't really blame her though. We act like we don't know she barely saved any insurance money for herself so that she could make sure the three of us could have a solid place to finish growing up and do anything we want to be happy, but we know."

"*Hudson.*"

He's not supposed to know.

None of them are supposed to know.

And here he is, telling a near-stranger who might like me or who might be buttering me up to destroy me.

I honestly don't know which.

Simon doesn't seem like an *I will destroy you* kind of guy, but then, he *did* write *In the Weeds*.

So he definitely has dark in him.

Even if he meant it to be a comedy.

"Did you truly sacrifice your own financial comfort for your brothers?" Simon asks me.

"No. I had what I needed. And this is a private family matter." I lock eyes with Hudson and point to the door. "Go buy yourself shoes."

"You know we're going to pay you back one day," my brother says. "So you can do anything in the world that you want to do. And by *we*, you know I mean Griff. At least until I'm world famous too."

"You have big dreams?" Simon asks me.

"She doesn't know what she wants to do because she hasn't had the chance to really think about it," the backstabbing little asshole replies.

the spite date

"Hudson—"

"When Mom and Dad died, she talked about opening their restaurant in their honor, but then she had to cook dinner for us every night, so she got tired of cooking and said one of us should learn so that she could just be the manager. Then she learned to drive a bus since the driver on our route retired and *someone* had to. Then she did whatever her latest boyfriend wanted her to do because it was easier than figuring out the hard things when she was already doing the hardest thing with handling the three of us." Hudson rises and stretches. "And it's a good thing she never got inspired to be an assassin for hire, or I'd be dead right now."

He dances around the coffee table, giving me a wide berth in the easy chair as he grabs his keys from the bowl on Daphne's small sideboard, which is carved to look like swan necks are holding it up.

She told me once that pieces like that could go from junk at a yard sale to a sought-after antique if the right furniture buyer scooped it up and convinced someone in her circles that it was worth something.

And the hilarious thing is, Margot eyes it funny every time she comes to visit.

Like she's wondering how Daph could afford it.

When Daph picked it up at an estate sale for fifteen bucks.

"We're talking later," I tell Hudson.

"I'm feeling like shoveling goat shit before the sun's up tomorrow. Good exercise."

So he's running away to stay at Ryker's tonight. "You're goat shit."

He grins, then glances past me at Simon once more. "She never actually got together with any of our friends' dads on those apps. She was too busy making sure Griff and I got to do every sport and club and take every kind of lesson we wanted to do. Later."

The door clicks shut behind him, leaving me alone with Simon.

Or him alone with me.

I'm not sure which one is more ominous.

"Apologies for abandoning you," he says before the silence can get awkward. "At the carnival. My security team didn't like the crowd we were attracting. I did offer to pay restitution for the broken glass."

I shift in the seat to pull my legs closer to my body, grateful that he's not giving me an inquisition over my financial situation and life goals. "It was faulty equipment. Not your job to pay for that."

"The world has given me more than I deserve. I enjoy helping those who are in the same kind of predicaments that I once was."

"You used to run a ping-pong toss booth that some jerk destroyed with a mallet head?"

He smiles brighter. "Goodness me, no. But I am familiar with being overworked and underpaid. So much so that I still use a dusty old computer when I'm working so that I remember normal people often have to wait a full minute for a sentence to appear on their screen and that their printers randomly spit out stacks of papers that they don't recall ordering it to print. It keeps me humble. Tell me—did all of the goldfish survive?"

See? He's either hilarious and awesome, or he's plotting my death. "They did."

"That's a relief."

"But you shouldn't replace the bowls. Everyone in town hates that game. You're a hero to everyone but those traumatized goldfish right now."

"That's definitely a conundrum then."

We stare at each other while I fiddle with one of the buttons on my blouse.

Oh god.

This probably looks like I'm offering to take it off for him.

And that has me shooting to my feet. "Would you like something to drink?"

He grimaces.

"Nonalcoholic," I amend. "Daph keeps a pitcher of raspberry tea in the fridge at all times during summer. If you like that kind of thing."

the spite date

And the smile is back. "Sounds delicious. Thank you."

He trails me into the kitchen, and my heart starts doing that annoying thing again.

It's bouncing in anticipation.

Eager to hang out with Simon.

In private.

No one listening in.

Just the two of us.

I haven't had a drop of alcohol today, but I still feel a fizzing in my veins like I've been guzzling champagne.

"Did the boys have fun today?" I ask him.

"Alas, despite winning four cakes, they failed in their endeavor to also be banned from musical chairs. They're currently in a sugar-induced stupor for having eaten their feelings with two of the cakes they did win."

That makes me smile too. "They're a handful."

He leans against the sink, watching me as I pour two glasses of tea. "They've had their worlds turned inside out."

"I hear moving is hard on kids." I've also heard his kids are here in Athena's Rest basically permanently since Lana's moving closer to care for her mom. Starting school here in the fall, with plans to stay through high school no matter what happens with her mom, since stability is important.

"Also rather difficult to suddenly be in the spotlight at school because of your father's job. And then difficult to make new friends when you're unsure who likes you for you... I suspect you can relate."

"A little. My family's some kind of famous—or infamous, maybe?—because of the fire, and truly, Griff's our current most famous resident. He's the first baseball player from here to hit the big leagues."

"And your roommate?"

"She can relate a lot."

"I recall you saying something about her coming from a family that runs—some kind of large business. Appliances? Why am I picturing her leaping out of a fridge?"

I'm smiling as I hand him a glass of tea. "Probably for a good reason. But her family runs hotels. One of the largest chains."

"And she was disinherited?"

"Yep." Our fingers brush, and I tell my entire central nervous system to *knock it the fuck off*.

He's a guy.

Just a guy.

And not one who'll be around for long.

He keeps leaning against the sink as he sips his tea.

And smiles.

Of freaking course he does.

"This is delightful."

He's like a giant puppy. *This makes me happy! That makes me happy! Oh, look, a new toy! A new friend! The sun came up! Everything is wonderful!*

No, *delightful*.

I like that he uses words like *delightful*.

"Are you honestly always this happy?" I've asked him before, but I still don't believe it.

And unlike every other time I've asked, this time, he cringes a little behind the smile.

It's so odd.

He's happily cringing.

"Usually it's easy, but—you were correct when you said that I have gaps in my memory of our evening together last night, and I'm afraid I may have been less than happy then."

And here we go.

I nod. "You want to know what you said."

"I suspect I said a few things that I rarely confess aloud, and I—well, possibly some things that aren't true as well."

"Like that your parents used you somehow while they cheated on each other?"

Yep.

We're going for that elephant in the room too.

the spite date

And he is *not* smiling anymore. "I said that? Exactly that?"

"You did. And that you didn't like me because I pretty much did the same thing to you with Jake last night. Putting you between us."

He looks down at his tea, then rubs his free hand over his face. "I do not dislike you."

"I'm not going to tell anyone your issues with your parents, if that's what you're worried about. Not my business, and I should've told you why I wanted to go to Jake's grand opening last night. You have every right to be mad at me."

"But I dislike being mad at anyone."

"Except your parents?"

The man smiles at me.

He *smiles*.

At *that*.

"You have issues," I mutter.

"We all do."

"Oh my god, *stop smiling*. That's just—why are you so happy about not liking your parents?"

"I have managed a remarkable achievement. I dislike my parents, so I set out to be as unsuccessful as possible while also being as happy as possible to spite them as I simultaneously disappoint them, and I've succeeded beyond my wildest expectations. And then the world rewarded me for my humble happiness with an ungodly level of professional success that I do *not* rub in their faces, though I could, and they know it, which means that I win. I am the bigger person, all while immensely disliking the people who raised me and being happy about all of it."

I don't even know what to say back to that.

I'm not sure I even followed it all. "You're getting back at your parents by being unsuccessful and then over-successful and you win because you're also morally better than they are?"

"Exactly. When one or the other wasn't angry with me for whatever I saw or didn't see with their flagrant affairs, they made sure that I knew perfection wasn't good enough, therefore I would never be good enough. It's remarkable how choosing to be happy has been the antidote to my entire childhood."

"I can't decide if that's the healthiest attitude I've ever heard or the most unhinged."

"Hopefully both. Are you aware that we've become the subject of gossip at a national level?" Simon says, switching the subject so quickly that I almost get whiplash.

"What? No. What are you talking about?"

"The executive producer of my show called as the boys and I were headed home. We've made a few gossip sites. He's asked that I continue to be seen in public with you. Good for continued high ratings while I write my next project."

"What's next?"

He winks. "It's a secret. Which us being seen in public would not be."

"And…you'll go out with me to spite your parents?"

"Absolutely not. My jolly existence is enough to spite my parents at this point. But I enjoy your company, and Lana tells me she's on your side and that I shouldn't be angry about the situation with your ex-boyfriend, as he's a total wanker. So it wouldn't be a hardship to take you on another date, unless you dislike me so immensely for the utter arse that I made of myself last night that you would prefer to never see me again."

I choke on a laugh. "It's a relief to know that being seen with me wouldn't be a hardship."

"I'm aware you have no interest in long-term plans. I am also never getting involved in anything long term, so we could simply…enjoy each other's company for the remainder of the summer. Or until you become fed up with me. Whichever might come first. Which I suspect will be you becoming fed up with me. It fits my track record."

Fuck me sideways, he's serious. "What makes you think I'd be fed up with you before you get fed up with me?"

That smile.

My god, that smile needs to stop.

the spite date

I'm starting to feel happy just because he's smiling, and that's easily four steps beyond noticing a man might have an attractive feature or two.

This is puppy attraction stage.

Not puppy love—god no, never puppy love—but definitely puppy attraction.

"I would be the person with the most to gain from a fake relationship—" he starts.

"Public friendship, nothing more. I don't do relationships, fake or otherwise. My brothers would flip the fuck out, and—"

"Would they punch me?"

Why does he look even happier about that? *Men.* They're so—just *men.* "Look, there's something you need to know about Griff—"

"He's taken up boxing when he's not playing baseball?"

"No, I was going to say he's very good with his bat. And he's the chillest of my three brothers until someone mistreats me. Then, watch the fuck out. He doesn't know all of the details about my breakup with Jake because he'd be a complete ass about it, and I think he has some teammates who would help him out."

"Do you go to see him play often? His home team is in Atlanta, correct? Not exactly driving distance, is it?"

"Ryker and Hudson and I went to a few games last year when his team was in New York or Boston or Philadelphia, and the team flew me to Atlanta once or twice because of how much the press loved his story last year. Big deal, orphaned rookie and all."

"I have this thing called a large bank account. It's fun to use it. I could take you to one of his games in any city you'd like. And we could hide from the press. They wouldn't have to know we were there."

Is it possible for eyeballs to gag? That's what it feels like mine are doing right now.

Gagging right out of my head.

"Simon."

"Yes, Bea?"

"That's not public friendship. That tells people I'm giving you blow jobs every day."

"We could negotiate that into our arrangement. Though I do insist on orgasm equality. My dream is that a former lover one day encounters my father and informs him that I'm better in the sack, and that dream will never come true if I don't uphold high standards for myself."

"I am so glad I wasn't drinking anything just now."

His eyes twinkle, and I want to kiss him.

I want to throw my arms around him and kiss him until I can't breathe.

I want to know if he's serious about equal orgasms.

I want to know if he's as capable as he's making himself out to be.

I hold a hand up as he takes a half step toward me. "We are *not* doing this. Thank you for stopping by. I'm glad you got out of the carnival safely after the incident. And thank you for forgiving me for putting you in an awkward situation last night."

"I would have forgiven far worse for the magic that is your willy—ah, corn dog."

I press my palm to my forehead. "Are you for real, or is this all an act?"

"You'll never know unless you spend more time with me."

I could do it.

I *want* to do it.

I want to be around someone this happy.

Not that Daphne isn't happy. Or our other friends. My brothers.

Okay, Ryker's not happy.

He's a grumpy-ass grump monster.

But he's consistent about it.

"What will Lana think?"

"She'll be highly amused. Especially if you attempt to teach the boys some of your brothers' tricks. For use on me only, naturally."

the spite date

"Oh, no. Hard line. I'm not getting involved in your kids' lives. I'm so serious when I say I'm not raising any more kids. And I'm not leading them on."

"The boys are well aware that I occasionally date and that none of my dates are serious."

"Are they, though?"

"My parents should have divorced before I was born. Lana's parents as well. We've been very clear with the boys that each of us will have romantic partners, and that they—the boys—will always come first until they reach the age of maturity."

Is it wrong to be in love with how he says things?

That's normal, right? For me to have a crush on his speech patterns?

For me to wonder what he'd say if we were naked and he had me on the brink of an orgasm?

Why is it so damn hot in this kitchen?

"If we do this—"

He angles closer.

Or maybe I'm angling closer to him.

Am I moving closer to him?

Huh.

I am. It's me.

I swallow and set my tea on the small patch of counter between the fridge and the sink that he's still leaning one hip against. "If we do this, it's friends only."

"Friends with benefits?"

"I—"

I enjoy sex.

I suspect I'd enjoy sex with Simon a lot.

And not because Jake would hear or because I want to hook up with a celebrity so that I can tell a story to my great-nieces and nephews one day.

I'd enjoy having a fling with Simon because he's fun. And despite my initial irritation with him over the whole jail thing, what other celebrity—hell, what other *person*—would have sought me out to apologize for the misunderstanding? And then *also* made his kids apologize?

He didn't have anything to gain from that.

I'm cautiously optimistic that he *is* a good person.

That he's not out to hurt me.

"How about this?" he says. "I'll kiss you, and if there's no spark, then we will be friends in public for the fun of it. But if there *is* a spark, then we will be friends in public with benefits in private for the fun of it."

"That's a lot of pressure for a kiss."

"If you find me sloppy and cold and disgusting, then I shan't even ask you to be my friend in public."

How is it possible that I'm smiling so much that my cheeks hurt?

I can't remember the last time I smiled this hard. "You're hilarious."

"I rather prefer the word *charming*, but if you wish to call me hilarious, I'll deal with it." His hand settles on my hip. Eyes still twinkling. Smile still shining bright. "I find you fascinating. I would enjoy spending more time with you. So I certainly hope I'm not a disappointment. There's quite a bit of pressure now."

There is.

It's in his crotch.

"Yes, I can feel that," I murmur.

"It's beyond my control when I'm alone with an intriguing woman. Your dimples drive me mad."

"If things beyond my control are all you like about me—"

"I've only begun to name the things about you that intrigue me."

Simon likes me.

Or, as Hudson would say, he *liiiiiikes* me.

Or he's pretending.

And so what if he is?

Neither of us is looking for a long-term relationship.

We're just looking for fun.

the spite date

That's what I'm thinking about—*fun*—when his lips brush mine.

Warm, soft lips that make my heart race faster and the delicious kind of shiver dance down my neck.

My eyes drift shut.

He suckles at my bottom lip.

I grip his shirt while he slides his hand around my waist and tugs me closer, that bulge behind his zipper pressing harder into my belly.

We're doing this.

I'm kissing Simon.

Not just tease-kissing.

No, this has rapidly moved to full-on making out, lips and tongues exploring while he turns me against the counter.

Apparently one of us is hungry.

Maybe both of us.

Because now that I'm kissing Simon, I can't see a world existing where this doesn't end with us naked and in my bed.

I want to lick his neck.

I want him to leave whisker-burn marks on mine.

Losing myself in this kiss, in the grip he has on my waist, in the way he's pushing me against the counter—*yes, please*.

I hitch one leg around his hips, and he lifts me onto the edge of the counter so I can wrap both legs around him.

Clearly, this kiss is going well.

I might have to pretend to be his girlfriend for the summer.

Or just his lover.

The way his erection is nestled between my thighs while I pulse my pelvis against it, the talent he has with his tongue, the steel wall of his chest—this man looks like a happy-go-lucky goofball, but *oh my god*.

When was the last time my lady bits were panting this hard, coiling tight so fast? He hasn't even touched my ass or my breasts or my neck or anywhere else that it usually takes to get me turned on.

He's just dry-humping me on a countertop while his tongue and his lips treat me to the best kiss of my life.

If he tried to touch my ass or my breasts or so much as breathed on my neck, on that magic spot behind my ear, I'd come on the spot.

I wrap my arms around his neck and weave my fingers through his hair, gripping the short strands and holding him in place.

He makes a low growl in his throat, and then he's deepening the kiss.

Yes.

Yes, *more.*

He slides one hand under my blouse, his fingers dancing up my spine and playing my body like he's been practicing for this moment his entire life.

Bedroom.

No, fuck the bedroom.

I mean, we'll fuck in the bedroom.

Later.

Right now, I need to get these buttons on his shirt undone and then tackle his pants, and then—

"Well, hello. Not what I was expecting, but I can go with this," Daphne says.

I shriek.

Simon yanks out of the kiss and loses his grip on me, which would be fine if I were on the counter-counter.

But I'm not on the counter-counter.

I'm on the edge of the counter in front of the sink, and *no one* has a small enough ass to be balanced there and then suddenly freed to go anywhere except back.

And that's exactly what I do.

I fall back.

Into the sink.

Dishes crunch and clank beneath my ass.

Water soaks into my linen shorts.

Cold, nasty, dirty dishwater.

"He needed to role-play a scene so he can write it right," I blurt.

Simon gives me a slow once-over.

He's returned to standing in front of the sink—probably so that Daphne can't see his raging hard-on, which my lady bits are missing right now—and his cheeks are flushed and his pupils are dilated and his breath is coming too fast.

"Do you honestly think she believes that?" he murmurs to me, those talented lips hitching up at the corners again and making all of me a little swoony.

The man is too attractive for my own good.

Possibly his own too, but that's his problem.

"I definitely don't believe that," Daph says. "Margot?"

"Quit being obnoxious," Margot replies. "We're leaving. Carry on."

"My ass is soaked with soggy cereal," I mutter.

Simon's grin grows.

I don't think it's a *serves you right* grin though.

I think he's just—well, *happy*.

Because that's what he's chosen to be.

Happy.

It's inspiring.

I want to be happy like that.

"We shall have to plan our next date better," he says to me.

"Casual summer fling date," I stutter in return.

"As you wish."

"Jake's gonna fucking lose his mind," Daphne whispers.

"That's his problem." Simon adjusts himself subtly, then pulls me out of the sink. "Do all of your issues revolve around water and plumbing fixtures? Toilets and fishbowls—"

"They wouldn't if you'd made out with her in her bedroom like a proper gentleman," Daphne says. "And the fishbowls were your fault, Romeo."

"She egged me on," he replies with a grin.

Margot sighs and looks at the ceiling. "I would love to help you out more here, Bea, but I have to get back to the city. My driver's waiting. Daphne—actually, I don't know what to say right now."

Daph slings an arm around her sister's shoulder. "I love you works."

Margot smiles, then squeezes her tight. "Okay. Then I love you. Don't let that cheese go to waste."

"Never."

"I should go as well," Simon says. "The boys—"

"Shouldn't be left for long," I finish.

"I'll ring you later."

Am I blushing?

I think I'm blushing. "Okay."

That smile. *Gah*. Again with that smile making me feel—well, things I shouldn't feel.

Like that he cares.

That he likes me.

That we'll be making out again soon. This time with advance planning.

And hopefully no falling into dirty dishes.

He squeezes my waist and kisses my cheek, and then he follows Margot out the door.

Daphne shuts it behind both of them, then looks at me.

After a minute, both of us squeal.

It's not *real*-real.

It's a temporary fling.

And I'm going to enjoy every minute of it.

Weird or not.

18

Maybe clothes are the problem

Simon

The weather is making me miss England, which is remarkable.

I rarely miss England.

But when it's this sticky and hot anytime I leave my house, I do.

I miss cold, drizzly days that don't feel as though they might melt one's brains.

Still, I'm smiling as Pinky and I approach Bea's burger bus at the far end of the car park where half a dozen food vans are set up on the opposite side of the lake from JC Fig.

This park area, Pinky has informed me, belongs to Austen & Lovelace College.

And today, it is teeming with adolescents in a summer nature program.

The car park is not as busy, as it's early for lunch, but I expect it will be full soon enough.

I pause at the window of Bea's burger bus and peek inside.

Ah, there she is.

Preparing burger toppings.

"Hello, Bea," I call. "Lovely day to sweat your arse off, isn't it?"

She doesn't answer, but she does shake that lovely arse in my direction.

I clear my throat and order my cock to behave itself.

And then I realize why Bea hasn't answered me, and why she's truly shaking her arse.

"*Get you better, get you bested, get you better, get you arrested,*" she croons.

I'm unfamiliar with the song, but I spot earbuds in her ears as her head bops with her rear end.

She dances about, organizing containers of lettuce and tomato and pickles.

I lean into the window and watch.

After a minute or so, she executes a dance spin, one arm in the air, head bopping, and then she spots me and screams.

I step back and applaud. "Brava. Have you considered backup dancer as a future career possibility?"

She pops her earbuds out, then fans her face with one hand and holds her other over her heart. "First, don't scare me like that, and second, I can't tell if you're mocking me or not."

"I only mock people who deserve it."

"That doesn't reassure me."

"I can assure you, your performance had a rather…moving…effect on me."

She stares at me for one more long moment, and then she half laughs while shaking her head. "I'm choosing to believe you enjoyed it."

"Good. Because I did."

"Burgers aren't ready yet."

"I didn't think they would be. I was in the area and simply wished to say hello."

"Oh! You enrolled the boys in the summer program?"

How is it that I feel as though I've only just discovered smiling every time I'm in this woman's presence? "I assumed a veteran parent of teenage boys wouldn't steer me incorrectly."

the spite date

We had a short text exchange once I returned home Sunday night, and she suggested I consider this summer program for the boys.

So that they could make friends, she said.

To ease their transition to this smaller town.

It meets once a week on Wednesdays.

Those dimples light up my entire world as she smiles back at me. "All of us loved that program. I did it. Ryker did it. Griff kept saying he had to do it again so that Hudson wouldn't be alone, but I knew he wanted in for himself."

"The minute the teacher said *get dirty*, I was concerned my boys might die of happiness overload."

"They have to be faced with too much happiness sometimes. How are they going to learn to live with it otherwise?"

"Good point." I peer around her again. "No Daphne today?"

"Daph has a day job. Environmental nonprofit that tries to convince animals to cross the roads in safer places."

I recall that she had a job, but not the specifics. "Truly?"

"It's a little more complicated than that, but yes."

"So Hudson will be along to assist you?"

"Nope. He has a thing with some friends. I'm flying solo today."

Oh, this is excellent. "Are you indeed?"

She props herself on the windowsill and smiles broader at me. "I am indeed."

"In that case, I shall have to assist you."

"Haven't exactly had enough foot traffic this week to justify paying a helper."

"My rates are rather reasonable." Truly, I would help her merely for a smile, but I wouldn't turn down a kiss either.

"Are they negotiable?"

"Indeed."

"What's your starting point?"

"That depends on the currency."

"Cash or burgers?"

The minx is playing with me. Her eyes are sparkling, though her pupils have dilated, and she's biting her lip as she awaits my response.

"Hand-holding in public or shagging in the back of your burger bus after closing."

She leans closer. "What if I wanted to pay you in chocolate syrup?"

"Then it would depend on the administration of the payment of chocolate syrup. Though I am far more fond of honey, if I'm to be the end consumer of the payment."

Pinky clears his throat.

Bea straightens and nearly clocks herself on the top of the window.

I glance over and spot a group of adults strolling to the food van beside Bea's bus. But when I glance back at Bea, she's making a funny face.

"Is there an issue?" I ask her.

She shakes her head. "No. It's just—it's been slow. I don't think I'll make enough to afford honey today."

"Not with that attitude."

"The Camilles—"

"Are no match for someone with as much experience at succeeding out of spite as I have."

I'm not fond of confrontation, but I am a fan of passive-aggressive warfare when necessary. And that Camille woman cornered me yesterday outside my new favorite tea shop to insist, again, that I consider a role in the community theater's production.

She was none too pleased at my response that my studio contract forbids community theater performances, nor did she seem to appreciate that I was unable to commit to attending her murder mystery dinner, as I need to keep my calendar open for my boys.

However, she was far more displeased when I suggested Bea's burger bus as the best new restaurant in town to a fan who stopped to ask me for an autograph too, though she didn't tell me to my face that I'd become sick if I ate there, as I've heard she's implied to others.

the spite date

Bea smiles at me again, but this one seems amused. And full of doubt. "If you don't have anything else to do, come on up. Just push the front door open."

I smirk at her. "I hope you're prepared to work your arse off selling out today."

"I hope you're prepared for disappointment when you find out even your star power can't overcome the doubts the Camilles have planted about me in the hearts of every person in Athena's Rest since Jake and I broke up. Because if it could…it would've by now."

"Would you care to bet on that?"

"Are you for real right now?"

"Completely serious."

"You realize I win either way, right? If I sell out, I win. If I don't sell out, you lose, which means I win."

"And once again, we're down to the terms of the bet. What are you prepared to offer me when you lose?"

She's once again shaking her head at me. "Best I can do is cook for you."

I squint at her. "Why am I suddenly craving risotto?"

That smile.

She knows something I don't.

"If you win, I'll tell you why you want risotto. *And* I'll make it for you."

"And if you win, I'll buy out the rest of your ingredients for the day and cook you burgers at my place."

She sticks her hand out of the bus. "Deal."

I shake. "Deal."

And then I hop inside her bus, which is approximately the temperature of the furnaces of Hell. "How on earth do you work in this environment?"

She grins at me and adjusts a fan so that it's blowing in my direction.

It moderately helps.

"You know how to take orders?" she asks me.

I straighten and aim a haughty glare at her. "I beg your pardon. I'll have you know I was a starving actor for well over fifteen years. What do you think?"

She cracks up as she points me to the tablet and card reader hanging in special containers by the window. "But are you young enough to adapt if the technology is different from what you're used to?"

I mock gasp, which sets her into another peal of laughter.

Well worth taking the digs to see her smiling and laughing.

I unhook the tablet and make a quick study of the app, then order myself a burger and fries.

"You can't cheat by ordering it all yourself," she tells me from the prep line behind me.

"Those were not in our terms."

"They are now."

"Fine. Are we done with terms?"

She turns and looks at me.

I keep a straight face.

I *am* a trained actor, after all. I could theoretically straight-face her all day.

"What else are you up to?" she asks.

"Why would you think I was up to something?"

"You have a look."

"I most certainly do not."

"You certainly do."

I could bicker with her all day.

Mainly because she's the one smiling now.

As though being in my presence makes her happy.

And that makes me happy.

"If the terms are settled, then I shall get to work," I tell her primly. "If the terms are not settled, then we need to settle them so that again, I may get to work."

"You're going to cheat, aren't you?"

the spite date

"My middle name may be *disappointment*, but my attitude is forever *win at all costs*."

"Okay, Peter."

I crack a grin at that. "Fine, fine, I only win at all costs when it comes to people who gave me *disappointment* as a middle name. Last chance to set any rules, Ms. Best, before I *best* you."

"At this point, I'm too curious to see how you plan to cheat to care what other rules I should add."

"Brilliant."

I whip my shirt over my head and contemplate if I could get away with stripping out of my shorts as well.

My undergarments would remain on, naturally.

But only because the studio's publicity team has instilled mortal fear in my soul.

"What are you doing?" Bea gasps.

"Cooling off and attracting more customers."

"You can't serve burgers naked."

"Why not? I'm merely taking orders. You're the only person touching food. But if you insist, then I'll wear an apron when we have customers."

Her gaze keeps darting to my naked torso. "If my food truck gets shut down by the health department—"

"Then I shall launch a campaign to have you reinstated. Thus far, all of my efforts to help you have been passive at best. Today begins a new strategy. Active endorsement and participation." I sense a presence, and I turn to find a woman gaping at me from the service window. "Hello, madame. How many burgers would you like today?"

"Are you Peter Jones?" she asks, her gaze also dipping to my torso.

"Only on television. The burgers here are quite tasty. My favorite in the States, in fact. How many for you today?"

"Does it come with an autograph?"

"Certainly, madame."

"One, please."

"Only one? There's no one else in your life who would appreciate the world's best burger? And I can vouch for the chips—sorry, sorry, *fries*—as well."

She bites her lip and stares at my chest, completely oblivious to the way I'm also using my accent against her.

I slide a look at Bea, who's glaring at the customer, which makes me smile broader.

"Two orders?" I ask the woman. "Or three? Coworkers? Friends who need a good burger?"

"Simon—" Bea starts, but she's cut off as the woman blurts, "Two. Two burgers and fries."

"Certainly, madame. And make sure to tip your cook well. She's adopted one too many kittens, and one has special needs."

"*Simon*," Bea hisses.

I ignore her and hold the tablet out the window for the customer to pay for two burger baskets. "Do tell your friends that I shall be here all day."

She nods at my chest.

Bea shoves an apron at me. "Two burgers and fries, coming right up," she says. "And when the kids are turned loose for lunch, you're putting your shirt on."

"Why must you be so prudish about bodies? They're natural."

"Yours could cause car accidents," the customer says.

"Why, thank you. Though I can hardly take credit. Most of this is genetics."

"I did my dissertation on your mother's artwork," she says.

Well.

This has certainly taken an unpleasant turn.

Must my mother have been famous first in her own right? "How lovely."

I wave at three people standing a short distance away from the food vans, seemingly contemplating which one they should pick. "Free autographs with burger purchases," I call.

the spite date

"*Simon*," Bea hisses again from the grill, where several burgers are sizzling happily. "I'm just starting to make headway with being friendly with the rest of the food truck owners. Maybe don't steal *all* of the customers?"

Bah. That's easily enough solved. We shall simply sell out first, and then I'll assist the rest of the food vendors.

Which I will tell her later. "You're very particular."

"I have to live here after you leave."

"But do you? You could move closer to your middle brother and travel the country with him to explore new places. Or attend university anywhere you wish if that's necessary for your goals. Or take a gap year and travel the entire world looking for unexpected adventures."

"Gap years are usually for college-aged kids. I'm a little older than that."

"It seems far more useful when applied to fully formed adults facing significant life changes though, does it not?" I ask her.

Our customer blinks at me. "You are *so* right. I should do a gap year when my daughter graduates high school."

I smile back. "You're welcome."

The three people who seemed undecided a moment ago approach the window.

"Do you have any secret menu items today?" one of the two ladies in the bunch asks.

I lean back. "Bea? Secret menu items?"

"Fish on a stick."

"Truly?"

"Yep. Limited supply. Ten orders total."

"Brilliant." I turn back to the window. "I'll answer your question if you each agree to tell two friends that they need to have lunch in this car park today."

"*Simon*."

"Are you aware if you chide me with my name three times, I only get worse?" I grin at Bea.

She fights a valiant battle but ultimately loses to the smile blossoming on her face.

"Can we really get autographs with our orders?" the lone gentleman inquires.

"Certainly."

"Can we get selfies too?"

"With extra orders of fries. Which are truly their own reward, but as I'm here today, I may as well be a side benefit."

I wait for the *Simon* to come, but Bea merely slides me an exasperated look.

Still with a smile.

"I told six friends you're working at the burger bus today," the third woman announces, holding up her phone.

"Brilliant. Fish and chips for you then?"

They all three order fish and chips, the gentleman with extra chips, so I pose for a photograph with him.

Bea bumps my hip with hers, and I step aside so that she can hand two burger baskets through the window to our first customer.

"My autograph?" she asks me.

Bea hands me a Sharpie, then returns to the grill.

Pinky appears with a stack of my headshots and a scowl aimed my way.

Good man.

He reads situations well.

"Bea's cooking us a feast this evening," I tell him.

"Only if I lose," she calls from the fryer station.

"Thought we were having a quiet writing day," Pinky says to me.

I smile at him. "Best laid plans, old chap. Bea, could you—"

Before I can finish my sentence, she's bumping me out of the way again and holding out a burger basket for Pinky. "I hope he pays you well."

"Well enough," Pinky replies.

"Oh, shit, this is *your* burger place?" the gentleman says to Bea.

the spite date

She looks him up and down. "Surprise."

He winces.

The two women with him square up and box him in. "You got a problem with Bea?"

"You know how much she's done for her family and this community since her parents died?"

"She's the reason my sons had busing in high school."

"If it wasn't for her, the PTA wouldn't have survived the baked bean scandal."

"She was also Margot Merriweather-Brown's inspiration for her generous donation to the mathematics department, which she denies because she never takes credit for herself."

"But if you want to listen to the rumors the Camilles are pretending they're not spreading about her since Jake dumped her…"

"Which won't get you any better roles with the community theater…"

I interrupt them by holding the tablet out of the window for payment.

The older of the two women taps a card to the reader with a very clearly dangerous look slid in the direction of her male companion.

And I continue to adore this town.

More so than even my continued inspiration, I adore my growing role in it.

"It really shouldn't be about sides," the gentleman says. "Good food is good food."

"Does character matter in this debate?" I inquire.

He grimaces once again.

"Character *always* matters," the younger of the two women tells me. "Especially when you realize it might not have always been what you thought it was. And we'll be back."

"Three secret menu baskets and an extra order of chips," I call to Bea.

She doesn't answer, though I'm certain she heard me.

I pretend I don't notice her dabbing at her eyeballs with the edge of her apron before she ducks to grab the fish from the fridge beneath the prep counter.

Sometimes a person needs to know they're appreciated.

It's unfortunate that I'm only now understanding how little Bea realizes she's appreciated by the entire community.

Not pitied for her situation.

But valued for her contributions and respected for the extra sacrifices she's made to participate in the community.

And also fucked sideways by this break-up with Jake Camille, who seems to be one of those men who portrays himself one way in public, and an entirely different way in private.

Much like my parents.

There are things in this world that I can fix, and there are things in this world that I cannot.

This falls into the *fix* column.

And it shall be my next project.

"Don't forget to offer the chef's table," Bea calls to me. "It's twenty bucks to sit and watch us work for half an hour."

"Marvelous. Consider it done."

19

Could you please knock first?

Bea

We did it.

We sold out.

We sold out, and not just because the kids in the college's summer program flooded the parking lot and Simon's boys alone ordered six burgers and finished off my fish.

And I have two new parties booked before the end of July.

Simon, of course, disappeared as soon as the last order was placed, leaving me to clean up on my own.

Probably just as well.

Between the way he brought customers in and then worked some kind of crazy magic that had over half of them asking for my newsletter and socials links so they could track where I was every day, I was in danger of jumping his bones if he hadn't taken off so quickly.

Everything's cleaned and put away, and I'm doing one final inventory check when he climbs into the back of the bus and pulls the door shut behind him.

Still shirtless.

Which is just—holy hell.

He told at least six customers that push-ups and jogging are all he does for exercise, but my god.

The man's abs are tight, with the subtlest of man-V's disappearing into his waistband. His pecs are delicious. And his shoulders—his shoulders are the reason shoulders exist.

Broad, with tight balls of muscle at the tops of his arms, holding up biceps of steel.

He's not bulky—more lean muscle—but he could've been successful as a model even if his face wasn't handsome as hell.

And don't get me started on his ass.

The twin dimples on either side of the groove of his spine right above his waistline.

The curve of his butt.

The way I've stolen glances at him all day long.

Simon Luckwood has been hiding the body of a god under his shirts.

He beams at me as he steps around the chef's table and approaches me. "Your competitors would like to invite you to their next barbecue and have requested that I inform you that you're to bring your own bean bags for cornhole, which is a request that I assume you understand better than I do."

Is he serious? "You—you *networked* for me?"

"I didn't want them to resent you for us selling out first, so I made sure to draw customers to the other vendors as well. Far better to be friendly competition than cutthroat enemies, no?"

I'm sweaty and smell like the worst part of a dirty gym bag. I got a burn on my hand from misbehaving fry grease. My feet ache because I need new shoes, just like Hudson, and also just like Hudson, I haven't prioritized them yet.

And I'm throwing myself at Simon and kissing him like he's just rescued me from a desert island.

Because in a way, I think he has.

He catches me without stumbling, wrapping his bare arms around me and slanting his mouth against mine.

Like he's been searching the high seas for me for decades and had almost given up hope.

Or possibly just like he's horny.

Or maybe he likes me.

He totally likes you, my vagina squeals.

She's such a hopeless romantic.

Of course he likes me, I tell her back while I thrust my fingers through Simon's short hair and hold him closer and kiss him deeper. *He wouldn't kiss me if he didn't like me.*

And that's what this is.

Mutual attraction.

Combustible mutual attraction leading to him pushing me back against the bus wall at the end of my kitchen while he grips my ass.

A window latch jams into my back. "Audience," I gasp.

He stares at me, dazed, his hair disheveled, his blue eyes unfocused and aimed mostly at my lips, which are tingling with the need to be attached to his again.

I tug at his shoulders. "Lower."

His gaze darts to my breasts, and I press my shoulders back without thinking.

Yes, please, kiss me there.

Like he's reading my mind, his head lowers to my left boob.

Wait.

Was that what I—*no*.

I meant—

Simon's mouth and hot breath land on my shirt just above my nipple, and my head rolls back against the window while an incoherent noise comes out of my throat.

He lowers his mouth to my nipple and sucks hard through the fabric, and my clit sits up and takes notice too.

"Why—magic?" I gasp.

"Why delicious?" He peels my shirt up, ducking lower to kiss a trail up my stomach to my sports bra—*a sports bra, Bea? Seriously?*—and then he slides his fingers beneath the tight band, making my skin shiver and quake with his touch.

Fewer clothes.

He's right.

Fewer clothes make this better.

"Better than my fantasies," he murmurs against my skin.

My lips ache with the need to kiss him back.

And—*windows*.

Right.

Right.

"Simon—"

His thumbs stroke the underside of my breasts. "Yes, darling?" he says between open-mouthed kisses to my stomach.

My eyes cross.

My brain goes blank.

Do I even have a brain?

Strip him! my vagina orders. *Strip him and ride him and let him be our sugar daddy!*

She and I don't see eye to eye on everything.

But—"*Oh god*," I gasp as his thumbs work their way up to my nipples.

He's pushed my sports bra up so it's choking the upper part of my breasts, but he's pinching my nipples and rolling them between his thumb and finger and *oh my god*, when he puts his mouth on one nipple and sucks, everything goes blinding white with pure, uncut craving.

Pants off.

Pants have to come off.

Ride him.

I'm wet.

I'm swollen.

I'm aching.

He sucks harder, still torturing my other nipple too, and I whimper. "So good."

Instead of answering, he hums softly, the vibration making my knees wobble.

I'm gripping his hair and I want to touch myself because it would only take three strokes to get me off right now, but I can't let go of him because my brain has forgotten how to brain, and also if I let go of my grip on his head, will he stop what he's doing to my breasts, because this—this is exquisite.

Exquisite torture.

I didn't know a man could do this to me just with his mouth on my breasts.

And yet—"Simon," I pant. "Please."

He releases my nipple from his mouth, then blows on the wet skin, and I gasp again.

"Please what, Bea?"

"I don't—know."

"No?"

"Feels—so—good."

"Naturally."

My eyes are half-crossed and my knees might give way, and here I am, laughing at the man now sucking my other nipple into his mouth.

"Oh god," I gasp again.

And that's before he grips my thighs and slides both of his hands up under my loose shorts toward my panty line.

I widen my thighs.

His thumbs trace the edges of my panties.

I'm so turned on, I can smell myself.

"Touch me," I whisper. "Oh my god, please touch me."

"Here?" he murmurs against my breast, his thumbs drifting farther from my pussy.

"*Simon.*"

"I rather like when you chide me." He licks the tip of my breast oh-so-lightly, the barest touch, making me shiver again even though it's a hundred degrees in here. "Perhaps I should misbehave more."

"You're misbehaving—plenty." Talking is hard. Breathing is hard.

Not coming is hard, but I can't come.

I'm not quite *there*.

He rubs his chin around my nipple, the stubble setting my skin on fire.

"If I were to misbehave more—" he starts.

"Please play with my breasts and stroke my pussy," I gasp.

"Your pussy?" he murmurs.

"Why is it so much hotter when you say pussy?"

"Because you haven't tired of me yet."

"*Simon.*"

A mischievous grin flashes at me, and then the man is sliding his hand beneath the cotton of my panties to stroke my hot, wet flesh, and—

"Bea!" someone bangs on the back door. "Open up. I have lettuce and tomatoes for you."

"*Oh my god,*" I gasp.

I'm halfway into an orgasm and *my brother is here.*

I shove Simon back and try to yank my sports bra back down, but it's stuck.

Of fucking course it's stuck.

It's a hundred degrees in here and I've been sweating like my sweat glands are waterfalls all day, and *oh my god*, that's Simon's first impression of me naked.

"Bea?" Ryker calls again. "It's too hot for you to have the doors shut."

Simon's eyes snap into focus.

He looks at me while I'm trying to pull the tight, wet material back over my boobs, then at the exit at the front of the bus, then down at his own bare chest.

"Why's the goddamn door locked?" Ryker yells.

Simon meets my gaze.

His blue eyes are black as midnight, pupils dilated. He sticks his thumb in his mouth and sucks on it, and that orgasm that was half-started makes my legs wobble.

He's tasting me.

My brother's trying to break down the door to get in here, and Simon Luckwood is licking me off his thumb.

"Bea?" Ryker yells again.

"Hold on, I had my head in the fridge," I yell back.

It's a gaspy, whimpery yell.

The kind that says something else entirely was going on.

"Where's your security?" I add to Simon, softer.

"Likely laughing their arses off nearby, conspiring with the universe to make me earn this," Simon murmurs as I finally get my bra straightened enough to yank my shirt down and head toward the back of the bus.

"I—sorry," I manage.

He grins. "Oh, don't be. I enjoy a good challenge."

How does the man keep getting even more attractive?

I shuffle on weak knees to the back of the bus and unlock the door to let Ryker in.

He's waiting in his usual overalls and dirt-covered T-shirt and boots, holding a waxed box of produce at one hip, and as soon as the door is fully open, he immediately looks past me.

"Hello, mate," Simon says behind me.

"Where's your shirt?" Ryker asks him.

"Did you know the women on this campus and in this town will buy burgers from a man who's not wearing one?"

Ryker's gaze wavers from Simon back to me. "You're peckering out your burgers now?"

"Sorry?" Simon says. "I'm unfamiliar with that term."

I would laugh, but my vagina is too busy crying over what almost was. "Do you know the restaurant Hooters?" I look back at Simon, who's flung himself into one of the seats at my chef's table.

Probably to hide the massive boner I glimpsed when I was panicked and wrestling my bra back in place.

And at that thought, my vagina whimpers once again.

We almost had that boner.

Simon's brows furrow. "Hooters? I don't believe I do."

He's lying.

The man is lying.

Like he wants to make me say it out loud.

"It's a restaurant whose main draw is that all of the servers have very large breasts and they wear tight, skimpy T-shirts." I gesture to my own breasts, realize they're lopsided because I couldn't get the damn sports bra back on right, and then cross my arms over my chest before Ryker cares to look close enough to notice.

I can play off every single sweat drop and smell in this burger bus right now as what happens after a long shift on the hottest day of the year, but I can't explain to my brother why my boobs are crooked.

Or why my lips are probably swollen.

Simon props his elbow on the table, chin on his fist, his thumb brushing his bottom lip, which reminds me once again where that thumb was just a minute ago. "Fascinating. And that has to do with me being shirtless...?"

"Rumor goes around every once in a while that someone's starting a restaurant called Peckers to compete. Where shirtless men in tight pants serve the ladies."

That smile.

That smile will live on in my dreams until the day I die.

Because when Simon Luckwood smiles that smile at me, I know he's thinking about when we can get together again. I know he's thinking about how much he enjoyed basically getting caught with his hands in my underwear.

the spite date

I hope he's thinking that he likes me.

"Seems a splendid idea," he says to me. "We certainly demonstrated how well it works today, did we not?"

"We'd have to test it with other men to see if it was the naked torso factor, or if it was the *you* factor," I tell him. "I'll put out a call on socials now that you've gotten me some new followers. See if any other guys around town are willing to work for tips for a day to stand in my burger bus shirtless."

He frowns.

Simon.

Frowning.

Look at that. He's hot when he's frowning too.

Ryker makes a noise. "You fucking will *not*."

"Oh, because you'll do it?" I ask him.

He ignores the question. "Will you take the damn vegetables and go home?"

"Yes and no. I'll take the vegetables, but I'm not going home."

He closes his eyes and sighs heavily. "Why not?"

"Well, old man, because I'm coming to your house. I owe Simon dinner for helping me sell out today. And you have the best grill and the most room for his kids and security team and Daph and Hudson too."

Ryker stares at me without blinking.

I give him my best you-love-me-and-you'll-love-dinner smile.

"This isn't a private dinner?" Simon asks.

Ryker growls. "Fuck, no. Bring the army to my house. Better cook something good."

"Do I ever not?"

My brother looks at me, then down at my crooked breasts, then over at Simon, then back to my face. "Guess we'll see."

20

One big happy family
Simon

This is undoubtedly the most charming farm I have ever visited. As we pull beneath the iron gateway announcing our arrival at Sunrise Fresh Farm, I notice rows of leafy green plants, a red barn, and a white farmhouse. Trees and a few buildings dot the rolling meadow, which is sectioned off by natural wooden fencing, with some sections having rows of plants, while other sections appear to be unbroken ground or simply grass.

Although the temperature is still fairly hot, the sky is a brilliant blue and spotted with thick clouds that may or may not drop rain and thunder on us later.

The charm doesn't entirely make up for the fact that my balls are still achy and unsatisfied after being interrupted with Bea, but at least my boys are happy.

And I certainly have new fodder for fantasies.

Which I will be acting out alone for the foreseeable future.

I nearly sigh, but catch myself as I remember where I am.

Namely, in a car. With my children.

About to have dinner with Bea and her family.

the spite date

Charlie is the first to realize how wonderful this place is, nearly as soon as he tumbles out of the car. "Dad! Dad, there's a *dog*!"

"Is it friendly? Can we pet it?"

"I want a dog."

"I wanted a dog first."

"You wanted one of those dogs that always needs to be groomed and looks like a pompous arsehole."

"I wanted a mutt!"

"You can only pet the dogs if you don't argue with each other, and you can't try to ride the dogs," Bea calls from a concrete slab set a reasonable distance from the house but somewhat close to the broad deck on the farmhouse's side, where she is monitoring a barbecue grill. "Sprite is the bigger one, and Digger is the furrier one."

The boys both dash after the dogs lying in the shade beneath a large tree between the house and a row of fencing holding in grass.

"Be nice to the animals," I call after them. "Your mother will have my head if either of you provokes a dog attack."

"They're pretty tame," Bea tells me.

"So long as your hooligans don't try to wrestle them or steal any of the goats," Daphne adds behind her.

"Got 'em, boss," Butch says. "Go and do…date things."

"It's not a date."

He grunts, a noise that clearly means *if you say so*.

Pinky shakes his head at me, also clearly thinking I'm daft for not realizing what this is.

Tank has the evening off, so he isn't here to comment.

With five adults already in attendance for this cookout, two security agents seemed more than sufficient.

Also, with five adults in attendance for this cookout—before Pinky and Butch—this comes nowhere near qualifying to be anything date-ish in nature.

Though the sundress Bea has changed into, showing off her legs and shoulders and arms and I daresay a hint of cleavage as well, which I shall have to inspect in more detail once I'm closer to her, is making me wish it were a date.

It's also making me think I should've brought all three of my security agents.

One more to help me remember we're not alone and keep me from blatantly ogling her this evening.

I give myself a mental shake.

This level of infatuation is rather unlike me.

A hint of woodsmoke and cooking meat lingers in the air—likely thanks to the grill that Bea is manning—or is it womanning?—and there are enough trees around the house to provide a break from the sun's heat.

She's applying sauce to the meat she's tending, but she keeps sliding looks my way.

Looks accompanied by small private smiles that make me rather glad smiling is my default.

I'd look like a lovestruck fool as I smile back at her otherwise.

Not that I'm lovestruck.

Smitten, possibly. Horny, most definitely. But never lovestruck.

"May I be of assistance?" I ask her.

"Nope. Go sit. Get a drink. Gird yourself for the other grilling that's coming."

I smile broader.

She smiles back again, but while my smile is easy, hers seems laden with apprehension.

"Second thoughts about the family dinner?" I murmur. When she explained what she was making—over text message, as Ryker hustled me out of her bus rather quickly, and my security man did nothing to help me—she added that it was impossible to cook her family's favorite meal without involving them.

And being the spitefully happy prat that I regularly am, I insisted I was ecstatic at the opportunity to get to know her better through her family.

"Not second thoughts, but definitely guilt," she replies. "Terrible, horrible, insurmountable guilt. You should've held out for a private dinner later. They're going to eat you alive."

"Are you worrying yourself over me, Bea?"

"It's more that I don't want to face the backlash from the town when everyone finds out you fled the entire state in terror because of my family."

"Have no doubts. I survived my own youth. I can survive an evening of uncomfortable conversation. Is this your magic sauce?"

Her cheeks turn a lovely pink. "Family secret magic sauce."

"It smells almost as good as you taste."

Her eyes go dark and her lips part as she draws in a quick breath.

"Drinks on the deck, you say? Lovely. I'm parched. And hungry."

I leave her gaping after me and climb the three steps onto the broad wooden deck.

Though I do agree with her rather strongly on one point—I should have held out for a private payback dinner.

A naked private payback dinner.

Which I need to *not* ponder much longer until I'm in private again.

"Heard you Magic Mike'd Bea's burger bus today," Daphne says as I join her on the deck. She's in loose jean shorts and a vest top. Her feet are bare, toenails painted a bright blue, her eyes hidden behind sunglasses, and her magically colorful hair tucked under a baseball cap.

I circumvent the long table adorned with a red checkered cloth and a basket of cutlery to lean against the railing in a position that gives me a view of both Bea at the grill and the boys in the garden. "Going shirtless made the temperatures more bearable, though I only danced when the tips were high enough."

"Must be nice to be a dude."

"The drinks are in the cooler, Simon," Bea says from the concrete slab below. "Ryker has everything from water to tea to soda to beer."

"I brought wine," Daphne says. "There's this pinot gris that I get at a winery up the road that pairs perfectly with the risotto. And it's local, so you know it's not fake."

Bea squints at her. "What? Why would it be fake?"

"Never mind. Want me to take over? Or do you actually trust Hudson with the risotto?"

"Gah. Two seconds…and done. This can sit for a bit. Wait. Simon. Drink."

"I got him, Bea." Daphne grins at me. "I want to pick his brain about people I used to know that he might know now."

"Do *not*—"

"Give him shit about being naked in your burger bus and Ryker suspecting hanky-panky? Bea. Am I your best friend or not?"

"That's a loaded question," I observe.

"Very loaded," Bea agrees. "Crap. The risotto. I'll be back."

She hustles past me to a side door, and the back door bangs in its frame as it shuts behind her.

"Sorry," she calls. "Forgot to catch that."

"He's here?" Hudson says inside. "Can I go torment him?"

"Fine," Bea says. "But he's welcome to torment you right back."

Daphne hands me a water bottle and then points to a folding chair at the head of the table that does *not* give me a view of both the grill and my boys.

"Is this the interrogation chair?" I ask her.

"Yep."

The back door bangs again.

Hudson's joined us.

"I get to go first," he says to her.

"No, you don't."

"He who sleeps on the couch is crankiest, and the crankiest deserves the little joys," he replies.

"Got a spare bedroom here," Ryker says from the ground behind me.

I don't jump in surprise, but only barely.

Daphne tosses a water bottle to Pinky, who's settled in a folding chair in the corner of the deck and is watching all of us.

Then she looks at me.

I oblige the silent demand and take a seat.

"So, Simon, are you the marrying type?" Daphne asks while Ryker circles the deck to join us.

"Absolutely not." It's less me answering, and more years of training answering for me.

"And is Bea aware of that?"

"Bea prefers it that way," Bea calls from the kitchen.

"When's the last time you were tested for STIs?" Ryker hovers close enough to be mildly intimidating but far enough away to not provoke Pinky into telling him to back up.

"Oh my god, are you serious?" Bea yells.

"I'm glad she lacked the foresight to see why volunteering to make Dad's risotto was a bad idea," Hudson stage-whispers to Daphne. "It's nice to have her occupied in the kitchen."

"I had my annual exam two months ago, and I'm fit as a fiddle without any detectable traces of infection, sexually transmitted or otherwise," I tell Ryker.

"Gonna need to see that paperwork," he replies.

Pinky growls.

"He says he's clear, Bea," Hudson calls.

"Clear of what?" Charlie calls from the yard.

I look at Hudson. "Oh, do go on. You have such strong opinions about what my children should and shouldn't know."

"Acne," Daphne calls to Charlie.

"I freaking hate that stuff," Charlie says.

"Don't say *freaking* when we're at other people's houses, dumbass," Eddie says.

"Ryker's house is your house," Daphne tells them. "Use all of your words. Then I won't feel bad for using all of mine too."

"Please attempt to use your more polite words first," I tell my children.

"Got it, Dad," Charlie says.

Eddie salutes me, then returns to hugging the smaller of the two dogs, which is still a sizable mutt.

"Ryker, please check the chicken," Bea calls from inside.

I start to offer my services, but both of the Best brothers and Daphne give me a look, echoed by Pinky, and I settle back the half inch that I managed to move before becoming the recipient of the *sit still* look.

"I *can* cook," I mutter.

"If you were on a sinking boat and could only save one of your kids, which one would you save?" Hudson asks me.

I choke on my water.

"Too soon," Daphne says to him. "He should have at least a glass of wine and a false sense of comfort before you spring that one on him."

"Simon, I'd apologize, but I think you probably knew what you were getting yourself into when you didn't argue about everyone coming to dinner," Bea calls.

"Is the risotto worth it?" I call back.

"It'll get a little uncomfortable when my brothers start moaning over it, but there's very little in life that can top this butternut squash risotto. Don't worry—no butter, only olive oil, so it's lactose-friendly. I used fresh sage from Ryker's greenhouse too."

I sit straighter again. "This is unlike what I expected of a farm. Do you not have acres of wheat and corn?"

Ryker slides me a look as he flips the chicken breasts on the grill. "Nope."

"He rotates crops every year and does crop shares," Hudson says. "Grows what people actually eat, like tomatoes and zucchini and eggplants. Except I don't actually know anyone who eats eggplants. Plus, there are the chickens and goats."

"All he needs is a wind turbine or two, maybe some solar panels, and he could live completely off the grid," Daphne adds. "It's so self-sustaining that I have farm envy, and I have never in my life wanted to be a farmer. What about you, Simon? Ever wanted to be a farmer?"

"Never given it much thought."

"Dad! Dad, look! There are goats!"

I peer over the deck railing at my boys, who are now racing further away toward a fence with goats on the other side, the dogs running along with them.

"But upon further reflection, I suspect farming would be a poor combination for me, my sons, and the animals," I tell Daphne as I rise. "Boys, remember to be kind to the animals."

Ryker looks at me, then at my boys, then at Hudson.

Hudson grins back at his brother. "Your animals, bruh. I'll flip the chicken."

I head after my children. Pinky follows me. Ryker overtakes me and reaches them as Charlie climbs onto the lower fence rung.

Even as the smaller of the two boys, he's much too large to need to stand on the fencing to reach over it to pet the goats, but he does it anyway.

"They bite," Ryker says.

Both of my children look up at Bea's brother, and while they're vastly different in appearance, they're identical in the way they jump back from the fence.

Eddie angles behind Charlie, which should be hilariously funny, considering Eddie is the larger of the two.

"How bad do they bite?" Eddie asks.

Ryker doesn't blink. "Took off my last girlfriend's finger."

"Whoa," Charlie whispers.

"Did she get it back?" Eddie asks.

Ryker folds his arms. "No."

"Dinner," Bea calls from the deck.

The boys look at each other and promptly break into a run toward the house.

Once again, the dogs follow, and I'm reminded of the fortune teller's suggestion that I get them a dog.

Rather unlikely to get that approved by Lana. Not as long as she's spending so many of her hours caring for her mother and I'm due to leave for four to six weeks for filming as soon as school begins.

I glance at Ryker. "I was under the impression you don't date much."

He stares me down much as he was staring down my boys a moment ago. "And now you know why."

Without another word, he turns on his heel and heads back to the deck.

I trail along, wondering less if his statement is true and more what it would take to make the man crack a smile.

It's suddenly a personal challenge.

A goal.

Secondary to finding an opportunity to be alone with Bea, naturally, but still a goal.

"Which one of these was the dog who disappeared?" I ask Ryker.

He slides me a look.

"Bea mentioned it."

"Roseanne. She didn't come back."

"Oh. Terribly sorry."

Once again, he doesn't reply.

I experience that unfortunate wash of emotions that tells me I'm not as impervious to the feelings of wanting to fit in here as I tell myself I am.

Not the first time I've encountered a family that made me wish I could belong in ways I never did as a child.

Likely won't be the last.

"Wash your hands first," Bea tells my boys on the deck. "Sink's just inside. Don't let the cat out."

"Yes, ma'am," they chorus.

Manners they clearly learned from Lana.

"You too," Bea calls to Ryker and me.

"She still mothers you?" I inquire.

As expected, he declines to reply.

Fair enough.

the spite date

I wouldn't answer me if I were him either.

Bea's issuing orders to Daphne to get the chicken off the grill and Hudson to start prepping to serve the food in the kitchen.

I follow Ryker into the kitchen, where my boys are attempting to squirt one another with the flexible-handled sink hose.

God help me, I both want to indulge in a water fight with them and also ground them at the same time.

"Boys," I begin, but before I can finish, Ryker's rescued the sprayer and has both of my children pinned against the cabinet with the sprayer aimed at them, but not spraying.

"Do you know what I have that you don't?" he says to my children.

"N-no," Charlie stammers.

Eddie shakes his head.

"Wisdom, strategic thinking skills, and a mortgage. You want to scrub this kitchen floor to ceiling?"

Now both of my boys are shaking their heads.

"Then wash your hands and go sit and eat, including your vegetables."

"But is corn really a vegetable?" Hudson says behind me.

In one swift motion, Ryker flips the sprayer around and sends a short burst of water at Hudson, who ducks behind me.

Not that he needed to.

Ryker was always aiming at me, I'm certain.

And I'm just slow enough to not duck myself, which means I take the full spray of lukewarm water square in the chest.

Eddie's eyes bulge.

Charlie gasps.

Ryker glances over his shoulder, inspects his handiwork, and smirks. "Whoops."

And me?

I smile.

You're bloody right, I do. "Jolly good shot, mate."

The back door bangs, and all of us turn to see Bea.

She looks at Ryker first, then my boys, then me.

And she heaves a sigh that would make my mother proud.

But on Bea—with her lips pursed together as though she can suppress the smile that I am certain she's suppressing, her dimples popping because she can't suppress them, and her eyes cast heavenward but also smiling—well, on Bea, that long-suffering sigh is nothing short of erotically appealing.

She shoves a container of barbecue chicken at Hudson. "Set this on the sideboard. Ryker, if you got water in my risotto, you're grounded." She looks out through the back door. "Daph, first glass of wine is mine."

"On it," Daphne calls back.

Bea points to all of us collectively. "I *will* take back all of the risotto if you don't behave. Understood?"

"I can make my own later," Ryker says.

"I can help him," Hudson says.

"I don't like risotto," Eddie says.

"Me either," Charlie agrees.

They share a look.

I don't like that look.

That look spells trouble.

Based on the way all three of the Best siblings are now glancing at each other, I suspect they're also familiar with this look and they know it means trouble as well.

"Better go light on Simon's," Bea calls to Daphne. She grins at me. "How would you say it? You need to have your wits about you tonight?"

"Indeed," I agree.

My children smile at me.

So do both of Bea's brothers.

Still doesn't count on Ryker's behalf though.

This isn't yet an actual happy smile.

It's a *you're in trouble* smile.

And I daresay he's right.

On many, many counts.

21

Never trust a teenager

Bea

The food is almost a success.

Hudson and Ryker are moaning over the risotto, as usual, though they're putting more of a show into it like they're trying to make Simon uncomfortable.

Daphne eats almost as much as I'd expect one of Simon's boys to eat, claiming it was a long day and she didn't have enough food for lunch. She splits her time at work between checking in with the outdoor crews and making phone calls to raise more money for the nonprofit, and today was an outside-all-day kind of day.

Those always make her hungrier.

Simon's offering praise between every bite and making me blush.

He's as far as he can get from me at the table. I'm the last seat on one end, he's the last seat at the other end, with Tank at the head by him and Pinky across from me.

Daphne and my brothers conspired on the seating arrangement, even if they're claiming innocence.

And Simon's children—both of them—have hardly touched their plates.

Midway through dinner, Daphne and I excuse ourselves to the kitchen under the guise of getting seconds. "Are the kids sick?" I murmur to her as we huddle in the kitchen beside the screen door, secretly spying on the men to see what they'll say while we're gone.

"You're asking the wrong person. I know nothing about kids."

"Hudson was only a little older when you moved in with us."

"Yeah, and we hung out. I didn't do the parenting."

"You drove him to guitar lessons and took him to the pool in the summer when you were off."

"Bea. You had to *teach me to drive* before I could take him places."

"You knew how to drive. You just didn't know how to do it without getting speeding tickets."

She ignores me. "I didn't parent. I helped to express my gratitude for your patience with the extra hot mess you took in to raise too."

I roll my eyes.

She rolls her eyes back.

Her eye roll is decidedly more pointed.

Not the first time we've had this conversation, and it likely won't be the last. "You know you saved my sanity?" I say to her.

"You saved my whole fucking life."

I give her a shoulder-squeeze hug.

The men are discussing the farm. The minute anyone stops grilling Simon, he asks a question of his own about how Ryker runs things out here. They've covered the goats, the chickens, the honeybees, the greenhouse, the barn, how the CSA operates, how old the farmhouse is, and a few other things I can't specifically remember now.

"I'm done doing parenting," I murmur as I glance at Simon's boys again.

Charlie's in a hoodie despite the temperatures, though he doesn't have the hood up, and Eddie keeps looking at his plate like he wants to eat, but won't.

"I'd do it," Daphne says. "Maybe. One day. With my own. If I get enough therapy to overcome my own childhood."

the spite date

"You don't think they're refusing to eat to make some kind of statement about me and Simon dating-not-dating, do you?" I ask her.

"Psh. You're not looking for long-term. He can tell his kids that."

"You know that. I know that. Simon knows that. But still—his kids aren't eating. And they usually eat everything."

"Ooh, you're nervous. Like you *like him* nervous."

"Am not."

Okay, I am. But what he did to me in my bus—of course I like him.

Wouldn't mind a little more of that.

Yep.

It's all physical.

Nothing at all to do with how much watching him smile now makes me want to smile too.

"It's okay to be nervous around a guy you like, Bea," Daph says. "He's hot, he's funny, and I think he really is that happy all of the time. That's good for you."

"So you're Team Simon now?"

"Maybe. He got you arrested, so that's still a mark against him. Is he going to dump you in another sink full of dirty dishes tonight, or do you think he'll actually treat you like a lady and rail you against a wall instead when he sneaks upstairs with you under the guise of getting a house tour from you?"

"*His kids are here.*"

"Yeah, and there are two security dudes who can keep them occupied."

"And my brothers are here. Pretty sure you know for yourself how excellent they are at cock-blocking." They already made him so uncomfortable at one point by pestering him about the new show he's apparently writing this summer that I thought he was going to bolt. They backed off though and changed the subject when they realized he didn't want to talk about it.

And I can understand it, even if I've never considered myself creative.

I've had my big dreams stolen from me. I can imagine Simon feels a protectiveness over his projects too.

"I can make a goat emergency happen in thirty seconds flat," Daphne says. "They'll be chasing Gustav and Rainbow and Merrick all over the farm."

"You know Ryker hates it when people name his goats."

She grins. "I'm willing to face his wrath if it means you finally get properly laid."

"Just for fun," I add.

"Well, duh, just for fun. You don't want forever. You've made that pretty clear."

I cringe. "Daph…"

She pins me with a look that has me glancing at the door to make sure we're still alone. "What?" she says flatly.

"It's just…I realized that my last three boyfriends happened when I was determined to just go have a fun time. So I'm starting to get worried that if we actually do this, I'll think I'm in love with him."

She grins broader. "Rocking chair test."

"Hey, kids, want to hear about the time I figured out my vagina always convinced me one good night of sex meant he was my soulmate only for me to get my heart ripped out of my chest time and time again when it ended because my vagina is a lying dirtbag?"

"See? You identified a problem and learned from your mistakes! If I need to have a talk with your vagina about Simon not being your soulmate, I'm happy to. But she's not a lying dirtbag. She's a hopeless romantic. I'd rather have a hopelessly romantic vagina than a suspicious vagina, and I say that as someone who knows suspicious is a smarter choice."

"Sometimes I wonder how I love you as much as I do, and then you go and say things like that, and I realize life wouldn't be the same without you, and I do mean that the complimentary way."

"You're welcome."

the spite date

I'm smiling as I glance at the door again. "We should get back out there before they come looking for us and catch us having conversations about my hopelessly romantic vagina."

She snickers.

I grab another scoopful of risotto for myself and follow her out the door, back to the table where Simon has noticed his kids aren't eating too.

"Are you sure you're not ill?" he asks Eddie, who's beside him.

Eddie stretches and fakes a yawn. "I'm tired. Must be getting ready to sleep and grow a few inches."

Charlie stretches and fakes a yawn too. "Same."

"Is this when we mention the strawberry shortcake for dessert?" Daphne settles into her seat. "Bea, do that thing where you tell your brothers they can't have dessert if they don't clear their plates."

"We don't do the clean plate club," Hudson says. "We do the *eat until you're not hungry anymore* club."

"I do the *only take as much as you'll eat* club," Ryker says.

"I can always eat more risotto."

"And that's why you're not staying at my house tonight."

"Will he puke?" Charlie asks.

Hudson grins.

Ryker scowls at him.

"No," I answer for them. "Sometime when we're not eating, they can tell you about the great Christmas plumbing disaster. For now, are you sure you're not hungry?"

"I might have some strawberry shortcake," Charlie says. "Sample it. Like I sampled all of this."

"We sample," Eddie agrees.

"It's good to sample when you're getting ready to sleep for thirty-four hours so you can grow two inches."

"I might grow three."

"I have to grow five to start to catch up."

The twins share a look, and they once again yawn in unison, both stretching their arms above their heads, both barely holding back grins.

Simon's looking between them—one across from him, one beside him—like he can't decide if he should ask to take some dinner home and bail or if he should see how this plays out.

Then he glances at me and catches me smiling broadly.

"You're enjoying this," he says.

It's an affectionate statement that makes my belly warm and tingly in ways even the best barbecue chicken and butternut squash risotto can't.

"Sometime later, I might tell you stories about things Griff and Hudson did after pretending to be tired, but you helped me out today, so I'm not going to give your kids any ideas."

"We *are* tired," Charlie insists.

"Exhausted," Eddie agrees.

"I might fall asleep on this plate."

"I should probably go lie down in the grass while you do boring adult stuff."

"I won't allow Bea to send food home for you if you don't behave yourselves," Simon says.

He's so bad at this disciplinarian thing.

I don't believe him.

I don't think they do either.

The boys share another look.

"We don't want food, Dad," Charlie insists.

"Yeah. We're not hungry," Eddie agrees.

"He's so fucked with something," Daph whispers to me.

I sip my wine and smile.

Simon makes eye contact with Tank, who rises as soon as Charlie darts out of his seat.

Pinky rises as Eddie gets out of his seat too.

"This is better," Charlie says.

"Yeah. You can talk about adult things while we sleep."

"I love sleeping in the grass. It's better than sleeping in the trees."

"How has he not sweated to death in that hoodie?" Daphne whispers to me.

"It's teenage boy magic," I murmur back. "Griff did it too. For *three* summers. And then he wouldn't wear a coat in the winter. But he survived. And now he claims it was training to help him play in any weather."

"Boys are annoying. Why do we like them again?"

"Evolution and genetics hate us."

"I can hear both of you," Ryker says to us as the boys dart off the deck with both security agents following behind.

I smile at my brother. "Good. Don't be a stupid boy." I move to Charlie's spot across from Simon.

Daphne moves to Eddie's spot between Simon and Ryker.

Hudson gets up for thirds.

Ryker slinks back in his chair and rolls his eyes at us.

Simon takes Charlie's plate, then shoots a look out at his boys, who are making a show of sprawling in the grass beneath a tree, next to the dogs.

"They're up to something," he says.

I giggle.

Daphne laughs.

Ryker smirks. "You think?"

Simon smiles a *what can you do?* smile. "Time will tell what."

Ryker looks out at the boys too, and then he sighs.

"Gonna put the goats up?" I ask him.

"Seems smart." He climbs out of his seat too. "Hudson. Get out here and help me."

"It's *risotto*, dude. Wait a minute," Hudson replies from inside.

Daph shoots to her feet. "I'll help."

I grab the belt loop on her jean shorts and tug her back into the seat. "Hudson, he's loaning them out for goat yoga tomorrow, and that can't happen if they're stressed."

"I don't stress the goats," Daphne says.

"You stress me, and that stresses the goats," Ryker replies.

Daph makes a face at him. "Everything stresses you."

I hide another grin behind my wine.

Hudson appears at the screen door. "Tomorrow's goat yoga day?"

Ryker hooks his thumbs in his overalls. "Thursday. Duh."

My youngest brother makes the face of every man ever forced to choose between more food and helping with something that might make its way back to a girl he has a crush on.

"Ooohh," Daph whispers.

"Now you're catching on," I say.

"Catching on to what?" Simon asks as Hudson disappears again.

"Hudson has a crush on the goat yoga instructor," I whisper.

"She works at his favorite diner on Sunday mornings too," Daphne adds.

"I'm giving up extra risotto for this," Hudson says as he pushes out of the house, work gloves in hand. "Make sure you mention that part."

Ryker rolls his eyes again.

"Do it," I tell him. "Mention that part."

He ignores me and heads off the porch, Hudson trailing behind slower.

Like he's already eaten too much chicken and risotto.

"Did the goats truly bite off his ex-girlfriend's finger?" Simon asks me.

"Whose ex-girlfriend?"

"Ryker's ex-girlfriend."

Daph explodes in laughter.

"Ah, I take that as a no."

"Who told you that his goats bit his ex-girlfriend's finger off?" I ask.

"Ryker. When the boys were attempting to pet them before dinner."

Daph's still cackling. "Dude. Ryker doesn't date."

the spite date

"He made that up," I agree.

Simon scoops another bite of risotto onto his fork. "I assumed as much. Thank you for verifying before I made a fool of myself in front of anyone else."

He bites into the risotto, and his eyes cross as he sighs happily.

"Don't thank us yet," Daphne says. "We're secretly recording the way you're eating Bea's cooking so we can post it on the internet if you piss us off."

He slides one eye open, smiles, and shrugs. "The world should know what it's missing."

"And what do you get out of letting us use you to tell the world what it's missing?"

I don't bother telling her to knock it off and leave him alone.

It's nice to have a friend who's willing to ask that.

And before Daphne, I didn't.

I was too young to really get along with most of the other parents, and too tired to make friends my own age to go out with.

Daph regularly reminds me that I saved her life by teaching her how to get by as a normal, often-broke person, but the truth is, she saved my life too.

Not with appliances, but with being a friend at a time when I didn't have the bandwidth to make friends. She was just *there*, with her completely different lifestyle and zero fear about anything and some soul-level understanding that we needed each other.

"Bea," Simon says suddenly, "did you tell Daphne what the fortune teller said?"

I wince.

His smile freezes. "Oh."

"*You saw Madame Petty without me?*" Daph shrieks. "What did she say? I have to know what she said. You know she told me I should hoard money two weeks before my parents disowned me, right?"

"She didn't say anything that made any sense," I tell her.

"But what did she say?"

I look at Simon.

He shovels another scoopful of risotto into his mouth, with far fewer manners than he's been using to eat the rest of dinner—seriously, adorable—and his eyes roll back in his head again.

"She just said you shouldn't do anything stupid," I say. "Which is dumb. Who's to say what's stupid?"

Simon eyes me.

If he tells Daph that Madame Petty said she wouldn't come home one day, my hopeless romantic vagina will be finding someone else to be hopelessly romantic about.

"That's seriously what she said?" Daph looks between us. "That's so vague."

"Does she—erm, that is, she also said that my boys would cease speaking to me, so I rather suspect she's a charlatan," Simon says.

"Honestly, Daph, he has a point," I say. "You know I love you, so I say this with love too, but that fortune she gave you about hoarding money? Anyone who'd ever seen a single article about who you used to be and the subsequent articles about your parents' heartburn might've guessed the same."

She squints at us, her gaze still darting back and forth between us.

And then she sighs. "You're right. Another fortune teller told me once I'd be arrested, and honestly, of course I was going to be arrested. It was inspiration, if anything." Her eyes suddenly go big. "Oh my god. Your mother's Naomi Luckwood, isn't she?"

Simon's face goes blank. "That is her name, yes."

"The painter?"

"That is what she's known for, yes."

"She was there."

"Excuse me?"

"Your mother. My mother went on this kick where she was thinking about buying some of your mother's artwork since she was Margot's fiancé's mother's favorite obscure artist for a while, and she was there when I got home after the first time I was arrested. They all were, actually. My mother, your mother, Margot's former fiancé's mother…"

"Fascinating."

If Simon thinks he's hiding how he feels about his parents with this neutral-expression thing he has going on, he's dead wrong.

I can *feel* Daph picking up on the vibes.

"You're not very much like your parents, are you?" Daph says.

"Strawberry shortcake?" I interrupt.

"Indeed." Simon rises. "Please. Allow me to assist."

"That's a fabulous idea," Daphne says. "I'm gonna sit here and be lazy and watch the sun set. Can you make sure my cream is extra whipped?"

Simon's eyes widen and then shift in the direction of his empty wineglass.

I tug his hand, and sparks shoot up my arm. "C'mon. Let's go whip some cream. For everyone else. Not for you."

"Whip it good," Daphne calls.

"Life is never boring in your circle, is it?" Simon murmurs.

"Never. And I love it."

The screen door bangs shut behind us.

And we're alone.

Again.

Just like this afternoon in my bus, except that Simon's in a shirt that's almost dried after Ryker got him with water, and I'm in a dress that he can very easily slide his hands under, and we have maybe four minutes before someone realizes we're alone inside together, because that's how my life goes.

He squeezes my hand and pulls me closer to him, away from the door and lone window. "That was the most delicious meal I've had in years."

"Hate to tell you, but that's the pinnacle of my culinary tricks. It's all downhill from here."

There's something different about his smile.

It's probably the smoky desire making his blue eyes darker. The way they crinkle at the edges. How he smells like patchouli and summertime sprinklers and old books. The brush of his shirt against my bare arm as he presses me against the countertop.

"Tell me there's not spilled food behind me," I say.

He smiles wider.

And it's impossible to not smile back.

"If there were?" he says as he lowers his lips to my neck.

"The answer to that question depends on what you—*oh god*, right there."

How does the man know the exact right place and the exact right pressure to put on my skin?

He nips at the sensitive skin behind my ear. "Is this the right answer?"

I angle my face into his neck and lick the tendon from his shoulder to his jaw, enjoying how he shudders against me. "Clearly yes," he murmurs.

"We have like three minutes."

"How could you possibly—"

"I raised three teenage boys and Daphne. I know my odds here."

He chuckles against my skin, and I know.

I know I am absolutely hopeless at resisting this man.

He's a bit of a mess, but so am I.

But mostly—it's the kindness.

"I apologize for my demon spawn's refusal to eat your food. I don't know what's got into them."

See?

In the middle of slipping a hand up my leg and under my dress, he's worried that his kids hurt my feelings.

Kindness.

I press a kiss to his stubbly jaw. "I don't take it personally."

"Would you like to take this personally?" He flexes his hips against mine.

the spite date

I arch back against his hard-on. "Yes, please."

"Good. Because I—"

"*Bees!*" someone screams outside.

Simon's head whips up.

He blinks at me as someone else screams.

"Oh, bloody hell," he mutters.

We both dash toward the door, get in each other's way, and I manage to get out first.

"What's wrong?" I ask Daphne, but she's not on the porch.

She's running after Charlie, who's running away from the tree and toward the barn.

"*Beeeeees*," Charlie hollers.

I run after Daphne and Charlie.

Simon overtakes us both as he sprints after his son.

Both Tank and Pinky are chasing Charlie too.

"It doesn't make sense," I pant at Daphne as I catch up to her. "Ryker's bees are on the other side of the property."

She stops so suddenly I almost trip over her.

And she turns around just as fast.

"What?" I gasp.

She doesn't answer.

But she does start to grin.

We're both huffing and puffing—clearly need to go running more—but she's smiling and changing course, running again, but this time, around the back of the house.

"Daph?"

I look back at Simon and Tank and Pinky and Charlie.

And that's when it hits me.

Eddie's not with them.

Ryker and Hudson are in the goat barn.

All of the other adults are running after Charlie.

I switch course too, following Daphne.

And when we circle the house and find Eddie, I actually gasp out loud.

His head whips up and he stares at me with the most comical *oh shit, I'm caught* expression.

Simon's son is attempting to dognap Digger.

He has the rear door of the SUV open, and he's using grilled chicken to try to lure the dog inside.

Digger's already halfway up.

"You are so busted, dude," Daphne says.

"The dog opened the car," Eddie blurts.

Digger does his part and finishes jumping his sturdy body up into the SUV.

I snicker. "Uh-huh."

"He did. I'm trying to get him out. Here, boy. Here, Digger-Digger. Get out of the car."

"Did you know Ryker lost one of his dogs a couple weeks ago?" Daphne says.

Eddie's eyes get big.

It's like looking at a mini-Simon.

A mini, not-smiling Simon.

And something melts in my heart.

It's a little something, but it's also not.

Because I know exactly what that feeling is.

Protectiveness.

And not for Ryker.

Not for the dog.

For Eddie.

Dammit.

"Lost him how?" Eddie asks.

"She ran away and didn't come back," I answer. "He used to have three dogs. Now he's down to two. And the cat. He'd be sad if he only had one dog. And the cat."

the spite date

Someone shouts in the backyard, and I pull my phone out of my pocket—best dress ever—and send a quick note to Simon. *Daph and I are with Eddie. He's fine.*

"Don't tell my dad," Eddie says.

I hold eye contact with him. "You're going to tell your dad."

"But—but then he'll never get us a dog."

"Have you asked him for a dog?"

"All the time, and he keeps saying no because Mom's too busy and he's about to be gone too much," he mutters. "But I can take care of a dog. Charlie and me both can. We can walk to the store and buy food and we can walk the dog and we can sleep with the dog and we can do all of the things."

"Like picking up dog poop?" Daphne asks.

"That too. We can do it."

I want to believe him.

Simon probably wants to believe him.

And he's still a thirteen-year-old boy.

As is his brother, whom I suspect just faked a bee attack to facilitate this attempted dognapping.

Which wouldn't have worked, by the way.

There's zero chance Digger would've made it to the end of the driveway without barking inside the car, even if they managed to hide him under a blanket or something.

He hates car rides.

He also smells like a dog.

Someone would've noticed in four seconds flat.

"Can you tell him?" Eddie says. "Can you tell my dad we'd take good care of a dog?"

"Have you tried showing your parents that you're responsible enough for a dog? Do you help with the dishes? And the cooking? Do you keep your rooms picked up? Do you do your homework on time?"

I feel four hundred years old as the words leave my mouth.

The number of times I had to say these exact words to my brothers—it's bringing back all of the feelings about being thrust into the parent role at nineteen.

My parents were amazing, and I was grateful that I could step in and let my brothers finish growing up here in Athena's Rest, but the responsibility wasn't without resentment that I wasn't getting to experience college and a job away from home and the parties and the freedom.

And the time to figure out who I wanted to be.

What I wanted to do with my life.

So I wouldn't be twenty-nine and still floundering, wondering what my purpose is.

"But a dog is different," Eddie says.

My brothers said the same thing. It's like reliving history.

"When I was your age, I wanted polar bears," Daphne tells Eddie. "My parents wouldn't let me have one either."

He makes another teenager face at her. This one's *you're stupid*. "Nobody can keep a polar bear for a pet. They'd eat you."

Daph puts one hand on her hip. "My parents had enough money to buy an entire zoo. They could've gotten me a polar bear. And a polar bear keeper. And I could've had a polar bear that didn't eat me because I could've raised it from birth to love me."

Eddie gapes at her while I swipe a hand over my face to hide a smile.

Footsteps pound behind us.

Eddie looks past Daph and me, and he cringes.

"What on earth—*Edward Richard Kent, are you stealing a dog?*"

I grab Simon by the arm before he can storm past me. "He wouldn't have gotten away with it."

"Between Bea knowing her brother's tricks and me basically being one of her brothers in my youth, we were on to him," Daph agrees.

"And Digger's a barker who poops in cars," I add.

Daph nods. "If you didn't hear him, you would've smelled him."

the spite date

"You said we could get a dog but we don't have a dog," Eddie says. "It's never going to happen if Charlie and me don't make it happen."

"*You don't steal someone else's pet.*"

Whoa.

Simon's actually pissed.

This is new.

No smiling or anything.

"She already lectured me," Eddie grumbles.

"*Especially* after they welcome you into their home and serve you good food and let you run loose and wild and pet their other animals."

Eddie scowls at him.

Simon's chest is heaving, and I don't think it's the running.

Pretty sure that's anger.

"Bea, please thank your brother for a lovely evening. I must return home with my hooligans."

"Simon?"

"Yes?"

Yep.

He's pissed. Fuming pissed. And clearly uncomfortable with anyone seeing him this way.

"Remember their brains won't be fully developed for another decade."

"Even people without fully developed brains shouldn't be booking secret parties and destroying the landscaping by digging for imaginary treasures and attempting to steal other people's pets."

"The man has a point," Daph murmurs. "But my brain's fully developed and I'd honestly go digging for imaginary treasures too, for the record."

Simon squeezes his eyes together.

Tank and Pinky stroll past with Charlie between them.

I let Simon's arm go. "I promise it gets better eventually."

He doesn't answer.

"Digger?" Ryker calls from behind us.

The dog barks once and takes off running for him.

Simon stares his boys down as they load into the back seat of the SUV.

"Good dinner," Pinky says to me.

"You ever want to drop off more of that risotto, we won't have you arrested," Butch adds.

Daphne snickers.

Honestly?

I do a little too. "Appreciate that kind sentiment."

He grins.

And then everyone's in the SUV, and they're pulling away from the farm.

And I'm sighing a sigh so deep, I feel it in my toes.

"I totally get why my parents hired nannies now," Daphne says.

"What the hell was that?" Ryker's joined us, clearly completely oblivious to the fact that Simon's kids just tried to steal one of his dogs.

"You remember the guinea pig?" I ask him.

He stares at me.

Then looks at Digger.

Then looks at the dust cloud kicked up from the departing SUV.

"Son of a bitch," he mutters.

Daph lifts a brow at us.

I shake my head. "Let's go do some dishes. And I need to pack up some of that strawberry shortcake."

Daphne smirks.

Ryker sighs.

I ignore them both and head for the house.

A summer fling is supposed to be more sex and less talking.

But we'll get there.

Hopefully.

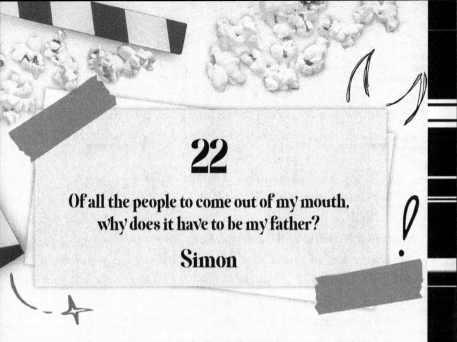

22

Of all the people to come out of my mouth, why does it have to be my father?

Simon

If, when I die, I become a star, I hope I have the decency to sparkle less brightly on nights when my descendants feel as though they are the world's biggest fuckup.

But these stars—these stars in the sky have the utter audacity to twinkle merrily. Even a lack of my glasses causing the stars to be blurry doesn't hide the fact that they're happily shining away without a care in the world.

Clearly my ancestors.

It tracks with how my parents would twinkle in the sky.

They'd be overjoyed at my failures and disappointments.

And they had the nerve to try to call once again this evening too, as if they were aware I'd fucked up and wished to revel in my failures.

One of these days, I should block their numbers. I never answer, and I have no wish to continue a relationship with them, but for some reason, I never make that final step to rid myself of them fully.

Possibly I wish to have the occasional reminder of the kind of parent I don't want to be.

Or possibly I enjoy torturing myself with the occasional spike in my own heart rate any time I see their names pop up on my phone.

Someone rustles in the dark, and I scowl at them too. "As I've made quite clear, you've been dismissed for the evening. I shan't be eaten by lions or tigers or accosted by stalkers in my own back garden," I snip at whichever security agent is coming to check on me after they should be off.

"Are you sure about that?" a woman replies.

I sit up straight. "Bea?"

"Stalker reporting for duty. Wanna be kidnapped? I bribed your guards with risotto and have strawberry shortcake for you. No cream. Just shortcakes and juicy, juicy strawberries that have been soaking into the shortcake since I left Ryker's house. It's undoubtedly delicious. Plus, fresh strawberries, right out of his garden."

I'm uncertain if I should bless her or curse her.

My cock certainly is on the *bless her* side of the scales.

The rest of me though—my children attempted to steal her brother's pet, and I was so embarrassed, and so very disappointed that a nice family evening had ended with my boys being complete hooligans, that I rushed us out of there without making a proper apology to him.

Were I her, I'd be delivering poisoned dessert to me right now.

She settles on the ground beside me, depositing a large, dark, rustling package on the ground before us as well.

"I waited outside the gate until I saw Lana's car leave. You okay?"

"Am *I* okay—excuse me, but your family were the victims this evening."

The bag rustles, and something inside clinks.

A bottle.

She's brought bottles in addition to strawberry shortcake.

The shortcake is likely made with cream and butter and will cause me a fair bit of discomfort, which I undoubtedly deserve.

"Root beer or a summer shandy?" she asks me.

I peer at her in the darkness. "Are you aware those are two of my favorite beverages?"

"I cheated and googled you. Like a good stalker."

the spite date

"Do you have a preference?" I ask her.

"In search engines for stalking?"

"In beverages."

She's smiling at me. I can sense it. "I like them both."

"Then surprise me, though I don't believe I deserve either this evening."

"Good answer. I don't think I can tell them apart in the dark. Also, I like that you keep yourself humble. It makes you more bearable."

That should be amusing, but I feel myself sighing. "Thank you for your kindness, but I'm afraid I intend to be rather poor company this evening."

She passes me a bottle, essentially setting it upon my knee since I cannot see her nor the bottle in the darkness. Not with my eyes being what they are in the dark.

I take it from her, deeply regretting how much I enjoy when our fingers touch.

I would like to kiss her.

To forget this evening happened.

Though I would prefer to have earned that honor rather than deserving to be verbally eviscerated for my failure to raise upstanding, law-abiding children.

"Maybe two months after my parents died, my brothers started asking for a dog," Bea says. "All three of them were asking constantly. I was barely keeping up with who had to be at band practice or play practice and who had to be at baseball practice and when Ryker's therapy sessions were and if they were all getting their homework done, so I kept telling them we'd talk about it later. But later came and went, and they got tired of the answer, so Griff and Hudson snuck into the elementary school and stole the kindergarten class's guinea pig."

I peer in the direction of her voice. "Truly?"

"Yep. That was my first run-in with the local chief of police. No, second. Ryker was the only one of my brothers home the night of the fire, and the police had a few questions for him, so at the ripe old age of nineteen, I was officially his adult to be present when they were questioning him as a minor at not-quite-sixteen. But not the point. Point is, kids do kid shit. Even bad kid shit when you think their consciences should know better. And eventually they grow up and become the kind of people who will host cookouts at their farmhouses for you even though they don't like using the grill because it's on fire or being around a lot of people."

I twist the top off the bottle and take a sip.

Ah.

I've got the shandy.

It's rather lovely.

The voice whispering that I don't deserve one of my favorite drinks whispers a bit softer, as though I might be loosening up on the self-flagellation.

"Then there was the year Griff didn't turn in a single assignment on time," Bea continues. "Ryker missed some occasionally, especially when his nightmares about the fire would come back, but not like Griff did his freshman year. I was getting calls and emails from the school about him failing classes *constantly*. And he kept rolling his eyes at me and telling me the baseball commissioner didn't care if he passed algebra, and he didn't listen to the softball coach at Austen & Lovelace who told him otherwise, but she used her network for me to get us a call with the local minor league team's coach who put the fear of the ghost of Babe Ruth in him for me."

I sip at my beer again and remain quiet.

Her voice is calming.

So is the message she's gently delivering, which is soothing parts of me that I never knew could be soothed.

That I never thought I deserved to have soothed.

Is this what true family is supposed to do?

"And that was the year that Hudson had a cold every other week, which meant he was at the doctor every other week because I didn't want to not take him if it was actually worse than just a cold because that would've been letting my parents down if I didn't get him diagnosed right and then he got that infection in his heart that sometimes happens with strep throat."

"Is that a thing?"

"Yep."

"Bloody hell. Charlie sniffled yesterday."

"Probably allergies."

I sigh deeply and stare into the darkness, idly letting the bottle dangle by my fingers. "Lana took the boys. She has no time or bandwidth, as she calls it, for them this week—her mother is being quite difficult, which she insists is not her mother's fault, given her memory issues—but I'm clearly inept at being a parent, so she took the boys."

Bea's hand rests on my leg, and she squeezes gently. "My parents were pretty awesome as far as parents go, but I still remember occasional nights when I was little when one of them would get angry and the other would tap in. And I can't tell you how many fights my brothers and I had the first couple years after our parents died because I didn't get a break and I needed one and felt guilty for not being able to live up to the example they set for us."

"My parents were bloody awful, and I was constantly berated for anything, sometimes even perfection not being perfect enough, and so I have no idea how to discipline my children without being my parents, but I was so fucking angry this evening, and all I could hear was my father's voice coming out of my mouth."

She scoots closer and settles her head on my shoulder. "I googled your parents too. I know you can't tell a person by their search results, but I'm pretty sure your father wouldn't be sitting in the grass beating himself up over worrying if he was a good father or not."

I want to sigh again, but instead, I take another swig of beer.

She's not wrong.

Generally, after berating me, he would seek solace in the arms of a mistress.

Occasionally in our own home if my mother was away.

And I'd hear him call whomever his flavor of the week was, and I'd hear exactly what he said when he asked her to come over—*the little twat has me by my last thread. I need relief*—and once again, it was my fault that my father was a philanderer.

Because I dared to make noise or ask for something or simply exist.

I dared to annoy him enough to want to fornicate with a woman who was not my mother.

"Did Lana say you're a terrible father because of tonight?" Bea asks.

"Of course not. She never says such things. Even when she should."

"Did you go out of your way to try to read it in her body language?"

That was rather pointed.

And correct.

"How many trips to the headmaster's office and police station did you make as you were raising your brothers that you would ask that question?"

"Enough."

"So that's to be my fate when I'm in town."

"Not necessarily. I know lots of families who never had to talk to the principal or the police. I think that's actually more normal. And the guinea pig was almost the worst thing my brothers did. At least, on purpose. And then there's Daphne, who's spent a number of nights in jail because of activism, which is completely different from spending nights in jail because of busting through a private gate in a burger bus to try to make kids eat fried fish on a stick."

"I never had run-ins with authorities when I was young. I suppose that's one thing my parents did well enough for me. Put the fear of consequences into my bones."

"But at what price?"

I take another drink.

That's the killer question.

"To them, or to me?" I inquire back.

"Either."

I lift my head to study the stars again. "I never wanted to be a father."

It's something I've said to myself, but never aloud to anyone aside from Lana, and to her, it was more of a *so you're getting rid of it*, which, again—not my finest moment.

Yet here, in the dark, with Bea, I feel as though I must confess it. For me.

"Do you still wish you weren't?"

"No." I shake my head. "My boys—even when they make me angry, when I have to fight how I was taught to parent in my own childhood—they are the best part of me. They're my chance to do better in the world than I had done to me. And I find I'm not doing better. I'm simply doing different, and now they're criminals."

"They're not criminals."

"They're well on their way."

"They're pushing to see how far they can go."

"Lana would have seen through why they weren't eating and realized they were plotting something before she'd finished a full bite of chicken herself. But they're stuck with me as their primary parent this summer, and I'm oblivious to what they're up to despite the hours we spend together, have spent together their entire lives, because I'm so afraid of being my parents that I'm inept in the exact opposite way."

"They're good kids at heart, Simon. Eddie looked way more guilty than my brothers ever did when Daph and I found him with the dog. They've had a lot of change this summer, but I think they'll be okay."

"It's kind of you to lie to me on their behalf."

"I'm not lying. He did look guilty." She kisses my shoulder. "You know the hallmark of a good parent?"

"Successful adult children?"

"Self-doubt. If you care enough to think you're doing it completely wrong, you're probably doing a lot right."

"Why am I confessing all of this to you?"

"Because you want in my pants."

God, she's funny.

And correct, though I'm some way off from being able to get out of my own head and simply enjoy having an attractive woman share a nightcap with me.

"Even before the show became ridiculously successful, I would not've confessed to anyone that I never wanted to have children. Or that I told Lana the same when she informed me she was pregnant."

"Ever get a woman thrown in jail before me?"

Heaven help me, she's actually made me laugh. "No."

"That must be the difference. You put me at my lowest, so now you're compensating by showing me yourself at your lowest. And Simon? You're a good dad. However you got here—it doesn't matter nearly as much as what you're doing every day. Your boys know they can count on you. They know you love them. Give yourself credit for that."

I swallow hard and don't reply.

My voice can't support it without betraying how much her belief means to me.

She shifts beside me, and the bag rustles again.

A moment later, there's another item being set on my leg.

"Eat your strawberry shortcake," she tells me. "And then let's see what else you want to confess."

I swallow again. "Did you make this yourself?"

"Nope. Hudson did it while I was in the shower. With orders to use coconut milk and clarified butter, and a threat of hiding his guitar from him and finding a kid with a cold to breathe on him if he didn't."

My heart softens as if it's a mound of butter on a sunny rock.

Remembering once or twice that I don't tolerate dairy well is one thing.

Consistently remembering—that's more than even Lana manages.

And it's making me feel more than a warm heart.

the spite date

It's making me suspect I should cut this evening short. I cannot afford to feel real affection for a woman who wants nothing more than a summer fling with a man who's leaving in a few weeks' time.

"Hiding your brother's guitar and giving him a cold is a threat?"

"He wants to be a rock star when he graduates college. And he finally got a few gigs lined up in town for the rest of the summer."

"You're allowing that?"

"He's a legal adult, and I convinced him to get a degree in education so he has a fallback career. I've officially set all of my brothers up for some kind of successful adulthood, and now I get to be the cool sister who doesn't nag them or give them life advice that they don't want. Also, I told him when he's famous, he has to get me concert tickets for my favorite bands from my own teenage years that he thinks are cringe. Just like Griff has to get me season tickets to any baseball team I want if I ever leave here and move to a city that has a baseball team."

"Would you be interested in raising two more young men? They've only six years left of their schooling before university, and I could pay in cash and orgasms."

She laughs. "Not a chance. Especially since these orgasms are still mythical."

"But are they? I seem to recall an encounter in a bus this afternoon..."

"My greatest performance."

"Oh, come now, Bea..."

"There's something else I haven't told you."

"And what, pray tell, is that?"

"I actually come from a long line of talented actresses. My mom ran the community theater and acted in all of their shows when I was growing up. I get a lot of talent from her."

"And she taught you to fake orgasms?"

I truly wish I could see her smile, though sensing it is almost as good. "Yep. Good thing I'm their only girl. Otherwise I would've had to teach my sister too, and that would've been awkward."

Ten minutes ago, I would've thought it impossible, but I'm laughing at the image of Bea sitting down a fictional sister to explain the ins and outs of faking orgasms.

Laughing.

Feeling lighthearted.

As though the world *will* turn out all right in the end.

My children will learn and grow and become mostly functional adults.

I may or may not have any more professional success—the more time I spend with Bea, the more I find myself brainstorming ways to change this script before I have to turn it in to the studio to hide the true inspiration—but it will be okay.

I have time.

And I have time with Bea.

"You are good for my soul," I say, and oddly enough, I don't instantly regret it.

"Give me five minutes and I can fix that." Her phone's flashlight flickers on. "Better. I can drink in the dark. I can't eat strawberry shortcake in the dark."

She grins at me, and her dimples pop, and then she forks a bite of strawberry shortcake into her mouth, making strawberry juice dribble down her chin, and everything else that's wrong in the world fades into the background.

I lean in to her and brush the strawberry juice from her chin, then suck the sweet taste off my thumb.

She watches me, close enough that I can see her clearly, her eyes wide, her lips parted, her breath coming quicker.

Her gaze dips to my lips. "You keep doing that."

"Haven't been disappointed yet."

Her tongue darts out to sweep her lower lip.

I set aside my strawberry shortcake and my beer.

Then I take hers and set them aside as well.

the spite date

"This wasn't my goal," she whispers as I thread my fingers through her hair and lower my mouth to hers.

"What was your goal?"

"Just to be a friend. I thought you might need one."

"Do you object to me kissing you?"

"No."

"Would you *like* me to kiss you?"

"Yes."

"Good. Because I would very much like to kiss you too."

She's smiling.

Her eyelids are lowered, and she's smiling, and her dimples have popped out, and I feel—

Free.

Safe.

Home.

Accepted. Warts and all.

I brush her lips with mine. "Turn off the light, if you don't mind."

She fumbles with her phone, and then all is dark again, the night lit only by the stars.

No moon.

No exterior house lights.

No neighbors close enough for their lights to intrude on the evening.

It's simply Bea and myself, her tongue making a slow inspection of my lower lip while she hooks one hand behind my neck.

Night sounds settle around us—crickets, frogs, a distant dog's bark—but I'm far more interested in the sounds coming from Bea.

Small gasps as I nip back at her lips.

Little moans when I slide my hand up her leg and beneath her dress.

"Are we really doing this?" she asks against my mouth.

"I shall fire or have arrested anyone who interrupts us this time."

That soft giggle.

That soft giggle will live on in my dreams for decades to come.

So will the feel of her fingers in my hair.

The way she tugs me to the ground beside her.

The feel of her leg around my hips, pulling me closer and making my cock swell eagerly as she nestles it between her thighs.

My eyes drift shut as she takes charge of this kiss, the slow, methodical glide of her tongue against mine building my anticipation with torturous leisure.

I can still taste the strawberry on her, and my tongue remembers the heady, delicious taste of her near-orgasm too.

By far the best torture I've had in ages.

Allowing me the time to learn her curves with my hands. To decipher her body's cues about where she enjoys being stroked.

If she prefers whisper-soft touches or aggressive pawing.

Both, it seems.

There's nowhere I touch her, no manner in which our bodies mesh together, that she doesn't respond by deepening the kiss, becoming more frantic in her own exploration of my body until she's clawing at the buttons on my shirt.

Her dress is up around her hips as I trace the skimpy undergarment covering her pussy.

Lacy.

Small.

Are they black? Red? Pink?

Any option makes my eyes cross.

I hook my thumb beneath the string waistband. "I'd like to bite these off you."

"Have you been a good enough boy for that?"

"Was parading naked to sell burgers for you not good enough?"

She palms my hard-on through my trousers. "It wasn't a private show."

the spite date

My cock swells harder as I imagine her splayed on my bed in nothing but black lace undergarments, teasing her own clit and playing with her own breasts as she watches me strip out of my clothes.

I should lift her and carry her into my bedroom and live out the fantasy, but I'm incapable of walking at the moment.

Not enough blood flow to my legs.

It's all stopped in my cock.

"I'm afraid private show bookings are sold out for the next week," I murmur against her neck.

She laughs. "By who?"

"Privileged information."

"You mean you're in the doghouse and this is your only night without your kids for the next week and there aren't actually any tickets available at all?"

She punctuates the question with another rub of my cock.

My eyes cross.

My balls tighten.

My lungs cease to work.

"Yes," I manage to reply. "Please don't stop."

"This?" she asks, stroking me through my trousers.

"Yes."

"But wouldn't it be better if I did…this?"

My trousers are suddenly unbuttoned, and she has both hands down my boxers, caressing me now.

"*Yes.*"

I'm gulping for air and I don't know what I'm doing with my hands or if my eyes shall ever uncross, but god help me, her smooth, warm hands on my cock, and—Christ— cradling my balls now too—I'd forgotten exactly how much I enjoy being with a woman.

More so being with a woman I appreciate rather than simply tolerate.

"Touching you is making me wet," she whispers against my neck.

"Beatrice."

"Yes, Simon?"

She's smiling. I can hear it.

And that too makes my cock swell harder in her hand.

Those dimples.

I could lick her dimples, but I cannot *see* her dimples.

"I don't—have—a condom," I pant.

"I wasn't planning this, but that doesn't mean I wasn't prepared." The hand cradling my balls disappears, which makes me whimper quite an unmanly whimper while the bag rustles.

And then her hands are back on me, and all is well.

"Your dress drove me crazy all evening," I gasp out.

"Did you fantasize about taking it off me?"

"Yes."

"All through dinner?"

"Yes."

"Naughty man."

"God, call me that again."

She grips my cock and slides the condom down it. "Tell me something else dirty."

"I hope you get grass stains on your knees."

Her hand pauses.

I grip it and guide her along. "Was that not dirty enough?"

"That was…double dirty. I'm impressed."

"You're welcome, darling."

Her laughter is soft and breathy. "Naughty, naughty man."

And then she's kissing me again, swinging her leg over my hips once again, her lace-covered pussy teasing my cock.

"You need to remove these." I stroke a finger beneath the band.

"Do I?"

"Beatrice Best, you are a terrible tease."

Her breath catches as I stroke inside her knickers. "I'm not the only one."

The hell with these.

the spite date

I tug them aside, and my cock glides along hot, slick skin.

My god, the way I'd love to feel her without this bloody condom.

While in my bed.

With fairy lights around the room.

Rose petals.

But the music of the night—the evening chirps and songs of the night insects—that, I would keep.

"This feels like we're hiding from our parents," she whispers as she slides her body onto my cock.

My eyes cross yet again at the sensation of her pussy squeezing me. "As if we're being bad?" I manage.

"So bad." She nips at my ear, and then my jaw.

I thrust up into her, and have the pleasure of once more hearing her breath catch.

"Do you enjoy being bad?"

She rocks against my body, riding my thrusts as we fall into the easiest of rhythms that also has my balls tightening too quickly and my cock straining too hard.

Cannot. Disappoint.

Not tonight.

Not the first time.

Not with Bea.

"Always—a good girl." She presses her hands to my chest and lifts herself, riding me harder.

"Always?"

She huffs out a laugh that turns to a gasp as I locate her breasts in the dark, jiggling beneath her dress as she rocks herself on my cock. "Al—*oh god*, pinch harder."

I oblige her and roll her nipples tighter between my fingers and thumbs.

Her body jerks, and she grinds against me, rocking against my cock with untethered abandon. "Oh god, that's so good."

Sweat beads on my forehead. My arse and legs strain to keep up as she jerks above me. My poor cock has nearly had enough, and it's becoming more and more difficult to hold out.

"Bea."

"Yeah?"

"You're not wearing a bra."

"You're welcome."

Her answer startles a laugh out of me, but laughing makes my cock teeter more precipitously on the edge of release, and I suck in a gasp to try to regain control. "Bea—"

"Is it as good for you?" She pushes my shirt aside and flicks her thumbs over my nipples, and it takes every ounce of control to not come on the spot.

"Yes," I manage.

"Simon?"

"Yes?"

"I'm about to—I'm right—it's there—"

She presses her hips hard against mine as her pussy tremors around my cock, and then she's squeezing me from the inside, the satisfied kind of whimper accompanying her internal spasms, and I drop my head back to the ground and let myself go with a groan of utter satisfaction.

The stars twinkle brighter above Bea, her soft chants adding to the music of the night. "*Yes, yes, so good, oh my god, yeessssss.*"

Most definitely agreed, Beatrice.

Coming inside her is the most exquisite experience I've had in ages.

I don't want this to end.

I want to simply exist here, in this moment, with Bea's pussy cradling my cock while we both ride a never-ending wave of orgasmic pleasure.

Except I'd like to see her face.

Witness her lovely green eyes heady with desire.

Watch her flush.

the spite date

Do her dimples come out when she's aroused?

I'm pondering all of it as her body relaxes and she sags down against me, head nestling into the crook of my neck.

The last of my own orgasm subsides and, breaking my own long-standing rule, I loop my arms around her back and hold her while we both catch our breaths.

I'm certain I did not deserve this tonight.

And I'm also certain I haven't a care in the world if I deserved it or not.

"Okay," Bea finally says quietly.

"Excuse me?"

"You passed the test. We can do this friends-with-benefits thing."

I blink up at the blurry stars for a moment.

And then the most unexpected thing of all happens.

I burst out laughing.

Perhaps Bea will be good for all of me.

As a friend.

For a short while only.

As it must be.

23

It was just good sex, not love

Bea

"Someone's cheerful this morning," Daphne says as she passes me to start the coffee maker Thursday morning. "I'm literally standing here still half asleep."

"With a smile."

I lift a block of cheese. "Even half-asleep me smiles over finding hidden rosemary and sea salt gouda in the fridge."

Daphne's hair is a wreck. She looks like she was battling demons in her sleep, and the bags under her eyes suggest she slept about forty-five minutes the whole night.

But she's still smirking at me. "Nice grass stains on your knees."

"Oh, shit, I thought I scrubbed those when I got home."

"How's the hopeless romantic vajayjay today?"

"She and I are negotiating terms of how much I can let myself like him knowing he's leaving at the end of the summer."

"You're fucked, aren't you?"

"No." Yes.

"I can hear you both," Hudson grumbles from the living room.

And now I'm three-quarters awake and smiling back at Daphne. "Still worth it," I whisper.

the spite date

Seriously, though. It is.

I know I'll get hurt.

That's no reason to not have fun in the meantime.

While pretending like I somehow won't get hurt.

Dammit, hopeless romantic vagina.

I raise my voice and change the subject. "Why do you look like you pulled an all-nighter?"

She wrinkles her nose and sticks her head in the fridge, clearly avoiding the question.

"Daaaapphhnneeeeeee," I whine. "What's wroooooonnnngg?"

"I hate your brothers for teaching you to talk like that."

"It was Griff, and I hate him too," Hudson says.

The living room lights are still off, and in deference to his sleeping habits, I only turned on the light over the stove, but the light from the fridge is making the kitchen even brighter.

I poke my best friend. "Come on. Out with it so we can solve it."

"You can't solve this."

"I'm superwoman. I can do anything."

"No offense, Bea, but having an orgasm doesn't actually turn you into superwoman."

"Again, I can still hear you," Hudson says.

Daphne grabs a glass storage container holding what looks like leftover lasagna and shuts the fridge while the coffee maker starts to sputter loudly.

"Your job?" I guess.

She grunts and shoves the lasagna in the microwave.

Pretty sure that's a *no* grunt.

"Friend issue?"

Another grunt.

"Family?"

"Freaking Margot." She stares at the microwave while the lasagna circles inside and the coffee maker gets louder. "Our father is insisting she give her ex another chance once his dad's out of prison, and I just—

they're not right together. Like, if they were truly soulmates, that would be one thing. But he's *easy* for her. He's not *right* for her. You know?"

"I think so. Does she want him back?"

"She keeps saying *well, I'm not dating anyone else and there would be strategic business advantages*. Like that's a reason to get back together with an ex who broke her heart."

"If he broke her heart…there was something there."

She wrinkles her nose. "Maybe. I've always thought she was more brokenhearted at the loss of the idea of him than she was at the actuality of him. Like, it wasn't *him* that she was mourning so much as it was mourning the idea of checking falling in love and getting married off of her to-do list."

"Oh. That's complicated."

"Yeah. She wasn't unhappy with him, and he hurt her a lot when he dumped her, but they were boring. And boring and not unhappy is never a good standard for a relationship."

"I'd take boring over toxic or abusive."

"No. You take being single. You never take being bored. And he is *so boring*. So boring. Like, he redefines boring. That's how boring he is."

"What's the dude in prison for?" Hudson ambles into the kitchen, apparently interested enough in gossip to voluntarily wake up.

"Not her ex. His dad."

"Whoever. What'd he do?"

Instead of answering, Daphne pulls up her phone, thumbs over the screen, and then passes it to him.

Hudson makes a strangled noise. "Oh, shit—your sister dated that family?"

"Not the whole family. Just the only son."

I peer over his shoulder and take in the headline from several years ago. "Miles2Go CEO Sentenced to Four Years in Embezzlement and Wine Fraud Case."

"They own gas station convenience stores, we own hotels…" Daph pulls a face as she takes the lasagna out of the microwave. "Margot's the good girl who always does everything Daddy tells her to, Oliver's the boring guy who always does everything *his* daddy tells him to…"

My body flushes involuntarily at the mention of *good girl*.

I told Simon last night that I was always the good girl too.

And then he gave me the greatest orgasm I've ever had.

In his backyard.

With our clothes still half on, which weirdly made it even hotter.

I shiver, smile, and realize Daphne and Hudson are both looking at me.

Crap.

Missed something.

"You can't control what your sister does, but you can be there for her to offer perspective when she's ready to hear it," I say.

"That's why *you* need to talk to her. Oldest daughter to oldest daughter."

Ah.

That's what I missed.

"I can try, but Daph, our parents weren't exactly running a multi-billion-dollar international corporation when they died… What Margot wants isn't what I might want. Or even need."

"Being rich doesn't mean you shouldn't want love above all else. And there's no fucking way Oliver can love her the way she deserves to be loved."

Fair enough. "Okay. When do you want me to talk to her?"

"We have a few weeks until the dumbass gets out of prison."

"Think she'll come visit again?" It's unlikely, and I know it. I moved in with Daphne four months ago, and last weekend was the first time I've seen Margot since.

So I'm not surprised when Daphne shakes her head. "We'll video call. Or—when's Griff in New York next?"

"September," Hudson answers instantly, which I knew too. We both know when we're going to see him play locally.

Daphne wrinkles her nose.

"Maybe Simon needs to take Bea to the city," my brother adds.

"We're just friends," I say.

Both of them stare at me.

And then both of them look pointedly at my knees.

I really thought I got all of the grass stains off in the shower last night. Clearly not.

"Friends who do…friend…things," I add.

Daphne cracks up.

Hudson grunts.

And my phone dings.

All three of us dive for it where it's sitting in the little corner of the kitchen where mail and phone chargers pile up.

Hudson gets there first, and he uses his height and his stupid inherent male strength to keep my phone out of my reach while he reads the text message in a terrible British accent.

"Would you like to accompany my children and me on the paddleboats at the lake after I've completed my writing on this terribly slow computer for the day? The boats are built for four, and I fear we should turn in circles were there only three of us."

"Physics was never my favorite, but even I know that's not how those paddleboats work," Daphne says. "They don't actually need you."

"You should go with Simon," Hudson says. "Jake's restaurant keeps selling out because not enough people know he's terrible. So use Simon's star power to pull in customers for the burger bus."

"Jake's restaurant is brand-new and everyone's still curious," Daphne says. "He might be able to move real estate, but I don't think he has the chops for the restaurant world. It won't last another month. Meanwhile, Bea had a stellar sales day yesterday."

"Because Simon paraded around naked for her and drew in a big crowd."

"See? That's what I'm talking about. Oliver would *never* parade around naked to sell vacation packages for Margot and Aurora Gardens. She deserves a man who'd use his body to help her when she's in a bind."

My phone dings again.

the spite date

Hudson makes a face, but he still holds it out of my reach. Doesn't mean I can't see the screen too though.

It's a picture of the strawberry shortcake with a short note.

Simon: *Also, thank you for breakfast. Quite tasty.*

And now I'm wishing I could have Simon for breakfast.

Yep.

I'm not instantly in over my head at all.

"Why can't I be a casual sex type of person?" I ask Daphne. "Why does my body have to try to convince me I'm in love with anyone who's halfway competent with his penis? And it was dark. I didn't even actually *see* his penis."

"Oldest daughter syndrome," she answers.

Hudson makes a gagging face and passes me my phone. "I'm going to take a shower."

"Before goat yoga?" I ask.

"Don't use all of the hot water," Daph adds.

He flips us both off and heads down the hall.

Daph frowns at me.

"What? What now?"

"I'm rethinking having you talk to Margot. If semidecent sex is all it takes for you to fall in love with a guy—"

"I'm not in love with him. My vagina is infatuated. There's a difference, and I know what it is now. Also, it was better than semidecent. It was top tier."

"Still reconsidering."

My phone dings once more.

It's Simon again.

Simon: *The boys have been sent to help tend the gardens at a care home under direct supervision of several of Lana's mother's neighbors and Tank and Pinky as well, so if I decide to catch up on my script this evening, I suddenly have the morning free. Do I recall someone mentioning goat yoga? Have you participated?*

I'm intrigued and would adore company if it fits your schedule.

"Maybe you're not in love, but..." Daph grabs a coffee cup out of the cabinet and pours herself a cup now that the coffee maker's finished.

"He told me the studio likes the attention he's getting from being seen with a woman. We're friends. With benefits. The end."

Once again, my phone dings.

Simon: *Apologies for the large number of messages. My fingers have minds of their own, which should be impossible after how much writing I accomplished last night after you left, but nonetheless, they keep typing and typing.*

"I can't decide if he's cute or annoying," Daphne says.

I'm smiling.

I can't help it.

"He's—well, I think he's *Simon*."

I text him back.

Bea: *Morning. I still have grass stains on my knees and apparently, I keep smiling. Are you up for something other than goat yoga this morning? Lucinda Camille always goes to goat yoga. She's annoying.*

My phone rings before he could've possibly had time to read my answer.

And once again—I'm smiling.

Daphne grins at me. "I'm going to eat in my room."

Before I can object, she's gone, the smell of lasagna and coffee left behind in her wake.

And I'm answering Simon's call. "Morning."

"Could we talk your brother into hosting a separate goat yoga session elsewhere without notifying that Camille woman?"

Yep.

Just the sound of his voice has my vagina doing flips and my heart making moon-eyes. "You can't declare war on the Camilles and then leave town."

the spite date

"So I shouldn't host my own competing murder mystery dinner since the woman keeps inviting me to hers"

"*No.* That'll only make it worse."

"Do you know what I despise most in the entire world?"

"Something between milk and letting your parents see when you're not actually happy?"

Silence settles between us.

That's unusual.

"Or...something else?" I guess.

"No, you were spot-on," he says. "Quite an astute observation. Well done. Even more spot-on than what I had intended to say, actually."

"Which was?"

"Bullies. I despise bullies."

"Mrs. Camille was very nice while I was dating Jake."

"Did she make you call her *Mrs. Camille*?"

"Yes."

"That's terribly awkward for a woman who was auditioning for the role of your mother-in-law. Even I'm allowed to call Lana's mother by her first name, and her mother dislikes me greatly."

I grab the teakettle and start filling it with water. "She doesn't like you?"

"Goodness me, no. She wanted us to get married, and I'm fully to blame for that not happening."

"Lana wanted to get married?"

"Absolutely not. I was a terrible catch back then. Still am, though I have a bit of fame and money going for me now."

The man cracks me up. "But it's still your fault you didn't get married?"

"Mother logic. Far better to blame me than to acknowledge her daughter wanted to be an unwed mother. So. What time does goat yoga begin? I'd like to make a point to this Mrs. Camille."

"Simon."

"Ah, excellent suggestion. I shall do it without my shirt. Thank you for the reminder."

"*Simon.*"

"You are aware that it's highly arousing when you chide me?"

My face flushes. "That'll make goat yoga more difficult."

"So glad you agree it's a good idea. Shall I see you there in an hour? Also, I've officially decided to host my own murder mystery dinner. It sounds like great fun, no?"

"Simon—"

"Oh, yes, please do say my name again."

"Your kids will still have to live here when you're away."

"My children? The children who plot parties that get people tossed in jail and who attempt to steal dogs and who are likely to manage some kind of mischief even while being supervised by six adults? Those children?"

I open my mouth, then close it again.

Hudson strolls back into the kitchen.

He's dressed for goat yoga in a T-shirt for his band and cotton shorts.

"What?" he says to me. "You have a look."

"Okay," I say to Simon. "I'll meet you at goat yoga in an hour."

"And you'll save the date to come to my murder mystery dinner."

I crack up.

I can't help it. "Sure. Consider me RSVP-ed. But if Mrs. Camille tosses flaming dog poop in my burger bus because you misbehave, you're buying me a new one."

"Deal."

24

Exes and Goats

Simon

"How did I not know this was here in Athena's Rest?" I inquire of Bea as I join her beneath a maple tree in a gated-off section beside what is clearly an outdoor drive-in cinema not far from my estate.

There's a large screen on a wooden frame against a backdrop of trees, though I suspect the screen is less screen material and more likely some kind of painted metal, and speakers on posts at regular intervals amongst the weedy, overgrown ground outside of the fenced-in area for the yoga class. A shack large enough to house a kitchen is behind our little goat yoga pen, undoubtedly the popcorn stand.

And it's utterly lovely.

"Because you don't pay close enough attention?" she replies with a smile.

She's in tight casual shorts and a pink vest top, with sunglasses on and her curly hair tied up in a messy bun, carrying a bag with a yoga mat sticking out, and I would very much like to kiss her.

I cannot, however, as a goat butts between us before I can come any closer.

She pats it on the rump. "Ryker let you come, hmm? Stay in your own lane during child's pose, got it?"

"Is this cinema still active?"

"It's been for sale for probably seven or eight years now."

"Has it?"

"Yep. I'd come out here all through high school with my friends, but it kinda died out not long after I moved back home."

Hudson joins us and sets down his bag with a yoga mat in it as well. "Rumor has it Mrs. Camille has been trying to get some investors together to buy it, especially so she can control weekends off when the community theater's performing."

"That's...quite the reason to buy a business."

"Daph's biggest regret is that she didn't buy it before she lost her trust fund." Bea grins at me. "She would've shown old horror flicks every weekend."

"And had a massive crowd," Hudson agrees.

The goat participates in the conversation by sticking its nose into Bea's crotch.

"Cut it out, asshole." She affectionately pushes him away.

"Does this creature have a name?" I inquire.

"Ryker doesn't name his goats," Hudson tells me.

"How does he tell them apart?"

"He numbers them," Bea replies. "This is number thirteen. See? It's on his ear tag. And he's a handful, aren't you?"

The goat lifts its front hooves onto her stomach and attempts to lick her face.

"Knock it off, Thirteen." Ryker joins us as well. He grabs the goat by one horn and pushes it back down to all fours.

"It's not his fault I'm irresistible," Bea tells her brother while the goat attempts to shove his nose between her legs once again.

Quite understandable.

I, too, should like to have my nose in her pussy.

the spite date

Both of her brothers peer at me as though they've heard my thoughts and now hope that the goat will step on my family jewels during yoga today.

"None of these poses have us on our backs, do they?" I murmur to Bea.

She grins at me, making those dimples pop even more, and shoves the goat away again. "Second thoughts?"

"Certainly not. But I am a fan of self-preservation."

"Should've stayed home then," Hudson says.

He shakes his black yoga mat out onto the ground. Bea follows his lead and places her soft blue mat next to him.

After pushing the goat aside, of course.

There must be a dozen goats here, most of them smaller than this number thirteen, but only Thirteen seems obsessed with Bea in particular.

"Simon? *Simon!* I thought that was you."

Even the goat cringes at the sound of Lucinda Camille's voice.

Bea recovers first. "Hi, Mrs. Camille. Beautiful day for goat yoga, isn't it?"

Lucinda's face suggests she's just eaten something sour, but she quickly turns a smile to me. "Come, Simon, I saved a spot beside me. I would love your thoughts on managing an unruly cast. And you'll get more goat time when you're with me. They love me best."

"There's no talking during yoga, Mrs. Camille," a chipper young woman I haven't met yet says.

"That's Molly Taylor," Bea whispers to me. "She's the instructor."

"Ah, Hudson's crush?" I whisper back.

She smiles at me, dimples dimpling even deeper with the mischief in her eyes. "You remembered. I'm impressed."

I smile in return, then call out a reply to Lucinda. "I must stay at the back of the class. Easier to escape should my man deem anything a security risk."

"Dammit, Simon," Hudson mutters.

"What? Merely stating the truth."

"And now she's coming to the back," Bea says.

We all watch as Lucinda whips her mat off the ground and hustles to the back row.

She's in bright pink spandex pants and a white sleeveless top not dissimilar to Bea's shirt.

Thirteen *baaah*s ominously.

"Are you fucking serious?" Bea mutters.

"Hell, no," Hudson echoes.

"I shall, erm, put her on my opposite side," I say to Bea. "And assist with distracting Thirteen."

But then I realize her issue isn't with Lucinda, or with any particular goat.

Her issue is that Lucinda's son, Jake—Bea's ex-boyfriend—has appeared in yoga attire as well.

And he is also headed in our direction, weaving amongst the attendees and goats alike, pushing aside any that dare linger in his path too long.

Goats and people, though the one person was merely a tap.

But the point remains.

He could have stepped around her instead of insisting that she move herself.

"Oh, dear," I murmur.

Internally, I'm fighting the urge to introduce his nose to my fist.

How could a man have treated Bea as abysmally as he has?

Although any man who insists everyone else clear a path for him is a particular sort of man who likely doesn't care how anyone else feels.

Jake scowls at me, then smiles, then scowls, then smiles, and he's so distracted by apparently deciding if he should still like me or not that he doesn't see another goat in his way.

He steps on it, and it *baah*s at him angrily and butts him in the kneecap.

the spite date

"Does he often come to goat yoga?" I ask Bea as Lucinda begins arranging her mat beside Butch, who has arranged both my and his yoga mats on the grass while I've been watching Jake.

By *both my and his yoga mats*, clearly I actually mean *both Pinky's and his*, as I don't believe I have a yoga mat of my own.

My security men deliver once again.

They're excellent at everything.

Bea shakes her head at me. "Jake's never done yoga a day in his life, to the best of my knowledge."

"Me either, but I assure you, the entire class shall know I'm inept. I don't intend to fake understanding tree pose or namaste."

She squints at me. "Didn't you play a time-traveling knight once who had to do a yoga class in one episode? What was that show called?"

"Beatrice! You know *Knight at Night*? How lovely."

She shoves Thirteen out of her crotch once more. "Like real lovely, or like that's what the studio makes you say?"

"No, that was quite possibly my favorite television series ever. Cast and crew enjoyable, ratings utterly abysmal." I lower my voice to a conspiratorial whisper. "And the yoga consultant was rather angry with me before the filming of the yoga episode was over. Truly, yoga is my worst subject."

"We're starting soon." Hudson bounces on his toes.

"You could do so much better for dating in this town," Lucinda says to me. "If I had daughters—"

"No talking," Butch says.

"Move," Jake says to Hudson on Bea's other side.

"Fuck off," Hudson replies.

Lucinda makes a noise I've heard my own mother make time and time again while she bends over and touches her toes, as if demonstrating that she can. "Such a shame their parents didn't make it. He would've been so much better off."

"Bea, we need to talk," Jake says.

Lucinda glares at him.

He glares back.

Both of them, glaring at each other across Butch, me, Bea, and Hudson.

And Thirteen.

Who is once again nosing Bea inappropriately.

"Have you hidden snacks in your knickers?" I murmur to her.

She smiles at me. Birds burst into song. The sun shines brighter. Rainbows and wind chimes crash together in a symphony of beauty and joy.

What is this magic in her smile?

It's unlike any smile I've ever had aimed at me before.

"Yes, Simon, I put carrots in my underwear," she says.

And truly, that answer only makes her more beautiful.

"Bea," Jake repeats.

"Back. The fuck. Off," Hudson growls at him.

"Such language," Lucinda says. "It's a wonder they all haven't spent time in jail."

"Is there a further-back back row?" I murmur to Bea.

"Yes. It's called the *not at yoga anymore* row."

Jake stomps his foot.

A grown man.

Actually stomping his foot. "*Bea*. We need to talk."

She squeezes her eyelids closed briefly while sucking in a large breath through her nose and simultaneously grabbing her little brother, then she shoves the goat away from her once again as she turns to her ex-boyfriend. "What?"

"You know he's just playing with you."

"And that's worse than dating someone to steal their dreams because…?"

Several other people around us suck in their breath or gasp softly, though I'm uncertain if the gasps are because she said it aloud, or that they were unaware of this detail.

the spite date

"Good morning," the chipper young woman calls as she faces the front row of yoga participants. Three smaller goats prance around her. "Two more minutes for stragglers, and then we'll get started. Nice to see new faces with us for my favorite class of the week. And one more reminder, there's no talking in yoga. Especially when the goats are here. Unless, of course, a goat steps on you wrong, which is one more reason we need silence. So that Ryker and I can hear if someone needs help."

"We'll talk later," Jake says to Bea.

"I don't want to talk to you," she replies.

"You're being—"

Whatever he intended to say is dashed straight out of his mouth as Butch steps between him and Hudson. "The lady said she doesn't want to talk to you."

"Such brutish behavior, Simon," Lucinda says. "Not that Jake can't do better too, but truly, I expected better from you *and* the people who work for you."

My shoulders bunch.

Bea lightly touches my hand.

So lightly, it's barely a brush.

"Are you trying to kiss up to him or drive him away so that I'll get back together with Jake?" she asks Lucinda.

Thirteen lifts his nose out of Bea's pussy of his own accord to look at Lucinda Camille as though he, too, is interested in the answer to this question.

Lucinda ignores her. "Now, Simon, I can forgive this transgression against my son if you would just—"

"Madame," I interrupt, smiling as only a man who learned to smile in the face of *so disappointed in you* all throughout his childhood can, "I barely have any inkling who you truly are beyond your name and a few anecdotes that have been shared with me—many unflattering, I'm afraid—so I have no idea why you would think your opinion of my life matters to me."

Bea makes a strangled noise.

Whispers and murmurs float through the crowd of yoga-goers.

Thirteen bleats his goat bleat as though he cannot believe his ears either.

"Holy shit," Hudson mutters.

I appreciate the reverence in his voice.

Of all the people in this town, I *do* wish to curry favor with Bea's brothers.

While we may be temporary lovers by choice, I'd like to remain friends with her when the summer ends.

Whenever I return to Athena's Rest, which will be often, as I don't intend to miss any more of my boys' childhood than is necessary to keep a foot in the door for my career while finally also providing for them as Lana has most of their lives.

Although considering the dagger-eyes Lucinda is aiming at me now, possibly the next town over would be close enough.

"If you've heard anything about me," she says in a tone ominous enough to bring Butch back to my side, "then you know you do *not* cross me."

"I really wanted to like you, mate," Jake says. "But you don't cross my mom. Especially over the woman who *will* come back to me when she realizes you're…a fake."

I ignore him as I stare back at Lucinda.

Still smiling.

Naturally.

I immensely enjoy battling my nemeses while smiling. "Your previous flattery means far less now as I'm realizing you clearly don't know very much about me either."

"I know you're burning through your money faster than it's coming in now."

I smile broader. I have heard those rumors as well. "I fought bullies and tormentors long before I had money to my name. And I enjoyed it. And I always won."

"How *dare* you."

the spite date

Jake growls from behind me. "My mother is *not* a bully, you dickhead."

Thirteen bleats loudly.

Butch grabs me by the shoulders and physically moves me all the way to Hudson's other side.

And Thirteen—the goat who could not get his nose out of Bea's pussy a moment ago—charges at Lucinda Camille.

"Leaving. Now," Butch orders me.

Lucinda screams and takes off running around the nearest tree.

"Mom!" Jake gasps, and he chases after his mother.

Presumably to catch the goat.

"But I'm rather enjoying this," I tell Butch.

The chipper instructor appears at my side too. "I'm so sorry to have to ask you this, Mr. Luckwood, but I think you're going to be a distraction, and as you can see"—she gestures to the tree that Lucinda is circling while the goat continues chasing her, and while Jake chases them both, and Ryker merely watches from a distance—"distractions are a little dangerous. I'd be happy to give you a private class, no charge, with whoever you want but no goats later."

"Molly's right." Hudson's chest is puffed out broader than a peacock's. "It's not personal, Simon. It's just—the goats, and Bea, and you—not your fault."

"We're leaving," Butch tells Molly.

"I'm staying," Hudson says. "Best behavior. And I'm moving so I'm not next to my sister's ex. Promise."

"Jake won't stay," Bea says. "He'll have to take his mom home so they can plot who they're suing over this."

I gulp. "Sincerely?"

She winces. "Maybe."

Molly shakes her head. "They signed the contract releasing the yoga studio and the farm of any liability that comes with taking a risk while being in an enclosed space with animals."

Hudson's chest puffs even higher.

It's rather adorable, though I won't tell him that.

"The contract is super ironclad since Damon Camille sued the yoga studio once before over this," he says mostly to me, but he keeps looking at Molly too.

"They'll still try," someone mutters.

"But we have crowd-funding to fight back now," someone else says.

"And Daphne," a third person adds. "She still hasn't gotten to use any of her connections in the city since she moved here."

Ryker whistles, and every goat in the park—including Thirteen—immediately turns toward him and runs.

"I'll have your farm for this!" Lucinda yells.

Her hair has fallen out of its bun, and her white vest top is stained with mud or dirt.

She must've fallen when I wasn't looking.

How unfortunate.

Bea slips her hand into mine as Molly heads toward Lucinda. "Wanna get out of here?"

"Less *want*, more necessity."

Butch has gathered our yoga mats.

"Though I will definitely be booking a private class," I add. "I remain fascinated by how this works."

Bea squints at me as she falls into line with Butch and me.

"Oh, dear. Have I breakfast left over on my face?"

"No, it's just—you really like to learn about things."

"Keeps life interesting. And I have a whole list of potential careers to try instead if I ever find myself in a position of needing to wait tables between gigs."

She's still watching me as we slip out of the gate, making sure to not let any goats out with us. "Can I see it sometime?"

"The list?"

"Yes."

"Certainly."

the spite date

"It's just—I don't know if I'm doing what I really love, but I also don't know what I want to do, and having to come home and take care of my brothers when everyone else my age was getting jobs or going to college and figuring out what they wanted to do with their lives—I still sometimes feel lost. Especially now that Hudson's in college and basically running his own life. So I don't know if my burger bus is forever, but I also don't know what I want to do, and I don't even know what's available." She freezes and looks at me. "And you didn't ask any of that."

I slip an arm about her waist. "Yet I enjoyed listening to every word. Have you had tea at this tea shop? I've only purchased loose-leaf to go for home. But I suddenly have an extra hour on my hands, and I believe you do too."

That smile.

I would do nearly anything to have that smile aimed at me regularly.

"I *love* the tea shop."

"Excellent. Then let us have tea."

And stolen kisses.

And a hurried tryst in the loo.

Though when I say it in my head like that, it sounds far less romantic and sexy than I believe it would be.

"You're thinking about being naughty again, aren't you?" she whispers.

"I simply cannot help myself."

"Good. I don't think I can help myself either. You look good in yoga pants."

Butch sighs.

Bea pinches her lips together, but her dimples are still popping as she gives me a conspiratorial glance.

I've never believed the perfect woman existed.

But if she did, I do believe she'd be on her way to have tea with me right now.

25

Family lunches and other awkward things

Bea

Being friends-with-benefits with a single dad is already reminding me of how difficult parenting is.

We didn't do tea yesterday. One of Simon's boys gets tangled up with a skunk and so Simon had to dash off before we made it to the tea house.

He had the boys last night, so his focus was on them, though he's texted me a lot.

The man is hilariously funny with a vulnerable vibe beneath it all that I can't help but appreciate, even if I'm wary of how much I'm enjoying everything about him right now.

And then there's the other weirdness that comes with being involved with a single dad.

Namely, his ex.

Who's now sitting at my chef's table, having a burger and fries while I wait on the occasional customer. I'm parked at the farmer's market, the only food truck here today, and traffic is slow enough to make me wonder if the Camilles are spreading more rumors, or if something else is going on that I haven't picked up on yet.

the spite date

I know my social media reach is being suppressed—Lana said she almost couldn't find my account to see what today's special was even after searching for my bus by name—but I don't know why or how to fix it.

It's frustrating, but I'll find a way to make this work. Or I'll find a new mission in life.

That's what I do.

"Can I ask a very personal question?" she says to me between customers.

"We're basically neighbors since we live in the same town again, I know your boys well enough to tell them to behave in public, and I'm sleeping with your ex, so sure. Let's get personal."

She smiles.

Beams, really. "I love your bluntness."

"Thank you. It comes and goes. And that wasn't a question."

"Right. The question. Why did you ever date Jake Camille?"

I look up from the burger I'm frying. "That's your question?"

"He just seems like such a dick to me. The whole family, actually. But I was one of few people who didn't like him in high school. Enough that I wondered if the problem was me."

I shake my head. "He's good at making people like him. When he asked me out, I felt like he was the first person who *saw* me in a long time. And it wasn't just the way he smiled at me, or the little presents and the flowers and the other normal dating things. He'd go to Hudson's band performances with me, hold my hand when I got nervous before all of those interviews about Griff, reassure me that Ryker would be okay when he was extra grumpy. Jake seemed to get that dating me meant dating my family. And I thought he liked all of us. Sometimes I still can't believe he's the guy who woke up one day and was like, *we both know this isn't working out, so let's just call it a loss before it gets worse.*"

"He seriously just flipped a switch like that?"

"If there were signs, I didn't see them. And believe me, Daphne and I analyzed everything either one of us could think of to analyze."

"Asshole."

"I hate that I sometimes question what I could've done to make him love me more when it feels so obvious now that he's just a user, and when I know I shouldn't ever have to beg anyone for their love, but I definitely see the whole family differently now than I did before. And now I'm mad that so many people around town still love them when I logically get it—they do a lot of good in the community, which reminds me of my parents too—but he hurt me. *They* hurt me. And now they're telling everyone I'm the problem."

"If it helps, nearly everyone here that I've ever heard talk about you else seems to love you too."

"Not enough to pick my burgers over his," I mutter. "The asshole's serving *bester burgers* at JC Fig for lunch today."

"Classic Camille family warfare. You only notice the poke if it's aimed at you, and otherwise, it looks like an innocent accident. Though *bester burgers* is pretty direct."

"It is. And the reason everyone loves me is because they think it's amazing that I left college to take care of my brothers. I could blow up a car on Main Street and kidnap everyone's puppies and they'd say it was because of the psychological trauma of losing my parents. They'd avoid me for it, but they'd make excuses for me too. Those people who think I'm great? Very few of them have gotten to know *me*. Don't get me wrong—I'm grateful for all of the support we've had the past ten years, but—"

I stop myself and shake my head.

"But your entire identity to the town is caretaker, and not person," she says softly.

"*Yes.*" I give her a wry smile. "Everyone asks about your mom first now, don't they?"

"Or the boys. Or something about Simon." She shrugs and lifts her last bite of burger. "It's the box we get put in."

Pretty sure by *we*, she means *women*.

"What's your favorite TV show?" I ask. Because it's not about caretaking. It's about making friends.

"Promise not to tell a soul?"

the spite date

"My lips are sealed."

"I watch *Panda Bananda* when I have five minutes."

"The kid show?"

"Yes."

"*No.*"

"You watch it too?"

I shake my head. "My brothers were past cartoons when I moved home. But—a kid show? When you could watch anything? Really?"

"You know the main panda? Jonas Rutherford does his voice. And one cannot grow up in Athena's Rest—"

"Without having a crush on one of the Rutherford brothers," I finish for her with a smile.

The Rutherford family owns the Razzle Dazzle TV movie empire. It's headquartered in Albany, which is close enough that one of them used to occasionally roll through town and cause a massive stir.

"Which one was your crush?" Lana asks me.

"Jonas all the way," I answer without hesitation. There are two Rutherford brothers, but only Jonas went into acting. His older brother is way more reclusive, and the people I know who say they'd pick him also say it's because they like the mystery of him. Not that it matters. They're both married with kids and not in Albany often anymore. "I fell asleep to the Razzle Dazzle channel nearly every night the first three years after my parents died."

"Simon's had small roles in a couple of their TV movies and says they're all super nice."

"Would he say any different?"

"No."

"Didn't think so."

"Two seconds. This this order's done." I settle the burger on its bun, top it with the lettuce and tomato from Ryker's farm, grab a handful of fries, and pass it out the window.

"You're being so screwed by the Camilles and what they're saying behind your back to anyone who will listen," my customer tells me. "Jake fucked up a real estate deal for me once, and it opened my eyes. I was the same as you before. Thought they were great. I hope Simon takes them down for you."

"What if I want to take them down myself?"

She gives me a look that suggests she wants to pat me on the head and call me adorable. "Sweetie…you're living with Daphne Merriweather-Brown, and it's been how many months since you and Jake broke up? If you wanted to do it yourself, you would've already done it. Where are you tomorrow? I'm making my husband and daughter come too."

I smile at her. "Thank you. I'll be lined up with everyone else at the parking lot at the lake. Paddleboating is half off tomorrow."

Lana's watching me when I turn back into the bus. "I think there are more people who'd speak out about them than we think they are," she says.

"Yeah, but at what price? The Camilles have decades of experience with making everyone think they're amazing. It's easier to just run a spite burger bus until I get tired of it."

She grins. "So it's true that this is a spite business."

"Where'd you hear it?"

"From Simon. Don't worry. I won't tell a soul."

I squint at her. "You're a lawyer?"

"Specializing in intellectual property. Keeping secrets is the biggest part of my job. I'm pretty good at it."

"Hello?" a voice calls at the window. "Do you have enough burgers left to feed an army of two teenage boys?"

Lana's gaze smacks into mine.

I'm positive I'm starting to blush.

She smiles.

It's definitely on the wicked side.

"Is this weird?" I ask her.

She shakes her head. "Simon's more like a brother who also happens to be my co-parent than he is anything else. If you're having fun, have fun."

"That's…really unusual and pretty cool of you."

"If I wanted more, I've had ample opportunity over the past fourteen years. But he's not the one for me, and I won't raise my kids the same way I was raised."

My face does the talking for me, clearly telegraphing I'm not entirely sure what she means.

"My parents shouldn't have been together as long as they were. Not a good example of a healthy relationship. I want my boys to know it's important for them to be happy on their own instead of expecting a woman—or anyone, really—to cater to their every whim."

"Hello?" Simon calls again.

"Hold on, I'm bracing myself for how much work I'm about to have to do," I call back.

"Quite wise. We've just come from the trampoline park, and jumping made them ravenous."

I glance at Lana. "Want them to join you? Or do you have to go?"

"Send them in. Believe it or not, I miss them. All of them."

"Come on in to the chef's table," I tell Simon as I lean out the window. "Fans are working, and I'll point them out the bus so I don't have to smell stinky boys."

"We don't stink nearly as bad today as Charlie did yesterday," Eddie tells me.

"It's impossible to ever stink that bad again," Charlie agrees.

Simon smiles at me while Butch and Tank hustle the boys toward the back of the bus. He's in a T-shirt advertising the cheese shop, which is hilarious considering he can't eat cheese, and a ball cap with the college's women's hockey team logo on it.

"You've changed your bandanna," he says

"I felt purple today."

"It does lovely things for your eyes, and I didn't think they could get lovelier."

And now I'm smiling and blushing harder.

His gaze flicks to my lips, then back up to my eyes. "At least twelve burgers, I'm certain. Would you like me to take my shirt off and call everyone else over too?"

"Maybe after you eat."

"Dad, Mum's here!" Charlie shrieks from the back of the bus.

Simon's brows shoot up. "Truly?"

I nod. "We've been talking about how annoying it is when people think you're funny."

He smiles broader.

"Oh my god, don't be happy about that! And we weren't. We wouldn't. You're honestly very funny. But we were hardly talking about you at all."

"Were you thinking about me at all then?" he murmurs.

"Yes," I whisper.

"Excellent. Glad to hear it. And we truly do want at least a dozen burgers."

The boys are peppering Lana with questions and hugging her, and for a split second, I feel the hardest longing.

It's the way she's smiling at them.

Like they're her whole world.

The best thing she's ever done in life.

Just like Simon said they were.

I raised my brothers, but I didn't get *that*.

"Any secret menu items?" Simon asks me.

"Do you want a secret menu item?"

"I have an insufferable craving for corn dogs."

"Just corn dogs?" I tease.

He grabs my hand and turns his face into my palm, pressing a light kiss to it. "Corn dogs made all the more delicious for the specific companionship."

Yep.

I'm in trouble.

I know it'll hurt when he leaves, I told Daphne.

I just hope it hurts less for knowing it's coming.

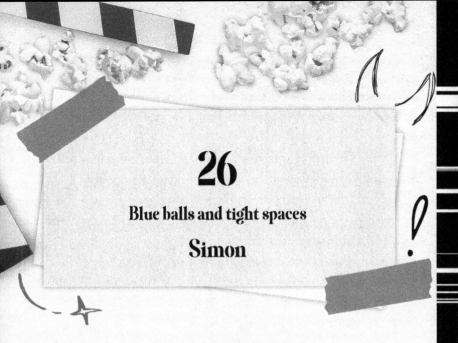

26

Blue balls and tight spaces

Simon

The next week passes in a blur of enjoying every moment that I can with my boys, continuing to modify my new television script to make the fact that Bea is my inspiration even less recognizable, running out of printer paper and ink because my blasted computer somehow gave itself orders to print seven copies of the movie script I'm supposed to be memorizing for the shoot in September, ignoring yet another call from my parents, making plans for my own murder mystery dinner since I *am* that level of petty and annoyed with Lucinda Camille, and texting and phoning Bea.

Texting and phoning Bea is my favorite part.

The woman makes me smile in new ways, which should be impossible given how much experience I have with smiling, and I shouldn't confess how many times I've re-read our text conversations.

I manage to join her late Saturday evening at a pub where Hudson is performing, and watching the pride and joy in her eyes when she cheers loudest in the entire establishment after every song makes something ache deep in my soul.

She loves him more than my parents have ever been capable of loving me, and she loves him every bit as much as I love my own boys.

And that—that deep capacity to love those whom she could so easily resent, her choice to continue loving them—that is what makes my soul ache with a desperate need that I've generally been able to ignore.

Until I'm texting with her, or phoning her, or arriving at her burger bus with my boys for lunch in the midst of our summer fun.

Then I feel it again every time—that longing for her—for *someone*—to love me for the absolute mess that I am the same way that she loves her brothers and her friends.

A smart man would recognize this is a fool's path.

But as I am not a smart man, and as it's once again Wednesday, and Bea is once again set up in a car park at Austen & Lovelace College, across the lake from the Monday car park.

My children are at their college program.

And I'm approaching the burger bus because I'm obsessed with wanting her to myself and increasingly desperate to find a way to see her.

Preferably finally naked once again, as I'm happy to lie to myself and insist this longing is coming from my cock and balls and not my heart.

I'm a man starved for his Beatrice fix.

But Tank and I are still at least five paces from her bus when a creeping sensation makes me slow my steps.

"Oh my god, it's Peter Jones!" someone says in a falsetto voice from inside the bus almost instantly.

Bloody hell.

She's not alone.

"Hello, Hudson," I say amicably.

A man who is very distinctly *not* Hudson, with brown eyes and curly light brown hair and a very familiar pair of dimples, appears in the service window and grins back at me. "Hello, Peter."

"Hey, Simon," Bea calls from deeper inside the bus. "Guess what? Griff showed up on my doorstep this morning. He decided to come home for the All-Star break."

"If I shake his hand, will he break every bone in mine?" I inquire.

"What kind of a question is that?"

"He was the victor when his team did the social media challenge where pro athletes have their grip strength tested."

Griff smiles broader. "You've been following me."

"Daphne was singing your praises, and my boys found the video," I tell him. "Lovely to meet you. I shan't be offering my hand to be crushed, but you may feel free to tell anyone you wish that I was a complete and total fool who's afraid of you if it helps your reputation or your ego."

Bea joins him at the window and smiles at me in a way that makes my lightheadedness once again go lightheaded.

She's clearly bewitched me.

I clearly have no objection.

"Are you Magic Mike-ing for me again today?" she asks, eyes twinkling and dimples dimpling.

"Only if your brother does too."

Griff's shirt flies out of the burger bus window.

That seems to be a yes from him, which means—

"Are you so for real right now?" Bea interrupts me from also stripping out of my shirt with her reaction to her brother's chest. "A parrot? You got a tattoo of a *parrot*?"

Griff points to the tattoo on his left pec. "Dude, this is Long Beak Silver. He's *famous*."

Bea lifts her eyes to the bus's ceiling. "Your body. Your body. Your body."

"Plus, I lost a bet," Griff stage-whispers to me. "Long story."

I pull my own shirt off and point to a small scar on my shoulder. "I lost a bet once as well. Though I suspect you have a far better story."

"Mine involves accidentally crashing a future-Hall-of-Famer breakfast. Multiple sports. Crazy road trip."

"Mine involves a friend in school not believing me when I said that my skin was fireproof."

Bea's moss-green eyes go the shape of saucers.

Griff rubs his chin. "You might actually win this one. I think that was dumber than thinking I could win a bet with the Berger twins and a bunch of Cooper Rock's old teammates too. Don't mess with hockey and baseball royalty when they get together, especially when most of them are bored in retirement. Hey, you want to trade autographs? Mine's gonna be worth more than yours someday."

Bea points to him behind his back and mouths something that looks like *huge fan*.

I, naturally, smile delightedly. Assuming I've read her lips correctly.

Though even if I have not, it's never a hardship to watch Bea's lips.

"I can see you," Griff says to her.

"Good. Go shake your booty and bring in some customers. But put your shirt back on before the kids get turned loose for lunch. You can take it off again after they've all gone back to their program."

And that's how I end up not having lunchtime nookie with Bea on Wednesday.

Though I am fond of this last brother of hers before she's sold out for the day.

He's rather amusing.

And less inclined to tell me to leave her alone than her other two brothers.

Yet, at any rate.

Likely because he's too busy talking to all of the locals who want to hear about his baseball career. And the young man does mention a time or two that he's seen a little of *In the Weeds*, which Bea informs me later means *all of it, multiple times*.

"So he has terrible taste?" I murmur to her.

She simply smiles, putting those dimples on display and reminding me that I still have not had the chance to lick them properly.

We've been heavy on the *friends* side of this *friends with benefits* situation these past days, despite my constant longing for more.

"Do you have plans this evening?" I ask Bea when Griff is distracted with three younger women as she's cleaning up.

"Griff's taking us all out for pizza."

"Welcome to join us, my dude," Griff says.

Clearly not as distracted as I thought he was.

Bea opens her mouth, but I leap in before she can say a word. "Brilliant. My boys love pizza."

"Griff—" Bea starts, but both of us look at her, and she shakes her head again. "Never mind."

"I suspect she intended to tell you that I can't eat cheese," I tell Griff.

He grins back at me. "She was going to tell you that I'm only using you because every good baseball player needs celebrity friends."

I smile broader at that. "I'm happy to be used for my talents before the world tires of them."

"I'm going to trick you into eating cheese."

"Truly, that's a relief. I hadn't expected Hudson to be harder on me than you were. And I enjoy a good challenge."

Tank glares at Griff.

Griff grins back at my security man.

And several hours later, my boys are ecstatic beyond belief to be having a pizza night out.

I sequester them at one end of the table, one across from me and one beside me, and tell them they can only escape to the arcade room if they actually eat dinner and behave politely, and I remind them that both Butch and Pinky are at the next table and can see them as well.

Daphne has joined the family dinner.

To my utter surprise, and the boys' delight, Lana takes the final seat at the reserved table with us.

"I invited her," Bea tells me. She's managed to sit beside me, and our knees are constantly brushing against each other. "Daph's sister is having a problem, and I have this gut feeling that Lana's a better person to talk to her about it than I am."

"With the hotels?" I inquire. "That's not Lana's specialty."

"No, it's a personal thing."

My boys are discussing pizza toppings with each other, so I lean in closer to Bea and drop my voice. "I rather miss being personal with you."

She visibly shivers as her eyes go dark. "Same."

"Dad? Can we try anchovies?" Charlie asks.

Hello, mood-killer. "On the side so that you waste minimal pizza if you don't like them."

The boys dive back into the menu, and soon we've all ordered—salad sans cheese but with chicken for me, all of the pizza that the kitchen can make for the rest of the table—and the conversations resume.

It's remarkably casual.

Easy.

Comfortable.

Almost unreal in how much this feels as though we're on the set of a family show where everyone gets along, and everyone likes each other, with Bea and her brothers including Lana without an ounce of awkwardness over the fact that she and I were once lovers who now share teenage boys.

Except this is real.

Completely real.

Another now-familiar longing hits in my chest. I pretend to ignore it. I'd generally never admit that I smile as a shield to my feelings, but when sitting in a place where I feel as though I've found a family to belong to, one that cares more about how you are than about how you perform—I've found the parts of life that have been missing.

That I've been terrified to embrace for fear that they'd be taken away again.

And with a woman I'm falling harder and harder for every day sitting beside me, soothing my soul with her easy acceptance of all of my quirks and flaws and enticing my body with her actions.

While Griff tells more of the story of his tattoo after the pizza and my salad have arrived, Bea drags a finger along my upper leg, getting very close to my inner thigh.

the spite date

While Daphne and Lana have their own animated conversation at the other end of the table, Bea brushes her foot against mine.

While Hudson tells a story about Ryker's goats, I intermingle my fingers with hers and draw hearts on her palm with my thumb.

Yes, yes, I'm that far gone.

I should be very concerned for myself, but I rather suspect I'll bugger this up soon enough.

Which is a thought that has my blood running cold.

I don't want to bugger up anything with Bea.

She's funny. She's sexy. She treats me as though I'm a normal human being. She spots my boys trading one of *those* looks before Lana or I do, and with one lift of her eyebrows, they both sink back into their respective seats and quietly grab another slice of pizza, but she also smiles at them and engages with them as the individual human beings that they are.

Bea has given me an opportunity to exist inside a bubble where family are tight and care about one another, even as they argue and tease each other, but ultimately are all watching out for one another. And with Daphne and Lana and myself and the boys joining them—it's the kind of family that grows without traditional boundaries.

The kind of family I never had.

Siblings. Inside jokes. Laughter. Love. Acceptance.

Their parents clearly did something right, and the injustice that two good parents have left this mortal plane while mine remain hits me square in the chest again.

Will my boys be this tight?

Are Lana and I doing anything right enough to give them a true sense of family?

Lana is, of course, my family as well, but she's rather stuck with me because of the boys, whereas with Bea—

With Bea, I feel as though she's choosing me.

When she has so many reasons that choosing me would not be in her best interest.

"You okay?" she murmurs to me.

I shake my head as I realize everyone else at the table is laughing at something while I'm *not* smiling. "Quite all right, thank you."

She watches me. "I've never seen you this quiet."

I squeeze her hand. "Merely admiring how well your family get along. I rather doubt another person could have done what you've done for your brothers and still liked them in the end. I certainly couldn't have. But you—you are a wonder, Beatrice Best. A wonder who holds your whole family together, blood relations and not, and I suspect you've no idea how attractive that is."

She blinks quickly, but not quickly enough for me to miss the way her eyes mist over. "I forget sometimes that I shouldn't take them for granted."

"You absolutely should not. Though you should give yourself credit as well."

"I did what I had to."

"At great personal cost to yourself. And I'm happy to see your brothers seem to recognize it."

She glances at them, Hudson laughing so hard that he's nearly choking, Griff smiling mischievously, Ryker smiling as well, more reserved, but still smiling.

"Worth it," she says softly, that lovely glow once again coming into her eyes.

How could a person see the way she loves her family and not want to be a part of her life?

"Dad, we ate three pizzas. Can we go play now?" Eddie says.

I swing my gaze back to my boys. "Each?"

"Together," Charlie answers.

"I tried anchovies and didn't like them," Eddie informs me.

"I could like them if I tried them two more times."

"You're just saying that."

"It's true! I didn't almost puke like you did. I think I like the salt. I just need to grow into it a little more."

the spite date

"You don't have to find gross things to like."

"Griff, how are your anchovies?" Bea asks.

He turns to stare at her in horror. "Gross. Who eats anchovies?"

"I do, dummy," Ryker replies.

"I don't, but I do sneak them onto Griff's pizza sometimes," Hudson announces.

Lana makes eye contact with me. "And now I'm glad we only have two."

"Indeed," I agree.

Bea giggles.

I glance at Butch, who rises.

He and Pinky have both finished their pizza.

"Got 'em, boss," he says to me.

"You may go and play," I tell the boys.

Lana pushes her chair back. "I think I'll go play too. Show them how *Centipede* is done."

Griff, who's been leaning back on his rear two chair legs, drops the front two back to the floor as my family races one another to the game room. "That's still here?"

"They're never getting rid of it," Ryker tells him.

"I thought it would've died by now."

"It did," Daphne says. "Right between you leaving for college and me being disinherited. I bought the new one and set up a trust fund for it in case they ever have to replace it again in the next hundred years."

Bea's brothers stare at her in utter reverence.

"In retrospect, I probably should've funneled my trust fund into a different trust fund but…eh. Live and learn."

"Why do some rich people who are complete douchenoodles get to stay rich, but you had to be disinherited when you were doing so much good in the world?" Hudson says to her.

"Excuse you, I'm still very rich. In character."

Bea's dimples are putting on quite the show as she watches them all.

I slip my arm around the back of her chair, my fingers brushing her bare shoulder. Vest tops are, indeed, my favorite article of clothing ever. "You're not friends. You adopted her."

"It's a little of both."

"Have you contemplated that your role on this earth might be teaching the world what family means?"

Those lovely green eyes blink at me. "Oh, I'm not *that* good."

She is indeed, and I file away her lack of recognition of the fact for contemplation later.

For now, I'm contemplating how close her face is to mine.

That she has a light dusting of freckles on her cheeks that I hadn't noticed the last time I saw her.

Has she spent time in the sun? Has that brought out her freckles?

"I would like to take you out on a proper date, just the two of us. Somewhere without a menu swimming in cheese, and with an empty house to return to later."

She smiles broader. "Can we keep the lights on this time? I heard a rumor you have a secret tattoo."

"Have you? Or did you start that rumor because *you* have a secret tattoo?"

She lifts her brows mysteriously and continues to smile at me.

If ever there was an invitation to kiss a woman, this is it.

I lean in, anticipating once again having Bea's lips against mine, when someone kicks me from across the table.

I yelp and straighten.

"Really, Griff?" Bea says.

"So I've been telling my teammates about your burger bus, and they want you to come do a cookout for us," he says to her.

"So this is how a middle child acts," I murmur.

"Be glad yours barely argue over who's the baby," she murmurs back, then she turns her attention to her brother. "I didn't think burgers were on the menu for most of your teammates during the season."

He grins. "Just the older teammates who don't still have metabolisms of steel."

"You're gonna flunk out of the majors if you don't stay fit," Daphne tells him.

"Flunking out of the show isn't a thing," he scoffs.

"That's the same thing at least three of my ex-boyfriends who flunked out of the majors said before their teams cut them for younger, faster, stronger players who ate chicken and greens instead of pizza and burgers."

I could be kissing Bea.

Sneaking her off behind the building to kiss her and touch her in the semidarkness, someplace without witnesses.

But as she joins the conversation about Griff's health, which turns to a discussion of Hudson's lung capacity on a stage, which turns to a conversation about Ryker's ability to continue chasing his chickens and goats, I'm unexpectedly content.

This must be what belonging feels like. Belonging without fighting it, without second-guessing it, without doubting it.

And it's oddly more satisfying than sex.

Or perhaps differently satisfying.

Yes.

Differently satisfying.

In a way that I suspect I'll crave far more than I shall crave sex long after I no longer have either.

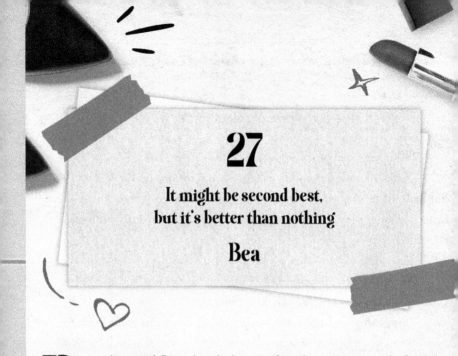

27

It might be second best, but it's better than nothing

Bea

Daphne and I are barely home after the pizza party before my phone rings.

She takes one look at my phone screen, smirks, and heads for her bedroom. "I'm going to put on my noise-canceling headphones and rock out for a while," she says.

"Don't stay up too late. You have work tomorrow."

She flashes a thumbs-up, like we're both thinking about her working and not about Simon calling me when we both spent all of dinner trying to touch each other any way we could in public.

At least, I'm thinking about touching Simon.

Daph was at the other end of the table. She might not have been thinking about me touching Simon.

Either way, she disappears into her bedroom.

I duck into mine, answering the phone on its fourth ring. "Hey."

"Do you have any idea how much I detest cheese?" Simon says by way of greeting.

I kick off my shoes and flop down onto my bed, which I neatly made this morning for once. "A lot?"

"It causes a level of discomfort in my entire midsection that I don't wish to contemplate, much less describe."

"Did you accidentally eat cheese?"

"No. But despite how much I detest cheese, I cannot stop thinking about how much I would enjoy eating melted cheese off your breasts."

I absently rub one of my breasts as the tingling starts. "You couldn't fantasize about honey instead? I thought you had honey fantasies."

"It's the oddest thing. I must have cheese on my brain. I definitely have you on my brain. But eating *cheese* off you? I fear something in me has broken from a lack of alone time with you."

"Are we having phone sex?"

"Very poorly if you have to ask. And if I'm thinking of cheese."

I'm simultaneously amused to the point of laughter and turned on to the point of frustrated. "What are your kids up to?"

"They're playing that bloody awful creature game Hudson showed them."

"At your house?"

"In addition to her mother's care, Lana has a client with a sudden emergency. She received the call the moment we left the restaurant."

"Do you know who's the best babysitter ever?"

"Mary Poppins?"

"Daphne."

"Your roommate and best friend and semi-adopted extra child? That Daphne?"

"She has the energy of a squirrel, the background to know all of the trouble kids can get into, and now the wisdom to prevent other kids from doing what she did."

"Excellent. When can she arrive, and when can I join you at your place? Wait. Is Hudson there? Wait again. Do we care if Hudson is there?"

"Griff got a suite at one of the hotels by the college. Hudson's crashing with him the next two nights."

"Only two nights?"

"All-Star break is short. And the only reason Griff can stay until Friday morning is because the commute to Toronto for his next game is short."

"Is Daphne free tomorrow evening?"

"Probably not. She has a very active social life. And it's a work night."

Simon growls softly.

"But she loves me, so she'll probably cancel her plans and watch your kids so that you and I can hang out here alone. Watch a movie. Eat popcorn. Maybe play some Scrabble."

"Beatrice."

I smile at my ceiling. "Yes, Simon?"

"I have never adored a woman who tortures me quite the way I adore you and the way you torture me."

"I like to set my expectations low so that I'm not disappointed."

"I would like you to set your expectations high so that we can improve this orgasm count."

An aroused shiver slinks through my body. "If my expectations are too high though, I might be disappointed. And so might you."

"Oh no, darling. I never underperform when expectations are high. Especially when exceeding expectations is so very satisfying."

"I thought you liked being a lazy bum."

"No, I rather overachieved being a lazy bum. There's a difference."

"Simon?"

"Yes, darling?"

"I think I adore you too."

"Quite the pickle, is it not?"

"*Indeed*," I reply, just like he would.

He chuckles, and another warm, delicious shiver makes its way over my skin.

"So tell me, darling," he says softly, "what *are* you wearing?"

Oh yes.

I am *all in* on this. "What do you want me to be wearing?"

"Preferably nothing at all, in my bed, but as that is not an option… tell me about those lacy bits of undergarments you had on when you were last here."

"My thong?"

"Yes. What color was it?"

"Red."

He groans softly.

"With little black bows."

"Will you put them on again?"

"Now? Or tomorrow?"

"Both."

I lift myself off the bed and eyeball the stack of laundry in the corner. My body is flushed, my hormones buzzing, and that thong is right on top. "I have something else for tomorrow. Something better."

"Impossible."

"I'm changing into my red lace thong now."

His breath comes through the phone, ragged and desperate.

"What are *you* wearing?" I ask.

"A cotton T-shirt, socks, and a pair of boxer-briefs."

"Is that how you always walk around your house?"

"No. My trousers are highly uncomfortable when I'm this aroused."

"Where are you?"

"My bedroom."

"What does it look like?"

"Emptiness and loneliness and bleakness."

I've shimmied out of my shorts and plain pink cotton panties, and now I'm dancing into the thong. "You could hire a designer to fix that."

"Having you here would fix that."

"What would your room look like if I were there?"

"It would look like a naked Bea splayed across my rumpled white sheets, which is my very definition of heaven. Have you changed your knickers?"

I finagle myself out of my tank top without dropping the phone. "Yes. I'm in my red lace thong."

"Are you still wearing anything else?"

"A completely not-matching beige cotton bra."

"Take it off."

"One strap at a time, or do you want me to reach behind my back and unclasp it so it falls off?"

"Bea…" His voice is getting hoarse.

"Yes?"

"I'm picturing your breasts and gripping my cock."

I want to see Simon's cock. I've felt it, but I haven't *seen* it. "Just gripping? Not stroking?"

"I fear it would take fewer than five strokes considering how turned on your voice makes me."

"I want to stroke your cock."

"I want to lick your dimples and tease your pussy with my fingers."

My legs squeeze together. "Simon?"

"Touch your pussy for me, Bea. Slip your fingers under that lace and play with your clit."

I lean back on my bed and do exactly as I'm told, imagining my fingers are Simon's, that he's rubbing my clit with his thumb while his fingers tease the slick, wet skin between my thighs. "Feels—so—good," I whisper.

"Are you wet?"

"Soaked."

He groans softly again. "I want to feel you."

"I want to taste you."

A strangled noise comes through the phone.

I slip two fingers inside myself. "Simon?"

"Yes, my beautiful minx?"

"Are you hard?"

"As granite, love."

"Stroke yourself."

"Bea, I am so utterly close—"

"I—am too."

"You should—come first."

My head rolls back on the mattress, thighs open, the lace of my thong soaked. "I wish you were here."

"God, Bea." He's panting.

Panting and gasping softly, and I want to be there with him.

I want to be jerking his cock. I want to cradle his balls and feel him on top of me, pumping inside me, kissing me.

"I want you to touch my breasts again," I whimper.

I'm close.

So close.

"I would like to worship your whole body." His voice is strained. I picture him with his eyes half-closed, watching me touch myself, and my entire body comes unraveled.

"Oh god, Simon, I—I'm coming," I gasp as I come in one hard, fast spasm. It spreads immediately into heavy aftershocks that travel from my toes to my fingertips to the roots of my hair.

"Thank fuck," he gasps, and then he's groaning softly again.

"Are you?" I pant.

"Yes."

"Want—more," I gasp while the tremors continue in my core.

"Soon, love. Soon."

It's not usually like this.

Dating.

Screwing around.

Whatever you want to call it.

Every time I've dated anyone, we've *dated*.

Evening dinners several nights a week.

Then his place. Then I'd get home late and hope my brothers didn't know what I was up to.

But with Simon—we have to fight for time.

Either he's with his boys, or Daphne or one of my brothers needs something, or I'm booked somewhere.

He's leaving soon.

I'm staying soon.

And we're still fighting for these moments of time between the other slices of everyday life.

And when we get them—they're electric.

"Simon?" I whisper as his breathing evens out on the other end of the phone.

"Yes, Bea?"

"You are my favorite part of this summer."

He makes a soft sound halfway between a chuckle and a sigh. "You are a most unexpected treat."

"Is it helping?"

"Helping what?"

"The publicity. Helping your career."

A long stretch of silence lingers on the other end of the phone.

"Simon?"

"I…have a confession."

I blink at the ceiling. "A confession?"

"No one suggested that I see you for the publicity or visibility or any other trickery involving any form of the press."

"No one—what does that mean?"

"I merely wanted an excuse to continue to see you…without having to confess to even myself how much I wished to continue to see you."

I sit up and stare at myself in the mirror over my dresser, watching my eyebrows try to settle between surprised and irritated and flattered, my jaw flapping open, my forehead wrinkling, my breasts chilling out, completely naked, nipples still tight from that orgasm, phone to my ear, and—

And I completely lose it.

Laughter overtakes me as I flop back on my bed.

"You… You're not angry?" Simon asks.

I can't answer.

I'm laughing too hard.

Laughing, and maybe crying just a little too.

"Bea?"

"You're a disaster."

He barks out a laugh too. "That I am."

"And you're perfect."

"That I am most certainly not."

"*Simon.*"

"Ah, do say my name like that again."

"Have you ever had a normal relationship with someone where you could just say that you liked them and they could say they liked you back and you did dinner dates and sometimes went to each other's houses to make out and watch TV and cuddle and have sex and cuddle more?"

The silence stretches longer this time.

"Simon?"

"You are the closest I have ever come to that level of perceived normality."

My heart squeezes.

My hopelessly romantic vagina does too, but mostly, it's my heart.

"And I've hardly seen you in nearly a week." His words are rushed, like if he doesn't say it quickly, he won't say it at all. "But I still—I miss you. I think about you constantly. I wonder what you're doing when we're not speaking. I feel a contact high from being in your presence even when we're both clothed and unlikely to be naked because I simply enjoy…you. And I don't entirely know what to do with that."

"Do you know my favorite thing about you?" I whisper.

"I'm honestly afraid to guess, and I rather hope it's slightly unflattering. I'm far more comfortable in the uncomfortable and awkward. If you could do us both the favor of insisting it's my British accent, that would be lovely."

"My favorite thing about you is that you're so very, very real, when you have all of the tools at your disposal to be anything but."

He's quiet again.

Am I wrong?

Is this *not* real?

The stories about his parents, about his spite smile, about his intentions to never have this level of success, his confession that he never wanted to be a father and he's afraid he's messing it up—who would say any of that if it wasn't real?

"And my favorite thing about you," he finally says, "is that I feel safe being real with you. Truly, it's a gift I cannot adequately thank you for. Regardless of what happens at the end of the summer, you, Beatrice Best, and your friendship have changed my life for the better."

My eyes water.

My heart—yep.

My heart's done it again.

It's fallen headfirst into love with a guy who will likely never fully love me back.

And my vagina smirks in an *I told you so* and swoons a little too.

I curl up on my bed and wish I was curling up next to him. "Simon?"

"Yes?"

"Tomorrow is Griff's last night in town, and I don't want to miss it. But I'll ask Daphne if she can hang with your boys on Friday."

"One would think two security men would be sufficient," he says with a sigh.

"Not one who's met your kids."

"Speaking of my children—I should check in on them."

"You're doing a good job," I whisper. "They're going to be the best people ever when they grow up."

"You're entirely too good for me."

"Doubt that."

the spite date

I can hear him smiling as he answers. "One day, Bea, you'll see the truth of the matter. And until then, I shall humor your incorrect opinions."

I'm smiling and rolling my eyes as we hang up.

He's wrong.

Simon and I?

Neither one of us is perfect.

Far from it.

But together?

I think we're bringing out the best in each other.

And *that* is the last thing I expected. But it's my other favorite thing about him.

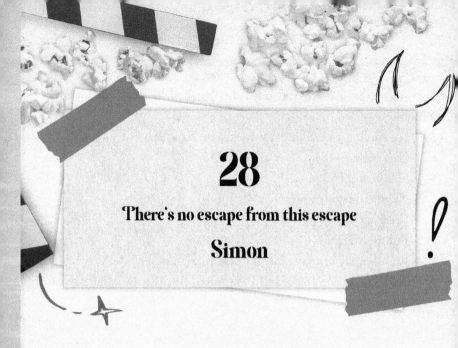

28

There's no escape from this escape

Simon

I'm unable to find alone time for friends-with-benefitting with Bea for another five days.

And today won't be my day either.

Not with what my children have requested and which I've agreed to because I do enjoy spending time with them, and I'm well aware that they could tire of me at any minute.

They *are* teenagers.

Though at least Bea is joining us, at the insistence of my children, who have seen her enough now between meals with her family and meals at her burger bus that I believe they're picking up on the subtle clues that I like her.

"So we'll give you up to three hints, and that's it," a lovely person with spiky black hair and a nose ring is telling my boys. "You have to be smarter than the escape room if you want to beat it."

"I'm smarter," Charlie says.

"*I'm* smarter," Eddie says.

"You thought serial killers attacked breakfast food," Charlie fires back.

Bea grins.

the spite date

It's an utterly delighted grin that turns into a small giggle, which has both of my boys looking at her and this attraction that I cannot deny for her growing stronger and stronger.

Usually, my involvement with women is physical only.

With Bea—well, with Bea, I've spent more time helping in her burger bus and having dinners with her family and helping her avenge herself against an ex-boyfriend while daydreaming about the next opportunity I'll have to see her smile.

I'm quite far gone.

Quite far.

Would I like to have an entire week with her, just the two of us, with nothing to do beyond each other?

Too bloody right.

I should probably spend some time talking myself out of these expectations.

But I'm too ecstatic beyond belief that she's here, with us today, where I can squeeze her hand and sneak kisses and just be near her to care about anything beyond getting to enjoy an hour's activity with her and my boys.

"Hudson and Griff had this same argument about serial killers right after our parents' funeral," she says to them. "You're going to have to try harder if you want to be original."

They share a look.

"Did you truly have to tempt them to argue more?" I murmur to Bea.

She giggles again.

And it's such a lovely sound, I can't even be annoyed with her.

"You ready?" our escape room guide asks.

I look at Bea. "This isn't too tight?"

"It's bigger than my dorm room was. I can make it an hour."

"We're ready," Charlie says.

Yes, he's still wearing that hoodie, and oddly, for once I don't blame him.

It *is* slightly chilly in this room.

Likely ambiance. We've chosen the room where we get to pretend to be bank robbers.

Quite fun to rob a bank, actually. I did it once for a television show.

And my character was killed in the robbery, so I didn't have to memorize very many lines.

Simply play dead.

"Lock us in," Eddie says to the guide. "We'll see you in five minutes."

"The confidence of youth is so inspiring," Bea murmurs. She's still grinning widely.

"How long would you estimate?" I ask her.

"Hudson's best time in any of these rooms is seventeen minutes."

"Good luck beating that in the bank," our guide says. "Your first clue—you only have so much time before the police notice what you're up to."

They leave a card with the clue on a faux marble worktop beside the door, meant to simulate where people would once stand inside a bank and sign their checks, I gather, and then they depart, leaving us locked into this room decorated to look like a bank.

My boys grab the clue and rush to the cuckoo-style clock hanging behind the teller stand. "So easy," Eddie scoffs.

"Such an easy first clue," Charlie agrees.

"Do you need assistance?" I ask them.

Identical eye rolls answer me. "Watch for the cops. We've got this."

Bea grins at me, and I take another arrow to the heart. I do love her smiles.

"You've done this before?" I ask her.

"Yep."

"This room specifically?"

"No. This one's new since the last time I was here." Her smile grows as she watches the boys. Charlie's climbed onto a chair to inspect the clockface. "But I've had a clock clue before…"

the spite date

"Are they warm?"

"Depends on if the staff changed up how the clue works. They do sometimes. But I think they're right to be looking at the clock in general."

"We should help them."

"We don't need help, Dad," Charlie says. "Look. The time's wrong."

He moves the clock hands until they're opposite of what the time actually is.

Nothing happens.

"That's backwards," Eddie says. "You have to put the long arm on the minute and the short arm on the hour."

He starts moving the clock hands differently.

"No, this is what time it is, dummy," Charlie says. "It's after four. I got it right."

I start to move in, but Bea holds an arm out, blocking me.

And a moment later, despite my children fighting over the clock's hands, moving them this way and that way, a panel beneath the clock opens, revealing a dangling clue.

The boys grab it, each getting a hand on it, and pull it to them, their heads together, both of their mouths moving yet not saying a word out loud.

Bea and I amble the short distance toward them.

"Are we not to enjoy the clue as well?" I ask.

"Shh," Charlie says.

"This is for your own good," Eddie adds.

"You can claim we held you hostage when the police get here."

"And then run away with half the money that they don't realize you're holding."

"It's a good plan."

"You should thank us for not involving you."

"If you smile any broader, I fear your cheeks will fall off," I murmur to Bea.

"Don't worry," she murmurs back. "They'll need us for something other than being the scapegoats eventually."

"The *scapegoats*? But they've said they intend to leave us innocent."

"In my experience, what they say and what they do doesn't always line up."

Charlie looks over at us. "Just because *your* brothers are terrible doesn't mean *Eddie* and I are terrible. We mean it. We won't utter your names to the police."

"Charlie! Look. Look at the clue." Eddie points to something on the index card. "It has a bone on it."

"That's not a bone. That's a key."

I frown. "Whoops."

"Whoops?" Bea repeats.

"I believe I was supposed to take one of them to the optician for an eye test."

"You're not really a parent if you don't forget to make at least one doctor's appointment every once in a while."

It's odd to realize how much I enjoy her company without a single item of clothing coming off.

Make no mistake—I would enjoy the hell out of locking Bea inside my bedroom for days on end—but with the difficulties in scheduling bedroom time, I'm still happy to be in her company, day or night, in person or on the phone or over text message.

She simply makes me happier.

"It's about the cash register," Eddie says.

"Banks don't have cash registers. They have cash *drawers*."

"How do you know?"

"I helped Dad practice a script once for a bank robbery."

Eddie's eyes pinch together, and he stares at me as if he's been slapped. "Why didn't I get to help with that script?"

"I believe you were bedridden with some kind of flu," I reply.

He scowls. "I miss all of the fun scripts."

the spite date

"You can help Dad when he has to memorize his lines for his new script," Charlie says. "Right, Dad?"

"Indeed. You're both welcome to assist."

"Do I get to be the bad guy?" Eddie asks.

"If you wish."

"Good. C'mon, Charlie. Let's crack this case and steal this money."

Bea wrinkles her nose at me.

"What? Have I leftover lunch on my face?" I ask.

"No, it's just—I forgot for a minute what your day job actually is."

And that as well—that has me smiling too. "Am I not handsome enough that you'd believe me a top-tier movie star even if we'd never met?"

"Gross," Eddie mutters while he and Charlie fiddle with a panel beneath the customer service counter in this fake bank room.

Bea sputters out a laugh. "You know you look a lot like him?"

"But better for the parts of Mom that I have in me."

"Also," Bea continues, "that's not the teller drawer. You're on the wrong side of the counter."

Both boys whip their heads up at her.

"Bloody hell," Charlie whispers.

"Don't say *bloody hell* in front of Dad's girlfriend."

I freeze.

Girlfriend?

Bea is certainly not my—

Oh, bloody hell indeed.

Bea *is* my girlfriend.

Not officially, of course.

But what else do you call a woman with whom you obsess over every waking moment when you're not together, whose schedule you arrange your own around in the hopes of seeing her, and whom you occasionally enjoy in-person or phone sex with?

She's smiling at the boys, though I'm incapable of that expression at the moment. "You can say anything you want in front of me, provided you're not using it to call me names," she says to the boys. "And really, a good *bloody hell* is way better than *fuck this shit*. It's like proper cussing. I like it."

They shoot her matching grins as they dash around the counter to the other side.

"She's bloody right!" Charlie crows.

"Bloody nailed it," Eddie agrees.

"Simon," Bea says softly, intertwining her fingers with mine.

I realize I'm swaying on my feet, eyes wide, my normal smile unable to form on my lips.

I shake my head, but it doesn't quite clear the stun I'm feeling at my boys calling Bea my girlfriend.

Will they become attached?

Will they expect that I marry her?

Why the bloody hell am I not having an instant panic attack at that thought?

"*Simon,*" Bea says again, this time in that tone that has my cock sitting up and taking notice. "They're going to live here for the next five years—"

"Six," I correct absently. "We held them back a year before kindergarten."

"—and I like their mother, and I know boundaries, and I can be one more safe adult in their life if they ever get in trouble, no matter what happens with you and me, because I have a fucking lot of practice with it, and I might as well embrace that."

Thank heavens.

I've found the world's most perfect woman.

I should say something pithy or something grateful, but all I can do is stare at her.

She blinks back, lifting her brows and making her forehead wrinkle in the most adorable way as she waits for me to find words.

"How do we know the code?" Charlie says to Eddie.

"We can guess."

"What's the bank's address?"

"I don't bloody know!"

"Why would they give us a keypad without giving us the code?"

I shake my head once more, and this time, my brain reengages, diving headfirst into a distraction that's an easy out for this conversation.

Which I would oddly like to have.

Namely, so that I can ask Bea how we might continue our, ah, situationship.

I believe that's what the younger people call it.

And the term fits.

We're not dating, though everything we're doing would fall under the normal classification of *dating*, which means—

"Do you think they used one of our birthdays?" Charlie says.

"How would they know our birthdays?"

"I don't know. I didn't fill out the paperwork."

"Dad did. Maybe he had to put his birthday."

Yes.

Distraction.

This works.

"Dad, what's your birthday?" Charlie asks.

"It's November fourth, duh," Eddie says.

"How do you know Dad's birthday?"

"How don't you?"

"He never celebrates it, for one."

Both of my boys look at me.

"Have you thought maybe the clues are tied together?" Bea asks before I can say anything.

Am I still gawking?

I am.

I am still gawking.

Being quite the prat.

"*The clock!*" both boys shriek at the same time.

"It's five-forty," Charlie says.

"It's eight-twenty-five," Eddie replies.

They stare at each other.

I make a mental note to have remedial clock training for Charlie.

"You could try both," Bea muses.

My children, the two boys who laughed with me until all of our cheeks hurt yesterday over our attempts at knitting to prepare for this weekend's adventures in Athena's Rest, knock their heads together with a distinct *crack* as they both dive toward the keypad again.

"*Owwww*," Charlie howls.

"Bloody freaking hell, that hurts," Eddie groans.

I don't even realize Bea and I have moved as one until she's squatting before Charlie, enabling me to direct my full attention to Eddie.

"You okay?" she says to him, touching him lightly on the red mark on his forehead.

"How badly does it hurt?" I ask Eddie, doing the same for him.

Both boys insist they're fine.

"I can shake it off," Charlie says to Bea. "I'm tough."

She smiles at him. "Clearly."

I, however, am not tough.

I am a bloody marshmallow being slow-roasted over a comfortable fire.

Or perhaps that's merely my heart.

Melting on the inside.

Have I—have I fallen in love with Bea?

It's the question humming through my mind as the boys work out the next three clues, until they've become stumped as we all four squat before a vault behind a hidden door.

"The gold is in there," Charlie's insisting. "That's what the clue says. That we have to crack the secret code for the vault if we want to have our riches before we depart."

Bea's sweeping her fingers over the edges of the door. "Maybe there's a hidden combination lock that's not on the vault?"

"That doesn't make any bloody sense," Eddie grouses.

the spite date

"Agreed, but there's not a combination lock on the vault either."

"There's a keyhole," I point out.

"But none of the keys we've found work," Charlie says.

Bea and I lock eyes.

"Safe deposit boxes," she says at the same time I blurt, "Both keys must be turned at the same time."

We grin at each other.

Clearly, we're on the same wavelength.

"The keys, please, Charlie," I say to my son. "Bea and I will show you how banks work."

"I mean, usually safe deposit boxes are lined up *inside* the vault, and you don't have to do the two-key method to get in exactly like this," she says.

"Have you worked in a bank? Are you quite sure there's not double keys for the safe entrance too?"

She shakes her head. "That's one career I haven't had, but I've been to banks enough. My parents had three safe deposit boxes. I kept finding keys in different places."

"*Three?*"

"They had a joint one, and then they both had a secret one they kept from each other where they'd hide nice gifts. Mom's had this gorgeous pocket watch and front-row tickets for the whole family to go see a hockey game in New York, and Dad's had the matching earrings to the pearl necklace-and-bracelet set he'd given her the two Christmases before. It was really sweet."

"But safe deposit boxes?"

"One of my grandpas was a banker before he retired and moved to Arizona. I think he gave them a family discount. You ready with that key?"

"Whenever you are, love."

Bloody hell.

I *have* to quit calling her that.

Especially with the way it makes my boys giggle.

"Three, two, one," she says, not reacting in the least to the pet name, as if men call her *love* all the time.

Probably she thinks it's a British thing.

She wouldn't be wrong, but she wouldn't be entirely right, either.

"...and *turn*," she says.

I turn my key in the keyhole we've located beside the teller counter drawer.

She turns her key in the keyhole on the right side of the safe, where she's balanced in a squat, knees up, making me think of yoga poses and goats.

There's a clicking noise, as if something has been unlocked.

"It should've opened," she murmurs. She runs her fingers along the edges of the door again, then gives it a slight push.

"It opened." Eddie crowds behind her.

"I heard it," Charlie adds, also crowding behind her.

"Must be a sticky door." She pushes once, twice, and before I can offer my assistance, she puts her shoulder into it.

The door swings open, into the safe, from hinges above the door.

And Bea follows the door with a gasp, her body propelled inward as though she's lost her balance.

I reach for her, but—

The door swings back shut again, and a red light flashes from somewhere above us.

I gasp.

Eddie gasps.

Charlie gasps. "*It ate Bea!*"

I shove my boys out of the way and get down on my knees, pushing at the door. "Bea? Bea, are you in there?"

Are you in there?

Bloody stupid question, Luckwood.

Where the bloody else would she be?

And why won't this door open again?

There's a muffled answer from inside.

the spite date

A muffled, higher-pitched answer accompanied by dull thuds from the other side of the door.

My blood runs cold.

How small is it in there?

How small is it in there?

"Charlie. Turn the key again," I order. "Bea? Bea, if you can hear me, we're attempting to open the door again."

Charlie and I count down quickly and turn the keys together.

The door doesn't open, but another light begins flashing as well.

"Stop turning keys!" Eddie says. "It's the wrong clue! The police are coming!"

"I don't bloody care about the police! Bea's trapped."

Charlie makes a face at me. "Dad, it's a game. They'll let her out."

Right.

Right.

"Bea?" I call. "Can you hear me? Are you all right?"

There's another series of thumps on the other side of the door, but no words answer me.

My heart is in my throat, beating madly.

My hands are getting sweaty. Clammy.

My breath can't come fast enough.

She's stuck.

Stuck in a tiny place.

And it's my fault.

"Ring the guide," I tell Charlie and Eddie. "We *must* get Bea out of here."

"Dad—"

"She's terrified of enclosed spaces. *Ring the bloody guide. Now.*"

Terrible time to realize one more reason to not do relationships.

Because when the woman you're suddenly afraid you've fallen head over heels in love with is in danger, and you cannot assist no matter the sheer strength you're putting into breaking down this bloody safe door, it feels as though your entire life is over.

I've hurt her.

I've put her into a small space.

And I can't fix this fast enough.

Is she hyperventilating?

Does she know I'm coming?

Will she have nightmares?

"Problem, boss?" Pinky says above me.

My father's voice and my mother's voice and the voice of every bossy nanny I had in my childhood comes out of my mouth as I rise and point to the door. "Bea's trapped and I've no idea what's behind this door and I want her out and I want her out *now*."

Pinky looks over his shoulder to the spiky-haired guide. "Open this door."

The guide frowns. "You did the key thing?"

"We did the key thing."

"That's supposed to open the door."

"It did."

"And leave it open."

"Bloody hell," I mutter. "*Open the fucking door and get my girlfriend out of there.*"

Yes.

My girlfriend.

Bea.

My Bea.

If she'll forgive me for this.

29

But my heart doesn't feel trapped

Bea

B*reathe breathe breathe*, I tell myself in the dark while I feel around the tiny space for a latch or a string or *anything* to help me get out of here.

I bump up against a bag of something that jingles like plastic coins pretending to be gold, and I find a stack of plastic something else that turns out to be fake gold bars too.

Yep.

Finally remembered my phone has a flashlight.

There's thumping on the other side of the door that tells me Simon's trying to get to me, but turning on the flashlight reveals just how cramped this space is.

I keep it on long enough to inspect the hinges on the door to see if I can pull out the pin holding them together, but it's in there solidly, and I don't have any tools on me.

I don't have cell signal either.

There are muffled voices on the other side of the door, but I can't tell what they're saying.

So after a few attempts to kick the door open, I shut off my flashlight, curl up in a ball, close my eyes, and attempt to stave off a panic attack.

Simon's coming. Hudson will freak out then laugh. Ryker will show up with fresh eggs. Griff will call. Daphne will take me to a field and let me stand in the widest open air that we can find.

I'm in a field.

I'm in an open field.

I'm safe.

I'm okay.

I'm stuck in a dark little cave in an escape room and Eddie and Charlie might not get to finish their escape room experience.

You're in a field, Bea. A wide-open field.

What if they're solving the rest of the clues?

What if I can't get out until they've opened the door?

What if help doesn't come?

Do I have enough oxygen in here?

I suck in a breath and order my heart to slow, but it doesn't work.

Because the memories are taking over.

Hide-and-seek with Ryker.

The old fridge at my grandparents' farm.

The way I started getting drowsy.

My parents panicking when I woke up from my nap, outside of the fridge.

Ryker standing over me, looking like a ghost.

Ryker dead.

But Ryker wasn't dead.

I almost was.

Not Ryker.

He was just scared.

Scared that I was dead.

You're in a field, Bea. Wide open. Plenty of air. Arms wide. You can twirl and not touch anything. The sky is high, high, high above you.

A tear slips down my cheek.

They're coming to save you. They know you're here. You're not hiding. They'll get you.

Another tear slips down the other cheek.

Be in a field, Bea. Be in a field.

My breath shudders out of me, and then a shaft of light appears.

"Prop that bloody door open *right now*," Simon orders. "Bea? Bea, it's all right. We've got you."

I suck in a breath and try to swipe my eyes before he can see me, but when I lift my head, it's too late.

The mixture of compassion and worry and *I will burn this whole bloody town down to save you* flickering in his blue eyes as he crawls into the space enough to grab my hand without getting trapped in here too—

I told you so! my vagina squeals. *He loves you!*

"No more escape rooms." Simon's voice is tight, but I can tell he's trying to be lighthearted. "Come on, Bea. Let's get fresh air."

I don't know how long I've been in here.

Maybe a minute.

Maybe ten.

Hard to tell when you're trying not to panic.

But as soon as I'm back in the room, with both boys looking on wide-eyed, all three security agents hovering, the escape room guide in here too—well, with that many people worried about me, it's hard to not let the tears slip out again.

Simon crushes me in a hug as soon as we're both standing. "Are you all right?"

I swallow hard.

Then have to swallow two more times before I trust myself to speak. "I found the bank's gold."

His breath whooshes out of him. "You scared the hell out of me. We couldn't get the door open fast enough to get you out of there."

I don't know if he can tell how fast my heart is still pounding, but I can feel his against my cheek, and it's racing.

And that makes my eyes hot and my throat clog again.

He remembered I don't like small spaces.

He doesn't even know why, but he remembered.

And I knew he would, because it's Simon.

He pays attention.

"Next game's on the house," our guide says.

"You're to close this room until it works properly and no one's in danger of becoming trapped inside a vault without their consent," Simon says crisply.

Bossy.

Commanding.

Not a hint of a smile.

"Yeah, management won't want a lawsuit," the guide says. "We'll get it fixed. Probably shut it down like the last setup they had in here. This room's cursed."

"Did someone die in here?" Charlie asks.

"Please don't answer that," Simon replies.

He's sounding a little more normal now.

But when I loosen my grip on this hug, he doesn't let me go.

"Boys, let's go and find dinner. And get Bea some fresh air." He scoops me up into his arms again and carries me through the building.

"I can walk," I murmur against his neck.

"You bloody well cannot until I say you can" is his gruff response.

A door *woosh*es, and warm summer air tickles my nostrils as he strides out into the parking lot.

"I didn't know Dad was that strong," Charlie whispers to Eddie behind us.

"I'm never carrying a woman like that. I'd probably huff and puff and drop her like I dropped you last week, and then she'd never want anything to do with me again."

"We should both probably run more. Or do push-ups when Dad does his push-ups."

the spite date

"Mom says we don't have to be obsessed with how our bodies look like Dad is though. She says we should get jobs where it doesn't matter what we look like."

"I want to narrate books when I get older. Then I can sit in a little closet and talk to myself all day."

I shiver.

"Perhaps save the small room talk until later, Charlie," Simon says.

"Whoops. Sorry, Bea."

I look over Simon's shoulder to smile at his sons. "It's okay. If it makes you happy, that's what counts."

"I think it's because I've always been the smaller twin," Charlie says. "I like being next to people in really tight—erm, I mean, I just like being crowded."

We reach the car, and Simon sets me down.

And then he looks at me.

And this time, when my breath leaves me, it's not because I'm scared.

Well, maybe a little.

Told you so, my vagina crows.

Because the way Simon's looking at me—a man doesn't look at a woman like that if he doesn't care.

A lot.

More than he should.

He brushes his thumbs over my cheeks, inspecting my face with both his hands and his eyes. "Are you all right?"

"You already asked her—*oof*."

"Let him have his hero moment, dumbarse."

His eyes pinch shut, but the teeniest of lines crinkle in the corners, and his lips turn up the smallest bit too.

"I knew you'd save me," I whisper.

His eyes open again, and *god*, they're so blue.

Like the wide-open sky.

All the space in the world.

"I'm cooking for you tonight," he informs me.

And when we get back to his house—manor? estate?—that's exactly what he does.

He mans the grill himself, making bratwurst and hamburgers and grilled chicken.

Insisting I do nothing more than sit outside in a chair by the grill, drinking a root beer and sampling the chips and raw veggies that he arranges neatly in bowls and on platters for sides.

And every time he looks at me—

Something's changed.

Something earth shatteringly monumental.

We make small talk, trading stories about his boys and my brothers, then stories of our own childhood mischief. On the surface, it's light.

But not when he looks at me.

It's like he's verifying I'm still here, and holding his breath for fear I'll disappear behind a door again, and also holding himself back from whatever it is that has his eyes so very, very serious, even when he's smiling and joking with his boys or the security agents who occasionally check on us while we're eating.

The boys volunteer to clean up after dinner, which has Simon smiling again. "You want to have video game time."

"We wouldn't turn it down," Charlie says while he gathers plates.

"Not if you're offering," Eddie agrees as he grabs the platter of leftover vegetables.

"Is that yours, or did it come with the house?" I ask Simon as I spot the flowery pattern, which is oddly familiar.

"Everything came with the house. Made moving quite easy. Though I did replace the mattresses."

"I think Mrs. Young used that dish to serve food at her husband's wake here."

"We're eating off funeral dishes?" Charlie whispers.

"Epic," Eddie says.

the spite date

He and Charlie dash for the back door with their arms loaded down. "Maybe we can make more friends if they know we have dead people's stuff," Charlie says.

Simon swipes a hand over his face, his smile a little more pained now.

"Do they need more friends?" I ask him.

"They've made a few in that program you recommended, but everyone could always use one more friend." He looks down at the table, still littered with chip bowls and a single leftover bratwurst and some cups and utensils, then lifts his gaze to me again.

So very, very serious. "Bea."

My pulse kicks into overdrive. "Yes, Simon?"

"I called you my girlfriend while we were attempting to rescue you today."

Swoon, my vagina sighs.

Shut up, he's breaking up with us, I tell her.

Because I know how this goes.

He doesn't want to date anyone.

He's leaving in a little over a month.

We've hardly had any time for the *with benefits* part of our friendship deal, even if I feel like I know everything about him with how much we've texted.

I know when the jig is up, and folks, this is definitely the end.

A slice of my heart screams in agony, and I slap on my best poker face.

"People say things," I say with a shrug.

Like it's not a big deal that he misspoke.

Like I won't go home and sob into my pillow.

Because I'll miss him.

Simon Luckwood is everything I ever could've wanted in a boyfriend. He can carry on conversations for hours. He's funny and he makes me happy. He doesn't have anything to gain from dating me—not his reputation, not a financial benefit, not inspiration for his next business venture—and so of course, I knew this moment would come.

With him staring at me so seriously as the sunlight fades from the sky, the same night insects that were chirping away the night we had sex on the grass beginning their music again, the perfect evening cookout making my belly content even while my heart is cramping.

He wanted to give me one last meal and make sure I'll survive before he pulled the plug.

"But I would very much like to be your boyfriend," he says.

The fake smile I've been holding on to in the face of our impending breakup cracks in two, and I squint at him so fast that my brain almost cramps. "What?"

"I had no intentions of developing feelings for you beyond friendship, but these past weeks of getting to know you, spending time talking and working at your burger bus, meeting your family, being *welcomed* by your family, and then today, when you were trapped and I was helpless to get you out fast enough—being your friend is not enough. And it's bloody terrifying because I don't do relationships, but when faced with a choice of having you as something more in my life or cutting things off completely, I—I cannot let you go. You mean entirely too much to me. Unless, of course, you wish to go. Then I suppose I will somehow get by."

"Oh my god, I thought you were breaking up with me," I gasp.

It's exactly what a woman should *not* say in this situation.

But this is Simon.

Simon, who's now giving me a wry smile that's still tinged in vulnerability. "I daresay that may have been the easier choice. But sadly for me and my very exposed heart, it's not the choice I made."

"Simon," I whisper.

"If you intend to turn me down, please do it quickly."

My heart twists. I don't want to turn him down. I *want* to be his girlfriend. I *want* to have more reasons to see him. I want *him*. But—"You're leaving in a month-ish."

"Not forever. This is home until the boys have gone on to university or whatever they choose after high school. And I'd be more than happy to provide transportation for you to come and visit me when I'm unable to leave the set for too many days in a row."

My pulse is creeping higher.

So is my hope. "I'm stubborn, and I like my independence."

"I adore that about you. You have no need for me to be any part of what defines you, and I am not looking for an additional co-parent for my children. You've earned your freedom from that responsibility. I only wish to complement you and your life, rather than rule it as my parents allowed themselves to rule one another and their deeds. You've shown me what family can be, how I can be a part of that, and I want—I simply *want*, Bea. I want you."

And now my eyes are watering and my nose is stinging, but not in the bad way. He's saying all of the right things, and even more right things than I would've expected him to think to say. "You are the most unique person I've ever met."

He leans into the table, hands folded before him. "I sincerely hope you find that appealing enough to let me intentionally call you my girlfriend."

I swipe at my eyes, then reach across the table to cover his hands with mine. "Do you really know what you're getting into here?"

"Of course not." A nearly real Simon smile pops out, tilting one side of his mouth higher than the other. "But I am rather excited to find out. I do enjoy a good adventure, and so long as fire and enclosed spaces are not involved, I suspect you do as well."

"I'm still figuring out what I enjoy."

"Do you enjoy me?"

"*Yes*. Very much so."

"Then it would be an honor to be part of your life as you explore all of your interests and hobbies and future career options, whatever they may be, for as long as you can tolerate me and my own unique challenges."

Something inside shatters loudly enough for us to hear it through the windows.

Simon winces. "Such as whatever that might have been. Which, again—I realize they're an extra complication. Which is a terrible thing to say about a person, or two people, especially children, but—"

"Shh. It's okay." I squeeze his hands harder and tip my head back and laugh. "Simon Luckwood, you have yourself a girlfriend."

He leans across the table and captures my lips with his, but it's a brief kiss.

Because the door bangs open, with Charlie's voice carrying over the patio. "Eddie broke the funeral plate!"

"I just found something new I like," I whisper to Simon as we break apart, me giggling, him lifting his eyes skyward with a massive smile.

"Children with terrible timing?" he guesses.

"Laughing while I'm kissing you."

He looks at Charlie, then back to me, and then he rises. "Let's get it cleaned up, then. Bea will be staying to watch a movie with me."

"Which movie?" Charlie asks.

"Something bloody and gory and terribly boring."

"Awesome. Can I watch too?"

Simon slides me a look.

And I feel another smile creeping over my face.

We are officially dating.

Dating-dating.

And I have a crazy feeling that finding alone time with Simon will continue to be just as hard.

Not that it truly bothers me that he has kids.

They're just little people. And they're not *mine*.

Not my responsibility.

Mine to enjoy as extensions of him instead.

"Worth it," I whisper to him as I link my fingers through his.

"You absolutely are," he agrees.

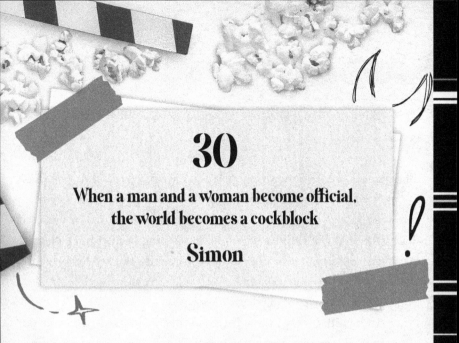

30

When a man and a woman become official, the world becomes a cockblock

Simon

After a week where Bea joins the boys and me for dinner several nights, along with an unexpectedly funny trip to the bowling alley and a full afternoon of the four of us playing MarioKart, finally—finally—the stars have aligned.

Even though my parents tried to ruin my day by ringing me—I sincerely need to block their numbers—I am giddy with glee.

I'm about to see my girlfriend.

Alone.

I can barely restrain my excitement as my car arrives beside Bea's burger bus.

My boys are staying with Lana for the first time in weeks on a night when Bea isn't also booked for a party, and so Bea insisted that I meet her at the old drive-in cinema, and honestly, it was sheer brilliance on her part to suggest a place this secluded and remote.

The large screen beyond the overgrown field glows with the moonlight, and everything is bright enough that I don't require my night glasses. I hand my phone to Butch with orders to not interrupt for anything short of fire, screams for help, or a random sharknado suddenly appearing in the vicinity, and I cross the short distance to climb into the back of Bea's bus.

"Shut the door," she says in a purring voice that makes my cock instantly hard.

We've seen one another at least every other day what with the dinners and play time with my boys, and we've texted and spoken on the phone far more about anything and everything under the sun. She's shared stories of her parents and told me why she's afraid of enclosed spaces and that she's always regretted not coming home from college to see what would be her mother's final community theater performance. I've told her stories about my career and side jobs, along with tales of my own parents that even Lana doesn't know.

And while I feel as though I know Bea inside and out, we've not been alone in person together for more than five minutes here or there, stealing kisses and very little more in those moments.

I'm starving for her touch.

For her unfiltered words shared directly into my ear rather than over text message or on the phone.

For that beautiful smile with those irresistible dimples aimed straight at me and only me.

I shut the door and realize a black curtain blocks my way.

I lift it aside, step deeper into the bus, and fairy lights flicker on around me.

Fairy lights against dark curtains hung all around the interior of the bus, blocking off even the kitchen portion of the food truck and making a cocoon of the chef's table portion of her mobile establishment.

"Bea?" I say softly. "Are you all right?"

This feels tight, and I hope she's okay.

"I am." The curtains to the kitchen part, and a bare leg sticks through it, mid-thigh down.

My cock strains against my trousers at the realization that I'm about to get a show.

From my girlfriend.

the spite date

Now, this—this is worthy of getting out my glasses.

Which I do in a quick flash.

I grabbed them in case the moon wasn't bright enough, but as it turns out—they're necessary for the full, crisp, clear enjoyment of whatever Bea is about to do next.

"Don't take anything off," she says. "That's my job."

My hand drops away from my belt buckle. "How—" I start, and then I realize I don't quite care how she managed to set up her bus like this.

"Sit on the edge of the table." One long, slender arm pokes through the curtain, pointing at me.

"Anything you wish, madame."

Her shoulder follows the arm, displaying a single black strap that I'm well aware is holding up something lacy and irresistible.

I may not have brought enough condoms with me.

Or possibly I'm about to come in my boxers, and this evening will be over before it's begun.

Bea's face pokes through the curtain, which she's holding so that I can still only see her leg, her arm, and her face. Her gaze drifts down below my waistband, and that smile—heavens above, I could drown in that smile.

Completely lose myself in her happiness.

For the first time in my life, I don't care if I succeed in having sex tonight.

I don't want to *have sex*.

I want to make love.

I want to be so close with Bea that I don't know where my body ends and hers begins.

I want to laugh with her.

I want to hear her tell stories of her customers and her family and anything she wishes to tell me.

I want to hold her in my sleep. I want to wake up to her sleepy face and marvel at whatever her hair looks like first thing in the morning.

I have somehow fallen head over heels, completely in love with this woman.

And it's not the terrifying, nauseating idea that one would think it should be, given my history with relationships.

Because she makes it so easy to adore her. So easy to believe she likes me for me. That she understands my faults and finds me worthy as a whole flawed-but-good-intentioned human being.

"You seem almost as excited to see me as I am to see you," she says.

"There's no comparison, love. I am *far* more excited."

"Where's your phone?"

"Behind the building with Butch."

"Does anyone know you're here?"

"Not a soul."

"If the sex is terrible tonight, are you dumping me?"

"Beatrice. The only way sex with you would be terrible is if—" I cut myself off, tilt my head, and smile broader. "As it turns out, even my wild imagination is unable to come up with a scenario in which neither of us leaves this bus fully satiated tonight, so—"

"Say that again."

"My wild imagination?"

"Satiated."

I love when she asks me to repeat random words.

I love it even more when she's watching me with her eyes dark as midnight and her lips parted and her bare skin nearly close enough to touch.

I jerk my chin at the fabric she's gripping. "I rather think that's worth a bit more of a show, don't you?"

"Take your glasses off and put them back on."

I don't ask why.

I merely do as instructed.

She bites her lower lip as I slide my glasses back up my nose.

"I like your glasses," she whispers. "I don't know why they make you even hotter, but they do."

"You have a thing for academic men?"

the spite date

"I have a thing for you." She angles her body, and one hip comes into view.

One hip with a small black strap hugging it and disappearing behind her.

I swallow as she shifts the barest bit more, exposing a small red bow tied to the triangle of fabric covering her pussy.

My cock pulses harder and my voice goes hoarse. "I have been dreaming of your skin and your mouth and your breasts and your pussy for weeks."

She drops the curtain a smidge more and runs a hand from her collarbone, down her breast held in skimpy black that barely covers the dark nipple that I can see outlined behind the lace, then lower, her fingers drifting over her belly and down to the better view that I have now of her lacy thong.

"This pussy?"

"Yes."

"She's missed you."

"I am here for the taking, Beatrice."

Her smile flashes brighter, deepening her dimples. "I never liked my full name until you said it."

"I never imagined I should get so lucky as to fall for a jailbird until I met you."

She tips her head back and laughs, exposing her slender throat, and in this moment, I would do anything to have this woman in my life forever.

Marry her.

Die for her.

Anything and everything in between.

"You've the best sense of humor," I tell her.

"No, you're just that funny."

"I'd like to be inside you more than I'd like to be funny right now."

"Ah-ah. Don't touch your belt. That's mine."

"Excuse the paranoia, but I'm struggling to convince myself we truly do have the time to fully enjoy this." We thought we did three days ago at her apartment when she finished early for the days and while my boys were still occupied in a program, and we were interrupted by Hudson and Daphne. And then there was a phone sex conversation last night that I stopped under suspicion that my children were too close, which also turned out to be an accurate concern.

The paranoia is well-founded.

Those warm green eyes crinkle as she smiles again. "I can't decide if having to hurry makes me more or less turned on."

"You should come closer so that I may help you make that determination."

"Are you sure you're ready for this?" She wiggles the curtains.

"Unless you've acquired a tattoo of a scary beast on your belly since I last glimpsed that marvelous part of your body, I'm positive I can handle anything you're hiding behind that cloth."

She hasn't stopped smiling.

I haven't either.

Though I'm also quite parched, rather achy in the balls, and eager for her to strip me of my clothing as she wishes.

She takes one step forward, the curtains gliding along her body, still covering her, but covering less of her.

Her belly comes into view. Her other breast. Second leg.

I attempt to swallow and find I've forgotten how.

"Were you wearing this the night of our first date?"

She closes the gap between us and runs her hands over my shoulders. "Define first date."

My hands are drawn to her hips, and I'm helpless to resist caressing her soft skin and bare buttocks. "With the red dress."

That smile.

Were I to perish in her smile, I would leave this earthly plane the happiest man to have ever died.

"I was wearing red panties"—she leans closer to me, her breasts brushing my chest, her lips hovering at my ear—"and no bra."

"I'd like to remove this bra with my teeth."

She shivers against me while her hands sneak under the hem of my T-shirt, her bare touch lighting my skin on fire.

"What else do you want to do with your teeth?" she asks as she pulls my shirt over my head.

"I should like to bite your inner thigh."

Another shiver, this one carrying the heady scent of her arousal with it. Her fingers glide down my chest and abdomen as she presses a kiss to my neck. "Why does that turn me on?"

"Because you know I'd be rather good at it."

Her hands reach my belt, and she makes quick work of undoing both the buckle and the button of my trousers beneath. "I didn't want to hurry."

"I'm content to hurry. The first time." My lips find her lace-covered nipple, and I suck it into my mouth, enjoying her soft gasp of pleasure while also enjoying the glide of her hands inside my trousers.

She strokes my bare cock with those magical hands, not chilly, but not hot either, silky smooth against my shaft, and I lose her nipple for the groan of sheer ecstasy that I cannot hold back. "Bea—"

"Do you know I've seen you shirtless four times, and this is the first time I get to touch you in the light?"

"I am *well* aware I've not had the pleasure of your hands all over my body nearly enough, though that's not what my shirt covers that you're currently stroking."

"I haven't seen him yet either," she whispers. "Is he pretty?"

"Beatrice—"

A dark-eyed, sparkly smile lights her face as she strokes me root to tip once more. "He feels pretty."

My eyes cross.

She pushes at my trousers, and I lift my hips so that she can fully push them down.

"Oh, he *is* pretty," she whispers. "I like him."

"He likes you too," I manage to force out. "Very much."

"Does he have a nickname?"

"No."

"That's a terrible nickname, Simon."

I'm on the edge of losing control. She's still in her lacy undergarments. And that teasing smile coaxing a laugh out of me—this isn't happiness.

It's more.

It's radiant joy. It's peace. It's finding where I belong in a world where I didn't even realize I was always on the sidelines, looking in.

I cradle her face and draw it to mine to kiss her, long and slow and deep, until she's shimmying out of her thong and pushing me further back onto the table, then straddling me with a hurried desperation, her knees on either side of my hips on the table.

I barely remember to dig out a condom and roll it on before she's sliding her hot, wet, silky core down on me.

Next time.

Next time, I will take this bra off her with my teeth.

This time, I barely have the control to unhook the clasp.

The cups fall away, and I cradle her breasts in my hands while she rides me, still kissing me, rotating her hips in a magical way that has me uncertain if I'll ever see straight again.

"You—amazing," I whisper against her lips.

"I missed you," she whispers back.

"Dreaming about this—every night."

"It's getting very obvious what I'm doing in the shower every morning."

The image of this beautiful body, wet and soapy, with Bea touching herself while thinking of me—"Bea…"

Her shoulders shudder. "This is so much better—than my fingers—"

"I'd love to watch you with your fingers."

I shift one hand lower, between us, to press my thumb to her clit, and clearly she's as close as I am, because her breath catches, and her eyelids lower, and her entire body trembles. "Simon—"

"Come for me, love. Let me watch you come."

A gasp wrenches from her core as her inner walls tighten around my cock. Her hips still, pressing down hard onto me as her climax overtakes her.

But she doesn't look away.

She stares into my soul as I join her in tipping over the precipice and into a deep, endless abyss of nothing but sheer pleasure.

I strain into my release, panting for breath while she cries my name, still holding my gaze, fearless and beautiful in her orgasm.

Fully sharing it with me.

Holding nothing back.

This—coming with Bea, our bodies in sync, our eyes wide open, nothing between us—this is unlike anything I knew could exist in the world.

I've discovered my life's purpose, and her name is Beatrice Best.

Giving her pleasure. Shielding her from pain. Laughing with her. Loving her.

Her eyes drift nearly shut as one last shudder racks her body, and then she's sinking against me, face in my neck, arms looped about my ribs. "Oh my god, Simon," she whispers.

The last of my own release trembles away, and I find myself panting hard as well as I lower both of us onto the table.

"I—" I start, but I don't know how to finish.

How does one say *thank you for giving my life meaning and my soul a place to belong*?

I suppose exactly like that.

But not now.

Not when it could be swept away later as a post-orgasmic high.

She twists her neck to press a kiss to my collarbone.

I squeeze her as tightly as my satiated limbs will allow, then smile. "Satiated," I murmur.

Her soft giggle is every reward I've never known I needed. "Thank you."

"My utter pleasure."

31

Naturally...

Bea

Simon's body is my new favorite wonder of the world.

I love learning everything about it.

Like that he's highly ticklish for a few minutes after sex. That he's genetically blessed, and that and some running and push-ups are all he claims it takes to keep his flat abs and biteable pecs and shoulders. That his penis is absolutely perfect.

It's bigger than I expected when I finally see it in the light. Not circumcised. Silky smooth and thick and beautiful.

And highly effective.

He's playing with my fingers as we cuddle on the table, my hand resting on his chest, my head too, listening to his heartbeat. "Your favorite movie is…*Honeymoon for One?*" he guesses.

We're at least a dozen questions deep in a game of *let me guess things about you*, and it's so perfect and serene and comfortable, I never want to leave.

I furrow my brow. "I don't think I've ever heard of that movie."

"Razzle Dazzle flick. Quite good. Features a studly young British man who aims a volleyball incorrectly and is rather an arse about it, hitting a lovely woman, thus setting up the plot for Jonas Rutherford's character to come to her rescue."

"You think my favorite movie of all time is a made-for-TV Razzle Dazzle flick that you had a minor role in?"

"You're my girlfriend, so by default, you're obligated to say yes."

I laugh so hard I snort. "You—you are the best kind of ridiculous."

"Bloody hell. Here I go, exceeding expectations already. We are doomed, Beatrice. Doomed."

"*Ever After*," I tell him. "My favorite movie of all time is *Ever After*."

"The Cinderella retelling?"

"My mom used to watch it all the time when I was growing up. It would get to the end, and she'd say, 'See, Bea? She saves herself. It's always a better movie when she saves herself,' and my dad would ask if he could please assist if she ever needed to save herself, and she'd say only if he followed directions, and then they'd both laugh, and it always made me feel safe and happy, like nothing bad would ever happen because my parents loved each other and me and my brothers too much for anything bad to happen."

"I suppose that's a reasonable second choice for a favorite movie." He hugs me tighter and kisses my hair. "And Bea? You've done a remarkable job of saving not only yourself, but your family too. I have no doubt they'd be incredibly proud of you. And grateful as well."

My eyes water, but I'm smiling as I blink the tears away. "So you know, my dad set the bar high. *Reeeeeaalllly* high. My expectations in this relationship are going to be absurd."

"Darling, I'm acquainted with at least one of your ex-boyfriends, and I'm afraid, despite the example you had set for you in your youth, you don't recognize the bar."

I poke him in the stomach. "*Hey*."

"And then you went and decided to invite this guy to a late-night rendezvous—"

"Booty call," I correct.

He ignores me. "When I've warned you time and time again that my greatest pleasure in life is underperforming expectations."

"Simon?"

"Yes?"

"If I told you I wanted pancakes for breakfast tomorrow, what would you do?"

"If I answer honestly, you're making a liar of me, and if I answer dishonestly, you'll know I'm lying."

I can't stop smiling. "How would you get me pancakes?"

"First, I'd secretly ask input from your roommate and brothers about your favorite kind of homemade pancakes, if there's a mix you're absurdly addicted to or if you prefer all fresh ingredients, and then I'd add sausage and bacon—both the American and the British kind, because I cannot make one without the other in case I ever convince everyone in my life of the superiority of British bacon—and likely a fruit salad, precut from the store for time's sake, and I would arrive at your apartment ready to cook a full hour before you usually awake, with a local diner on speed dial in case I bungle it all to hell."

I shift onto my elbow and lift myself to look at him.

He purses his lips together and looks away, which cracks me up.

"You're a terrible bad boyfriend."

He looks at me again. "You're merely saying that because I discovered your secret love of those horrific marshmallow treats and made sure you had enough that you'd make yourself quite ill on them, thus never desiring them again."

The way his eyes twinkle as he says it, the way he's tucking my hair behind my ear, the way this is just so comfortable and easy even while it's not easy at all to find private time together right now—there's no *I could fall in love with this man.*

There's *I'm already there.*

"Why have I not taken you up on that offer to have your roommate supervise my children so that we can see each other more often?" he murmurs while I settle back against him.

the spite date

"Because she's been distracted and busy and stressed about her sister. I'm not sure she's sleeping more than three or four hours a night right now. And also because you know you're going to miss your boys when you leave in a few weeks."

"But I shall miss you too."

"I can come see you easier than they can. And I'll have you all to myself then."

"I'll be terribly busy for some of those weeks."

"Griff's playing a series in LA not long after you leave, and I've never seen LA at all. Vacations haven't been a high priority the past ten years." And things have finally been picking up for the burger bus, so I could afford to take a week or so off.

"Why are you so very perfect?"

I shake my head. "That's the afterglow talking."

"No, I've thought it to myself more than once lately. When you showed Eddie how to throw a baseball after lunch the other day. When you bandaged my finger after my failed attempt at cutting a watermelon. When you sent me that very kind text message reminding me that every parent has hard days, harder when they're flying solo. And then that other text message about touching your own breasts and thinking of me. That was top notch as far as perfection and text messages go."

"Those are little things that anyone could do."

He shifts on the table to face me, as serious as I've ever seen him, short of when he was mad after that dinner at Ryker's place. "But I trust you have pure intentions when you do them. You take in family and give them a place to belong in your heart. Not just your brothers. Daphne too. Me. My boys. Their mother. The world I grew up in, the world I've known my entire life—this idea of *family* was quite foreign. Even the relationship I've had with Lana—while we're rather good friends, were it not for the boys, I dare say she would not choose to be part of my life, and I could hardly blame her. But you have family. You make it, you have it, and you give it, you make me feel as though you *want* me to be part of it, and it feels wonderful to belong to something I never thought was real."

I blink against another wave of hot eyes and stinging nose. "You are a good man, Simon, and you deserve the very best family. It's an honor to share mine with you."

"Yours is the best for you being the heart of it."

"You're very good at making a girl feel special."

He smiles and kisses the tip of my nose. "You *are* special."

I snuggle closer to him, feeling his cock harden against my thigh as I kiss his neck. "You are too."

"Nowhere near as special as you."

"*Simon.*"

"Do you know every time you chide me, I think of ten more things I would like to do with you? And not all of them involve being naked."

"Just most?"

"Naturally. Though I am hoping that you arrive at my murder mystery dinner party in that red dress you wore on our first date."

"I still can't believe you're—no, wait. Yes, I can."

"I've been working on the script for it. It's terrible."

I laugh and press myself against his erection. "Is it?"

"The worst thing I've ever written."

"Simon."

He slides his hand over my hip, smiling. "Truly. You wearing the red dress will be necessary to distract everyone from realizing it's rubbish."

There's a knock at the back door.

"Bloody hell," Simon mutters.

"Boss? Just heard on the radio that a police cruiser is headed this way."

I growl softly.

Probably Logan.

He's hung out near my bus a few times this summer, scaring people away. It would fit for him to be the one to catch us out here.

Simon smiles at me. "Will you growl at me like that the next time we have an hour alone? I quite like it."

How is it possible that I'm both irritated and the happiest I've felt in ages? "I quite like you."

He scoots off the table and reaches for his pants. "Do you have a list of secret parking places so that we might do this again tomorrow night?"

"I'll work on that."

"Have you other clothes?"

"Floor of the kitchen."

"Good. I wouldn't want anyone else to have the pleasure of seeing you in only your lingerie."

My breasts tingle. "Say *lingerie* again."

"Tomorrow, when you send me the secret midnight bus location. Though I suppose I could simply buy this place instead. Then I would give us permission to be on the land."

"*Simon*."

He grins.

And then he pockets my underwear.

Both the thong and the bra.

Butch knocks at the door again. "Got about three minutes, boss."

Simon disappears into the kitchen and reemerges with the rest of my clothes. We rush through getting dressed, and then he's kissing me hard and fast before dashing out the back door.

"We'll follow you," he calls. "Just in case you have trouble."

He's my trouble.

My favorite trouble.

And I don't mind at all.

In fact, I think I love it.

32

Nothing swoonier than murder

Bea

By the time Simon's murder mystery dinner arrives, I've almost forgotten that his whole intention was to upstage Lucinda Camille. I've been too busy seeing him and his boys at every opportunity to even care why he wanted to do it in the first place.

But the day of the dinner, I get a very solid reminder.

"Logan Camille seriously sat in the parking lot next to your burger bus *all day*?" Daphne says as she drives us to Simon's place now that the dinner is upon us.

"All day. Someone would start to approach, he'd make noise or stretch or something, and four out of every five potential customers recognized him and essentially ran away. Worst day I've had in like two weeks."

"Such a fucking *dick*."

"Either he's mad that Simon's upstaging his mother by hosting an invite-only version of her favorite event tonight, or Logan thinks it's my fault traffic has slowed down for Jake's restaurant. Which is crazy. I've hardly thought about JC Fig at all since Simon took me on that spite date, and I definitely haven't said anything. Not anywhere near the way the Camilles trash-talk me."

the spite date

She grins. "Who wants to think about a dumbass ex when you have the perfect rebound man coming by every day?"

I stare at her.

She slides a look at me. "What?"

"I don't think this is a rebound."

Her smile grows bigger. "Yeah, for the amount of time you're spending with his kids too? It's definitely more than that. Just wanted to make sure *you* knew it."

"He's just—he's fun. And funny. And kind, but not in the way that makes me think he's putting on an act so that I'll like him. He'll give me shit and also tell me I'm *brilliant* or *marvelous*, and sometimes he says things that make me feel like I'm...well, special."

"Bea. Boyfriends are supposed to make you feel special."

"And he's doing a better job of it than any other boyfriend I've had before."

"Impressive, considering how much you *haven't* had sex since you started dating."

"Lana's mom's went into the hospital with an infection a while ago. She's freaking out because she doesn't know what's happening, so Lana's had to be at the hospital more or less full time. It's so sad, and so hard. So Simon's been on solo parenting duty practically the whole time since he asked me to be his girlfriend."

"She deserves an entire spa week for what she's been through."

We lapse into silence because both of us know the only time Lana will ever have a full week to herself will be after her mom passes.

We make it to the driveway entrance before Daphne speaks again, and I'm not surprised when she changes the subject.

"According to my sources, there are at least nineteen rooms in this mansion, excluding the bathrooms. According to my knowledge of teenage boys, they won't leave the basement if it has food and gaming systems, which it definitely does because Simon's loaded and enjoys being able to buy his kids whatever they want for the first time in his life. So that leaves like a dozen rooms for you two to sneak off to for a quick shag."

"Daphne. I've been in the house before."

"Do the bedrooms have locks? Asking for me too. I'm fucking tired and might actually need a nap."

There's something going on with her that she's not telling me. Something more than worrying about Margot.

I haven't been pushing it when she lies to me, because I know she'll talk to me when she's ready.

Daph's complicated sometimes. Who wouldn't be with how she grew up and then was basically kicked out of her family?

She pulls to a stop at the gate, rolls her window down, and grins at Butch, who's waiting with a clipboard. "Hey, I was just thinking about you."

"I'm not interested in a second job as your on-site chef," he says.

"His burgers are almost as good as yours," Daphne tells me. "If he ever figures out your secret ingredient, you're toast."

I wave at him from the passenger seat. "Hey, Butch. Did you win or lose to get the gate job tonight?"

"Won."

"Nicely done."

"Thanks for driving a small car instead of your bus. Pull on through to the house."

Daphne follows orders, and we wind our way up the driveway to park her Camry next to Ryker's truck. We climb out of the car and follow a family of four toward the front door.

Simon's home here is a three-story mansion, with a stucco exterior, a red-shingled roof, the courtyard and lawn behind where I've spent several evenings, and landscaping that hadn't been kept up over the years before he bought it.

Now, the flower beds are freshly turned over, most of them brimming with young plants that make the beds lining the curved brick walk to the front door feel fresh and new. The stucco needs repainting, but it's low on Simon's priority list.

He has at least six years of living here when he's not off doing his famous actor thing.

Which is still weird to think about.

He doesn't feel like a famous actor.

He just feels like my very funny, very sexy, very kind, hot British boyfriend.

Daphne and I pass through a second security check at the door, where we're each given manila envelopes with our names on them, and then are directed through the foyer to the hallway on the left. The octagonal brick-colored floor tiles and the flowery wallpaper is the same as it was when Mrs. Young opened the house for Mr. Young's wake.

"Remind you of your family's vacation house in the Hamptons?" I ask Daphne.

She shakes her head. "Right size, wrong vibes."

"How so?"

"It's like someone died in here. And not in a murder mystery."

"You don't know?"

"Know what?"

"Mr. Young *did* die in here. Had dementia pretty bad in the end. Mrs. Young cared for him at home until he passed, and then she had his wake here."

She points to a framed photograph sitting on a knitted lace doily on one of the side tables. "Is that them?"

"Yep."

"Why does Simon still have their photos up in the house?"

"They were selling the house as-is, furnishings and all, and he's put his focus on fixing up the bedrooms and the basement for a game room for the boys ahead of taking care of the common areas."

"It adds quite the ghastly touch, does it not?" Simon strolls out of a room on the right to join us. He's in a black suit with a crisp white shirt, his hair styled to look like he's just rolled out of bed.

And he is, naturally, smiling widely in a way that makes my belly dip and my own smile pop out back at him.

"Welcome to the Grand Persimmon Hotel," he says. "I see you've received the information about your rooms and your stay. I am Archibald Ninnington, and I shall be your host this evening. If there is anything you require, anything at all, please do not hesitate to request assistance."

He puts one hand to my waist and kisses my cheek, and my entire body flushes with the contact. "And you may call me anything you wish, of course. That dress will never cease to be stunning on you."

Yep.

The dress.

The red dress.

With the new panties he hand-delivered yesterday.

They're also red.

The lace is more sheer.

And I'm not wearing a bra, because his kids are headed to a sleepover when the murder mystery dinner is over.

"Is this place haunted, Archie?" Daphne asks. She's in a killer black dress that highlights her curves, and she spent an hour on her makeup and had her hair's green and blue highlights touched up too.

"Certainly not." Simon winks at her. "Or perhaps I should say, not yet."

"I was going to ask if I could be the dead body, but I think I'd rather be the ghost."

Simon still has his hand on my waist, and he's drawing circles on it with his thumb and lighting my entire body on fire. "Four people have already asked to be the dead body."

"How many want to be the ghost?" Daphne asks.

"Only you." He shifts to look at me again, and his smile widens even more, as if he's aware of the effect his hand is having on me. "Bea? Would you also like to be the dead body?"

I smile back. "Nope. I want to figure out who did it before anyone else. And I can't do that if I'm dead."

"Marvelous." He beams at me.

I get tingly in all the good places to be tingly. I am so gone for this man.

"Are you the dead body tonight?" I ask him.

"Alas, my security team would have my head if I fooled them into thinking I were dead, so I must remain alive and healthy." He drops his hand from my waist and gestures for both of us to go ahead of him. "Do come in. We're waiting for a few more guests before dinner can begin. I highly recommend becoming familiar with all that our resort has to offer. And, of course, your roles."

"Is there a prize for best actor?" Daphne asks.

"Does your host have two teenage boys who wish to be rewarded for everything from waking up in the morning to not breathing on one another when it becomes annoying?"

I smile so hard I'm almost laughing. "So the kids are participating?"

"Bah. The children have all escaped to the basement to play billiards and table tennis and air hockey and video games while gorging themselves on the entire supply of pizza from two different restaurants."

"Good."

"Indeed."

I smile at him.

He keeps smiling at me.

Daphne pokes me. "C'mon, Bea. I smell appetizers. I don't miss a lot about fancy parties, but *the food*. The food better be good. Like, you have no idea where my expectations are."

Simon and I break eye contact.

Or more, he breaks eye contact to look at Daphne, blinking once like he's forgotten who she is and why she's here.

"The food is marvelous. As is the company." He snags Daphne's envelope. "I just remembered this packet is incomplete. I shall join you shortly with corrections."

"Do the corrections require your computer?" I ask.

He barks out a laugh. "No, it's been hung up worse than usual today, so I borrowed Lana's laptop to put the finishing touches on our murder." He smiles at me once more and presses a kiss to my forehead. "I'll join you again momentarily."

Daph and I both watch as he strolls the other way down the hallway and turns into another room that, if I'm remembering the floor plans right from my days of spying on the house's listing, should be his office. I haven't made it much past the living room or kitchen when I've been inside here yet.

"Is he turning me into a ghost?" Daph whispers.

My heart does that thing where it feels like it's hugging itself.

I know he wrote the script for the murder mystery himself.

He told me so.

Called it *grand fun* in a text, in fact. And also confessed that it was putting him behind on his deadline for his contractually obligated script, but said that the break was good for his creativity and revisions.

He ignored me when I told him again to get a faster computer.

"I think he might be," I whisper back.

And it's making me swoon just a little more.

This is *not* a rebound.

This is the best relationship I've ever had.

33

Is that a dead body in your dining room, or are you just happy to see me?

Simon

This murder mystery dinner is going swimmingly well.

We've moved past canapes in the sunken living room and are now dining on a feast of lobster rolls and a fresh garden salad. The serving staff are keeping wine glasses full, and dessert of lemon drizzle cake is awaiting us.

Two dozen guests are situated at the long table in the formal dining room, all of them laughing and dining and drinking and speculating on who will die and who will figure it out, with the occasional question about when or if I intend to redecorate.

All of the furniture stayed in the house, and as my boys would say, the vibes in this room are vibing for a murder mystery tonight. Add in the thunderstorm that has rolled in since the evening begun, with lightning illuminating the windows along the wall overlooking the overgrown gardens that have not yet been tackled, and they are quite correct.

There are old plastic flower arrangements for centerpieces—no candles, of course, in deference to Bea and her siblings—and Pinky found the most ancient lace tablecloth that perfectly fits the monstrosity of a dining room table.

Truly, the table seats all twenty-four of us. This room is large enough to justify coats of armor and national flags, as if it were a king's summer palace dining room.

I hate it normally—the physical space reminds me too much of the emotional space in my childhood dining room—but it suits my purposes this evening.

Bea's brothers have been entertaining Lana with stories of things they did in their youth so that she might be more prepared for things that our boys might do. It's lovely to see her getting a break, as she looks quite on the verge of a breakdown if she didn't have a night off from caring for her mother.

The parents of several teenagers are talking amongst themselves, sometimes pulling Lana or me into their conversation.

Daphne is flitting about, being every bit the agent of chaos that I expected her to be, which was what made rewriting her part into a ghost remarkably easy.

Quincy Thomas is sneaking photographs of everything while his partner, Wendell, chides him.

The doors to both the bedroom hallways and the bedrooms themselves are locked, as is my office door, as I was quite aware of the risk I was taking in inviting the man Bea tells me is the town gossip.

The potential rewards outweighed the risks though. No doubt the entire town will be aware of this event before morning, which is half the point.

I've once again put myself fully in the willful position of irritating Bea's ex and his whole obnoxious family, who have continued to interfere with her desire to simply serve burgers out of a converted bus alongside the other food vans in town on the days when I'm not assisting her.

And then there's the best part of this evening.

Bea herself.

She's glowing. Her makeup is not nearly as pronounced as it was on our first date, and her hair is down instead of up, and she is absolutely radiant. She has allowed me to fully monopolize her attention, making me regret inviting anyone else this evening.

It's difficult to keep my hands to myself as she and I trade parenting horror stories and while I pretend I'm not plotting every way that I might steal her away to mess her lipstick and peel that red shimmery fabric off her to discover if she's worn the undergarment I gifted her yesterday.

Being near her makes me so very happy, and when she smiles back at me—how have I never known before how wonderful the world could be?

"Wait until your boys hit the quacking stage," she's saying as the temporary staff I've hired for the evening begin to remove the dinner plates.

I pull myself back to the present. "I beg your pardon?"

"The quacking stage," she repeats. "There was a week one summer where Hudson and Griff refused to say anything to me unless it was the word *quack*. And it wasn't as many summers ago as you'd think it would've been."

"That's…" I trail off, oddly at a loss for words, and only partially because my mind was occupied with fantasies of stripping her naked.

"Weird," she supplies, her eyes beginning to twinkle as though she is aware of my thoughts. "It was very weird."

"Wherever do they get the ideas for their madness?" I ask her.

"I think there's a secret handbook for teenage boys."

"Terrifying."

She hums softly in agreement as she sips her wine.

Her eyes meet mine again, hot and hinting at her own desire to leave the guests behind and slip away for our own private dinner, and I once again kick myself for making this a public spectacle.

Lana rises from her seat, and the lights in the dining room flicker off.

Lightning makes a dramatic entrance from the side windows in a gift from the heavens that I could not have timed better had I scripted it in, and then all is dark again.

A woman screams.

Gasps follow, which are quickly drowned out by the thunder crashing upon the house.

Bea grabs my thigh.

My cock springs to attention so quickly that I get a pain in my gut.

Naturally.

I've been fantasizing nonstop about Bea touching me more, and now she's grabbing my leg, quite high in fact, and I would like to pull her into a dark room and kiss her until we're pawing each other's clothing off and going at it like rabbits.

But her breathing is suddenly unsteady, and while I'm having fantasies of her naked and sweaty, she might be on the verge of a panic attack.

"It's part of the event," I murmur, leaning into her and inhaling her perfume as a thump sounds. "All is well."

She blows out a slow breath. "Right. Right."

She doesn't move her hand from my thigh.

So I take advantage of the moment to cover her hand with mine while the thunder subsides and my guests murmur amongst themselves.

Such soft skin. Capable hands. I'd like to trace her fingers with my tongue.

Again.

And then I'd like to trace every other part of her with my tongue as well.

I'm cataloging those parts in my brain when thunder crashes outside again and the lights flicker back on.

Lana is gone.

Daphne is gone.

And I have a raging erection that is preventing me from rising and announcing the start of the murder mystery.

Everyone stares at me, and it's as though I'm a fledgling thespian who has forgotten to memorize his lines.

And I realize there's a problem bigger than my flagpole of a cock.

My dead body is missing.

It's supposed to be draped across the center of the table.

"Ah," I start, only to be interrupted.

"Wooooo*ooooooooo*," a creepy voice woo-woos from the hallway. "I am the ghost of Devyn Persimmon, the first person murdered in the Grand Persimmon Hotel, and I am here to tell you—"

"Ahhh! She's dead!" Quincy Thomas screams.

He flings his chair back, toppling it, and I forget all about the boner situation as I leap to my feet too.

Lana is supposed to be—

"*Oh my god*, don't kill me for real," Lana gasps.

She sits up behind Quincy, covered in fake blood with a prop knife sticking out of her chest, having barely missed being squished by his chair.

"Sorry," Quincy says. "Sorry. Sorry."

He straightens his chair.

Lana gives him a hard glare that I've been the recipient of more than several times. "Can I be dead again now?"

"You really should've fallen in the middle of the table. That would've been more dramatic."

She was supposed to fall in the middle of the table.

Perhaps the lights came back on too quickly considering the costume change necessary. Or possibly she was afraid of the lightning showing her position too soon.

Or possibly she enjoys making me squirm when things don't go as scripted, which is equally likely.

Lana glares at Quincy harder, and I feel a trickle of that glare bounce off his shirt buttons and deflect towards me as well.

"I really, really like her," Bea murmurs to me.

"Yes, yes," I say to Lana. "Do carry on being dead now."

"Thank you."

The mother of my children flops back onto the rug behind her chair, splaying herself dramatically in what I am quite positive is a mockery of the way that I tend to die while in various roles.

Legs askew, one arm over her head, hair splayed out, tongue hanging out, blank eyes staring at the ceiling.

People are gawking now.

"That's creepy," one of the parents of two boys hanging out with mine says.

"Is it just me, or is she laying exactly the same way that Simon died in that one episode of that cop show?"

Lana snickers. As much as she can while pretending to be dead.

Bea giggles.

"Wooooooooooooooooooooo," Daphne says. "Death has come again. And if you don't find the killer, this will not be the last death of the evening."

"Bea did it," Hudson announces.

Bea straightens and gapes at him. "*Excuse* you?"

"Jealous lover. It's always the jealous lover."

Ryker shoves him. "Your knife's missing, bro, and she's all the way across the table on the other end from the body."

Wendell Thomas rises on Quincy's other side. "I'm a detective! I'll get to the bottom of this."

"You made Wendell the detective?" Bea whispers to me. "Quincy's gonna hate that."

I grin at her. "I thought it might add some tension to the evening."

"Now it bothers me the way you smile when you're diabolical."

"Don't touch the body!" a woman yells.

"Quincy! Don't touch the body!" Wendell echoes.

"Wooo*oooo*, touching the dead body will put a currrrrsssse on yooooouuuuuuooooooouuu," Daphne moans.

Bea leans into me and squeezes my hand. "Thank you for making her a ghost. She's in heaven right now."

the spite date

"Far be it from me to disappoint a lady." I clear my throat and raise my voice. "If everyone could please stay calm, I will ring the authorities. Pinky. My phone, if you please."

"Cell towers are down, sir," Pinky says from the doorway.

His performance is woefully lacking, exactly as he informed me it would be when he lost whatever game the three of my security agents performed to decide which one of them would have to play a role and which two would be allowed to merely observe.

"Ah. Then do bring me my phone if the towers come back up," I reply.

He grunts and leaves the dining room.

Everyone stares at me.

Everyone except for Quincy, who gasps again. *Ryker's gone.*

A thump sounds in the next room.

And after a moment of staring at one another, half the guests flee toward the hallway.

"Is he murdered too?"

"Or did he do the murder?"

"He noticed Hudson's knife was missing."

"Where did that noise come from?"

"Stop! Stop! You're contaminating the crime scene! Everyone has to stay here!" Wendell stomps his foot, then rushes after everyone fleeing the room as though he might stop them.

Bea remains at the table, watching half the guests go, her hand inching higher on my leg.

"Did you see what happened?" Hudson asks her.

He, too, is among those lingering behind.

She frowns at him as he stops behind her chair. "Did you have a knife at the beginning of dinner?"

"Nope."

"Why didn't you ask for one?"

"Bea. It was lobster rolls and a salad."

"You didn't want to cut your cucumber?"

He starts to chuckle.

She waves a hand. "Never mind. Of course you didn't. Neanderthal. By the way, you have some dressing still on your shirt."

She grabs her serviette and dabs at it, unfortunately taking her hand off my leg in the process.

He bats her hand away. "Seriously? Is this part of your role, or are you being Bea right now?"

"So this part never changes?" I ask her.

She grabs his arm tighter and attacks the balsamic stain on his white shirt with a serviette dipped in ice water. "This part never changes. I wiped gravy off of Ryker's shirt last Thanksgiving, and he's the oldest. With a now fully developed prefrontal cortex."

Hudson takes the cloth from her and finishes cleaning himself. "Want to go look at the body?"

She grins at him. "Of course. Simon—Archibald—whoever you are—are you coming to look at the body too?"

"*Wooooooooooooooooooo*, more death lurks in the corners," Daphne intones.

But her voice—it's coming from the walls.

Tinny.

As though—well.

That's fascinating.

"Does this house have an old intercom system?" Bea asks.

"It does, though I confess, I had yet to figure out how to work it."

"Hope there's nothing else in here you haven't figured out yet because Daph will, and you might regret the next thing."

"So I should *not* mention that there's supposedly a pool with an electric cover that will slide off somewhere in the garden?"

"Seriously?"

"Yes?"

"Why did you say *yes* like it's a question?"

"Because there is, but now I suspect I should pretend there is not?"

"I disabled it," Lana says from the floor. "You don't even want to know the nightmares I had when I found out about it. I can only sleep at night for knowing the boys have no idea it exists."

"I think I just had all of the same nightmares," Bea replies. "Thank you. You can go back to being dead now."

"Can you do me a favor and move my body into a normal sleeping position? Maybe get me a pillow too? If I have to be dead, I'm taking a nap."

"Absolutely. I heard it's been hell in the hospital."

"For your sake and mine, I'm not going into details."

"*Don't move the body!*" Wendell shrieks. "My god, it's bad enough it's talking."

Bea smiles, making those adorable dimples pop broader in her cheeks.

She's so bloody addictive, and I sincerely hope I can convince her to stay the night.

Lana's been banished from the hospital and needs sleep, but the way she hugged the boys when she arrived first suggested she might need them more.

"Why don't you get some photos of the body since Quincy's going to want to share them all over socials tomorrow anyway, and then we can make her, ah, final resting position more comfortable?" Bea says to Wendell.

He sighs heavily. "That's why you invited us, isn't it?" he says to me.

"I made him because Quincy was the only person in high school that Jake and Logan got away with torturing more than they tortured me, and if you're going to war against the Camilles, you fucking go to war," Lana says. "Plus that other part where we're nice to people who can see through their act just on principle."

Wendell growls and pulls out his phone. "Look really good and dead. I need to get all of this prop blood. The business association's murder mystery dinner doesn't have bodies that look as good as you do."

Several other guests snap photos of Lana as well as I trail Bea around the table so that she may also get a better look. Some of the guests who had fled to the sunken living room return to study Lana in her role as the dead body as well.

"What's in the living room?" Hudson asks one of them.

"Not your brother. But an old statue fell off the buffet."

"*Wooooooooooooooooooooo*," Daphne says over the intercom. "The killer left a clue on the knife. Woooo*ooooooooooooooooooo*."

Bea squats in her dress, the fabric riding up her thighs, and I have to swallow hard.

Hudson glares at me.

He's returning to school in a mere two weeks, so I let him have the fun of glaring.

Rather suspect I'll miss him when he's gone. Not that I'll be far behind in leaving, but he's an enjoyable chap, and I'll return long before he does.

"Hmm," Bea says.

"What's *hmm*?" one of the dads of some of the children downstairs says.

"It's not Hudson's missing dinner knife, unless he's the only one who didn't have a knife that matched the rest of the set."

"Or unless a prop knife can't look like the rest of the knives," the dad says.

They both look at me.

I stare back in full offended glory, which makes Bea laugh, which makes me smile because I will never not smile when she laughs.

She squints at the knife attached to Lana's abdomen again. "Do we get fingerprint kits?" she asks me.

"Surely the sheriff or the police will bring some, but we intend to solve the crime before they get here."

She snags a serviette off the nearest chair and uses it to touch the knife.

"Ow, ow, my stab wounds," Lana says dramatically.

the spite date

"*Don't mess with the crime scene!*" Wendell shrieks.

"Or reanimate the body," the dad says. He squats next to Bea. "You're Bea Best. We didn't get to say hi earlier. I'm Torrence. Flying solo tonight. My ex—"

My eye twitches. "Have you inspected the body to your liking, Torrence?"

Hudson coughs.

Lana snickers.

"The *dead* body," I add. "The very dead body."

Bea grins up at me. "I'm good. And I should go find my other brother."

She rises, and I watch Torrence to make sure he doesn't try to sneak a peek up Bea's dress.

He quickly looks back at Lana's body, and I realize I need to growl again to make sure he's not checking out my ex's breasts.

I should have only invited single mothers when I could not invite a married couple.

No single fathers.

Bea slips her hand around my elbow. "Will you show me to the parlor, Archie? I'm afraid of being alone with a killer on the loose."

And just like that, I no longer care about Torrence.

Or dead bodies.

Or the way the lights have flickered again with another booming crack of lightning and thunder that come near-simultaneously.

Bea is touching me.

She's here.

Having a lovely time.

Nothing else matters.

34

Secrets, secrets, secrets

Bea

I don't want to go back to the living room with the other guests. But I do want to solve the murder.

Maybe not as I want to convince Simon that we need to pull a Ryker and disappear too, but I can do that after I solve a murder.

"What's Ryker doing?" I murmur to Simon as soon as we're out of earshot, his hand warm and solid in mine.

"Exploring the secret passages of the house, I presume."

"*Secret*—" I cut myself off as I realize I just shrieked that, and lower my voice. "Secret passages?"

"Yes, his role is to spy on the evening's festivities from the secret passages around the house. He has my phone number in the event he encounters any unexpected occupants."

"There are secret passages?" I'm flushing hot and cold at the same time.

Secret passages.

But also, tight, enclosed spaces.

I shiver.

Simon squeezes my hand tighter and pulls me into his body. "They're quite cramped, so I had no intention of assigning the secret passage spy role to you. Nor Daphne. I don't wish for her to know how to navigate my home without my knowledge."

"But Ryker can?"

"Do you truly think it likely your more reclusive brother would enjoy that?"

"Is that why you gave him that role? So he can have a break from people?"

He smiles.

My eyes get hot. "But he can still be here to tell you to—"

"Keep your goddamn hands off my sister," someone says in the wall.

Simon turns to a painting of Mr. Young that's missing an eyeball, which you would only notice if you looked closely.

"Oh my god," I say when I'm supposed to tell Ryker to back off, that *Simon is my boyfriend* and *he has permission to touch me.*

Which Ryker knows.

"Fucking cool party trick," my brother adds. "Do your kids know?"

Simon shudders. "I prefer my head to remain on my neck, and it would not if their mother knew that they knew."

"But if not for their mother?" I ask.

"We would play hide-and-seek for hours and I would have to replace my security agents every other week because of their frustration with us."

He turns away from the photo as a couple I only know a little bit heads our way from the sunken living room. "There aren't any clues in there," the man reports. "I need a better look at that body. Hey. What does your sheet say? Do you know who Lana was having an affair with?"

"I know who you're having an affair with," I reply. "In the script. In the script, I mean. I know about your affair in the script. Not real life."

His wife is grinning at me as she gasps in mock horror. "Gerald! How could you!"

She pretends to slap him.

"Brava," Simon murmurs.

"If you weren't such a cold fish, Nancy, then maybe I wouldn't have had to find comfort in Lana's arms!" he bellows.

Simon beams at both of them as more people come running.

"Gerald was cheating on Nancy with Lana," someone says.

"You bitch!" Quincy screams at him. "She told me she was only sleeping with *me*!"

Wendell gasps. "You cheated on me *with a woman?*"

"It was your snoring, Wendell. I cannot live with your snoring anymore. It makes me want to plunge a knife into your body the same way I plunged it into hers to get you both out of my life!"

"Are you fucking serious?" Daphne says over the intercom. "Quincy. You're not supposed to confess."

"Maybe I'm not confessing! Maybe I'm not working alone! Maybe I'm so brokenhearted that my lady boo was snatched from me by this Neanderthal that I'm speaking in overemotional metaphors!"

"You know this is why they never let you be the killer at the business association murder mystery," Wendell says.

"I did not know that," Simon murmurs to me.

"Could've asked."

"Next time."

"Is he really the killer?" Hudson asks Simon.

"I think he is," I answer. "The killer's left-handed. You can tell by the knife angle."

Simon lifts his brows at me. "Truly, you figured that out?"

"She's watched too many of those shows where an amateur detective helps the police solve crimes, and dude, the left-handed killer thing is really too easy," Hudson says.

"I thought that too, but I didn't know if the knife angle was intentional, or if any of us were supposed to be pretending to be left-handed," one of the women says.

"Also, Lana was sleeping with me as well," Torrence says.

"And me," another man adds.

the spite date

"And your wife," Lana herself says from the doorway. "I was actually sleeping with half of you."

It's creepy seeing her coated in blood with a knife sticking out of her dress but still walking around fully alive.

And weirder to see her smiling about her role.

"I warned her she had to have enemies if she were to play the dead body," Simon murmurs to me.

"Good to know what you do to people in your scripts," I murmur back.

He winces.

"So you have to handcuff me now," Quincy says to Wendell. "That comes next, right? The detective has to get pushy and handsy with the murderer?"

"Or we may all retire to the dining room or living room to finish enjoying dessert," Simon says quickly.

"Can I keep being the ghost?" Daphne says over the intercom.

"Can you truly hear us?" Simon says.

"That's my secret."

I look at the painting that was hiding Ryker a minute ago, but instead, I see my brother standing next to it. "She's listening in through your phone, isn't she?"

He smiles at me.

Ryker.

Smiling in public.

A real smile.

"Victory," Simon murmurs.

Ryker's smile almost dips a little, like he doesn't want to admit Simon gave him a thrill in letting him in on the secret, but he can't suppress it.

I blink quickly as my eyes start to water. I haven't ever dated anyone who went out of their way to get Ryker to smile.

Not that any of my other boyfriends had a secret passage in their house, but Simon didn't have to show it to him.

The boys rush in from downstairs asking for more food, and some of the other guests grab Simon's attention with more questions about the house and his plans.

Someone touches my arm, and I turn to find the mom of one of the boys who's been hanging out with Charlie and Eddie. "Bea? You have that new burger bus, don't you? And you do parties? My husband's fortieth birthday is coming up, and I was thinking surprise block party."

The next hour or two is a steady stream of questions about the burger bus and town gossip and whispers about Simon and the house while we make eye contact and smile at each other across the room, and eventually, I realize half the guests have left.

I knew Ryker would take off early, and he did hug me goodbye before he departed, but I don't realize how late it's gotten until Hudson hugs me too. "He's my favorite," he whispers.

"Your brother?"

"Your boyfriend. He's nice, but not too nice. That's good for you."

"What does that even mean?"

"He can keep up when you get petty."

I snort-laugh. "That's possibly not the healthiest part of a relationship. And I don't do petty *that* often."

"Still, a guy who'll show you his flaws is a lot better than a guy who pretends he's perfect and then dumps you after stealing all of your hopes and dreams." My brother hugs me again. "Have fun. Be safe. Call if you need me."

He takes off, leaving me pondering how unexpectedly right he is about relationships, and wondering if that's why he hasn't yet gotten up the courage to ask Molly out.

But that all takes a backseat to the butterflies fluttering in excitement in my belly as Simon appears at my side again. "My children are about to depart," he murmurs.

"I heard."

"I would very much like to check for myself on the status of that present I left you yesterday."

the spite date

"I think I have time to help you with that."

His eyes light up, and my god, the swoon happening in my belly and my starry-eyed vagina right now...

I am so utterly gone for this man.

Daphne yawns beside me. "Wow, I am *so beat*. Must be time to go."

And I love her too.

Simon presses a key into my hand. "Slip into my office. It's just beyond the front door on the right. I'll come and get you when everyone else has left."

I'd ask if we need to be secretive, but the boys aren't gone yet, and we're still easing into me being a part of their lives. Hanging out at an escape room or for a dinner party with two dozen people is one thing.

Them knowing their father is making plans to shag me is another.

"Next time you do a murder mystery dinner, call me beforehand," Daphne says to Simon. "I have ideas."

He smiles at her. "Can the world handle the two of us conspiring together?"

"If not, it'll be a fun way to go."

We say our goodbyes to the remaining guests and head for the front door.

Daph hugs me and leaves.

I dash the last few paces to the door on the right and use the key to let myself in.

And when I turn around and take in the office—I crack up.

Leave it to Simon to have left even the office the same.

There's an ancient wooden desk. A modern office chair that seems lopsided. Plastic plants and sagging ancient bookshelves that I suspect are lined with books that have been here for a few decades.

The only things clearly new here are two closed laptops and two printers, one of which has overflowed itself and is blinking an out-of-paper message.

I used to find Griff's printer like this too. Practically every day of high school.

If it wasn't homework—and that one year, it definitely wasn't—it was baseball plays.

He loved having it in a physical form that he could hold.

And after years of picking up after Griff's printer, habit has me squatting to grab Simon's papers that have fallen to the floor, musing that this is probably why his computer was running slower.

He told me it regularly prints things all on its own.

I don't mean to look at the papers, but as I flip the pile over to put it on his desk, the title catches my eye.

```
              The Mad Corn Dog Ambulance
                   By Simon Luckwood
                    Pilot: Betrayal
```

The...*what?*

Is this—is *this* what he's been working on?

Put it down, Bea. Walk away. Ask him later.

I ignore myself and keep reading.

```
                         Act One
    An ambulance converted to operate as a food van parked
                  on a country road — dusk

      A woman with red hair and a T-shirt bearing the logo
      for Mad Emergency Corn Dogs cleans up inside the
      converted ambulance after a long day without enough
      customers. A man steps out of a truck and approaches.
                    She does not see him.


                       PORTER JACQUES
    Sell more corn dogs when you don't betray people, Mad.

    Madonna "Mad" Bigley jumps in surprise, then aims her
                   cleaning spray at him.


                         MAD BIGLEY
    Get lost, Porter. You can scare my customers away for
    one day, but you have no idea who you're dealing with.


                           PORTER
    Everyone knows who they're dealing with when they deal
    with you. Fancy city girl who had to come home to raise
```

the spite date

```
her brothers. Thinks that makes you special. Well, it
                            doesn't.
```

My heart starts a familiar beat as I scan the rest of the page, then the next.

It's not butterflies fluttering my heart.

It's not swooning.

It's not eager anticipation or infatuation or love.

No, my heart is cramping.

It's cramping the same way that it cramped when Jake told me it was over and I realized he was taking my restaurant.

It's cramping the same way it did when Will told me I spent too much on groceries to make him gourmet meals every night and it just wasn't going to work.

The same way it did when Andreas took off to do the Appalachian Trail, solo, because *you're just a bummer with all of this worry over everything with your brothers, Bea, and I need to find the good parts of myself again. I thought someone who did something selfless would be less self-involved.*

It might even be cramping the same way it did when my phone rang in my dorm at midnight with Ryker calling to tell me the house burned down and that Dad didn't make it out after going back in for Mom. That neither of them made it out.

I scan three more pages, confirming what the burning in my eyes and the cramping in my stomach are already telling me.

Simon's secret project?

The one he's been working on all summer? The one he's told me he'll share with me once he's put the sparkling finishing touches on it?

It's about me.

About my life.

He's telling my story, *without permission*, for his own personal gain.

It's Jake all over again, except worse.

Because Simon knows what Jake did to me.

He knows what Jake stole from me.

And he willingly did it too.

I snap photos of the first two pages of the script, and then I call Daphne. "Are you still here?"

"Oh my god, Bea, what's wrong?"

"*Are you still here?*"

"Just left the driveway. I'm pulling over."

"I'm coming. Wait for me."

I don't say goodbye to Simon.

I just leave.

Because betrayal?

Again?

Fuck that.

35

When a man does something stupid...

Simon

It takes forever for the last of my guests to leave, and the moment the door is closed behind the last one, I dash toward my office.

My girlfriend is waiting for me.

I get to show her my bedroom.

Have her to myself the entirety of tonight.

No interruptions.

Just me and Bea and hours and hours and hours of enjoying her body and her laugh and her sighs and her moans and her smiles.

The boys are set, off to a sleepover with Tank trailing them to sit outside the house all evening.

Extra precaution.

Hopefully unnecessary.

And Lana left almost immediately after the boys as well.

There is no one who needs me for anything, except for Bea.

"Boss—" Butch says, but I cut him off with a wave of my hand.

"Everyone's gone. Bea's staying. All is well."

"Boss—" he says again, but I rush into my office, smiling in eager anticipation, only to find it empty.

I spin in a slow circle. "Bea?"

She's not here. Has she found one of the secret passages?

Unlikely. I warned her that they were cramped, and the entrances aren't immediately obvious, nor is there an entrance in my office.

Far more probable that she's gone in search of my bedroom.

And that thought has me smiling even broader as I backtrack, spinning to leave the office.

But Butch blocks the doorway.

"She left."

I stare at him dumbly. "Excuse me?"

"She left. Half hour or so ago."

I dig my phone out of my pocket and find zero waiting messages from her. "What? Why?"

He shrugs.

"Did she say anything?"

"Looked like she was crying."

I stare at him. "*Crying*?"

He nods, and my heart thumps ominously.

Did something happen to one of her brothers?

I dial Bea's number, and it instantly diverts to voicemail.

I try again.

Same result.

My heart shudders, and the tinny taste of adrenaline floods my tongue.

I dial Daphne's number.

She answers on the first ring. "Go fuck yourself in the ass with a rusty hanger."

And then she hangs up.

Panic claws at my throat. I look at Butch again.

He shrugs again.

"Her brothers—" I start.

"No accidents reported tonight."

I rub my chest over where an ominous feeling is growing.

the spite date

If something happened to one of her brothers, she would have told me.

Something clearly didn't happen to Daphne, because she answered and was quite angry.

Which suggests she's angry with *me*.

That *I've* done something wrong.

"Did she leave straightaway with Daphne?" My voice has gone hoarse with worry.

"Went into your office with the key."

"Yes, I gave her the key. How—how long was she in here?"

"A minute. Maybe three, tops. Not long."

I spin in a slow circle on shaky legs.

What on earth could she have—

It takes a moment to register the blinking printer light, and the papers haphazardly piled on my desk that should not be there.

With planning the murder mystery on top of my usual work, my office has been a terrible mess, but I picked everything up before dinner.

Dread makes my feet weigh a ton each as I cross the room to my desk.

I spy the first page of the first draft of my script, and everything around me spins in slow motion.

"Did she—did she print this?" I ask Butch.

But she couldn't have.

Not if she was only in the room for a minute or two.

Not when the script is only on my crotchety, slow, good-luck computer.

Slow or not, it's what I've used since I wrote *In the Weeds*.

Not even my boys will touch it. They complain it takes orders before you see the orders that you've given it, which puts homework assignments at risk of deletion and the wrong websites at risk of printing.

Which means I must have printed the first draft through some incorrect push of my mouse button or keystroke earlier today.

Bea could not have.

She could not have even pulled the document up on my laptop in two or three minutes, even if she'd known immediately where to look.

Not if Butch's timing is correct.

But if I accidentally printed it—then she could have picked it up.

I dial Lana without thinking.

"Simon, I have a high level of affection for you due to the fact that you're a very good co-parent, and for the fact that you got me a sober ride so I could get blitzed, and for an unexpectedly fun evening, and I completely understand how hard it's been for you to see Bea the past couple weeks, but if you're calling to tell me one of the boys puked and needs to be picked up, I'm sorry, you're going to have to handle it. I just got home and I am *dead* tired and I don't know how my mouth is still operating."

"Have you heard from Bea?"

Silence answers me.

The loud kind of silence.

Not the kind of silence that says she's fallen asleep.

The kind of silence that says she knows this is not a logical question that I should be asking if everything were perfectly fine in my world.

"*Have you heard from Bea?*" I repeat.

"Oh my god, was she in an accident?" Lana whispers.

"No. No, I don't think—no. Definitely not. I hope. I—I think she read the first draft of my script."

More silence.

Louder silence, if that's possible.

I sink into my desk chair, forgetting that it's wobbly, and topple right over.

"What was that?" Lana asks.

"You good, boss?" Butch says as he eyes me splayed across the floor.

"I'm fine." I'm not fine.

Bea's left.

Daphne wants me to give myself tetanus through my arsehole.

And I think I've fucked up the very best thing I've ever had.

"Why do you think Bea saw your script?" Lana asks.

the spite date

"It printed during dinner and was stacked oddly on my desk."

"You have *got* to get a new computer and printer system."

"I'm bloody well aware of that."

I push myself to sitting and slump against the desk drawers of the bloody awful desk that I should have prioritized replacing months ago.

The handles poke me in the back, but the discomfort is nothing compared to the roiling in my stomach and the pain in my chest.

My eyes burn. "How—how badly do you think I've fucked up?" I ask Lana.

"You need to go talk to her."

"She's not taking my calls."

"That's why you need to *go talk to her in person.*"

Of course.

Of course.

"Thank you. I don't—Lana, I don't know how to do this."

"Yes, you do. Quit thinking you don't, and do what your gut is telling you that you have to do for someone you care about."

My gut is telling me that I'm a fuckup who never should have tried a relationship in the first place.

But my heart is telling my gut to sod off.

I bolt up. "I'm going out," I tell Butch.

He and Pinky fall into step behind me on my way to the garage.

And I realize I don't even know where the keys are stored, so I slump into the vehicle's back seat like the idiot that I've become. "To Bea's apartment," I say.

When we arrive, my heart attempting to crack my ribs, they insist on accompanying me all the way up to her apartment.

Her bus is in the car park.

Daphne's car is as well.

I knock politely the first time.

More insistently the second time.

By the third time, I'm pounding, and a neighbor across the hall pokes his head out of his apartment. "Dude. It's like, after midnight."

I glare at him.

He slinks back inside his apartment.

I bang on Bea's door once more, and this time, a very cranky Daphne opens it just wide enough for me to see her face.

"Did you use Bea's life as inspiration for your script?" she demands before I can utter a word.

I am so very, very fucked.

"I'll throw it away," I tell Daphne. "Please. Please, I need to speak with Bea."

Daphne smiles.

It's not a friendly smile, nor a kind smile.

This is the feral smile of someone who has absolutely no use for me. "You'll throw it away," she repeats.

"The entire thing."

I will.

Fuck the script.

Fuck the studio.

Fuck the money and the consequences.

Daphne's no longer smiling, even a feral smile. "Here's the thing, Simon. This world you live in? The one where you have security around the clock for you and your family? The one where you can afford to throw money around and people recognize you out in public and want to be you? I've lived that life. I've known Hollywood *it* people like you before. And you can stand there and tell me all you want that you're different, that you'll really throw away a script that we both know you've already pitched to your studio, but I don't believe you. And I'm not letting you anywhere near the woman who saved my entire goddamn life right now because she deserves better."

I can't catch my breath. "*I will throw it away*. It—it means nothing to me—"

"Well, I can promise you, Bea's life means something to her. Having people like you use it for your own gain—that means something to her too. *I* don't deserve her. I know that. And I've never stabbed her in the back like you have."

the spite date

"It won't—I've fixed it. That was the wrong—"

"You never should've written it in the first place. You should have asked her. You should have fucking *asked her*."

"Please. Please let me speak with her."

"If she wants to talk to you, she knows how to find you. Until then, *leave her the fuck alone*."

The door slams in my face.

I lift a hand to knock again, but Pinky grabs it. "Let her sleep on it, boss."

"Got an audience," Butch adds quietly.

I swallow the bile rising in my throat.

I want to tell myself that this is why I don't do relationships.

Because I fuck them up.

Because there's always a stupid misunderstanding and unrealistic expectations.

But that's not what this is.

I have fucked up, yes.

This *is* my fault.

I should have told her. I should have told her where the script began and how I've changed it so that no one—*no one*—will ever realize she was the original inspiration. That my final drafts seldom resemble their original incarnation, generally because I *do* take inspiration from real life, and I am very, very aware of how much danger I would be putting myself and subsequently my boys' well-being in were I to ever be accused of malicious intent with one of my scripts.

Being broke is one thing.

Being destroyed is something else entirely.

And destroying the privacy and sanctity of someone else's story—someone I love—is an unbearable thought.

I have to fix this.

I have to fix this for her.

If she'll let me.

36

Secret menu item today is leave me the fuck alone

Bea

My head is a gelatinous mass of dull throbs and slushy slowness as I set up the bus for one of the last Monday food truck days at the lake this summer.

"You don't have to do this today," Hudson says to me.

He, Ryker, and Daphne haven't let me have a moment to myself since Saturday night unless I was in my own bathroom, and even then, they wouldn't let me take my phone with me.

They didn't make this big of a fuss when I broke up with Jake. Or Will. Or Andreas.

So either they think Simon hurt me more or our breakup is international gossip and they don't want me to know that the story of my life is once again tugging at heartstrings across the country.

Except this time with me as the cranky witch who dumped Simon. Because he betrayed me.

My eyes water. "What else am I going to do?" I ask Hudson.

"I don't know. Go blow shit up in a video game. Play with goats at Ryker's place. Bug Daphne at work. Take Griff up on his offer to fly you to Atlanta to see his games this week."

"And who'll run the bus?"

the spite date

"Me."

"I can't ask—"

"You're not asking, Bea. I'm telling. I'm telling you I'm a grown-ass adult with friends who can run a burger bus without getting arrested or shut down by the health department while you go take a vacation and clear your head and decide what you want to do."

Decide what I want to do.

That's always the question.

Well, Bea, you're primary guardian for your three brothers now, so what do you want to do?

Ryker's out of the house and you have more time, Bea, so what do you want to do?

Griff's gone too now, Bea, so what do you want to do?

Hudson's all grown up. Time to decide what you want to be when you grow up too, Bea.

Except there's never a forever answer.

There's a *right now* answer.

At first, it was *I want to survive.*

Then *I want to be involved like Mom and Dad were so that my brothers don't feel cheated, and it's not like I don't have the time.*

Followed by *Guess I'll drive a bus or volunteer with the PTA or use some of those free classes the college still gives me or take a pity job from one of their friends' parents to have something to do to bring in a little extra cash and plump up my resume.*

And then there was *I'm going to make my dad's dreams come true with the man I'm going to marry.*

Except it wasn't my dream.

Not really.

It was the same thing I've done since the call came.

I buried myself in looking for something that would fill the hole my parents left and help me walk in the shoes I had to fill, time and time again.

I keep trying to find ways to keep them alive.

Their memories.

Their dreams.

Their hopes for all of us.

Including their hopes that I'd settle down with a solid guy who loved me and live a life that made me happy. I thought they'd like Will. I thought they'd like Andreas. I thought they'd love Jake.

And now—now I have a spite food truck and a betrayed heart.

Broken dreams of my own.

And the worst part?

I still don't want to believe Simon used me.

I want to believe there's a logical reason for what I saw that's something more than *he used me*.

Because that's also what I always do.

I always believe that somehow, I made a mistake. That it was my fault. That I did something wrong. That I read something wrong.

And *I didn't*.

I have the photos of the script.

And one day…one day, I'll be strong enough to ask why.

Today, though, is not that day.

Hudson sighs. "Bea. Go home. I've got this today, okay?"

"I don't want to be alone," I whisper.

He doesn't tell me to go hang out at Ryker's like he probably should.

Instead, he shakes his head, grabs an apron out of the box that also houses the curtains that Daphne insisted I get for those times when people wanted a high-end, private burger bus experience—so far only used by me for the purposes of seducing the man I don't know if I ever want to see again—and he hands it to me. "Then at least put on your uniform. And don't like, cry in the burger meat or anything. You won't keep repeat customers if your burgers make them sad."

"That's not how that works," I mutter.

He snorts.

I snort back.

the spite date

And then the asshole does the worst thing he could possibly do.

He hugs me.

He hugs me, and he says, "I'm sorry he hurt you, Bea. I really thought he was smarter than that. And I wanted him to show you the whole world. After everything you've done for Ryker and Griff and especially me—I wanted you to have it all. One day, I'll make sure you see the world myself. You deserve it."

"Dammit, Hudson." God, it's hard to not cry. "Just let me work and pretend this is all about Jake again, okay?"

"What about me?" a man says in my window.

I rear back.

Hudson shoves me behind him. "Get fucking bent," he snarls at my ex-boyfriend.

Because there's Jake.

Standing there looking like he pressed his jeans and had his hair cut and his beard trimmed just to show up at my burger bus looking like a cover model while I'm in red-rimmed eyes with crusty lips and that constant, thudding ache in my head.

"I posted about your bus on my socials so that you'll get more customers," Jake says. "You're welcome. Now, can we please discuss what it's going to take for you to come to your senses and come back to me?"

Hudson looks back at me, utter disgust etched on his face.

Probably a good thing most of the weapons in the bus are things like ketchup bottles and burger flippers.

He could do some damage with one of the fry baskets though.

"Was he like this when you dated him?" Hudson asks me.

"Probably."

"*Probably?* That's a yes or no question, Bea."

"You overlook a lot when a guy's offering to help you make your dreams come true. And he probably hid a lot while getting all of my ideas out of me."

"I don't have to be here offering to take you back," Jake says. "My mother's opposed. She thinks you're unsophisticated and that you use your parents' death to get everyone's sympathy, and you really overstepped with throwing a competing murder mystery dinner. But the sex was good enough, and you can cook. Doesn't mean the offer doesn't expire though."

"Is he for real?" Hudson asks me.

"Don't know, don't care." I lean around my brother and lift a middle finger at my ex. "You're slime, Jake. Get lost."

"You're going to die alone and miserable."

Hudson blocks me again. "Projecting is a bad look on you, dude. You heard Bea. Go away. She doesn't want you."

Dying alone doesn't sound so bad right now.

No one can hurt you if you're alone.

But Jake—Jake doesn't get to see that, so I grab a ketchup bottle and point it at him. "I will use this again. Go the fuck away, and if your family doesn't quit talking shit about me, I'll destroy all of you. You've spent your whole life fooling people, but you've fucked up one too many times and made one too many enemies. We. Will. Take. You. Down."

He shrinks.

It's a small shrink, but it's a shrink.

"I knew you weren't smart enough to know what you had when you had me," he says as he turns to walk away.

"A gaslighting prick?" I say.

He turns back, and I let a squirt of ketchup fly in his direction, which sends him running, calling something about me making a mistake over his shoulder.

As if I care what he thinks.

Not long after, Ryker shows up with a box of vegetables that I don't need until tomorrow, which means he's checking in on me and I know it.

"You wanna come play with the goats?" he asks me. "Hudson and I have the bus. You can take my truck."

I scowl at him and don't answer.

He stays to help cook.

the spite date

We're serving fish on a stick as the secret menu item today.

I completely forgot or I would've changed it.

Because fish on a stick makes me think of Simon admiring it the first day we met.

Was that the day he decided to write a TV show about my life?

I shake my head and go back to my burgers.

Ryker runs the fryer so I don't have to touch the fish.

Hudson takes orders and he and Ryker jointly agree we're not selling spots at the chef's table today so I don't have to face customers with my face in the shape it's in.

Namely, depressed and sad and brokenhearted.

Hudson's not wrong.

My face is bad for business. Or it would be, if I showed it.

We're thankfully busy, and we even sell out before it's time to officially shut down.

Hudson and Ryker convince me to let them clean up and to let Ryker drive my bus home—he drives farm equipment, so he can drive my bus. And that means I take Ryker's truck back to my apartment.

The plan is for me to shower so I can be a clean lump on the couch when Daphne gets home with the Chinese takeout she promised before she left for work this morning.

I can handle being home alone for shower time.

I might even peek at socials to make sure I'm not the subject of gossip anywhere. Locally or beyond.

If I need to start checking my bushes for paparazzi, I deserve to know.

I'm so focused on the bushes and random trees where people could hide when I get home that I don't pay close enough attention to the cars around me.

And that's when the ambush happens.

I'm sitting in Ryker's truck, taking a hot minute to pull up socials and see what Jake actually said about me, when the passenger door opens and the man who just wrecked my heart slides into the seat.

"Please," he says in that posh British accent that still makes my vagina a little swoony, damn her. "Please, may I have two minutes of your time to explain myself and apologize?"

I squeeze my eyes shut tight and my legs shut tighter. "Go on. Say what you need to say so we can just get this over with."

He inhales loudly, but he doesn't immediately speak.

I count to five, staring at the last family picture we had taken before Mom and Dad died. It's been the background of my phone for over eleven years now.

And I'm realizing it might be time to change it.

"Clock's ticking," I say, hoping my voice doesn't sound froggy like I've been crying.

Simon takes another deep breath again, but this time, he fills the silence. "The day I met you is the day my entire world changed. I failed to recognize the magnitude of your impact on my life until I'd already begun changing the script so as to not resemble anything that would impede on your family's privacy, but I was wrong to not tell you that you inspired me. I was wrong to not tell you that you inspired me in more ways than simply sparking the idea of a story that has shifted and woven its way into being something entirely different, and that I've nonetheless informed the studio I will not be delivering after all."

The sun is beating through the truck's windshield, heating the interior of the cab and making me a little sweaty.

Or possibly that's the effect of Simon sitting next to me.

Saying all of the right things so far.

"It's not simply your family's tragedy, Bea. It's you. You inspire me. Your determination to make anything work, good or bad, once you've got an idea in your head. The burger bus. Our revenge date against your wanker of an ex. Seeing to it that your brothers have every opportunity regardless of the time or expense required. The way you can so easily reassure me that I'm not a fuckup of a parent for having had your own experience. Your refusal to accept less than you deserve from those of us who want to exist in your orbit. You—you are the best person I have ever known, the only person who could make me believe in family, who could make me believe that I, too, belong in a family, and the best person to complement me and all of my own hang-ups and traumas and stubborn ideas."

My breath wobbles.

My eyes burn.

I want to believe him.

I want to forgive him.

But I don't know if I can trust him.

"You should have told me," I whisper.

"I should have," he agrees. "And I would very much like to make this up to you if you'll let me. I want to prove to you that I can be the man you deserve. The man I've always been afraid to be, but the man that I know I need to be."

If I sit in this truck one more minute, I'm going to start crying.

And I absolutely do *not* want Simon to see me cry.

I don't know if it's my own pride not wanting him to see me hurt, or if it's worry that he'll feel worse if he sees me hurt, and that makes me mad too.

I don't want to care if he's hurt.

But I can't help myself.

He's still in there. In my heart.

My hopelessly romantic heart.

"I don't know."

It's all I can force out without completely losing control of my emotions.

I reach blindly for the door handle and stumble out of the truck.

"Bea?" Simon says.

"*I don't know,*" I say again, and this time my voice cracks. I spin to face him as he climbs out of the truck. "I don't know, okay? *I don't know.* Say I take you back. Then what? Then I just ride along doing whatever you're doing because I still don't know what I want to do for myself? That you're the next man whose life defines mine so that I don't have to decide who I want to be or what I want to do?"

His chest moves slowly, like he's controlling how fast he inhales and exhales so he doesn't lose his shit either. "I would be honored to be the lucky bastard who gets to watch you discover all the different places you might find your joy in life."

I rub my eyes, then sigh, barely able to look at him for knowing he's hurting. "I can't do this right now."

He blinks several times, then methodically nods.

"You have my number." Dammit, his voice is froggy now too. "You can call me anytime. Day or night. To yell. To talk. To breathe. It's only you, Bea. It will only ever be you."

My nose burns and I can't swallow right and the entire world is disappearing behind a waterfall.

I want to hug him.

I want to believe him.

But I'm too raw, and more than not knowing if I can trust him, I don't know if I can trust myself.

Because this *is* just like every other boyfriend.

I sill don't know who I want to be.

And how fair would that be to him?

So I give him a jerky nod, and I retreat into Daphne's apartment. Alone.

The way it needs to be.

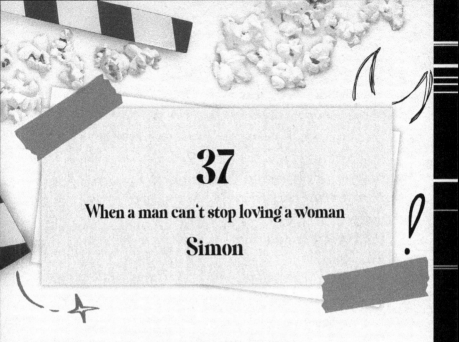

37

When a man can't stop loving a woman

Simon

"Has he moved all day?" Lana asks one of the boys two days after the last time I saw Bea.

"He put on sunscreen every thirty minutes and drank two beers," Charlie reports.

I had a temporary above-ground pool installed while waiting for the in-ground pool that was hidden beneath decades of leaf decay to be properly cleaned, filled, and balanced—even my money wasn't enough to fix it immediately when I decided the hell with it, that I wanted a pool—and my children have been enjoying the novelty while I've been enjoying the privacy that comes with not leaving the house.

"I also served you lunch," I say without opening my eyes.

Opening my eyes hurts too much.

There's sunshine and blue sky and happy children and complete uselessness because there is not also a Bea.

"He told us where to find the boxed macaroni and cheese to fix ourselves," Eddie says.

"You know how to operate the stove," Lana muses.

"But it's summer vacation."

"And you've made friends and had a blast at that summer program your dad found for you, and I know for a fact he's cooked for you or taken you out to eat practically every other meal this summer."

"Not breakfast," Charlie says. "I had to pour my own milk on my own cereal *every day*."

It's a joke that should make me laugh.

Instead, I stare despondently at the back of my eyelids and wish I could simply sleep until it no longer hurts.

Until what no longer hurts, you ask?

Everything.

My heart hurts. My sinuses hurt. My head hurts. My skin hurts. My feet hurt. My legs hurt. My arms and hands and fingers hurt.

Everything hurts.

"This is new," Lana says, much closer now. "Are you going to actually make it through this, or are you just going to lobster away at the pool?"

I could ask if she's making a joke about me getting sunburned, or about lobsters mating for life, but I don't have the energy.

So I simply grunt something.

"Mom's meds are working better," Lana says. "She's being transferred from the hospital to the memory care unit at Shady Acres tonight. It's finally about to be done."

I peel my eyelids open to look at her. Time to pretend to be human. "And how are you with that?"

Her shoulders sag. "Sad, but relieved, and then sad, and then depressed, and then relieved, and then guilty, then sad, then relieved, then sad. I should've forced her into the memory unit weeks ago, but when you know that she'll never see her own home again after that decision… it's just fucking hard."

I stare at her far longer than I should have to in order to form a coherent thought. "Emotions are terrible bastards."

"Emotions are what make life worth living."

the spite date

I grunt again and close my eyes. "We've an easy routine here. Take your time with resting and recuperating before the boys invade your house once more. They'll be with you full time for a spell again soon enough."

"You gonna recover well enough to head out to California on schedule?"

"I shall do what must be done."

"I saw Daphne today."

I simultaneously tighten every muscle in my body in preparation for hearing an onslaught of my worst traits while bracing my heart against any news that might give me the slightest bit of hope that Bea would consider taking me back.

She left things rather open-ended on Monday afternoon.

I don't know is a far cry from *Never speak to me again, you backstabbing twat*, but it's an equally far cry from *I miss you, I forgive you, I want you back.*

And with every second that ticks by without a word from her, I fear it means the former rather than the latter.

"She started a protest over the source of the meat at JC Fig last night," Lana says. "Jake had to close the restaurant because of the number of calls he got demanding to know where he got off participating in the inhumane treatment of animals."

The news doesn't make my body loosen.

"He apparently showed up at the burger bus on Monday and told Bea he'd take her back again. She attacked him with ketchup and told him she'll destroy him and his family if they don't leave her alone."

I squeeze my beer can so hard that it crushes in on itself.

There was still a half beer left, so now I'm coated in fizzy, beer-scented liquid.

"And Logan's apparently harassing her—hanging out near the bus every other day to chase away her customers—so Daphne put in a complaint to the police chief."

If I could crush my beer can again, I would.

"It would probably make more of an impact if you called to complain about him too," Lana muses. "And there are rumors floating around that Damon Camille is planning to sue Bea for false advertising."

"Damon Camille? Which brother is that?"

"He's Jake and Logan's father. The ambulance chaser. Sues everyone for everything around here."

Wonderful. "What is your point?"

"If you want to be her hero, you're missing out on a lot of opportunities by sitting here feeling sorry for yourself instead of proving to her that you mean it when you say you're sorry."

The grand gestures.

I've written a script or two in my lifetime.

I'm familiar with the concept.

Clearly terrible with the execution though. Which every woman in my life should know by now.

"Perhaps this is my sorry montage," I say dryly.

She ignores my comment. "Is it true that you didn't remind Bea that she lied to you about the reason she wanted you to take her to the restaurant's grand opening when you went to apologize the other day?"

I lift one eyelid just enough to verify that she's watching me. "What of it?"

"Simon, do you understand how people fight?"

"Yes, I believe I had it demonstrated for me by my parents every day of my childhood. Thank you for the reminder that they called me, by the way."

"Did you answer?"

"And let them have the joy of knowing I'm in such a state? Certainly not."

She sighs.

"What?" I grumble.

"If I was dating someone and we both fucked up and then we had a fight about it, I'd absolutely throw it back in his face that he wasn't innocent either."

the spite date

"And what should the point there be? To continue fighting? I don't bloody care if she was wrong. She apologized for it long ago, and that date was one of the best dates of my life. Cheese-filled monstrosity of a menu and the broken doorknob and missing the conclusion of it for passing out drunk on her table and all. So no, she has nothing to apologize for. That lies solely on my shoulders. I've apologized. She doesn't know what she wants. And so I'm forced to the sidelines to show her that I respect her wishes even if I hate them."

"If you were still dating her right now, no questions, no hesitation on her part, what would you do for your next date?"

"I can't bloody well force her to go on a date with me."

I don't need to open my eyes to know Lana's glaring at me.

"You know I'm terrible at relationships," I grumble.

"You know that's a shitty excuse when you love someone."

I wince.

She is not incorrect.

"Boys, anyone want chicken wings?" she calls. "I have a craving for something hot covered in ranch dressing."

"Me! Me!" Eddie yells.

"Me too!" Charlie chimes in.

"You're not invited," Lana murmurs to me.

"I assumed as much," I reply.

"That said…if you do pull your head out of your ass and want help, I have my own feelings to avoid."

"Bye, Dad," Eddie says. "I'd hug you, but you're covered in beer."

"We'll bring you back some wings if Mum lets us," Charlie adds. "But for real, you should shower first. It's always better to be clean when you're eating."

"I have missed you two *so much*," Lana says.

Again, I don't have to open my eyes to know what's happening.

She's hugging them fiercely, because she has far bigger problems than mine, none of hers self-inflicted.

As their voices fade, I slowly open my eyes.

What would I be doing with Bea right now if I hadn't made the worst mistake of my life?

I'd be planning a surprise.

Truth be told, it's already in motion.

I lift my head.

My brains slosh around inside my head, but I put my hand to my phone, lift it so that I may see the screen, and pull up my email.

I've a task that needs completing.

Imminently.

Regardless of the cost.

And then I shall decide if I want to continue with the rest of that plan.

Even though there's no question.

Of course I'll finish the plan.

It's for Bea.

Whether she wants me or not. She should have this.

Because it will make her happy.

And isn't *that* the point of feelings?

The point of life?

To find one's happiness?

I don't need a giant house. I don't need a pool. I don't need a huge career.

But I do want to know that I've left the people I care about in this world happier than the people who were supposed to care about me ever tried to make me.

Lana's right.

It's time I stop wallowing in my own sorrows and start doing something productive.

38

But is this scary scarier than that scary?

Bea

This is the week that will *not* end.

It's a mixed bag of good and bad.

The good—I've sold out every single day, and it's not because Jake posted about me on socials.

It's a combination of Daphne's protest outside of JC Fig every day this week with the reputation I have for being associated with Simon.

And the customers who tell whoever's manning the window in my bus that they're checking me out because of Simon don't say it's because I'm his girlfriend—*was* his girlfriend.

They say it's because he personally told them my burger bus is his favorite place to eat in town.

Or that they heard from a friend that he and his boys were always eating here.

Or that they saw pictures of him in a Best Burger Bus T-shirt on his socials.

That's crazy.

We don't even *have* Best Burger Bus T-shirts.

Daphne takes Friday off work and joins Hudson and me to work the bus. And she's as agitated as I am, though I don't know if she's agitated because she's sleeping worse and worse, or if she'd be agitated regardless of her own issues.

"I'm not mad at him anymore," I tell her as we work. "So you don't have to be mad either. I'm not saying I know if I want to try again with him, but I'm not mad."

Daph and Lana have become pretty good friends, and Lana relayed the information that, as someone in Simon's circles with more than a passing understanding of intellectual property and defamation laws, plus a vested interest in him continuing to provide for the twins, she's read the final draft of his script that was based on my life and it is actually nothing like my life.

It's now about four people—two men, two women—who grew up together under the care of a woman they called Aunt Zelinda, and who are now operating a honey stand and solving murders at the farmer's market.

The ultimate inspiration he drew from my life was about found family and how much he wanted to murder Jake on my behalf.

And also apparently that honey fantasy that we never tried, which I would know, but no one else would.

Lana also reiterated that Simon had told the studio he was wrong, the script was trash, and he was going to miss his contracted deadline for new material.

She didn't say he felt terrible.

Or if she did, Daphne didn't pass that part along.

"It's not Simon," Daph grouses. "I have to go home."

"To the apartment?"

"*No.* To New York. The Hamptons, actually. Margot's about to do something really, really, really stupid, and I can't stop her, so I have to stop *him.*"

I open my mouth, then close it again.

Daphne hasn't been back to the city or to her family's summer home in the Hamptons since her parents cut her off.

the spite date

It's not that I want the money, she told me once. *It's that I want to belong, and I don't. I never have, and now I know they don't want me to. So I'm done, and I'm never going back.*

And she hasn't.

"Daph—"

"You should give Simon another chance, Bea. He makes you happy. He makes you laugh. He makes you look more alive than I've ever seen you. *That's* what Margot deserves too. She's family, even if my parents aren't. And when you love people, you have to do the things that you might not like and the things you might not want to do when you know it's what will make them happy."

Hudson's staring at her now too.

My brother and I make eye contact, and we both keep saying nothing at all.

Him, likely because he wants to tell her Simon doesn't deserve me.

Me, because I'm suddenly back in Madame Petty's fortune-telling tent, where she's telling me that one day, Daphne won't come home.

Not even for the first time this hour, my eyes start stinging. "Just—just be careful, okay?" I grab her in a hug. "You're *my* family, and I don't like seeing you hurt either."

"I want to be wrong, Bea. I want so bad to be wrong that she's taking him back. How can she really trust he won't hurt her again? Even if she's serious when she says it would just be a business arrangement, how can she really think she'd be happy?"

I swallow hard. "How do you know Simon won't hurt me again?"

"Because he's sorry. Oliver's not. Simon's a normal guy who got accidentally rich and famous in his mid-thirties. Oliver's had a silver spoon in his mouth since before his mouth even developed. Simon could lose his career by not turning in this script, but he canceled it for you. Oliver couldn't handle dating and his job at the same time, and he picked his job over Margot. They're not the same. Not anywhere close."

My heart cramps again.

But it's not fear for myself.

It's worry for Daphne. "I'll come with you."

"No. *No*. Bea. Stay here. Where it's safe and people love you and no one will care if you show up to a party in a dress that's *so last year*. I just—I have to do *one thing*. I'll be back before the sun's up on Sunday morning."

"But will you be okay?"

"I'm Daphne fucking Merriweather-Brown. There are some things my family *can't* take from me. Like who I am."

"She's really scary when she says stuff like that," Hudson muses.

"We're lucky she's on our side," I agree.

Daphne laughs. "Of course I am. You're the best family I've ever had."

"Does this mean you're not protesting at Jake's restaurant tonight?" Hudson asks. "I was really excited for the signs about how he fucks over and cuts out his business partners."

She shakes her head. "I'm heading to the city to stay with an old friend before the party in the Hamptons tomorrow night. But I think a few people are carrying on without me."

I swallow the *we should've just protested the restaurant in the first place*.

Because it's not true.

I don't regret asking Simon to take me there for dinner. It's the first time in my life I've stood up and took a stand for myself against the shitty ways my exes have treated me, and honestly?

Jake deserved it.

In the past week, three of Jake's other ex-girlfriends have contacted me to tell me about the ways he stepped all over their hopes and dreams and plans while they were dating too, spurred on by Daphne's protest of the restaurant and the whispers that have started in town about where the idea for JC Fig truly came from.

He's gotten away with thinking he's *the man* for entirely too long.

Being someone who made him uncomfortable?

Someone who's regularly telling him *no* now?

It's powerful.

And Simon knew what I was doing that first night, and he went along with it anyway.

Even when he was mad at me for it.

I keep circling back to our conversation in Ryker's truck.

Where he didn't say a word about anything I've done wrong.

Shouldering the entire blame.

Just like he was taught to do as a kid who deserved so much better.

We sell out early in the burger bus again.

And as I'm standing in my bedroom in my robe after showering, looking at the wardrobe I've systematically hung up and sorted while I've been processing my feelings this week, debating if I'm brave enough to take the risk of going to see Simon and talk about everything that still worries me, Hudson stops and lounges in the doorway.

"You hear?" he asks quietly.

My heart thumps at his tone. "Hear what?"

"Somebody bought the drive-in. Stole it right out from under Lucinda Camille and her investors."

I gasp.

Then go a little lightheaded.

Then tingly in my extremities.

But I don't think it's dehydration or working too hard or anything other than a gut feeling that the drive-in being sold is life-changing.

"Who?" I ask.

"No one's saying. But the grand opening is tonight."

He stares at me like that's supposed to mean something.

I do quick math.

Not my birthday. None of my brothers' birthdays. Not Daphne's birthday either.

No significant anniversaries come to mind.

Griff's playing Copper Valley at home in Atlanta tonight. Not an insignificant rival, but not Atlanta's most hated rival either.

"Secret show," Hudson continues. "Have to go to see what's playing."

And then it hits me.

Tonight is the first night of the community theater's summer show. I gasp again. "*No.*"

Someone is stealing Lucinda Camille's audience.

My brothers and I all have the same identical evil smile. Doesn't matter that half of us have Mom's mouth and half of us have Dad's mouth.

We all grin evilly the same way.

Hudson's aiming that diabolical smile at me, and I know I'm giving it right back to him.

"So. Wanna go see a movie?" he asks.

My toes tingle. My fingers too.

And my heart.

My heart is tingling a little.

I tell it to chill out.

That it's probably Daphne.

Maybe she's not going to New York at all. She still has the connections to organize a hostile takeover of a college town's closed-up drive-in movie theater.

She *has* launched a full-scale war against the Camilles since Logan started showing up everywhere my bus has been this week and since Jake posted that ridiculously condescending *just because she's not a great businessperson doesn't mean a town like Athena's Rest shouldn't support her* social media post on Monday, and since the whispers started about Damon Camille, patriarch of the assholes, wanting me to change my business name because of false advertising.

This is absolutely something Daphne would do.

But she's not the only person in town who would do it.

And that's what has me undecided on what to wear right up until Hudson tells me he's going without me or taking me in the robe, my choice.

the spite date

I grab the first sundress my hand makes contact with, belatedly realize it's the same one I wore when I made barbecue chicken and risotto for Simon at Ryker's farm, almost burst into tears, and then put it on anyway.

When I dash to the front of the apartment, it smells like Chinese food.

"We're not going?" I ask Hudson.

He lifts a soft-sided cooler. "Post said to bring your own food. I heated up leftovers."

Once again—I almost cry.

My brother grins at me. "Remember that time Griff ate the last Chinese leftovers when you were taking those classes that had you super stressed and you collapsed in the kitchen and cried for an hour and then Ryker drove home from college just to bring you more sweet and sour chicken?"

I flip him off.

He jerks his head to the door, grinning wider. "Yeah, I remember that time too. Let's go. I want to know what they're playing. I hope it's *Rocky Horror*. Iconic, you know?"

I care less what they're playing and more who else might be there.

Specifically, if it's Daphne.

Or if it's Simon.

Daph's right.

I need to give him another chance.

Will he hurt me again?

Maybe.

But will it hurt worse if I don't try?

That's what I keep falling back on.

I've spent the past ten years trying to live up to the example my parents set.

Why would I not take a chance at making things work with a man who's made me feel more alive, more free, more like myself than I have at any time since I left college?

A man who wants to stand beside me while I figure out what I want to do.

He's not perfect, but he tries.

He always tries to do right by the people he loves.

Hudson sings along to the radio as we drive out to the theater.

And it is *packed*.

He giggles.

I don't, but only because this line is too long and I don't know if we'll make it into the drive-in.

"Did Daphne do this?" I ask Hudson. "Did she set this all up? Is she *not* going to New York?"

"If she did, she kept me totally in the dark. I think she's really going back for her sister. I think the protest was all she planned. I mean, that and the rumor that Damon Camille is sleeping with his sister, which I can't prove was Daph, but it sounds like something she'd start."

My leg bounces.

He shoots me a look. "You wanna get out and walk?"

I blink at him. "Yes."

"Bea—"

"Call me if you get a spot. I need—I need to go look for something. Lost it in goat yoga."

"You can't just—"

I ignore him, unlock the door, and dash out of the car and onto the shoulder.

He's still at least twenty cars back from the entrance, and then there are ten more cars lined up before getting to where you pay, and cars are already being directed into the last line in the lot, and it's getting dark and the movie will be starting in the next five to ten minutes.

So you're damn right I'm walking.

I start slow, but my pace quickly accelerates as I duck under an open part of the fence and start looking closer.

Black SUVs. I'm looking for black SUVs.

Specifically, Simon's black SUV.

the spite date

I can't find it and it's getting darker and darker and the cars are *packed* in here, which is crazy because there are only so many speaker poles—except then I realize what's different.

The speaker poles are gone.

A giant QR code flickers to life on the screen.

Scan here to be connected to audio. The show will begin momentarily.

I walk even faster.

Row after row.

Black SUVs that aren't Simon's.

I'm halfway to the front row when the movie screen flickers again.

It's not the familiar sight of the beginning of *In the Weeds*, which would have been so on-brand for Simon to buy a movie theater to show his least-favorite TV show just so that he'd know that I'd know that he was pulling a giant joke on everyone.

Maybe I'm wrong.

Maybe Simon didn't—

Chords of familiar music hits my ears, and I gasp.

Ever After.

The inaugural show for the drive-in's grand re-opening is *Ever After*.

The movie that I told Simon was my favorite.

Because she saves herself.

I stand there blinking at the screen, feeling my mom with me while the opening scene begins, and then I'm in motion.

Simon's here.

He has to be.

But where—*there*.

Of course.

The booth.

I duck and weave around the cars, racing faster and faster toward the booth in the middle of the drive-in.

I reach the booth and I stop at the door long enough to wipe my wet cheeks, and then I charge in.

No knocking.

This isn't a night for knocking.

This is—

"*Motherfucker*," I gasp as a tiny woman with dark blond hair glances up from the computer that's clearly running the show.

Lana starts, then smiles at me. "Hey, Bea."

"You—you did this?"

A laugh bursts out of her as she shakes her head. "Bandwidth not there for doing *this*. Not the *this* that you mean. I'm just operating the computer."

"Simon," I whisper.

She nods.

"Where is he?"

She winces. "Paying a little more for his sins?"

"He's not—he didn't—he's paid enough."

"You'd think so."

"I—I love him," I whisper.

"Good," she whispers back. "I was really, really hoping you would. He's needed someone like you."

"Where *is* he?"

"Don't yell."

"I'm not yelling."

"I mean when I tell you. You have to let me tell you the whole thing before you yell. And also, I'm blocked in. I can't leave."

"Lana. Where. The ever-loving *fuck*. Is Simon?"

She purses her lips together for a hot second, glances at the screen where our mothers are chatting on stage, and then she answers me.

And she's right.

I want to yell.

Howl, in fact. And then I want to go save Simon.

But first—first, I need to save myself, and I finally—*finally*—know how.

"Why are you smiling like that?" Lana asks me.

the spite date

Oh my god.

I am.

I'm smiling.

"Because I'm going to take down Jake Camille. And then I'm going to save Simon too. And then we're going to live happily ever after." I wince. "If he still wants me."

Her own smile grows. "He still wants you."

Gah, my heart.

It's beating in anticipation and hesitant joy.

Running to Simon right now—it's everything I want to do.

But I told him I needed to find myself. To figure out what I want to do with my life. To not ride his coattails or just follow him around in his own career.

I can't tell you what I want to do six months from now.

But I can tell you what I need to do today so that I can be free to find what I want to do six months from now.

And before I can go to Simon, I need to put it in motion.

For me.

And for our future as a couple without anything holding us back.

39

Fuck this shit

Simon

It's likely a good thing my security team is here.

They'll prevent me from killing my dinner companions so that I may continue to see my children grow up without finding myself in the exact situation that I put Bea in just before I met her.

And now I'm thinking about Bea.

Would be far more pleasant to think about Bea if I knew if she'd been made aware of the special show at the drive-in theater this evening, and if she went, and if she liked it, but I know none of those things.

Because my parents unexpectedly arrived on my doorstep at the exact moment that I should have been leaving for the drive-in theater myself, and the only way to keep them from terrorizing my children was to agree to have dinner with them.

At JC Fig.

Where we've been given a private room—over my objections—so that there are no witnesses now to my parents' horrific nature.

"You owe us, that's bloody why," my father is sniping at me as Aileen, the same server that Bea and I had, hovers in the doorway of this upstairs dining room as though she's afraid to approach the table to refill our water glasses.

the spite date

Tank takes the metal pitcher from her and does it himself.

I wonder what it would take for my security agent to justify homicide in my defense?

Clearly, I wouldn't want Tank, or Pinky, or Butch, to end up behind bars on my behalf, but what if it were justified?

"All of those years that we supported you while you were dilly-dallying with that silly career," my mother adds with a sniff.

"All of those times you made up stories about what your mother was doing when she was at her book club," my father growls.

"And the stories you would make up about your father while I was away on a commission," my mother adds.

The both of them.

Pretending that I lied about their affairs.

Because they're broke.

Flat broke.

That inheritance they claim to have taken away from me to bestow upon my sons instead?

Even their home is mortgaged to the hilt.

They're penniless.

Paupers.

Maxed the last of their credit cards to fly here to the States to badger me for money.

Probably expecting they'll be staying in my home too.

Not bloody likely.

They continue to prattle on about my terrible misdeeds as a child, making up their own stories about the things they never did to support me, while I smile as pleasantly as if I were eating—

Well, I was going to say a Sunday dinner of roast lamb and carrots and potatoes, but I find I'd prefer a very particular barbecue chicken and butternut squash risotto.

God, I should be at the theater.

Not that I expect Bea would fall into my arms in gratitude for showing her favorite old movie, but so that I could watch her watching the show.

So that I could see that I haven't fucked this up further by plunging her into the depths of grief by reminding her that she'll never again watch it with her mother.

Would you look at that?

I've drained my wine.

Again.

Is that the fourth? Or the fixth?

Fixth?

Is that a number?

"Well?" my father booms. "What do you have to say for yourself?"

"Well, what do you have to say for yourself?" I mimic back in a high, whiny voice.

My father's eyes bulge.

That's it.

I shall act out until he has a stroke.

And then I shall use my magical powers vested in me as a father of two teenage boys who steal animals and eat ridiculous numbers of hamburgers and have very fine women sent to jail, and I shall annoy my mother to death as well.

I burp.

The overwhelming churning in my gut thanks to the butter and cheese in the pasta that I requested plain comes out of my arsehole in a long, deep fart that reverberates throughout the room.

'Tis a good evening to have consumed dairy.

This will aid in my plan to murder both of my parents without laying a hand on them. "How's your—*hic!*—blood pressure?" I ask my mother.

Smiling, of course.

Waving my wine at her.

"What the hell is wrong with you?" my father snaps.

"*What the hell is wrong with you?*" I snipe back, falsetto.

This is fun now that I'm getting into it.

"You will cease speaking to me that way *right now*—"

I interrupt his tirade with another long, satisfying release of the gas bubbles tormenting my midsection.

"*Stop that right now,*" my mother snaps.

"*Stop that right now,*" I parrot.

Except that's not me parroting my mother.

I have not, in fact, opened my mouth at all, other than to sip wine, and it would be impossible for me to be parroting my mother while drinking wine.

Which means that someone else has parroted my mother.

Clearly this is the case, because they're both gawking at something over my head.

"How *dare* you," my father roars as my mother half rises and adds, "Who the bloody hell do you think you are?"

"Fuck off," comes a very cheerful, very lovely, very painful-to-hear voice.

A voice that makes my drunken heart pitter-patter and my pride have its first self-flagellation at the next long toot to come from my arsehole.

I'm terrified to turn around.

Both to discover that it is, and also that it is not, Bea.

She is Schrödinger's Bea.

She both exists behind me and simultaneously does not.

My mother looks around and waves viciously at poor Aileen. "Who's in charge? How *dare* the staff speak to us this way. Do you know who we are?"

"You're nobody," Bea's lovely voice says above me. "Absolutely fucking *nobody*. Because only *nobody* would speak to another person the way you're currently speaking to the best man I have ever known in my entire life. And my father set the bar high when it comes to judging men. Very, very, *very* high."

I would like my arsehole to stop answering for me now.

And for me to find my courage to look up at the angel currently hovering over my shoulder.

I can see her.

This room is full of mirrors, and *I can see her.*

Or her mirage.

Possibly she's a ghost.

"Are you a ghost?" I ask the woman in the mirror angled perfectly to show her lovely face to me.

Dimples pop out of her cheeks as she dashes her hands over her eyes.

All five of them.

Dimples and cheeks and hands.

Bloody hell, I've forgotten how to count.

Gentle hands settle on my shoulders. "Who fed you dairy? Did they do that too?"

I point in my parents' general direction. "I told you they were—"

My arsehole interrupts me.

"—dreadful," I finish, and even the wine can't give the word enough gusto to recover from the utter wanker my arsehole is making of me.

"Butch?" Bea asks.

"Right here." My security man shoves two supplements into my hand.

I leap on them as though they are a gazelle and I am a lion.

"What the *fuck* are you doing here?" a new voice says.

"Jake, meet Simon's parents," Bea says. "They're paying the bill."

My mother gasps.

My father goes the kind of red that makes my red wine look pink.

"Also, for your information, I just posted about your business on socials too," Bea continues, her face aimed toward Jake. I think. The mirrors and the wine make it so bloody difficult to keep up.

"I don't need your help," Jake sneers.

Bea squeezes my shoulder when I attempt to rise.

the spite date

"I'm not helping you," she says. "I posted about how you had no interest in opening a restaurant until we drove past Ada Jane here and I told you what my father always wanted to do with the old house, and about how you stole my dream from me when you dumped me. Griff shared my post. Daphne did too. Six people have already commented with ways that you've fucked them over too, and I have a feeling we're about to hear from many, many, *many* more."

"You can't do that," Jake sputters.

"Oh, I think you'll find I put in enough of the *in my opinions* and *the way I felt*'s that your father can't sue me for defamation. And even if he did, I know an attorney or two myself, and Daph's lining up backups as we speak."

How amusing—Jake's head has become a tomato.

A very ripe, very mushy tomato.

And the woman of my dreams—she has taken complete control of all of the unpleasant people in this room.

Pride swells my chest.

"Get the fuck out of my restaurant," Jake growls.

I start to rise to take part in defending the woman of my dreams, but the wine is acting as terribly as bubbly does, and I sway while my arsehole protests Jake's demands for me.

"I'm leaving, but only because I'm sick of your face, and I don't want anyone to think I would ever endorse your restaurant as a place to eat good food." Bea follows her announcement by waving her hand toward my parents. "And you two. If I ever, *ever* hear of you contacting Simon again, I'll write my own damn movie script about what terrible people you are, and then I'll have my brothers and their friends make it into a YouTube series, and you'll never be able to show your faces in public again. No. Shut your mouth. You're done talking."

She leans into me, her breath on my ear. "Now, can we please get out of here?"

"I've drunk six wottles of bine," I inform her.

"That's very restrained of you if it's been like this for the past hour."

"In—*hic!*—deed."

"I'm sorry I wasn't here sooner. I had to so a little saving of myself first. *Ever After* told me so."

She got the message.

She understood.

"I love your dimples," she tells me. "They—*hic!*—horn me makey."

She smiles, those beautiful pools of moss and trees and grass and every good green thing ever shining down on me as though I deserve to be smiled at. "I adore you, Simon Luckwood."

My eyes water. "I do not deserve you."

"You deserve every good thing in the entire world and so much more." She tugs on my hand. "Come with me."

I don't recall my feet working.

I do recall my arsehole making its presence known twice more before we reach the door.

There's some kind of yelling about a bill.

Butch makes a comment about dishes that makes Bea laugh, and also makes me wish I'd made whatever comment that was.

We step into the crickety night air, all crickety with the crickets cricketing, and warm arms circle me as other bodies move around us, carrying signs I cannot read in the dark.

"Simon," Bea whispers. "We have to keep walking."

"But I love you here," I tell the angel holding me up.

"I love you everywhere," she replies.

Some distant part of me realizes this is monumentous—monumental? Momentous? Good god, words are stupid—but the utter relief at no longer being in my parents' presence, the warmth of her body tucked against mine, the effects of the wine, the fresh air, and the thought of willy dogs has me content to do nothing more than bury my head in her hair and hold on so that I might stay here long enough to sober up and understand what, exactly, is happening.

Why I feel like sunshine in the darkness.

the spite date

    How I am the moon spinning about the earth and an immovable rock rooted through the earth's crust at the same time.
    "Beatrice?"
    "Yes, Simon?"
    "Please be real when I wake up."
    She squeezes me tighter.
    My arsehole responds as it must this evening.
    And everything draws darker in the musical sound of her laughter.
    If this is a dream, then I never wish to wake up.

40

This time, I'll bloody well get it right

Simon

My head is a sour lemon that has been squeezed one too many times and has now turned into petrified cotton.

Is petrified cotton a thing?

Why must alcohol make me so bloody miserable?

But—"Bea!"

I bounce to sitting so quickly that the room spins.

Was it a dream?

A nightmare?

The show.

I missed the show. At the drive-in.

Surely it was a nightmare. But—

"Whoa, hey, easy," a feminine voice, husky with sleep, says nearby.

It's followed by a gentle hand on my arm.

A very real hand belonging to a very real woman whose head is on the pillow beside mine.

I think.

Everything is still swimming.

"Bea?" I whisper.

the spite date

She sits up beside me, a whirl of color in the soft morning light poking through my curtains. "How's your head?"

"Are you real?"

She presses a water bottle into my hand. "Drink."

Memories float back to the surface, coming easier than they do when I've got pissed on bubbly.

"My parents—"

"They're gone, and they know what'll happen if they come back."

I stare at the woman in my bed. "Are you real?" I repeat.

She smiles, but the light is too dim for me to see more than a blurry flash of white teeth in the general shape of a smile.

Stupid eyesight in the dark.

I reach for her cheek, feeling—yes.

Yes, there it is.

A singular dimple.

"The next time you decide to drink, we're staying home," she tells me. "I was afraid to leave you alone."

My vision clouds, but it's not the wine, and it's not the lingering effects of that horrific pasta—oh, bloody hell.

"You saw me on cheese."

"Simon. I went through the full teenage boy experience twice, plus another half experience with Ryker. You on cheese doesn't faze me."

"I was…quite rude."

"You were in pain, and whoever served you dairy deserves your hangover. How's your stomach today?"

I take stock and find it tender, but no longer anywhere near the same level of uncomfortable. "Better. How are you the perfect woman?"

"You have very low standards."

"Bea—"

"You bought a drive-in movie theater and showed my favorite movie," she whispers.

I swallow hard. My nose burns, and my vision clouds again. "I did. And I would do it again if it would make you happy. Ten times over.

Every day, even, until I could no longer afford it, and even then, I would find a way."

She leans into me, looping her arm around my body. "I was trying to figure out what to wear to come here. To ask if I was too late or if you would still give us another chance even with me being a mess. Before I knew about the drive-in. You didn't have to—but you did—because you're you—and I love you and I want to make us work. I meant what I said last night. You are the best man I've ever known, and my dad set the bar so high, most of us mortals can't even see it."

"I didn't dream that."

She kisses my shoulder. "You didn't dream that."

"You told my parents to fuck off and threatened to make a terrible documentary about their life."

"They were being unnecessarily rude."

"Bah. It's simply how they—"

"*Simon*. No one—*no one* gets to speak to you like that. Ever. For any reason. And God help them if they try it in front of me."

"You told Jake to fuck off."

"Yes."

"You told the world what he did to you?"

"I did. And I'm renaming my bus. It's re-opening this week as Spite Burgers. I started new socials for it and shared where the name came from and I already have seven hundred followers."

My heart swells as my smile stretches my cheeks at this news, and I cannot hold it in any longer. "I love you," I say, my voice going hoarse with the magnitude of the words said exactly in that order, to exactly this woman, who will own me, heart and soul and body and mind, for all of eternity.

"I didn't wait too long?"

My head is sloshing about. My body aches as though I've run six marathons and lifted a car off someone.

I don't want to move.

I want to flop back onto the bed and lie perfectly still until everything stops spinning.

But none of that matters as much as pulling her into my lap and breathing in the scent of her hair and her skin and her morning breath, which is just as perfect as every bit of the rest of her. "I would wait for you to the end of my natural life, and then some."

She shudders against me. "I don't know that I deserve you."

"Will you chide me in that schoolteacher voice at least three times a day?"

"*Simon.*"

I rest my head on her shoulder and draw lazy hearts over the fabric covering her side. "Yes, like that."

She huffs out a laugh. "We're working on your standards and expectations for yourself and all of the good things you deserve."

"Quite a bit of trouble when I'm exceedingly content with my life exactly as it is now."

"Headache and all?"

"Perhaps that part could see itself out."

She runs her fingers through my hair and brushes a kiss on my forehead. "I'm sorry I got so mad."

"You should have been angry. I knew it was wrong of me to continue to draw so much inspiration from your life without your knowledge, and yet I persisted longer than I should have."

"But the final script was nothing like my life?"

"No one would recognize it for the leaps my mind took in revisions."

"Can I read it?"

My hand stills. "I've told the studio I won't be delivering it to them."

"But can I read it?"

"Certainly, if you wish. I have no desire to hide anything from you, no matter the consequences."

"What if the consequences are that I think it's amazing?"

"May I remind you, darling, that I was the head writer for *In the Weeds*?"

She laughs.

I cringe at the noise. How can something be so perfect and so painful at the same time?

Blasted alcohol.

"Maybe a little more sleep?" she says softly. "Lana has the boys. You don't have to get up."

"Only if you stay."

"There's nowhere else I ever want to be."

41

Happily Honey After

Bea

Euphoric is my new favorite word.

Simon murmured it as he was waking up midafternoon, and I've made him repeat it six times since.

After a leisurely and orgasm-filled shower, and then an early dinner of berries, bacon, and pancakes—my dad's recipe, adapted with a milk substitute that won't upset Simon's stomach—Simon insists on giving me a full tour of his house.

We make it to the first guest bedroom and no further.

Both because I can't stop laughing at the froggy wallpaper, and because me laughing apparently turns Simon on, and a turned-on Simon is absolutely irresistible.

And talented.

And dedicated to his craft.

And by his craft, clearly, I mean leaving me a satiated puddle of happiness.

But then he notices the time, and the setting sun, and the next thing I know, I'm being ordered to get dressed—Pinky made a run to my apartment and gathered a few things, and when I remembered Daph is gone, I didn't ask questions about who picked my clothes and underwear.

"Doesn't being the owner of the drive-in come with some perks?" I ask him as he tries to help me with my pants. "Like maybe we can watch this show another day?"

"No," he tells me.

Very bossy.

Very un-Simon-like.

So I decide to trust him.

And then I laugh as we pull into the theater and see that tonight's movie is once again free. "You know you can't run a business by perpetually giving away the product, right?"

"The very astute lady that Lana insisted I hire to manage my finances for me last year was quite irritated with that, but it seems this town loves to donate more to a cause than they would have paid had I set a ticket price."

I blink at him, and then I crack up again. "Are you serious?"

"Quite serious. I may have accidentally acquired a low-effort, high profit business."

"Simon."

"Yes, yes, the town's initial excitement at the novelty of having their drive-in cinema open again is giving me false hopes. Thank heavens. Otherwise, I should have done something else my parents might be proud of."

"Simon."

He drapes an arm around me and kisses me soundly, and I don't notice the car inching along with the other cars to find a parking spot.

Not when he's kissing me in the back seat.

I do notice when we stop though.

Or possibly sometime after.

Because someone starts banging on the window. "Get out here," Hudson calls. "They're showing *Rocky Horror*. Bea! *They're showing Rocky Horror.*"

I smooth my hair, then Simon's. "Did you know that's his favorite movie ever?"

the spite date

"I may have sought out that information."

Hudson and Ryker and Lana and the boys join Simon and me, and we spend the next one and a half hours enjoying *Rocky Horror* to its fullest. The cars aren't jammed in as tight tonight, which clearly is so that we have room to dance in the late summer evening.

And after the show, when everyone else is leaving, Simon insists that all of us stay for a private showing of something else. He breaks blankets and popcorn tins out of the back of the SUV, and once all of us are settled—Simon and me, my brothers, his twins, and Lana—he gives a signal to his security man in the booth, and then something that's clearly not a professional production flickers to life on the screen.

I squint.

It's a stage.

Like—like a community theater stage.

A woman strides onto the stage as if she owns it, and my gasp is echoed by Ryker.

"Sweetheart?" a very, *very* familiar voice echoes around the parking lot.

An achingly familiar voice that I haven't heard in over ten years.

"Sweetheart, have you seen my bag?"

That's my mom.

My mom, on the community theater's stage.

The video is grainy—it was clearly never intended to be shown on a screen this size—but *that's my mom*.

And if I'm not mistaken—that's my mom in the only show of hers I never saw.

"Simon," I whisper.

He scoots closer to me. "Lana found the recording. My role was simply in providing a venue."

"Your mom's last show was my mom's first show," Lana tells me. "She got into theater later in life."

"Of course I never put it away the same place twice. What would the point in that be?" my mom says on screen to her costar, prompting laughs from the audience.

And one laugh in particular—that's my dad's laugh.

Ryker and Hudson suck in matching breaths.

They know it too.

"Thank you," I whisper to Simon."

"As I said, merely provided a venue."

"Look, boys," Lana says as someone else joins my mom on stage. "That's your grandmother in the pink pants."

Eddie and Charlie crack up.

"*Pink pants*," Charlie crows.

"Shush and watch the movie," Hudson says. His voice is thick, and I'm not surprised when a box of tissues appears.

Several boxes, in fact.

"Griff should be here," Ryker says during an extra-long laugh from the audience that has the show pausing.

"We can show this—or any of her recorded shows—again anytime," Simon tells him.

Ryker stares at him. "If you hurt Bea, they'll never find your body."

"I should hope not. You've the land and the tools to dispose of me correctly. It would be a pity to cost Bea both her heart *and* her brother to prison."

"Oh my god, Simon." I tip my head back and laugh.

Ryker cracks a smile. A real one. "I'm pissed that I might actually like you."

Simon merely beams.

The show continues on the screen, and after it's over, when Lana's packed the boys off and taken them home, Hudson calls Griff, whose game is over for the night too, and we sit in the field in front of the screen sharing stories about our parents until long after midnight, with Simon wrapped around me from behind.

the spite date

Eventually, Ryker grumbles about the chickens waking him too early, and he takes off.

Hudson pauses long enough to give Simon a hug. I hear a *thank you*, but I don't make out whatever else my brother whispers to my boyfriend.

And then it's just Simon and me and the night air and the crickets and the fading moon.

Tank and Pinky have made themselves scarce, though I know they're somewhere close by.

I loop my arms around Simon's neck. "Is that projection shack empty?"

He runs his hands down my side. "If it's not, I'm acquainted with the management, and I do believe they've succumbed to my charms."

"We should go check."

His smile is brighter than a full moon. "Should we? Whyever should we do that?"

"Because I stole the honey from your kitchen."

I don't know which of us pulls the other faster to the little shack, but as soon as the door is closed behind us, all of our clothes go flying.

I pull the honey bear from my bag.

Simon slaps a strip of condoms on the projection table.

And then he's squeezing the life out of that honey bear while he attempts to drizzle honey onto my chest.

Attempts being the key word.

He squeezes.

And he squeezes.

And my breasts stand there, perky in the half-moon light, waiting to be covered in honey so he can lick it off.

But the honey isn't coming.

"Why do I have to squeeze so hard?" he murmurs.

I'm giggling so hard I almost can't answer. "Old honey. Crystallized."

He screws the lid off, dips his finger into the bear's head, and smears the grainy substance all over one of my nipples. "This shall do. I'll purchase fresh honey first thing in the morning."

I'm still giggling.

At least until he lowers his mouth to my breast, and then I'm not giggling anymore.

I'm gasping.

Because Simon's mouth is magic.

His tongue knows more tricks than a circus dog.

And his hands are sticky with honey that he's smearing down my belly too, following it with that mouth and that tongue, until he's sticking his face between my legs and making me absolutely fall apart against the projection window.

"Mmm, better than honey," he murmurs against my pussy, which pushes me over the edge into a full-fireworks orgasm that has me gasping his name.

This man.

He's had me arrested.

He was my partner in revenge.

My biggest burger bus fan.

Sometimes a hot mess.

Always kind.

So kind.

And now he's staring into my eyes as he pushes his thick, hard cock inside of me while I balance on the table against the window of the projection room of the drive-in theater that he bought for me.

"I love you far more than I ever thought I could love a person," he whispers.

I grip his hair and hold on while I meet his thrusts. "You are all of the goodness and happiness and perfection that I never thought could possibly exist in this world."

"Only because you've shown me that I can be."

"*Simon.*"

That smile flashes again, and he thrusts into me harder. "Chide me again, love."

It's impossible to not smile back at him, even while my body is warning me that I'm on the edge again. "I love you so much."

"I never knew those words could heal a person's soul."

"Only when they're true."

"Indeed, my love."

He kisses me, thrusting deeper and deeper inside me while I rock my hips to meet him, and I shatter into a million rainbows of orgasmic bliss as he comes too, straining into me and staring deep into my eyes and murmuring all of the *I love you*s.

I blamed him for putting me in jail.

But I think I'd been in my own mental jail cell long before I met him.

And now he's helped set me free.

He's my future and my hopes and my dreams and the man that I intend to love every day for the rest of my life, no matter what else I find to do with my life in the meantime.

He deserves that and so much more.

Epilogue

She's in love... but where did her bestie go?

Simon

This may be my first Sunday with Bea, but I have decided that every Sunday from here forward shall be my favorite Sunday ever, so it is simply my first favorite Sunday.

We laughed through washing all of the honey off her in the shower when we returned home sometime after two a.m., slept in, had a leisurely breakfast with lively debate over whether tomatoes should be served with breakfast, and now we're lounging by the pool while the boys and a few of their friends splash about.

I've provided the script she requested yesterday—printed from a newly acquired, state-of-the-art, current-model computer and printer that I bought this past week as well—and she's smiling and giggling her way through it as I scribble notes for a new concept that struck me in a dream.

"This isn't what I thought it would be," she says when she's halfway through.

"I *am* a professional, darling," I say with the barest degree of haughtiness that has her smiling at me again.

"I know." Her eyes gleam with more mischief, though not nearly as much as they should. "I mean, I do *now*."

I take her hand and press it to my mouth. "But you didn't know my process when you stumbled upon the first draft. And you've had experience in being betrayed recently. I would have come to the same conclusion."

She bites her lip. "Can I tell you something?"

"Always, my love."

"I think your dialogue is a little saggy here. I mean, compared to the rest of the script. What if she said something more sarcastic like *so you're an expert on wildflowers now too?* It just feels like it would be hilarious with the dry delivery I'm hearing in the rest of her lines."

I blink at her.

She holds her face in a cringe. "Or not. You're the expert."

"No, no, that's excellent. Much better line."

"Simon. Don't humor me."

"Truly, I hate the line because it makes the scene better, and you know how much I detest being anything above adequate."

She's smiling as she rolls her eyes. "*Regardless*, you should give this to the studio," she tells me.

I hold her gaze. "No."

"*Yes*. It's funny—"

"Which suggests the studio will undoubtedly have some dreadful director in mind who would insist upon converting it into a space drama."

She raises a brow. "Aren't they giving you producer credits? Doesn't that mean you have some sway on who the director is?"

"Yes, yes, fine, I have sway. Infernal success has made them believe I have some modicum of show business sense."

"You should give this to them," she repeats. "If it's a success, you're just going to have to learn to live with that. Possibly even enjoy it. For yourself. Because you deserve to honestly take pride in your work without giving a second thought to who else might have opinions about your success."

We embark on a staring contest.

She doesn't waver.

This is the Bea who kept her brothers in line at much too young of an age, when she should have been out going to parties and driving young men mad with those dimples and exploring all of the courses in the world to discover what her path should have been.

The Bea who will not take no for an answer because she knows in her heart what's right.

What's best.

"If I send this script to the studio and they accept it, which I would only do if you also tell me what else is wrong with it, because I prefer my co-writers to pull their weight—"

"*Oh my god*, I gave you *one* suggestion. I'm not a script writer."

"How do you know? Have you tried it before?"

She opens her mouth, then closes it again.

I smirk. "I thought not. What if this is the professional path you've been missing? You owe it to yourself to at least try, darling."

It's remarkable to sit beside a woman and know that her brain is spinning with possibilities, with objections, with worries, with fears, and then to see—

"You know what? Why not? And if it doesn't work, I still have my spite bus."

I beam at her. "Excellent."

"Simon, if I'm terrible at this—"

"Bah. All of us are terrible at it. Some merely better than others at fooling the studios into thinking audiences will love our clumsy attempts more than others. Also, you should know—there will eventually be a red-carpet premiere, and you will have to attend in a new dress and be photographed publicly with me if we do this."

She grins. "Will you pick that new dress for me?"

"If you wish."

"You have excellent taste."

"I have excellent fantasies."

She leans over and kisses my cheek. "I like living out your fantasies with you."

I clear my throat and drop my notepad over my suddenly hard cock.

She smiles and goes back to the script, though the second half is clearly not as well-done as the first half, because she keeps checking her phone.

I eventually lift my brows at her. "Is this a good time to point out that I clearly need your guidance, if your lack of enjoyment is any indication?"

She shakes her head. "No, it's Daphne. I just realized what time it is. She had to go home this weekend, which is similar to if you had to go back to London to see your parents."

I grimace hard enough that Eddie calls to ask if I'm okay.

"Bea has a theory that she can find things to make me not smile," I call back.

"Girlfriends do that?" Charlie asks.

"Indeed, and often. They're quite terrible. You should never have one."

Bea cracks up.

The boys grin at me, and they go back to their games.

"So her family is awful?" I ask Bea.

"I mean, they disinherited her, and she *did* have a real trust fund that had more zeroes than I'd see in a hundred lifetimes. She doesn't talk to them anymore. Margot's pretty cool though. Her sister. You met her. The day that you dumped me in the sink. Daph loves her, but she still lives a different life than Daph now, so…"

"I'm glad I never had a sibling," I muse. "What a terrible life for someone else to live."

Bea slants a look at me. "You would've gone overboard trying to protect them from what you went through."

Quite likely.

the spite date

She smiles as though she knows I'm agreeing with her in my mind but would rather not say so aloud.

"When is Daphne due to return?" I ask.

"She said she'd be back first thing this morning, but she hasn't answered any texts since yesterday afternoon, and her phone is going straight to voicemail."

"That's not good."

She bites her lip. "Tracking her phone is bad, right? I try not to track my brothers' phones either, even though we all share locations, because they deserve their privacy, and she does too but—"

"If she was due back and you cannot reach her, you're hardly invading her privacy to verify that she hasn't been in an accident. Or perhaps she simply misplaced her phone, and you would be doing her a favor to locate it."

"I'm going to ask you later to say *privacy* again, but for now…" She taps her finger over her phone screen.

And then squints one eye.

Tilts her head.

The pulse flutter at the base of her neck flutters faster.

"Bea?"

"This isn't right."

"What, love?"

"Her phone last pinged six hours ago in eastern Pennsylvania."

I sit straighter. "Where is her family?"

"She was going to the Hamptons. The tip of Long Island. Which is *not* eastern Pennsylvania."

She holds the phone to her ear for a moment, wrinkles her nose, and sets it down again. "And it's still going straight to voicemail."

"Butch has former army friends across the country. Shall I ask him to have one of them check on her?"

"Simon," she whispers. "Do you remember what Madame Petty said? That one day, she wouldn't come home?"

My heart thumps in dread.

I swallow hard.

"Surely not," I say, though my mind is also flashing to Madame Petty saying that a man would betray Bea, and I certainly did that, did I not?

She blinks hard and fast, but it's not enough to clear the shine from her eyes. "Okay—" she starts, only to be interrupted by her phone ringing.

She wrinkles her nose at the readout—not a number in her phone—and then swipes to answer. "Hello?"

My heart starts beating again as I lean in to listen closer.

"Bea. It's me."

"*Oh my god*, Daph, *where are you?*"

"I'm okay. I'm safe. I'm voluntarily doing what I'm doing."

"Why is your phone showing in Pennsylvania?"

"Shit. You weren't supposed to see that."

Bea squeezes her eyes shut and presses a hand to her forehead. "*Daphne.*"

"The reason I don't go home? I don't go home because then I'm the Daphne who was an epic fuckup and things just *happen* that aren't supposed to happen because I have the worst timing ever, and something happened again, but *I am okay*, and I'll be home…sometime…and I just didn't want you to worry."

"There is nothing about this conversation that isn't making me worry."

"Remember when I moved in with you? When you had to teach me to drive and how to do laundry and grocery shop on a budget?"

"Yes," Bea says while I file away my own questions for later about how she taught Daphne to drive.

"I have to do that for someone else right now."

"Who?"

"I can't tell you that."

"Daphne—"

the spite date

"Bea. Listen. I love you more than I love anyone else on this planet. You saved my life, and I would literally die for you, but I cannot tell you who I'm with. It's—it's sensitive, and it's just easier if you don't know, okay? But I'm okay. I'm on a little unplanned road trip. My phone is, um, temporarily out of commission, so I got this burner phone. I'm going to have it off a lot, but if you *need* need me, you can call me on this number or my other cell. I'm…working on getting it…working again."

"What about your job?"

"I'm calling in sick for the week. If Margot calls—if Margot calls, just tell her I got twitchy and had to go camping off-grid, and that I'll call her back in a week or two, okay?"

"Daphne—"

"Did you make up with Simon?"

"Yes, but—"

"For real?"

"He's right here. Want to say hi?"

"No, I need to go. He's going to notice that I'm taking longer than I should in the bathroom."

"He? Who's *he*?"

"Bea, I really have to go. But quick—are you happy?"

"Other than my best friend disappearing with an unnamed *he* and being really cryptic about it? Yes. Very happy."

"I'll be home as soon as I can."

"Madame Petty told me you wouldn't come home one day," Bea blurts.

"Fuck Madame Petty. I'm coming home, and then I'll tell you everything. I'll call you every other day or so. So you know I'm still alive. Gotta dash, Bea. I love you."

"Daphne—*dammit*."

Bea throws her phone down and stares at it in the grass.

"She hung up?" I ask.

"Did you hear that?"

"Every word. Has she…" I'm not certain how to finish.

"Done something like this before?"

"I was trying to find a more polite way to word that question."

"Not since she was disinherited."

"Bea?"

She looks at me, worry lines grooving her forehead and between her eyes.

"You taught Daphne to drive?"

The barest smile tilts her lips up. "Not exactly. But you want a good script for another show? I can tell you *aaaaall* about how much I had to teach Daph when she moved in with us the first time. Rich girl suddenly poor without a clue how to get along in the real world. I have some stories."

My hand hovers over my heart, which has begun beating wildly with excitement at the scenes taking place in my head. "Don't tease me, darling. That would be brilliant fun to write together with you."

She taps the script in her lap. "Give this to the studio, and I'll start talking. *If* Daph agrees. Which she will. If I tell her to."

"Beatrice Best, you are a wicked woman."

"The stories probably aren't really script-worthy. Especially not the one about dish soap at the laundromat. Or the one about her first time trying to dye her own hair. Or the one about when she discovered bulk beans on the internet."

"You are a veritable smorgasbord of life experiences that belong in a television series."

Her smile is growing, even as she glances at her phone again. "Thank you," she whispers.

"For what, love?"

"For reminding me of all the reasons Daphne's going to be okay. She's come a long, long way, and if someone from her former world needs help learning the same things she did, they're in good hands."

I toss aside my notebook and pull her into my lap. "She will be more than okay. As she said, she'll be home soon. She's doing a good deed."

the spite date

Her nose wrinkles. "He better appreciate what she's doing. And if he hurts her—"

"As I believe I've recently noted, your brother has all of the resources necessary to solve that problem."

She snuggles into me, her face in the crook of my neck, exactly where I like it. "I love you," she whispers.

"I love—" I start, but I'm interrupted by a giant wave of cold water splashing across us.

Bea shrieks and prances out of my lap. "Oh, that's how it's gonna be?" she says to my boys, an impish grin taking hold of her face. "You have no idea who you're playing with here."

They grin back at her.

She jumps into the pool, executing the most perfect, splash-tastic cannonball that I've ever witnessed, making my boys and their friends shriek with glee.

My eyes mist over as I watch them all water fight each other.

I didn't think love was the reason I came to Athena's Rest.

But as it turns out, love is the reason I've done nearly everything in my life since the boys were born.

The difference is, now I choose to embrace it instead of hiding from it.

And that is how a true happily ever after is made.

Bonus Epilogue

It's a very merry family Christmas

Bea

In the five and a half months since Simon's kids accidentally had me arrested, they've become some of my favorite people on the entire planet.

And that's making this Christmas better than any Christmas my brothers and I have had since our parents died.

"*No way.* A water bottle rocket? What even is this?" Charlie crows.

He hit puberty hardcore in September, and his voice is almost as deep as Eddie's now, but still scratchy.

He's also grown four inches.

And he's in shorts and a T-shirt while the rest of us are in long-sleeve Christmas pajamas because that's what kids who wear jeans and hoodies in summer do when winter hits.

We're in the room formerly known as the dining room, which currently has the world's fattest Christmas tree in the center, with space still for a foosball table and an air hockey table and a pool table, where Simon and the boys and I spend hours when they're staying with us.

This will be the dining room again at some point, whenever we finish renovations on the house and open it as the Athena's Rest Lodge, which is an idea Simon came up with when I went to visit him on a set in Calgary for a short shoot last month.

The cast and crew had fully taken the vacation rentals, and he and I ended up in an old-fashioned bed-and-breakfast.

"You take in strangers and make them family regularly anyway," Simon had mused. "Why not convert that monstrosity of a house to an old-fashioned inn? You and I and the boys hardly need that much space. I merely bought it to be ostentatious in the hopes my parents would see, and now I don't rightly care what they think."

So that's the long-term plan.

Because we're taking it slow.

And by *slow*, I mean I moved into his house as soon as Daphne got back from her road trip, and he's shown me Los Angeles and his favorite parts of New York and film locations in Canada Washington state. He's taken me to a few of Griff's games and gave his opinion on the people I interviewed to manage the burger bus so that I could keep one hand in the business and also enjoy traveling and dabbling at writing screenplays with him.

I'm debating if I want to take Spite Burgers into a physical location, or if I want to buy a second bus.

The rebrand has been massively successful. I'd expected business to slow down in winter, but I've had so many party requests both in Athena's Rest and the surrounding areas that I've hired more staff.

I needed to anyway.

Turns out, writing scripts is fun, and I like doing that more than I like flipping burgers.

For now, anyway. And if one day I want to do something different, that's okay too. I don't think my purpose in life is to settle with any one thing. I think it's to explore and try as many things as I can.

Also, the Camilles are no longer the family to fear in Athena's Rest.

After my social media post went so viral that I was slightly more famous than Simon for a hot minute, with countless comments from people who had also been screwed by one member or another of the Camille family mixed in with the thousands of comments in support of me, Damon retired from ambulance chasing and Lucinda retired from teaching fourth grade. She also turned over control of the community theater to Molly Taylor, whom Hudson still hasn't worked up the guts to ask out, mostly because he says he doesn't want his college dating experience to be fully long distance.

Logan Camille took a job in Wisconsin after one too many complaints to the local police chief.

And Jake—Jake is still running JC Fig, but only barely.

Simon's waiting for him to be desperate enough to sell that we can get the building at a bargain, and then he intends to turn it into a museum with a gift shop and a snack bar featuring some of my dad's favorite recipes.

He still has the drive-in, which he named the Best Drive-In.

He thinks I don't know the biggest box under the tree is actually seven wrapped boxes nested inside each other with an envelope with the deed to the drive-in signed over to me, but the boys can't keep secrets.

And it's not like I couldn't have guessed.

"If I were to ever screw up so monumentally with you that Ryker did, indeed, bury me somewhere on his farm with no one the wiser, I should wish for you to have every opportunity in the world to continue finding yourself, and that means you should have a diversified business portfolio of already successful businesses to support you while you explore," he told me over dinner last month when we were arguing over whose name would be on the lodge.

You know.

When it's done in three years.

"Why is my present making noise?" Lana asks, pulling me back to Christmas as she shakes the wrapped present Ryker just handed her.

The boys giggle.

Of course she's here. She's family too. She and Simon have a solid friendship, with regular exasperation on her part that she tells me is less since he started dating me, and I adore her more every time we hang out. She's rapidly becoming a sister of my heart.

"Remember when Mom got Dad those dinosaur slippers that roared?" Hudson says to Griff.

"Those were fucking awesome," Griff replies.

"He said the fuck word, Mum," Charlie says.

"He's a grown man who lives in locker rooms, so we'll have to overlook his terrible language," Lana replies.

"I actually learned it from Eddie," Griff says. "No one curses in locker rooms anymore."

Eddie gasps.

Charlie snickers.

My brothers are less uncle and more brothers to the boys.

It's pretty awesome.

And when it comes to the boys, I'm more doting aunt than stepmother-ish.

Simon refuses to ask for help with doctor appointments and school pickups and homework assistance, but I do go see the school plays when Eddie's running the soundboard, and I go to the middle school art exhibits and *ooh* and *ahh* over Charlie's artwork, which we all agree is brilliant on a level that none of us completely understand.

In short, I get the fun part of being a parent figure without the responsibilities.

I get to enjoy them for who they are, with a little bit of being a role model and disciplinarian thrown in when necessary.

"Boys, are you so for real right now?" Lana says as she tears the wrapping paper off her gift.

She cracks up.

Simon snickers.

I clap a hand over my mouth to keep from gasp-laughing.

"That's terrifying," Hudson says.

Lana points the talking Eddie doll at Simon. "I *told* you, *no more than a hundred dollars.*"

the spite date

"I am highly offended that you think I would break our bargain," Simon says with a sniff. "The boys made those as art projects at school."

He's lying through his teeth and we all know it.

"I love my mum the best!" the Charlie doll announces.

It's creepy and weird and terrifying, and also hilarious.

The dolls are each about eighteen inches tall, with cloth bodies hiding the sound boxes and porcelain heads that have been perfectly sculpted to capture the boys' faces as they are exactly right now.

I've heard about them—though the conversations I've overheard have mostly been giggles from all three of the Luckwood gentlemen—but this is the first time I've seen them too.

"I got your back, Lana," Griff says. "Unlike some people in this room, I was taught to live like a pauper during profitable times so that I can retire like a king at thirty. And I got this wicked cool endorsement deal for a fried chicken chain too, so *king* might be underestimating how rich I'll be. The sky's the limit with whatever you want to do to get them back."

"Thank you, but I think I'll enjoy vengeance best when I do it solo," she replies.

Simon scoots closer to me and wraps an arm around my shoulders. "Bea is innocent, so please do bear that in mind whenever you decide to do something you cannot take back."

"Bea won't suffer."

"Bea might help," I agree. "I don't have to be the adult in the room anymore."

All three of my brothers look around like they're just now realizing Daphne's not here. As if she'd be another adult in the room.

"She's coming later," I tell them.

They give me the trademark Best feral grin.

I grin back.

We are definitely having fun when Daph gets here.

If she can.

Snow's coming, and it looks like it's already started pretty thick.

Ryker notices too.

He rises quickly. "I have a present."

"You mean you have one to open or one to give?" Charlie asks.

"It's a very important distinction," Eddie agrees.

"One's selfish."

"One's not."

"You're not usually selfish."

"But Christmas can do things to people."

"All of those wrapped boxes…"

"It's irresistible, even for mature teenagers like us."

Ryker stares at the twins.

They grin at him.

He tries to suppress a smile, but he can't quite get there.

Simon won Ryker over with the exact thing he's going for now.

The secret passageway.

We all know about it. I've even been through it, with Simon and Tank and three industrial-grade flashlights.

It's pretty cool.

If a bit tight.

And it doesn't go to our bedroom or Simon's office, and they're both slated for renovation at separate times so that we don't have to worry about using a room connected to the secret passageways, ever.

"No fair—you said we couldn't hide presents in there," Eddie says to Simon.

"Sometimes life is utterly miserable," Simon replies, deadpan.

Ryker reemerges from the secret passageway. He balances a lidded file folder box on one hip while he tilts the wall sconce that's the secret mechanism to open and shut the door, and the door closes again.

Something rustles inside the box.

I blink fast because my eyes are getting hot.

This one's kind of a big deal.

This one's going to need more from me than what I've had to give to anyone since Hudson left for college.

And I'm stupidly excited about it.

Ryker deposits the box in front of the boys. "I hate wrapping so I hid it instead," he lies. "Merry whatever. Don't be dicks."

Griff snorts.

Hudson does too.

Ryker's said *don't be dicks* to them every single Christmas since he was fifteen, when he gave Griff a pie-in-the-face game and Hudson some game called *Exploding Kittens*.

He did it again the year after Mom and Dad died to keep the normalcy, and it's stuck.

Eddie and Charlie both dive for the box.

"Don't hit your heads together," Lana yelps.

The box yelps back.

The boys gasp, and they switch to seamless, in sync motions to pull the lid off.

"*It's a puppy!*" Charlie screams.

"Oh my god oh my god oh my god." Eddie wipes his eyes. His chin is trembling. "Is this real? Is this really our dog?"

"Can't have you stealing mine," Ryker says dryly.

The boys look at Lana.

She nods.

They look at Simon.

He nods too.

They look at me, and my eyes get misty. "I'm backup when you need an extra hand with her," I tell them.

"She's a she?" Charlie lifts the pup out of the box, staring in wonder at the golden retriever puppy.

"She's a she, and she's your responsibility first and foremost," Simon says.

"Can we name her Buttercup?" Eddie asks.

"You have to agree on a name, and you have to potty train her, and you have to take her on walks and pick up her poop," Lana says.

"We're gonna be the best dog dads." Charlie's voice cracks. "This is the best day of my life."

Simon kisses my shoulder. "Thank you," he murmurs.

"It's the very, very, *very* least that I can do for you and them."

Lana's not ready for a dog, and Simon still travels a lot. So this is only possible because I convinced them both that I'd be the dog's primary backup caretaker when I'm not traveling with Simon, and Ryker will cover when I'm gone.

She's a family dog. For the boys.

"It's far more than the least you've done," Simon insists.

"Maybe a smidge."

"*Oh my god, she's peeing on me!*"

I snicker.

"You've been chosen," Hudson says.

"Dogs only pee on people they like," Griff agrees.

"I don't miss you during baseball season." Ryker grunts as he moves back to the boys. "She needs to go outside every time she pees so she associates peeing with going outside."

They both jump to their feet.

My brother trails them out of the room.

Lana furrows her brows at me. "He didn't even make a face at you for what you signed him up for too."

"Because Bea's the best," Griff says.

"We made a pact to never get mad at her for anything," Hudson agrees.

"Plus she's making Dad's honey puff pancakes for breakfast."

"We don't get honey puff pancakes if we misbehave."

"And that includes making faces at her."

"And not helping when she gets her boyfriend's kids a dog for Christmas."

Lana stares at them. "Are you two for real?"

"Good god, they're like Eddie and Charlie," Simon says.

I can't tell if it's admiration or horror in his voice.

the spite date

Probably both.

Usually is when he discovers one more way his kids are similar to my brothers.

And sometimes I think that's what he likes most about me.

That I've done this parenting thing.

With kids super similar to his.

So I can assure him—and I regularly do—that he's not fucking them up.

"Dad?" Charlie calls. "We lost the dog in the snow."

"Of course they did," Lana says.

Simon rises quickly.

I hold out a hand, and he helps me to my feet. "Are you sure you're ready for this?" he asks again.

"For family and fun and stories to tell their kids one day when we're sitting on our front porch in our old people rocking chairs?" I grin. "Absolutely."

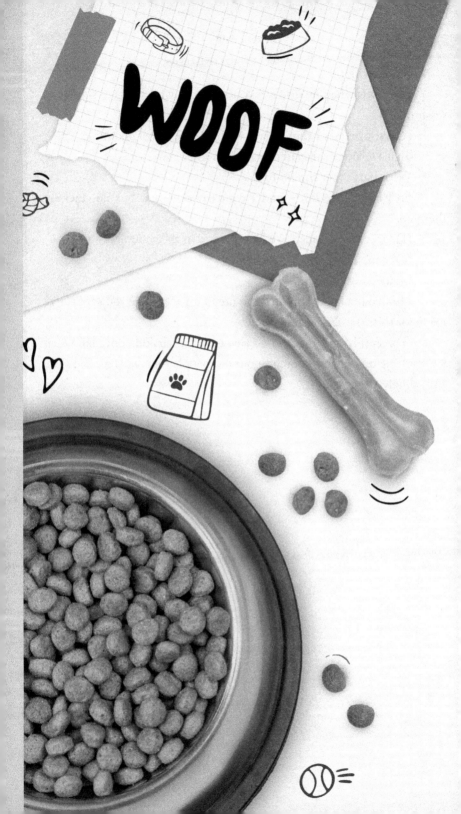

Bonus Bonus Epilogue
Buttercup,
aka a dog who's still a puppy and has the best life ever

Flowers are yummy.

I love flowers.

And there are *so many flowers*.

Pink flowers and red flowers and purple flowers and yellow flowers.

Or so my boys say. I can only see the blue and yellow flowers, but I know the rest of those are colors, and that's what color they say they are.

They're wearing fancy clothes today, and their shoes taste extra good.

And now my boys are walking me down a weird carpet outside—why do people put carpets outside?—and trying to keep me from eating the flowers on the chairs.

Why are there flowers on chairs?

They never put flowers on chairs.

Especially flowers that taste good.

"Come on, Buttercup," the shorter boy says. Everyone calls him Charlie. "You have to get the rings to Dad."

The rings!

I forgot they put the rings in a little case on my collar.

I have a big job today.

The taller boy—the one they call Eddie—said so.

And it's all for my favorite lady.

For my Bea.

She's so pretty today, wearing a fancy dress and carrying more flowers that I hope taste good.

She's behind us. I saw her.

The guy who's always putting his paws on her, the funny guy who sounds different, hasn't been with us all day, but that other lady—her human best friend, Daphne—said that he was going to cry when he saw how pretty she is today.

I lift my head and trot to the funny guy, the guy they call Simon, who's spiffed up too.

Oh! And there's my favorite guy ever! The one who sometimes takes me for rides to a farm where I get to run with goats and chickens and other dogs and alpacas.

I bark and run for him. *Ryker! Ryker!*

He shakes his head at me as Eddie and Charlie run along with me, and when I pant up at him, he rubs my head. "Sit."

I sit.

I sit because I get treats when I sit, and also because I'm a good girl.

I'm the best good girl.

And my favorite guy slips me a doggie treat.

I wag my tail so hard I almost pee, but I'm a good girl.

I don't pee on people's shoes anymore. I pee outside in the right place for me to pee.

The music changes, and I tilt my head.

Oooh, one of the boys is playing the guitar.

AND THERE IS MY FAVORITE HUMAN EVER!!!!

Bea's at the other end of the weird outside carpet, behind all of the chairs that aren't usually here.

And she is so pretty that I can't stop wagging my tail.

"If you hurt her…" Ryker says to Simon.

the spite date

"I deserve to spend eternity buried beneath the manure piles," Simon replies. "She's so bloody gorgeous."

"And you do deserve her, man. Just wanted you to know. I know I won't have to bury you under the manure piles. Happy wedding day. Glad to call you brother."

My favorite lady's favorite man wipes his eyes. "It's an honor to be part of your family. More than you will ever know."

Both of the humans sniffle.

I lunge on my leash because I want to love all over my favorite girl human, but my favorite guy human holds my leash tight.

I whine at him.

It's been *two whole minutes* since I saw her last.

And she's sniffling too.

Sniffling and smiling like the sun is inside her, making her smile, and like she'll never not smile again.

"I told you no crying," Bea says as she gets to Simon, who greets her with a kiss on the cheek.

Like I said.

He can't keep his paws off of her.

"There's too much happiness to hold it inside, love," he says.

I don't know what that feeling in my heart is, but it's squishy and happy and I want to feel it forever.

I bark.

"Shh, Buttercup," Eddie says to me. "You save the toasts for *after* the wedding."

Toast?

These wedding things come with toast?

Why didn't he say that?

"Sit, Buttercup," Charlie says.

They're both by Ryker and Simon too.

I sit.

If there's toast, I am *all in* for the sitting.

My favorite humans are talking again, telling each other how much they love each other, and it's making my heart do the warm and squishy things again.

I sigh happily.

The sun is shining. The flowers are delicious. Toast is coming.

I do my part and sit like the bestest dog ever while they get the rings from my collar.

Everyone is crying.

This is the best family.

I hope I get to be their dog forever.

And I hope they get more dogs too.

More dogs, and more boys to play with, and more flowers, and more toast.

My butt is getting tired.

I don't want to sit anymore.

I look up at my favorite guy human. At Ryker.

"They'd be so happy to see her this happy," his brother who's not around much says. I forget his name.

"She deserves every bit of it and more."

Bits?

I like bits!

Bits are what fall off the table!

Usually from the shorter boy and the taller boy.

My favorite lady throws herself at the guy with the paw hands and funny voice, and they do their kissing thing again while everyone cheers.

I bark.

It's my way of cheering.

But no matter how long I wait, and how many times I'm a good girl who sits, no one gives me toast *the whole day*.

I'd be mad, except I get to sneak off and eat flowers and shoes when no one's watching.

And when everyone but my main humans leave, they give me steak for dinner.

the spite date

"You were such a good girl today," Bea tells me while she rubs my head and my back.

I bark in agreement.

And then I puke up a shoe on her.

Maybe that wasn't such a good idea.

"Oh, dear," Simon says.

"Dad? I can't find my shoe," Charlie announces.

"Maybe not the best girl," Bea says, "but you're still young. We'll give it to you. Hey, Ryker? One last wedding present? Can you take Buttercup to the vet?"

I flop to the ground and pout.

No toast, *and* a trip to the vet?

At least I still have my humans.

And they're happy.

And if I'm lucky, they won't get rid of all of the flowers while I'm gone.

But even if they do, I still have my boys.

And they still have me.

Lucky humans.

ABOUT THE AUTHOR

Pippa Grant wanted to write books, so she did.

Before she became a *USA Today* and #1 Amazon bestselling romantic comedy author, she was a young military spouse who got into writing as self-therapy. That happened around the time she discovered reading romance novels, and the two eventually merged into a career. Today, she has more than 50 knee-slapping Pippa Grant titles.

When she's not writing romantic comedies, she's fumbling through being a mom, wife, and mountain woman, and sometimes tries to find hobbies. Her crowning achievement? Having impeccable timing for telling stories that will make people snort beverages out of their noses. Consider yourself warned.

FIND PIPPA AT…
www.pippagrant.com

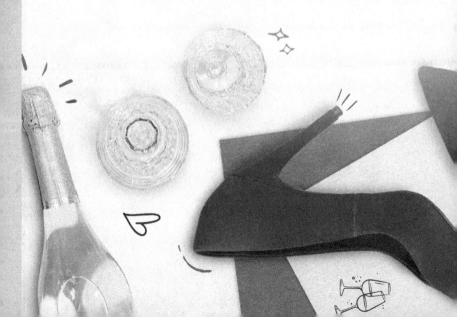